A TEAM OF TWO

AN UNSANCTIONED ASSET THRILLER BOOK 2

BRAD LEE

1

CAPTURE/KILL

TUESDAY MORNING

Outside Tampico, Mexico

2:33 a.m.

This is what we get for invading a friendly country, Axe thought.

The mild November temperature of coastal Mexico made the hike easier than usual for the SEALs. But the stress of infiltrating the area without permission, combined with the humidity on this dark, moonless night, left them drenched in sweat.

He brought up the rear of the column of the sixteen-man platoon, his tall, lean body clothed in desert camouflage fatigues, spec ops helmet, and chest carrier with ammo, grenades, and other essential gear.

Everything needed to capture or kill the target.

Axe hadn't shaved in two months. While he disliked the gray streaks in his messy beard, he now blended in better with the other SEALs. He was fit enough to handle the op but slower than the younger front-line men. He knew it—and they knew it. Despite all his efforts to stay in shape since retiring from active duty, he wasn't the young buck he'd been when he first joined the Teams fifteen years before. He rolled his shoulders, loosening them up, grateful they didn't creak and crack like when he got out of bed in the morning.

Getting old isn't for wimps.

He had three things going for him: the group he embedded with was his former Team, so they knew and mostly welcomed his addition; the op wasn't a wild 'run and gun' mission; and the Commander In Chief had specifically ordered Axe be allowed to tag along.

And when the boss spoke, people listened.

Axe took another careful, silent step, maintaining his distance from his former team lead, call sign 'Red.' Red's two-hundred-twenty-pound bulk moved just as quietly—and even smoother—than Axe.

The world glowed green in Axe's night-vision goggles. Patchy grass, scraggly shrubs, and the occasional small tree covered this part of Mexico, eight miles inland from the Gulf.

Ahead of him, the men spread out, taking cover as best they could behind the small bunch of trees previously selected as the last chance to survey the target before the attack.

Red and Axe stopped further back and huddled together, laying in the grass after using both the night vision goggles and their sense of smell to avoid any of the pasture's cow patties.

A quarter mile ahead was the ranch: an old house, a barn, and what they knew from daytime surveillance photos to be a brightly painted children's swing set, complete with a small plastic slide, tilted slightly off-kilter.

They all prayed no children remained on site. That would complicate matters.

"Kilo One, Kilo One, this is Bravo Actual," Red whispered into his mic. "How copy?"

Axe listened to the command channel through his earbud. "Solid copy," a quiet, assured female voice responded immediately.

"Tequila. Say again, Tequila."

"Copy Tequila. Stand by."

In the C130 Airborne Battlefield Command and Control Center flying parallel to the Mexico coastline many miles behind them, there would be a last-minute check of intel, including real-time drone and satellite scans of the surrounding area.

There would also be another crucial step in an operation of this magnitude. The President of the United States had to provide the approval to attack a civilian compound of an allied country.

Central Analysis Group (CAG) Headquarters—Operations Room
Alexandria, Virginia

Haley closed her eyes for a second, wishing she had more to offer. Her long blond hair fell over her face until she absently tucked it back behind her ear. In her khaki pants and simple black blouse, she felt underdressed for tonight's events. But after being abducted months before, and her experience in the field, she could no longer deal with a pantsuit and sensible heels. She now only wore clothes she could fight in.

Besides, this outfit made it much easier to hide the 9mm pistol in the concealed carry holster at her right hip. None of her colleagues had remarked on her change of appearance—or the minor bulge from the gun—but she suspected they discussed it behind her back.

Gregory Addison, her boss and mentor, stared at her through his round, fashionable glasses with one eyebrow raised. Despite the early morning hour, he looked focused and fresh, his decidedly longer-than-standard gray hair perfectly in place.

She had nothing to add. She shook her head slowly and shrugged in defeat. "Sorry, Gregory."

He took a deep breath, seemed to think about arguing with her—again—but stayed silent before turning to the large monitor on the wall. She looked as well.

The TV showed the White House Situation Room with many of the nation's top military and intelligence personnel, including the directors of the CIA, the FBI, Secretaries of State and Defense, and the National Security Advisor.

At the head of the long table sat the President of the United States, James Heringten—a man known to Haley for the past twenty-one years of her life simply as "Uncle Jimmy," a fact known to a few people in both rooms but acknowledged by none.

"We have no new information at this time," Gregory said in a quiet, firm voice over the video conference setup.

Diego Samuels, the Director for Counterterrorism, forty-four years old and a favorite of the president, acknowledged with a nod. "Understood. Anyone else?"

No one spoke up.

"Is this an ambush, Mr. Addison?" the president asked.

Gregory stared into the lens of the camera at the top of the large screen. "There is that possibility, yes, sir. But all our data points to the target being present at the ranch, surrounded by a manageable force protecting him."

In the situation room, the president's eyes flicked to his Chief of Staff, who nodded at the director of the CIA. A dour African American woman in her mid-60s, she hesitated, coughed in an attempt to hide her discomfort, then spoke. "Ms. Albright? Your input, please."

She knows I'm Uncle Jimmy's niece... and doesn't like asking me directly, Haley thought. *Too bad.*

Haley appreciated the president's ongoing charade that she was merely an ordinary analyst and not his adopted niece—or the person who had helped save New York City from destruction only six months earlier.

Haley glanced at Gregory only long enough to see the look of irritation at his newest, youngest analyst being asked a direct question in the middle of an international op.

"It's likely an ambush—a ninety-eight percent chance, in my estimation. But it doesn't matter. We have to go in, whether there's a two percent chance of catching the man or not. Whatever happens will lead us forward."

She'd spent the past few months working harder than ever. Combined with two other analysts assigned to her, she looked for threats to the country, but they also had a goal they worked on whenever possible. They were tasked with tracking down Todd Burkley, the man behind the planning and attack that killed hundreds in

New York, blew the power to Manhattan, and nearly caused the magnificent city to suffer fallout from a nuclear meltdown.

Every day saw the city improving. Solar panel installations on countless buildings had helped bring back essential operations, the bridges and tunnels were repaired, and power lines were being restored. But it remained a shell of its former glory.

Burkley had disappeared off the coast of Long Island. Lost to the sea, some in the office claimed. But Haley felt him out there —somewhere.

The only lead she had developed was of the small, run-down ranching compound in the dry farmland of northeastern Mexico, where the SEAL platoon, along with Axe, waited for the president's go/no go order.

It felt like a trap. Once again, she had no evidence. Nothing to convince her small team, the larger group of intelligence analysts, or her boss, Gregory. But she knew the best action was to walk into his potential trap and, as her asset and friend Axe frequently said, "Shake the tree."

One of the military men, decked out in a uniform cluttered with ribbons, growled from the end of the table—nearest the camera in the Situation Room. "You're willing to risk my men for a lousy two percent chance at—"

"They knew what they signed up for, General," the president cut in.

"Yes, sir," the man responded instantly, his tone not aligning with his words.

"Proceed with the operation," the president continued. "And make sure we're standing by to call the President of Mexico in case this goes to hell."

2

GO/NO GO

Outside Tampico, Mexico

Axe looked at Red, able to read the frustration and unhappiness in his body language. They'd been on countless missions together over the previous decade. They knew each other's silhouettes, the way they moved when confident, cautious, or anything in between. The entire team did. This knowing had saved their lives repeatedly in dangerous situations around the world.

It also made it difficult to keep secrets.

Red didn't like waiting and absolutely hated ops with direct supervision from the brass, let alone the Commander in Chief. They would all rather go after an HVT—High Value Target—on their own, left to do their jobs as the "quiet professionals" they were, than be monitored and babysat every step of the way.

Red turned his head to whisper to Axe when the radio in their ears came alive.

"Bravo One, Bravo One, this is Kilo One. How copy?" The woman's voice seemed less dispassionate than before, more excited.

"Bravo Actual. Solid copy," Red replied.

"The bar is open. Repeat, the bar is open. Drink up."

"Copy the bar is open." Red started to his feet. "Next round is on us."

"Copy, Bravo Actual. Party hard."

Axe switched his radio network as Red did, standing with him. "Party time."

"Party time," came replies from the fireteam leaders.

The group split in two. They would hit the compound from the northeast and northwest simultaneously.

Axe trailed Red to the group of trees, taking the cover other men had used moments before, then turned to face their rear. He wouldn't be part of the primary mission, no matter how much pull he had with the Commander in Chief. He was no longer a SEAL.

At least I'm along on the op, Axe thought. *I can't imagine how horrible it would be stuck in a room, watching instead of participating.*

———

The White House Situation Room
Washington, D.C.

President Heringten leaned forward and rested his arms on the table. In front of him, the scene on the monitor changed from the inside of the Central Analysis Group's operation room, switching from the view of his niece and her boss to a live drone feed. The black and white view of the ranch in Mexico and surrounding area had a level of detail that impressed him. He could make out individual blobs of light—the SEALs he had sent into danger, showing up as heat sources on the night-vision camera—as they maneuvered into position.

What I wouldn't give to be back on an operation one last time, the president thought. *To lead men in the field instead of from behind, sitting at a table, watching others act.*

He'd taken care of the treasonous vice president, which had been a covert op mission if there ever was one, and he'd gotten away with it. But it wasn't the same as attacking a compound, surrounded by a team of trusted fellow warriors.

We all age out. I need to appreciate where I am right now because in a few years I won't even have this. I'll be sitting at a desk back home in my study, alone. The only war I'll be fighting will be over what to include in my memoirs.

Outside Tampico, Mexico

Axe scanned the surrounding area, noting every small dip in the ground, the sparse grass, the location of the scattered bushes. Near, middle distance, far. Constantly searching. Doing his job.

A few feet behind him, Red received a last report from the team. The groups were in position.

"Thermals negative," came the whispered report from Hector, AKA 'Thor.' "Looks like cows in the barn and two, maybe three people in the house."

"Nothing here," Ronbo added.

It feels great to be working with my old Team again—especially Ronbo, Thor, Red, and Link.

"No change in the intel. It's probably a trap," Red said

"What else is new?" asked Ronbo.

"Yeah. Been there, done that," added Thor.

And got the scars.

"Okay then, exactly as we planned. Let's get some."

Quiet clicks confirmed the order. They were on.

The White House Situation Room
Washington, D.C.

The president and his advisors watched in silence as the attack played out on the big monitor. Two small teams of men advanced simultaneously, moving smoothly over the terrain. They lost visuals when the men entered the barn and the house. They could only listen to the radio feed, patched directly from the field into their system.

James frowned.

Our first lead in six months. If we don't get him tonight...

He wondered if hiding Todd Burkley's involvement in the attacks had been the right move months ago.

Could we have caught him earlier with a full-court press?

In the days after the terrorist attack, the search had centered on the man called The Boomer. He was a terrorist long known to the United States and easily recognized by his brilliant, piercing blue eyes. A few gunmen who shot people on the bridges of New York City had been caught and interrogated. All implicated a man matching The Boomer's description.

All the blame fell on him, which James did nothing to contradict, though he knew better. Axe's hand-written report of what he saw and overheard on Kelton Kellison's mega-yacht was the only source of the truth. The only people who knew Burkley's role, besides Axe, Haley, and himself, were Kelton Kellison and the vice president.

And if the VP or Kellison had talked, they would have implicated themselves in the crime.

Chad David, his Chief of Staff, came up with the idea. "Burkley's too rich and smart to get caught by a beat cop or the average Joe on the street," Chad argued. "He's likely holed up in a luxury hotel under a fake name, recovering from a cosmetic surgery. Putting out his name and role makes us all look bad."

"If it comes out..." James had said, worrying about the upcoming election.

"We create a cover story. Blame him for a crime people will care about. The police and public will be on the lookout for him. You'll have political cover. If necessary, we say due to the sensitive nature of the investigation, you held back essential details to lull the true terrorist into a false sense of security while the worldwide manhunt went on behind the scenes. We get the word out to all intelligence agencies that he is priority one because of suspected terrorism. But tell the public a different reason for wanting him."

They tossed around ideas. Arson. Blackmail. Computer hacking. None fit.

They sat in silence, contemplating their options.

James retrieved the folded yellow pages of Axe's report about the night on the yacht from his suit coat pocket. He pored over it, searching for an answer. Then he had it. A twist of the knife based on what Axe had overheard. A nickname sure to rub salt in his wound. They would dub him "The Assistant."

Chad leaked the story to a reporter. Within an hour, Kellison's company had picked up the idea and run with it, pushing the word out via their extensive publicity department.

And that quickly, they put a plan in place to draw Burkley out while covering their asses.

Now, at last, he was in their sights.

We get him tonight.

Outside Tampico, Mexico

The quiet sounds of breathing on the team network ended abruptly with the dull pop of suppressed gunfire.

First round of guards gone. So far, so good.

A minute later, Thor reported. "Barn, all clear. Nothing here except two dead guards."

Ronbo came next. "House, all clear. Three guards down."

What the hell? All this for a few guards?

There was a momentary pause while Red digested the report and thought of their response. "Confirmed, barn and house all clear. Search for The Assistant. Closets, cupboards. Also—intel. You know the drill: computers, maps, notes. Beware of tripwires."

Axe didn't hear a sound but felt Red move next to him. He glanced over. Red faced the compound, his rifle up and ready, but whispered his way. "What the hell, Papa?" The Team had changed his nickname from 'Axe' on his previous op with them.

Axe shrugged and whispered back their shared mantra from many years of experience together. "The intel is always wrong."

"Wrong? That's the understatement of the—"

"Contact—house!" Ronbo's voice competed with the sound of his weapon as he fired shot after shot. "Multiple hostiles."

Automatic gunfire broke the silence of the night from dozens of weapons.

Where did they come from? They cleared the area.

"Contact—barn. They're coming up from below." Thor's team joined the battle. The sound of more firing came from the compound, each quickly silenced by a shot from the men's suppressed rifles.

From below? There must be tunnels.

Axe never stopped scanning his sector. It was on now, and danger could come from any direction—including back this far to the rear.

A section of ground near him seemed to shudder in the green glow of his goggles. The ground shifted and rose into the air as a square of earth tilted upwards.

It's a damn trap door!

A head rose from the ground, looking right at Axe. In an instant, Axe noted the night vision goggles similar to his own, the rifle swinging his way. He hesitated. The last thing he wanted to do was kill one of his own men. As the man's rifle came to bear, Axe squeezed his trigger, putting a round into the man's face.

No fatigues, and a different type of chest rig than we all have. He's an enemy. Or was.

"Contact—rear," Axe said, keeping his voice in control. "There's a tunnel entrance—"

He shot the next head to pop up.

"Behind us, my sector."

Axe waited, focused mostly on the dark opening in the ground. When no more heads appeared, he quickly scanned the surrounding area.

To his left and right, further away, the earth moved again. Two more trap doors opened.

He put shots into each, then back into the first one as another head popped up.

"Falling back to waypoint Lime." Axe barely heard Thor's report over the noise of gunshots.

"Lime," Ronbo repeated.

Well, shit.

Waypoint Lime was on the other side of the compound from where he and Red were.

Red's gun added its quiet pop to the night. "Contact—west."

Axe fired rounds at each of the three openings, momentarily preventing the enemy from emerging.

The ground in the distance shook, looking like an earthquake. Axe's heart pounded, and he fought for control. In the 180 degrees he watched and from as close as fifteen feet in front of him to as far as he could see, trapdoor after trapdoor opened. Men clambered out, faster than he could shoot.

His training kicked in and he started firing. "Contact—everywhere!"

The White House Situation Room
Washington, D.C.

The president and his advisors watched the screen as white blob after white blob appeared all over the ranch. It looked like a scene from a horror movie where zombies crawl out of the earth.

Several of his military advisors had never been in combat, despite their years in service and high ranks. They glanced at him with concern to see if he would abort the mission.

"Stay calm, people," James said. "Let them do their jobs. They have a plan."

Onboard *Mine, All Mine*
Isla Mujeres Yacht Club
Isla Mujeres, Mexico
22 Miles East of Cancun

Todd Burkley sat with his glass of Scotch and a large cigar in a crystal ashtray on the rear deck of his yacht. The night he'd been waiting for had finally arrived.

He'd had his doubts. Would that little bitch Haley Albright find his breadcrumbs? Would she believe them? And most of all, would the mighty United States of America, his homeland—well, former—fall for the trap he'd set? Send in a team to capture or kill him... sweet, innocent Todd?

Chuckling, he leaned back on the comfortable loveseat facing the stern and looked up at the moonless sky. He had suspected they wouldn't be able to pass up a mission on this, the darkest night of the month.

He sipped the Scotch while adjusting his earbuds. The cigar had to wait until this part of the operation was complete. He wasn't a smoker, but he'd had a cigar or two to celebrate milestones. Tonight would be well worth celebrating. The death of at least some of the men pursuing him. The humiliation of President Heringten. And the beginning of the end for the analyst he blamed for all his problems. The one he couldn't wait to make suffer: Haley Albright.

The top-of-the-line earbuds were tuned to a private livestream available only to him, broadcast via the internet from seven hundred miles due west. Through them, he heard every word spoken, every shot fired.

If only I had risked a drone. I would love to watch from above. Like a god.

But it would have been noticed and the trap blown.

"Team Three, finish off the two in your area. Then sweep in. Spread out and make sure you don't miss any. And remember, any you find alive, disarm. We want all the bonus money available, right, boys?"

The sound quality on these really is incredible. It's like I'm right there.

Todd took another sip of the excellent Scotch and put his feet on the five-thousand-dollar coffee table with a contented sigh. The bonus money the mercenaries were so looking forward to was chump change to him. It would be worth every cent. When the mop-up operation began, he'd paid extra to ensure the mercenaries recorded video of the executions. He frowned, lowering his expectations slightly.

Or at least video of the dead bodies. One could only hope for so much.

Outside Tampico, Mexico

"Smoke out." Axe tossed a smoke grenade thirty feet ahead, then immediately pulled another grenade from his chest harness.

"Frag out," Axe said as he tossed the grenade into the open hole fifteen feet in front of him, nailing the shot. He dropped prone behind the thin tree trunks, shooting at men spilling from the other holes.

The second grenade exploded, flinging a severed arm out onto the dirt.

He killed several more enemy, carefully placing round after round on target.

Red lay next to him, shooting his own tangos. His sector didn't have as many tunnel openings, but there were enough to keep him busy. The enemy had planned well: draw them into the buildings, spring up on the outside of the compound, flank the attackers, and kill them. It was a hell of a trap.

The first grenade spat out thick smoke, giving them temporary cover. "Moving right." He rolled a few feet from their previous location, firing on another enemy through the smoke. Red rolled after him, shooting at his own contact.

"We're never going to make it across these fields. There's no cover. I've got a plan. Follow me."

"You and your plans, Papa," Red said over the shooting.

Axe low crawled as fast as he could, knowing Red would be right behind him. Bullets snapped all around him.

The smoke was dissipating. They had only a few seconds. "Going in." He didn't know how far the drop would be and didn't care. He and Red had to get off the deck before the smoke cleared and the enemy figured out their disappearing act.

He dove into the hole, praying for a soft landing. He heard Red right behind him.

This might hurt.

A second later, he landed on something soft and wet, hitting first with his shoulder, immediately tucking and rolling into the tunnel, desperate to get out of the way of Red's bulk.

He sprang into a crouch, rifle pointing down the tunnel, grateful he'd tightly buckled his helmet and the attached night vision goggles.

Red rolled and crouched next to him. "You hit?" he whispered.

"No."

"You smell like you're hit."

Axe kept his eyes glued down the tunnel but took a deep breath through his nose. The unmistakable smell of fresh blood flooded his senses. How had he missed it?

"You're bleeding." Red put pressure on his back.

Nothing hurt. "All good."

"You're covered in... Ah. Okay. It's not your blood. We landed on the bleeding dead guy."

He tapped Axe on the shoulder, indicating his readiness to move out. Axe stood, careful to not bump his head on the low ceiling, and moved forward.

Outside Tampico, Mexico

"Team One, report," the gruff voice of the captain called in Owen's ear. He ignored it. After all, he was only a grunt. He had to focus on killing the targets in his area. He'd almost gotten them, but one had thrown a smoke grenade. Though he'd poured a full clip into their position, he suspected they escaped.

Just his luck.

"We've got them on the run, and may have hit one," the lieutenant from Team One reported. "They're moving east, toward the water."

"Team Two?"

"Right next to Team One. They're running like scared little girls. We're on them!"

"Team Three?"

Owen's lieutenant spoke. "I think we shot the two on this side."

We got them? Not that I saw. But the little prick's trying to make us look good, which is fine by me.

Owen slapped a fresh magazine in his rifle as the smoke finally cleared. He scanned the area where he'd last seen the two enemy, but they weren't there. He crawled forward several feet and stopped to look again. Nothing.

He scrambled ahead, desperately searching for a sign of the men he'd fired at, but stopped. He wanted to be out front but didn't dare get ahead of the rest of his team. Any of them might get trigger-happy and put a round into him. Though every enemy captured alive was worth ten thousand dollars per team member, every enemy killed paid five thousand. Many of the men were likely to play it safe: shoot first and figure out who they hit later.

And if they had only two enemy in their sector, they'd better get both. The money he'd received for sharing the cramped, smelly room under the barn for the past three weeks was fine, but he wanted the bonus money. Hell, they all did. It's what had kept the days bearable. But they had to be alive to spend it.

He felt a presence next to him and rolled to his side, bringing his rifle to bear, finger tightening on the trigger.

"Whoa, hold on, Owen. It's me. Curtis."

The man's dark skin didn't show in the NVGs, but there was no hiding the full lips and flat nose of his African heritage. Curtis was the closest thing he had to a friend in the group, because of their assigned proximity for the past twenty-one days in what they dubbed 'the hole.' He and light-skinned, fair-haired, blue-eyed Owen seemed like an odd pair, but they had both come from farm families, joined the Army, then gone to state colleges after discharge. They clicked.

The gunfire around them slackened as the others in their team gave up shooting wildly and searched the area for the two enemy.

"Hey, Curtis. Did you see those two? Where'd they go?" He

continued looking in the area he'd last seen the men, searching for a clue to where they'd run.

"I only saw one. He got two guys before I got up the ladder. But I don't see him now." He asked hesitantly, "Wanna stick together?"

Owen knew what he was suggesting. The racism in the hole had been less than subtle. Curtis had confided that if a firefight ever came, he wasn't convinced he could trust the other mercenaries to not flat-out shoot him.

"Sure, let's go. We're not making any money laying here talking."

They crawled forward, a few feet apart, hunting.

3

LIME

"Passing Salt." Thor's words crackled in Axe's ear. The man sounded like he was out for a jog in the park—his breathing only slightly labored. He seemed completely relaxed. From his voice, no one would ever guess he and his men were being pursued by a horde of mercenaries, vastly outnumbered, in a running retreat for their lives, killing as they fell back.

"Salt, Salt" echoed Ronbo, sounding the same.

Just another day at the office for the SEALs.

The tunnel stretched ahead of Axe. He led the way, crouched in the tight, low space. Red walked backward behind him, matching his steps.

They had opted for speed instead of stealth, keeping their rifles up and ready instead of switching to knives. So far it had paid off—they'd encountered no one.

He figured they must be getting close to the area under the barn and house. The way was lit by a bright white light another twenty yards in front of them. He heard a man speaking but couldn't make out the words.

Axe stopped. Red instantly halted with him. Axe flipped up his

NVGs and gave his eyes a moment to adjust to the brighter light ahead. He started moving again, slower than before.

Slow is smooth and smooth is fast.

The last few feet were in slow motion. Movement caught the eye. Pressed up against the left wall of the tunnel, still stooped to avoid hitting his helmet and goggles against the ceiling, Axe edged closer to the brightly lit open space ahead.

A smooth glance around the corner revealed a large briefing room. Dozens of chairs ran in neat rows facing a whiteboard with a decently drawn map of the compound. A 30-something man in pressed fatigues and a fancy headset with attached microphone paced at the front of the room.

"You said you got 'em!"

Axe pulled back before the man turned in his direction, listening to him berate someone over the radio. An American accent. Southern, maybe. Possibly from Texas. A man used to being in command and frustrated by what he heard.

The man paused before he continued in an exasperated tone. "Fine. Leave behind four guys to sweep the sector again. Take the rest of your men and hustle after Teams One and Two. Double time—they're getting away."

Owen ran along the edge of the gravel road in a crouch, covering ground quickly to catch up to the other teams. Curtis ran two steps behind. The long driveway connected the ranch to the highway ahead. It curved to the right—south—twenty yards ahead. He slowed as they approached, reluctant to come up too quickly behind the other mercenaries. Sporadic gunfire came from around the corner. It sounded to him like the invaders had either been mostly killed or escaped.

They stepped left into the two-foot-deep ditch next to the road, which would offer cover if needed. A few more feet and he should be able to see the teams. They would be moving slowly, on alert.

He inched forward, crouching lower, angling for a view around a small group of bushes.

All hell broke loose.

He and Curtis hit the ground as the night lit up around them. He risked a look over the lip of the ditch and saw a horror show unfolding.

What looked like at least two dozen men were spread out on the road, caught in the open. The mercenaries he had lived underground with were being mown down. His mind instantly identified the cause of the mayhem: machine gun fire.

Round after round poured into the men. Tracers lit the night, coming from two machine guns in textbook ambush positions. Regular rifle fire complemented the machine guns.

In the driveway, a man jerked like a marionette before the rounds finally flung his lifeless body backward.

It was a show of overwhelming force that seemed to come from all directions at once.

Owen pressed his face to the earth, his mouth filling with dirt.

Over the noise of the guns, he heard the choked voice of Team One's lieutenant. "We're getting mowed down! We need reinforce—" A grunt, then nothing.

The thought of firing his weapon never crossed his mind.

"Shit, shit, shit." It sounded like the man leading the enemy was speaking right at them—and having a very bad night.

A pause followed. Axe waited patiently, knowing his Teammates had just sprung the ambush. Red had planned carefully, holding eight men—and their two machine guns—back at the first waypoint. The long driveway curved there, and bushes had been planted along the road. Someone—probably the drug cartel that owned the ranch—had planned to use the position as an ambush point for people coming into the compound.

Red had repurposed it for their own ambush in case the operation was a setup.

Axe nodded to Red in the light spilling into the tunnel from the main room, each thinking the same thing: it pays to be a winner.

Axe moved his head slowly, one eye barely peeking around the corner. The commander made a smooth pivot and started pacing away from them. Predictable. And careless. But understandable. He had other things on his mind.

Axe and Red stepped into the room, silently stalking their prey as he continued to speak into the headset mic.

"Send the quick reaction force. Yes, all the trucks! I think everyone is dead but me and maybe four men to the northeast of the house, so shoot anything that moves. And be careful—these guys are good."

He reached the far end of the room.

Before he could turn and walk back, Axe took a final silent step behind him. He brought his six-inch knife blade against the man's throat.

The man froze for barely an instant before his hand reached for the pistol in the holster strapped to his leg.

"Nope." Axe pulled on the knife as he brought the man tighter into his body. A line of blood appeared on the man's neck. A few drops of blood sprang from it.

"Nope, sir, you mean," Red told Axe, eyeing the pressed fatigues.

"What's your rank?" Axe asked.

"Captain," the man said stiffly. Axe felt him tense, preparing for another move. He hadn't given up yet, despite the immediate risk of the knife.

He thinks I won't slice his throat.

Red noticed, too. He grabbed the pistol from the man's holster, sliding it into the waistband behind his back.

Axe felt the man bring it down a notch after losing the gun.

"At this point, you've lost most of your men, Captain Asshole," Red began, moving in front of him.

"Except the QRF." Even with Axe pressed against him from behind and Red crowding from the front, the captain hadn't given up.

"True, but we'll take them out just as easily. So. Information. Now. What was the gig?"

The man spoke gruffly but came clean. "Hide out here. Three weeks underground. I was told at some point the compound would be attacked, probably last night or tonight. Then we'd spring the ambush."

"That didn't work out too well for you, did it?" Axe couldn't resist commenting.

"Who hired you?" Red watched the man closely, intent on picking up any sign he was lying.

"All done online. Aliases. I have no idea who it really is."

"Bounties?"

Nods.

"Asshole," Axe muttered. "You're American?"

"Yes."

Axe put more pressure on the knife. The man's neck bled freely now. Axe surveyed the room, noticing for the first time the screen of the laptop computer on a desk at the far side of the room.

"I didn't know it would be Americans. They implied a drug war. I figured a rival cartel. A worthwhile mission—ridding the planet of scum."

A line pulsed across the screen with every word the man spoke.

Red pursed his lips and glanced at Axe. "Anything else?"

The line moved, less noticeably, when Red asked his question.

It clicked in Axe's mind. He couldn't help tightening his grip on the man, the knife digging deeper and causing an involuntary grunt of pain from the captain. The line on the computer screen spiked at the sound, and again as Axe spoke. "You asshole! Are you broadcasting this?"

On the gravel road, the shooting finally stopped. What seemed like hours could only have been several seconds. Nothing moved.

From behind him, Owen heard Curtis' barely audible voice. "Let's get the hell out of here!"

Owen considered their situation. An unknown but large group of enemy lay ahead, each one worth five grand.

But they had just taken out more than twenty men.

Then again, they didn't know Owen and Curtis were there. If they came out of their ambush positions to check the bodies…

Or… He pictured the way the road curved. They could sneak forward via the ditch.

Very carefully.

He spoke as quietly as he could, hoping Curtis could hear him— and the enemy couldn't.

"We could flank them."

"Just the two of us?"

"The QRF is probably on the way already."

"Those assholes will shoot anybody they see. They don't care about us."

"Think of the money."

"Can't spend it if you're dead."

Truer words were never spoken. "Let's lay here a while and see what shakes out."

He felt a tap on his foot as Curtis agreed with him. He pressed his face back into the ground and played dead.

Onboard *Mine, All Mine*
Isla Mujeres Yacht Club
700 Miles East of Tampico, Mexico

Todd hyperventilated, out of his mind with rage, listening as his hand-picked mercenary was captured and interrogated.

All his work. All his plans. The money invested. For nothing.

They had won again.

And he had lost.

He was a loser.

The glass tumbler shattered as he squeezed it, his mind caught in a loop.

Loser. Loser. Loser. Loser. Loser.

The pain broke the cycle. He stared in fascination at the long sliver of glass protruding from his palm and the blood springing from the wound, dripping on the pristine white deck of his yacht.

He was not a loser. No, he had merely sacrificed a pawn to gain intelligence on the enemy.

He was a winner. A master planner.

He had contingencies in place for this.

And contingencies for the contingencies.

It was far from over.

The White House Situation Room
Washington, D.C.

"Sir. Trucks converging on the compound." A military staffer called out the obvious. "Also, if we widen out the view," he said, using the mouse at the workstation in front of him. The main screen changed to show a larger section of the Mexican coastline. "You can see twelve vessels cruising into the area where the SEALs' recovery boat is."

James stared. It had to be Burkley. This was too well planned to be a drug cartel lab they had accidentally stumbled into.

The Chairman of the Joint Chiefs of Staff, a pale, bald man in his 70s, chimed in. "Mr. President, the trucks they can handle. The boats… they could take them out…"

"But it would change the cover story from a drug cartel dispute to something else. Like an incursion by a foreign power."

The Chairman offered a grim nod.

"Give me the damn executive order to sign," James said. The op was no longer a military incursion into an allied country without informing them or receiving permission. With the stroke of his pen, he would temporarily assign the SEAL Team to the CIA, making it a covert operation in an ally's country. It didn't seem like much difference, but the law was the law. If things went bad, a blown intelligence operation would have less fallout than a failed military action. If they were going to follow the last-ditch plan, it had to be this way.

"Get the boat out of the area. Avoid confrontation at all costs. And roll the bus, then update the Team."

Outside Tampico, Mexico

Captain Asshole chuckled. "Yes, we're still broadcasting. They've heard everything. And unless you want to kill me right now, cool it with the blade, will you?"

Axe hesitated, then eased the pressure on the knife against the man's throat.

"Kilo One to Bravo One." Axe glanced at Red as the call came over their network.

"Bravo Actual. Send traffic," Red replied, locking eyes with Axe.

"Multiple tangos converging on your position by road from north and south. Eight, repeat eight large trucks with men and two technicals with machine guns. Total of five, repeat five vehicles from each direction. How copy?"

"Solid copy. Five and five. We'll handle."

"Orders follow. Don't drink and drive. Repeat, don't drink and drive."

"Copy don't drink and drive."

"It's time, Papa. We gotta go."

"Copy. First, let him listen," Axe said, making sure the line on the computer monitor moved as he spoke. "I'll give you a choice. Right here, right now. Come along. Tell us everything you know, voluntarily. No enhanced interrogation. The man who hired you is a known terrorist. Do the right thing. Help us catch him."

"What about immunity from prosecution?"

Axe shook his head. "Prison. A few years and you're out."

"Screw you. Live in a cage? I'd rather die on my feet than—" He twisted his body mid-sentence, bringing his hands up and pressing them against Axe's knife hand with all his might.

Axe barely resisted, letting the knife move away from the throat as the man fought against him.

Red's knife slid smoothly under the Captain's rib cage and into his heart. For a single moment, the captain stood firm, his eyes widening as his attention switched from Axe's arm and the knife near his neck to

Red standing in front of him. He sagged, impaling himself further on Red's long knife.

Axe and Red eased the dead man to the floor.

"Be careful what you wish for, brother," Red whispered to him.

"He's dead, Burkley," Axe said loudly, looking down at the captain. "They're all dead, and you're next. Hide in your hole, little rat. Savor every moment. Because it's only a matter of time until you're either locked in a cell or cold in the ground."

By the time Axe and Red rejoined the Team, the mayhem was over. The trucks had driven straight into the ambush. They burned brightly, the skeletons of fried enemy combatants visible in the flames.

"Headcount," Red demanded. The fire team leaders reported. All present, arrayed in a defensive perimeter. No injuries, no deaths.

A large, expensive tour bus came slowly toward them from the north. It moved onto the wrong side of the road, avoiding the burning vehicles, and slowed to a stop as Red rose from the ditch and waved.

"Our ride is here. Hustle up."

The men emerged from the area and quickly boarded the bus. Standing in the narrow aisle, they stripped off gear and dirty fatigues, stowing all in duffel bags from the overhead racks. While they cleaned off the grime and dirt, they grumbled about 'spy shit,' and how warriors didn't exfil disguised as a soccer team.

Axe climbed the three stairs into the bus, feeling tired. The young guys would be fine once they got some food and a bit of sleep. But for a few days, he'd feel the hike, all the crawling through the dirt, and the dive into the tunnel.

Red nodded at the bus driver, a retired Army Ranger based in Mexico the CIA used occasionally. The man closed the door and put the bus in gear. As they navigated a careful multi-point turn to head back north, Axe eased himself into the front seat above the stairs. Next to him, standing in the aisle, Red watched the men finish their transformations, shook his head, and pulled two duffels down from the rack above, handing one to Axe.

"The matching tracksuits are a nice touch. Your idea?"

Axe shook his head. "Partner."

"Your partner, or your girlfriend?" Axe had mentioned Connie, his relatively new girlfriend, to him.

"Partner. Haley. Come on. The girlfriend doesn't get operational details."

"Good. Well, she's clever, this partner. A blond, right? When you going to introduce me?"

"Never." The idea of Haley dating one of the Team didn't sit right with him.

"We'll see."

A few hours later, they'd pull into a marina to meet a chartered fishing boat for a relaxing cruise home, courtesy of the CIA.

As much as Axe wanted to sleep, the operation wasn't finished yet. He and the rest of the Team kept themselves awake and alert, weapons hidden but nearby. You never knew.

Red looked over at him. "We're no closer to the terrorist than we were before."

"Maybe. But now we know for sure he's out there. He's actively gunning for us. Before, we thought he might be living in the lap of luxury on a beach somewhere. And besides, I picked up a souvenir from my Mexican vacation." He patted the duffel bag where he'd stowed the laptop taken from the underground planning room. "Haley's going to love it."

Owen and Curtis lay in the ditch, the darkness covering them. It had been a while since they'd heard machine gun fire along the highway, as well as RPGs, followed by vehicles blowing up.

Curtis' voice was quiet but hopeful. "You think we got 'em?"

"Are you nuts? No way. Those guys were top-notch. SEALs, I'd guess."

They shared a long pause as they consider their options.

"What should we do now?" Owen asked.

"I say we ditch the gear, walk into town, buy some tourist clothes and get the first bus out of here," Curtis said.

Owen could picture it. The first half of their pay had been deposited upon arrival at the ranch. It would keep him going until another contract came along. "Hang out in a beach town," he agreed. "Drink for a few days. I'll get a wicked sunburn, then we take a bus home. Just a couple of ordinary asshole Americans."

"You got your wallet? Passport?"

"Yeah."

"Okay then."

"Wait." The partial salary would be nice, but... "What about the bonus money?"

"You think we actually killed any of them?"

Owen thought back to the way the two men flat out disappeared from the area at the start of the firefight. "Probably not, but it doesn't matter. To get it, we'd have to go back, see if the captain made it. And eventually, the police or Mexican Army are going to show up asking questions. We don't want to be around when that happens. We can't spend it if we're locked up."

"Or dead."

They stood slowly, arms up in surrender—just in case. When no one shot them, they stripped off their gear and fatigues, leaving them both in boxers and t-shirts. Clutching their wallets and passports, they hurried north, parallel to the road, their way made easier by the dying glow of the QRF's burning trucks.

Onboard *Mine, All Mine*
Isla Mujeres Yacht Club
Isla Mujeres, Mexico
700 Miles East of Tampico, Mexico

Todd spent the night pacing the stern of the yacht, his cigar untouched. He finally gave up when the leader of the flotilla sent him a coded email. A fast ship had outrun them as they converged on the area. From the timing, however, there was no way the SEALs could have been on it.

There was no report from the quick reaction force he'd thoughtfully put together and housed at great expense near the compound for weeks.

He assumed they were all dead.

The SEALs, including the one who had taunted him on the radio, had simply vanished.

His carefully laid trap, the first step in his plan, had failed.

Spectacularly.

In a few hours he would watch an amazing sunrise over the marina. He loved it here. It had high-speed internet and the locals were friendly without being nosy. They lived their lives to the fullest. The other gringos were mostly Canadian, along with a few Europeans, all good for a wave or smile but otherwise keeping to themselves. People who wanted to show off went to Belize. Those who wanted to party or snorkel went to Cozumel. Only the cruisers who wanted lazy peace and quiet came to Isla Mujeres.

Nothing in his past connected him to the location. It was an excellent base of operations.

He reviewed the long, detailed email addressed to Chang, the CEO of Happastology, and copied to a dozen of his VPs. The man Kellison had tasked Todd with unseating as the fiftieth-richest person in the world would finally have his revenge.

Dear Mr. Chang, it began. *My name is Todd Burkley, formerly of Cottswoth-Goldentech, and I have a confession. At Kelton Kellison's behest, six months ago I orchestrated an attack on your company. Kellison ordered me to arrange the killing of your programmers and managers to destroy the launch of your virtual reality platform scheduled for that day.*

Simply put, he made me do it all so he could be richer than you. All the attacks on New York City were designed by him to sabotage your company while disguising the intent.

I have been in hiding from both the authorities and Kellison's paid assassins. I have only surfaced to contact you with the following information I have spent the past months compiling. It contains all you need to bring down Kellison and his company, from backdoor passwords for his systems to many embarrassing personal details about Kelton.

Also below are facts only I could know about the attacks he made me commit. I trust you have the resources to verify them, proving what I say is true.

Due to the sway he had over me, Kelton ruined my life. He tried to do the same to you. I hope, for both our sakes, you will use the attached information to do the same to him.

I live with shame and regret. I beg your forgiveness, though I do not deserve it.

Below the note, he included all the company's vulnerabilities, dirty secrets, horrible stories, and shady business dealings from his time running Kelton's company.

Much of the information was true, though the bad actions were all his own doing, not Kelton's. The man didn't have a clue about all Todd had been up to.

Other details were false, though impossible to disprove, and too salacious not to use.

He reviewed the entire email, sent it, and sat back with a smile.

How long will they wait to act?

His hand throbbed under the white gauze bandage. He'd removed the piece of glass, cleaned and dressed the wound. Now, he took his right thumb and pressed it against his left palm, directly on the cut. Pain shot through him.

He smiled as his eyes flooded with tears.

Let the pain come. He deserved it for his failures.

Soon, others will feel pain. Haley. Kelton. Like this—only so much worse.

A part of his mind fought for control. A small voice inside tried to explain he'd gone over the edge, that it had been coming a long time. If he'd only listen, they could get out of this, salvage what was left. Save his mind, if not his soul.

He pressed harder. The voice went away as the pain increased.

He finally eased off, fascinated by the fresh blood seeping out from the edge of the bandage, then returned to enjoying the sunrise.

4

HOME

Haley let her head rest against the seat. The car warmed up slowly as it defrosted both front and back windows. The predawn darkness made the early morning still and peaceful.

She felt exhausted but relieved, with Axe and the SEALs safely out of the conflict zone, on their way home via a pleasant fishing cruise in the Gulf of Mexico.

As tired as her body felt, her mind spun. Burkley lived. Tonight's operation proved it. She'd never doubted, but others had. It was only through her diligent efforts—and those of her new team—they'd stumbled upon the trail of clues leading to the ranch.

Not to the ranch. To the ambush.

She'd warned them but still felt responsible. Thank goodness none of her guys, as she thought of them, had been hurt or killed.

It was a trap all along. Todd planted those crumbs for me to find. And I fell for it.

But it was over now. She would go home, sleep, then return for work a few hours later than normal, which Gregory had approved.

After resting, she could focus better, see if shaking the tree had any effect.

Haley pulled out of the nondescript Class A office complex, leaving behind the guards at the gate. Though the average American didn't know the upscale building housed an elite intelligence division, security rivaled the campuses of the CIA, NSA, or Pentagon.

It had been a long day and night. Her brain worked slower than normal due to the stress, lack of sleep, and information overload. She wanted to go through the latest intelligence from Mexico, but once the SEALs were safe, she called it a night.

There would be telephone call logs to sort. Maybe someone called someone who called Burkley with an update. She could use voice analysis. Look at internet traffic. Her mind churned with possibilities, but not as fast as usual. She needed rest.

At least she no longer lived so far from the office. The home she had purchased through an anonymous shell company to hide from Burkley could be reached in fifteen minutes... if she went straight there. Which she couldn't. It would be too easy to stake out the office and tail her when she left. For the past six months, she had conducted a surveillance detection route, or SDR, every night after work.

Tonight, despite her tiredness, would be no different. But she had long before run out of new routes to take. There were only so many roads to and from the area of the office. She would fall back on a shorter one and just stay vigilant.

Haley made turn after turn, eyeing the familiar streets, looking for tails, memorizing license plates. In an hour, traffic would be busy, but only a few cars were out now, and none of them went in her direction for more than a few blocks.

There were no cars moving on the streets behind or in front, and the road beckoned with green lights. Satisfied she wasn't being followed, Haley cut the SDR short. She would be home, showered, and in bed soon.

5

TRACK

Suburban Arlington, Virginia

His given name was Toby, but no one in the business used it. People asked for "The Tracker," or "Track" for short. He was a short, ordinary man in his late fifties with a scraggly salt and pepper beard and graying ponytail. The extra pounds he carried on his belly made him look harmless.

He only got called in for particularly difficult cases—and charged accordingly.

He had been a cab driver for years and knew the streets of the D.C. and Alexandria areas backward and forward. His lack of curiosity about current events—he didn't read the papers or listen to the news—came in handy for everyone. After he presented his reports to the agency he worked for, he never heard what happened to the people he stalked… including the many violent deaths.

Track could sit for hours without boredom, happily waiting and watching.

This morning he slumped in his car, parallel parked on the deserted street. He'd waited all night and thought he had missed her.

The silver sedan drove by as he froze, his eyes mostly closed.

He felt it. Tonight, his waiting might pay off.

He let his target's car get several blocks ahead, then he pulled onto the empty street. He would follow for a few turns, watching the woman's surprisingly effective detection efforts, narrowing down the location of her home a bit more. The same as he had done every night for weeks.

Tomorrow, he would select another likely location—further away from her office—and wait to see if she drove by. It might take a few more nights, but there were only so many streets. Eventually, the net would tighten enough for him to follow the last few blocks right to her house, all without arousing suspicion.

The agency's directives had been clear. Find the target's home, but under no circumstances could he be detected.

Once he found her base, he'd report, receive his bonus, and move on to the next assignment, without wondering or caring what happened to the young woman.

The first week on the case, he had suggested adding additional vehicles and air support, but his ideas had been vetoed. The target might see or sense a larger operation, he'd been told.

They wanted him to hunt his way.

One night at a time.

Playing the odds, closing the net a little more every evening.

Picking away until he found her home with his slow but effective method... or she made a mistake.

Track drove the main street, following nearly a mile behind the sedan, easily keeping her in sight with the straight road and lack of traffic.

She made no effort at subtlety or evasion. Out of habit or tiredness, he suspected, she even signaled a right turn, though he couldn't discount a potential trap being set for him.

But if that happened, it happened. He had nothing incriminating on him, didn't have any operational details, and could keep his mouth shut. He was a harmless guy out for a drive to the store or breakfast.

He saw in his mind the streets ahead and recalled routes the target had taken previous nights in the area. As her car swung out of sight, he turned abruptly, parallel to her path, and floored it down the smaller road. He had a hunch she was exhausted and had been lulled into a false sense of security. Tonight he had picked her up several miles from her office on a route she used too often, probably subconsciously, though the street was one of the main thoroughfares and hard to avoid if she needed to end up north of her office.

The Tracker bet she had done her usual expert job of turns, double-backs, and running red lights for several minutes near work. Now, believing she was in the clear, she would head directly home.

If he hurried, he could turn in front of her car and "follow" her.

If not, he would still be much closer to her location than before.

He turned left, carefully running a stop sign, and sped toward the street he'd seen the target turn onto. Had he gotten ahead of her?

He looked left as he slowed for the red light.

There.

Her sensible, three-year-old car approached. The light changed to red, forcing her to stop.

As the light turned green for him, Track signaled and turned onto the road in front of the target. He swung into the right lane as if he drove the route every morning.

Seconds later, the light behind him changed. The silver car followed him.

Track stayed three miles under the speed limit, letting the target car slowly overtake him.

Moments later, she signaled a left onto Cottage Street, he noted. Track continued on his course as the sedan made the turn down the narrow residential street.

Once she was out of sight, Track made a sharp left, not bothering with moving into the other lane first, down a residential street, three blocks away from the subject.

He had found her neighborhood. Given the lack of turns, he felt confident she lived nearby. She was going straight home.

There were too many fences and small, older homes set close together to see three blocks, so he once again sped down the street to the first stop sign. He ignored it, turned left without signaling, and barreled back toward her street.

Track slowed one block away and drove sedately to Cottage, where he stopped completely, signaling a right turn.

A turn he didn't make. He snapped off the signal immediately when he saw the light wink off over the side of a small red brick house halfway down the block on the far side of the road. Inside, lights turned on behind blinds.

He noted the address and continued forward.

Once again, he had successfully tracked his target.

What happened next wasn't his concern.

6

THE MOVEMENT

Rebecca Dodgeson—Bec—sat at her workstation in the muted light of the control room, rethinking her life choices.

Behind her, Stefan Conroy—or Pioneer, as they had been instructed to call him—stood atop his platform. The room had supposedly been modeled after NASA's launch center control room. But she'd enjoyed enough sci-fi reruns to recognize the layout as an expanded version of a starship's bridge, complete with a raised captain's platform and throne-like chair. At first, the idea of Conroy—or rather, Pioneer—being their starship captain had been amusing. Cool, even. They were boldly going where no one had gone before, working differently, creating a product and business to help the world.

But it's more than that now. The man fancies himself a god.

Conroy was one of the richest men in the world, a certified genius, and her employer—for now.

She saw his reflection in the corner of her monitor, standing arrogantly on the raised platform, legs spread wide, hands on hips, with his core group of three: his right-hand man and two right-hand women. The ultimate inner circle.

Bec's eyes flicked away, nervous about making any eye contact, even on the shiny surface. She pushed her oversize, black-frame nerd glasses higher onto her nose and ran her hand through her short, dark hair, hoping her androgynous looks would keep Pioneer's attention off her. It had worked so far.

She stared into space, occasionally moving her hand on the mouse to appear busy, and remembered the weirdness of the previous evening.

Monday Night

Pioneer Park Soccer Stadium
St. John, United States Virgin Islands

Sitting in the semi-darkness of the soccer stadium, Bec saw nothing but eager faces waiting expectantly to see their hero and guru, Pioneer. She forced her mouth into a fake excited smile to fit in.

There were about seventy-five hundred men and women in the stands, from early twenty-something techies like herself to boomers who had dropped out of society to come to the promised utopia.

There were all shapes, sizes, and colors attracted to Conroy, but women outnumbered the men.

Pioneer. I have to get used to calling him by the title, not his name.

With her short hair, baggy clothes, and tomboy demeanor, Bec was unique. Every other woman, from stunning to mousy, took pains to look feminine. The way Pioneer preferred.

Eight months earlier, on her twenty-fifth birthday, she had turned her back on Silicon Valley, enticed by an offer she couldn't refuse: one of the first hires at the startup tech company run by the brilliant, reclusive billionaire Stefan Conroy.

Around her, people continued to fill the padded seats of the gleaming new facility, practically quivering with anticipation. Just as they had every Monday night and Saturday morning since she came to the island. Except back then, there had been her and a handful of other people meeting in a conference room at the Center, Conroy's high-tech concrete bunker on a mountain in the middle of the island.

He used to sound much more like a visionary leader. Now he sounds like…

She didn't want to think about what he reminded her of.

Tonight, the stadium held more and more of the long-time island residents.

Well, they'd have to. Lots of pressure on them to either come… or go. Sell out like most of the others already have, leave the island, and never return.

She wondered which Pioneer preferred—a few more souls to hang on his every word, or the possibility of buying yet more of the houses and land from the locals.

Is this job, the money, the lifestyle, worth… this?

Conroy had been a prodigy, programming incredible software and creating amazing products as a teenager. As he entered his twenties, he focused on taking existing technology and making it ten, twenty, one hundred times better, then patenting those improvements. He had patents for the guts of half the important tech the world now used. At twenty-two, he became a billionaire.

Then he disappeared. Took his money and dropped off the face of the earth for ten years.

Bec remembered it well. She'd been a computer nerd in high school when it happened. It was headline news: One of the greatest minds of the century quits his (quite luxurious) rat race and disappears.

Rumors swirled. He traveled to the great libraries of the world and spent weeks reading one-of-a-kind manuscripts in search of knowledge and enlightenment.

He worked twenty hours a day on the technology and logistics of colonizing the galaxy.

Or he quietly bought up land on Caribbean islands, had a harem of women, and forty-two children.

She saw him now, recognizing him from behind as he stood in the shadows of the stadium's team tunnel, talking to someone out of her view. Others in the crowd noticed too. An excited murmur swept the stands. It wouldn't be long now.

Bec recognized the ploy for what it was: a way to build anticipation. Dally off-stage, unavailable yet in view, building the crowd's desire. Offer a person a glimpse of what they can't quite have, and they'll want it even more.

Bec slid her glasses back into place and made more of an effort to fit in, smiling at the woman next to her and raising her eyebrows in a reasonably believable show of excitement. She loved the island, the weather—which was better even than California's Silicon Valley—and her job. She worked on a small team identifying vulnerable network systems. The sales team would contact the companies and make a deal: if we hack your system, you use our new cloud-based, AI-assisted monitoring and protection cybersecurity suite.

She got paid to be a "white hat," good-guy hacker and to advise the programming team on security improvements. It was her dream job.

Plus, she was in on the ground floor. When this thing went public, her stock options would make her at least a millionaire. She could leave and do whatever she wanted with the rest of her life.

This morning had dawned a spectacular day, as every day did on the island of St. John, and as the sun set over the stadium, the night air had the perfect amount of warmth and humidity. The natural beauty of the place had attracted her as much as the job's salary, and she had overlooked the adulation heaped upon Conroy, in part because she also shared in it to some extent. The man was brilliant.

In the tunnel, Conroy finally turned, finished with his conversation —or rather, with building suspense. A few hundred people started clapping and chanting in unison. *Clap-Clap-Clap,* "Pi-o-neer," stretching the man's nickname-slash-title over three beats while they stomped their feet in time. More joined until the entire stadium rang with the noise. Bec joined in despite herself.

Clap-Clap-Clap, "Pi-o-neer."

Clap-Clap-Clap, "Pi-o-neer."

Pioneer bounded up the five steps to the empty stage in the middle of the soccer field, high-fiving one of his security detail standing nearby. As usual during these "talks," he was barefoot, with the stage covered by a large, thick rug. He seemed to glow as the spotlights hit him, his barrel chest, bulging arm muscles in a tight black t-shirt, and carefully groomed dark beard appearing larger than life on the jumbo screen at the far end of the stadium.

The crowd roared with approval and stood as one, clapping, forcing Bec to her feet to fit in.

The thought had been gaining strength in her for a few weeks, but she had successfully pushed it aside over and over. Surrounded by the screaming crowd though, she could no longer deny it.

She had inadvertently joined a cult.

Mom is going to be so disappointed in me when I tell her.

Stefan stood barefoot, the plush rug comfortable against his feet. He enjoyed the crowd's wild cheering for another few seconds, smiling benevolently at his people. Allowing them to express their adoration cemented his hold over them further, but he had an additional consideration tonight: the countless viewers around the world who he needed to entice to his cause.

"My friends," he began. Instantly, the energized crowd fell silent, though they remained standing.

"To those of you in this beautiful stadium, please join me in celebrating and welcoming for the first time, our viewers, your fellow Pioneers worldwide." He gestured to the cameramen arrayed on the ground around the stage, then up at the jumbo screen at the end of the field. "That's right, we are finally broadcasting to our brothers and sisters who are unable to join us here in Paradise Found. Welcome!"

The crowd of believers erupted again. He noted a few of the women in the section directly in front of him at midfield, already had tears of joy streaming down their faces.

Wait until I get going; they'll cry so much, by the end of the night they'll be dehydrated.

He smiled at a long-haired blond in the front row, his favorite disciple so far. So plain looking on the outside. But wild on the inside… and so desperate to please. His pulse quickened at the thought of her, and he vowed to keep the evening's talk to only one hour.

Stefan adjusted the tiny microphone running from over his ear to his mouth. Once again, the stadium quieted quickly.

"Let me begin with this: there is nothing inherently wrong or evil about technology. It made me who I am today. It brings my image and voice to you, my brothers and sisters sitting at your computers or listening on your phone during your endless commute. Many of you will stream it over the next days and weeks, relying on the blessing of on-demand technology to provide you with the inspiration and education you seek. You will share it with your friends and family via social networks so they too can discover the joy in these messages." He looked directly at the main camera.

"No. Computers, the internet, cell phones, social media are not to be feared or reviled. We rejoice in them!"

He offered a big smile for the crowd, which went wild once again, but calmed quickly. They needed to hear his words.

"But when these blessings are abused, it is a problem. When we ignore our communities, become disconnected from real life, avoid the beauty of our natural world so we can stay inside and live an ultimately unfulfilling digital existence… what shall we call that?" He paused, first looking at the camera, then at the live audience in the stadium.

"Evil," many in the audience called. They'd been well educated over the months.

"Wrong," others called.

"Heartbreaking!" the blond in the front row cried out desperately.

He nodded sadly, knowing the audience at home had heard the crowd, and his special friend in the front, via the microphones he'd had installed specifically for that purpose.

"Exactly. Evil, wrong, and especially heartbreaking."

His speech revved up from there. He had the crowd in the palm of his hand, as usual, as he listed the terrors of dedicating one's life to technology at the expense of living an authentic life.

Nothing too far out, nothing too controversial for this first broadcast. Thousands of people watching at home needed merely to have their interest piqued. He couldn't take a soul from A to Z in one lesson. What he needed at this stage were the curious. People he could convert over the next few months to serious followers. When the time was right, soon, they would be the ones he would rely on to be the ground troops his true believers would lead.

He didn't need thousands more on the island. He had his army assembled here already, and more true believers swamped St. Thomas, a mere thirty-minute ferry ride to the west. Hundreds of more true believers already filled many major cities and several smaller ones, in the countries around the world through his efforts over the past years.

The new viewers would make the end game easier. Every one was precious.

Stefan artfully brought the evening to a close with the argument he and his tiny inner circle had agreed would persuade the most people to take a simple action. The first small step down toward eventually worshiping him.

"To join this booming movement, do you need to make a sacrifice? Send a donation? Disconnect from your friends and family? Of course not! Just the opposite, in fact. This is what I ask of you: physically visit with a friend, a family member, or a neighbor. That's right, in person!" He leaned forward to whisper conspiratorially, with a sly smile. "If you must, use social media to make the arrangements."

The stadium crowd laughed in delight, though none of them could make any arrangements via social media or speak with any family not already on the island. They had renounced and abandoned their cell phones, tablets, and computers when they joined him in Paradise Found, known to the rest of the world as St. John.

"But meet them in person, preferably in a beautiful, natural place on this amazing planet. My community will set aside this Wednesday morning as a time to detach from technology, enjoy nature, and socialize. We ask you to do the same. Is that difficult, a tremendous sacrifice?" he asked, looking earnestly at the camera.

"No!" the audience screamed.

"No. If you like, you could go a step farther. To show your commitment to our planet, to your serenity and sanity, you could take twenty-four hours off from any electronics aside from electricity. No need to suffer! Just... unplug for a day. Would you at least consider that? For me?"

Out of the corner of his eye, he caught a glimpse of his rugged, handsome face on the huge monitor, but forced himself to keep his eyes imploringly on the main camera broadcasting his image around the world.

"And last, ask yourself a simple question: what would you be willing to do for a quieter, more peaceful, more fulfilling life?" He smiled gently at the camera. "For such lives are possible, if we try."

The live audience sighed with happiness. It was the life they were living now. They were happy tending the gardens, fishing, or for the many tech workers he'd recruited, working hard to grow his empire during work hours but unplugging and enjoying the natural bounty of the island after hours. His dream realized. His utopia. His people.

One island now. One planet soon.

"With that, I will leave you for now. I will see you again, hopefully live and in person or, if necessary, via the technology we give thanks for while we control it—not allowing it to control us. Goodnight, my friends."

He bowed his head humbly for a moment. The red light of the camera broadcast cut off as the feed switched to a screen showing bullet points summarizing the action steps he'd requested at the end, along with the offer of a free video course to those who filled out a simple online form.

The crowd in the stadium clapped their hands three times, then called out PI-O-NEER while stomping their feet. Over and over. He basked in their adulation.

Tonight was the beginning of the end. The plans laid over the past ten years were almost ready.

In no time at all, he would rule the planet. Not as a politician, dictator, or king.

He would rule as a god.

The Control Center
St. John, United States Virgin Islands
Tuesday, 8:07 a.m.

"Pull up the top twenty-five," Pioneer ordered from his platform.

Bec snapped out of contemplating the weirdness of the night before. While there were nineteen other men and women at workstations around her, all about her age, the command was directed at her. She had compiled the list based on the input of the others, along with her own research. In a way, it was her baby.

A quick click of her mouse brought the list first to her monitor. A shortcut keystroke flung it to the huge screen in the front of the room.

"Tell me more about number twenty-three," Stefan commanded, looking down at his core group of hackers in the control center with him.

One of his subjects, the woman who sat next to the tomboy, stood from her workstation and turned to face him. She blushed; he could see the red spreading even from his command station. Her long brown hair needed the split ends trimmed, and she looked as mousy as ever in a flower-print summer dress a half-size too loose on her. But he'd enjoyed her company twice in the past month. She wasn't frumpy in his bed at night.

He smiled benevolently. "Report."

"Pioneer," she began, blushing more. She had coined the name for him months ago when he invited her to visit his bed the first time. After finishing with her, she had blurted out her belief that his people should no longer address him by his name. He loved the idea and told her so, right before he kicked her out. No one slept with him. It would destroy the illusion he worked so hard to maintain that he needed merely a single hour of sleep each night. The next morning, he had told Gunther, his right-hand man. Within a few days, the title had caught on.

"Report." He added an edge to his voice. He deserved to be

worshipped, but at the moment, he had an important decision to make. Or at least, appear to make.

"Pioneer," she began again, more focused, though her face appeared no less red. "Target number twenty-three is a main freshwater treatment and distribution facility for the County of Los Angeles, containing, of course, the city of Los Angeles. It has mostly physical vulnerabilities. My esteemed colleagues have probed for cyber weaknesses but have found only minor ones so far, though they have not been directed to apply the full force of their efforts, pending your final decision. They are cautiously optimistic that, in time, they may discover some, or create one."

"Elaborate on the last."

She stared directly at him, her expression rapturous to be reporting to him on the target she had selected and researched. "They are confident a social engineering hack is possible due to the bureaucratic tendencies of several of the workers at the site. Barring that, or in conjunction with it, a Trojan horse email has a high percentage of success."

Stephan nodded, giving her a small dose of his charm. She beamed back at him. He would enjoy her again tonight. He glanced to his left at Gunther, who nodded discreetly, knowing exactly what he wanted.

"Potential reward?"

"The state and county have rare budget surpluses. Their system is essential and must be protected at all costs. The water must flow, or the city will grind to a halt. Civil unrest. Hundreds or thousands of deaths. Fear, confusion, rage. A mass exodus, taking property and sales tax revenue with it. My colleagues and I predict they will happily pay to upgrade their security once we point out their vulnerabilities and offer our product as a more robust solution."

He stared at the huge monitor. The business side didn't matter to him in the least. Big deal: a few million dollars for finding and fixing a problem before it got out of hand—after manufacturing it themselves, of course.

The cyber part also meant nothing. But appearances had to be maintained. Most of the techs were uninitiated into the inner circle of true believers.

"Excellent report..."

"Tina," Gunther muttered.

"Tina." Stefan chastised himself, not for his lack of knowledge of her name. His place on Earth did not require him to remember the names of his subjects. No, he kicked himself for using her name at all.

He turned his attention back to the screen without another thought of her. "Report on number nineteen."

Despite listening to the summary of the next several potential targets, Stefan had made his decision a few weeks before when the Los Angeles authorities had begun an investigation into his past. The state he had called home would suffer at his hand. It was the perfect pre-test before the actual target. If the device worked, it would be a joy to watch.

Of course it will work. I designed it.

Bec worked her keyboard, facilitating the presentation. She glanced at Tina sitting next to her. The connection between Tina and Pioneer was plain. The rumors about the man selecting female workers to join him after hours were probably true.

No, thank you. Not interested. I can take my salary and go back to California.

Well... after a few more months. The island was magical and the gig easy. She did her work, avoided attention from Pioneer, and spent her off hours living in a paradise quieter, more beautiful, and with better weather than California. Waiting made sense. See if anything changed with these kooky people. She could play along.

So what if it was a cult? As long as the money kept appearing in her account and they left her alone, no problem. No one had tried to recruit her. Aside from the mandatory Monday night meetings, and the optional—but strongly encouraged—Saturday morning ones, that is. But then again, she kind of shared the beliefs. Less screen time, more time in nature? Yes, please. More time with people she liked, the trail runners, paddle boarders, and snorkelers? Absolutely.

Was she living in denial? Maybe. But she'd made up her mind for now. And she had a lead on a publicly traded company with lax security she might be able to exploit by the end of her shift.

Bec got back to work, half listening to the ongoing report to Pioneer while her fingers danced on the keys, probing for weaknesses on the distant company's system.

In a few hours, she'd be off again. She could bike to Salt Pond Bay and swim with the turtles.

As long as they don't ask me to do anything weird, I can live and let live. Besides, how bad can they be?

7

AFTER ACTION

Central Analysis Group Headquarters
Conference Room C
Arlington, Virginia

Haley lowered the cheap white metal blinds first, then used the swivel wand on the left side to spin them fully shut. It annoyed her when the rest of the squad of analysts shot glances across the room at her team. She couldn't decide if they were curious, envious, or resentful. The obvious solution: shut them out.

She'd slept a few hours, then come right back in. Going over the previous night's op was the priority for the day.

"Right, about last night," she started, looking at the man and woman at the small conference table. After calling the New York City attack correctly, working with Axe and Admiral Nalen to help stop the attack on the nuclear power plant, and leading the task force to find The Boomer, Gregory had given her a perk: a team of two analysts.

If he only knew about the report Axe and I wrote for the president about the vice president's role in the attacks... I'd be managing the whole group.

But no one knew—only herself, Axe, and the president. Exactly how they wanted it.

Her two team members sat across from each other; Nancy on the left, Dave on the right. It bothered her. The table wasn't much bigger than a four-top at a cozy restaurant, but it forced her to swivel back and forth to face them.

Lately, a lot of little things bothered her more than they should. At night she lay in bed thinking about it, wondering if she chafed at being stuck inside as an analyst after her recent success in the field. Usually, she chalked it up to that.

But part of her wondered if she had unresolved issues about the men she'd killed on the operation with Axe.

She always pushed the thought down immediately, burying it deep.

She was fine.

Nancy went first—as usual, the more spontaneous of the two. She and Dave were in their fifties, which Haley struggled to not think of as old. They'd been analysts for years and had successfully mined data which resulted in protecting the country. Neither seemed annoyed at being assigned to her, despite being more experienced and thirty years older. Nancy's brown-going-gray hair stuck out wildly this morning, like she had been running late and didn't use product.

Dave's full beard needed a trim; it was bushier than most people wore theirs these days. In the months they'd worked together, Haley had noticed more and more gray whiskers. Here and there, bright white ones had grown in recently, too. He looked distinguished and smart in a college professor way, but the gray showed his age.

"Let's start with what went right. We called the ambush successfully," Nancy said matter-of-factly.

It had been a true team effort. After careful analysis of suspected cartel sites, they agreed there should either be many more guards—or none, if the site were abandoned. Five warm bodies on the thermal scan, only occasionally outside the house, didn't make sense. If Todd were actually there, protected by his own security detail or by arrangement with a drug cartel, it would have looked different. Five men were not enough, or too many. Burkley would either use his millions to surround himself with goons or be all alone, anonymous, incognito. Haley believed he was holed up somewhere quietly, keeping to himself.

"And you called the boats attempting to intercept the exfil if it ended up being a trap," Dave told Haley. It sounded like he was kissing her ass, but she had eventually realized he wasn't—he just told it like it was. Credit where credit was due.

Haley nodded. "Great idea on the fancy soccer bus," she told him. The idea of getting the SEALs out disguised as a traveling American soccer team had worked like a charm. His mouth twitched in as much of a smile as she'd ever seen. He wasn't in the business for praise, advancement, or money. He loved the battle, staying one step ahead of the bad guys.

"The SEALs picked up some intel," Nancy continued. "A laptop. It's been safety checked and is being couriered here now. We should have it in a few hours. I have the geeks standing by."

They had gotten a flash report from Axe and the SEALs. The man leading the ambush, who they called Captain Asshole, had been broadcasting his team's radio calls onto the internet, presumably for Todd Burkley to enjoy the ambush. No one had much hope of discovering a clue, given Burkley's resources and technical prowess, but they turned over every stone.

Dave looked down at his notes but didn't speak. Nancy clicked her pen in a heartbeat rhythm, *click-click, click-click.* Neither looked up.

"Now, what went wrong?" Haley waited, turning to look at each of them, wondering what they'd say.

"The SEALs did an incredible job. No injuries. Body count from the enemy on-site we put at eighty."

"At least," Nancy added.

"A few combatants got away. We're confident none of them were Burkley, however. We tried tracking them but lost access when the Mexican Army finally dropped by to check things out."

"Now—what went wrong?" Haley asked.

"We didn't get Burkley," Nancy said.

"We sent our boys into a trap." Dave's lips pursed together in anger.

Haley took a deep breath. "That's all on me. I followed the clues. I pushed for the assault."

Neither of them contradicted her.

"But now we know he's out there. Especially given the broadcast of the play-by-play. He's actively gunning for us, using his considerable resources to get revenge. Which means he's within touch of civilization. Comms—a cell phone, or at least internet. He can't plan an operation like this via snail mail."

"He's been in contact with people," Nancy said, warming to the idea. "A broker for the mercenaries. Captain Asshole didn't pull this together."

"Money changed hands." Dave made notes on a clean sheet of his yellow legal pad, adding small open circles next to each bullet point. Haley had seen him do it before. He'd put one line through when he started working on the idea and another, forming an 'X' in the circle, when complete. "Lots of money."

Haley watched as they fed off each other's ideas. The office rumor mill claimed they were long-time lovers. Seeing them work together again this morning finally convinced her it may be true.

"Email, at a minimum," Nancy said. "A deal like this though, probably required either in-person contact with an intermediary or a large sum of money upfront as proof of intent."

"Which would mean at least a familiarity ahead of time," Dave added. "No one would take a risk either sending or receiving money for an armed ambush in Mexico, the heart of cartel country, without some pre-established trust."

"If he's setting traps for SEALs," Nancy said, "he's after you too, Haley. And the president."

Haley nodded and patted her right hip. Today she wore a loose, dowdy cardigan which mostly hid the telltale bump of her pistol. None of the other analysts carried. She had started after the New York City attack, and no one said a word.

It made her a hit with the security department. They liked the idea of at least one of the brainiacs who worked in the building knowing their way around a weapon. It didn't hurt that she spent time at the same range the guards used... and could out-shoot several of them already.

"I've taken precautions. The presidential detail has been informed and is, as ever, top-notch. And the Mexico ambush was most likely for the asset. He and Burkley have history, as you are aware."

There were plenty of secrets in the world, and Burkley's lead role in the New York City terrorism had been quietly, thoroughly covered up. Instead, a worldwide alert had gone out, an ongoing, full-court press to find Todd Burkley, suspected embezzler, and terrorist financier. Nancy and Dave, along with Gregory of course, knew all the details.

"What about Kellison?" Dave asked.

"He's surrounded by highly trained professionals. My asset hooked him up with reputable, reliable people. He'll be fine."

Two sharp raps on the glass door of the conference room made Haley jump.

Not as sure about my safety as I claim, am I?

The door opened. Gregory walked in, looking fresh despite leaving after Haley earlier in the morning and returning before her. His eyes, however, were bloodshot.

The three of them stood quickly.

"Nancy, Dave, I need the room with Haley. Do you mind?"

"No, sir."

"Not at all."

"You know what to look for," Haley said as they hurried out the door. "Let's meet again when the tech guys finish with the laptop." She remained standing as Gregory shut the door behind them and stood opposite her at the end of the table.

"I've been thinking," he started. He treated her differently lately, was more respectful. She hadn't decided why he changed his tune: whether he finally acknowledged her ability, feared the connection she had with the president, or respected her time in the field.

Of course, it could be my less-than-subtle threat to have him killed if he didn't shape up. That'll change an attitude.

"There are other threats out there than the Assistant."

"We came close last night." It was a misrepresentation and they both knew it.

"It made sense to go after him, but I didn't give you a team to remove three of my pieces from the board until we find the man." She saw through his act. The earlier deference was a nice touch, but it was a velvet glove covering the iron fist. In the end, what he said was what she had to do.

They both knew that, too.

He nodded to the door, indicating the cube farm where the analysts did their work. "Dave and Nancy are solid. Proven records. Even more important, they are thorough. They're like dogs with bones; they aren't letting go. More than you, even," he said, then lowered his voice, speaking under his breath, "if that's possible."

She fought to keep a smile off her face.

He cleared his throat and shifted. Another part of his act? She didn't think so. He felt uncomfortable. "You and your team nailed the Boomer three months ago. Great job. But Haley, I need you back looking full time for other threats. Six months ago, the Assistant did his damage in New York. He will be caught, sooner or later. Hopefully by us, possibly even by you and Axe. But," he hesitated again, then continued, his eyes meeting hers and his tiredness showing more clearly. "Despite your lack of ability to follow the rules and provide proof of what you discover, I trust your gut. And we need it—both our department and the country."

He hates having to say this.

She wanted to revel in the admission, but the grownup part of herself she had discovered working with Axe, the side that had killed to protect her partner and her country, stopped her in time.

This is no time for ego or power plays.

"Absolutely, Gregory. I'm on it. Thank you for so much freedom to pursue Burkley." She hadn't dedicated all her time to him, of course, but she could be gracious.

"I've sent a file to you with odds and ends that need to be followed up. Weird stuff the others won't have the patience or imagination for. And," here his face changed into a small grin, "I have directed the various agencies to flag your name if they have any strange items or wild goose chases."

The funny thing is, he thinks he's just stuck it to me. But I live for this stuff.

"Bring it on."

"Spend the majority of your time on other threats. You can work the Burkley angle another hour this morning to run with the leads from the abduction attempt. After that, no more than five percent of your time on him. Understand?"

Haley nodded and they left together, Gregory back to his spacious office down the hall, and her to the desk at the edge of the cube farm, convenient to nothing, but containing everything she wanted and needed. She had access to the country's data, from Ultra Top Secret to what the beat cop's Confidential Informant said about Russia's plan to invade Texas—and everything in between.

Pure, unfiltered data she could lose herself in, then come out the other side with what she needed to fulfill her personal mission: to protect the United States of America from all enemies, foreign and domestic.

8

PUNISHMENT

Aboard *Mine, All Mine*
Isla Mujeres Yacht Club
Isla Mujeres, Mexico

Todd woke, gasping from the nightmare, drenched in sweat, tangled in the luxurious bamboo bedsheets. A glance at the clock showed he had only slept a few hours. His hand throbbed from the deep cut.

He sat up and hung his head, trying to get ahold of himself. The dream was always the same. Paperwork filled his inbox, endlessly piling up, while he stared at a closed door behind which, he knew in his dream, a great man worked.

On his desk, a cheap plaque read: The Assistant.

The morning sun shone through the curtains of the yacht's master suite.

He didn't have nightmares about the death and destruction he'd ordered. In fact, he'd been fine until he'd seen the first news report after making his escape in the mini submarine.

Todd swung his legs over the side of the bed, willing himself to ignore the memories. But in the luxurious room, his mind took him for a ride. Back to six months before. The morning after it had all gone wrong.

Six Months Earlier

Aboard *Mine, All Mine*
The Atlantic Ocean Off the Coast of New Jersey

With the yacht cruising south along the coast on a beautiful spring day, Todd used the slow satellite internet connection to read the latest news.

He expected to see reports of mayhem.

New York City in chaos.

Kelton Kellison dead.

The nuclear power plant north of the city either in a radioactive heap, if his drone criminals had gotten lucky, or at least severely damaged. Either way, people throughout the region would be terrorized.

Instead, he saw true disaster. Not for his intended targets, however. For him.

Kelton somehow lived, resting comfortably in a hospital. He told a ludicrous story of Kelton's mega-yacht coming under attack the night before by the same terrorist group that wreaked havoc on New York City. How he bravely fought off the men with the help of a dedicated personal bodyguard, getting shot in the process.

Kelton provided information on the man wanted for the attack: a known terrorist called the Boomer. The man Todd had scouted, recruited, paid, and directed.

Nothing at all about Todd.

He was stunned.

There had to be more… but there wasn't.

He had only one consolation: the sight of Manhattan. As he made his escape from Long Island, motoring south in the dark of the early morning, the New York City island would normally have been visible, glowing brightly in the distance. Instead, he saw nothing but darkness. Euphoria had flooded him. The island was dark because of him.

He had succeeded.

For a time, he searched the various news sites compulsively, then he set his tablet down.

Still nothing.

He tried to laugh it off. Reporters needed time to get the facts straight. There would be investigations. The truth would come out.

He didn't want to get caught. But he had prepared for the escape with the same focus and forethought he put into planning the attacks. He had disguises, plans, a passport, and credit cards in a fake name. Millions of dollars the government would never find.

Most importantly, he had a boat with enough range to go far between stops, allowing him to live in luxury while avoiding almost all contact with people. A boat that people would fuel or stock on command without ever expecting to see the mega-rich owner. A boat no one would ever tie to him.

Plus, just in case, he already looked different. Now he was bald, his head shaved smooth that morning. Contacts changed his eye color. An insert in his mouth, which still felt strange—but he would get used to —modified the shape of his face. His skin tone had changed thanks to a pricy bronzer applied after shaving his head. He used a cane and walked slowly with a limp, even onboard—you never knew who was watching, from Coast Guard patrols to drone and satellite surveillance. And soon, the steroids he had started injecting would completely change his body shape, from fit and thin to hulking.

He'd be fine. No one would catch him.

Despite believing in his heart that the entire operation would be a success, he had prepared for a manhunt. Because even in failure, what he wanted—what he deserved—was recognition.

Respect.

Some people—most, he assumed—would call him a monster. But there would be a subtext of admiration for his logistical skills for pulling off such a huge attack.

Some would also cheer him on. Root for the underdog as he got away with it. Vanishing without a trace.

The hours went by. There were more accolades for Kelton, who implied he would help the authorities track down the Boomer.

Still nothing about him and his efforts.

His success.

His frustration grew until he risked putting his name in a search engine.

Several stories appeared.

Finally. I must have missed them earlier.

He chuckled to himself. He'd merely gotten obsessed with the Kelton coverage, that's all. He would have to monitor his state of mind closely. A part of him remained self-aware enough to realize his obsessions were becoming stronger and more distracting.

Standing at the helm of the yacht, navigating, he clicked on the first story.

As it loaded, he dropped into the captain's chair in shock at the headline.

Kellison Assistant Wanted for Questioning in Embezzlement Probe

He read further.

Brooklyn, NY—Despite the terrorist attack on New York City, crime never sleeps. The Brooklyn-based Cottswoth-Goldentech company released a statement this morning in conjunction with the NYPD. In it, they revealed that one of CEO and founder Kelton Kellison's assistants is wanted for questioning for suspected embezzlement from the company's travel fund.

"Todd Burkley has been a valued, lower-level employee for many years," a spokesperson said. "A recent audit showed some irregularities we would like to discuss with Mr. Burkley, who has not been to work in several days."

The spokesperson for Cottswoth-Goldentech refused to provide specifics, but indicated the dollar amounts were, "relatively small change, in such a large company, but worth pursuing."

Mr. Kellison is currently recuperating in a Long Island hospital after bravely thwarting some of the same terrorists who recently attacked the bridges and tunnels of New York when they appeared on his mega-yacht off the coast of Long Island last night.

"Mr. Kellison has been informed of the financial irregularity but had little contact with Mr. Burkley, as he was one of many assistants to serve the company."

Todd jerked his head up from the tablet in time to correct his course, making a turn to stay in the channel instead of steering the boat onto a spit of land ahead.

Assistant. Assistant. Assistant.

The word thundered through his head.

No. This is all wrong. He can't do this to me.

Todd hit the back button on the browser, waited for the slow connection, then touched the next headline: ***Kellison Assistant Duped!***

The story, from one of the more sensational New York papers, repeated the main allegations, including the word 'assistant' four times in five paragraphs.

Todd wanted—needed—to turn the boat around, travel to Long Island, and kill Kelton. Preferably in an extremely painful manner. But he gripped the helm until his hands ached, keeping the yacht on course.

The assistant is suspected of using the stolen money to unwittingly help support the attacks by the terrorist known as "The Boomer."

"No, I'm sure there's an innocent explanation," insisted one coworker, who asked to remain anonymous. "He seemed like such a nice man. I don't believe he knowingly gave money to a terrorist. Honestly, he's just not the brightest guy in some ways, you know?"

Todd's right eye twitched uncontrollably.

Not the brightest guy...

The pesky voice of self-awareness tried to calm him, explaining it was merely a ruse to get him wound up, but the blind rage coursing through him easily drowned it out.

Present Day

Todd lurched to his feet and hurried to the ensuite bathroom, where he dry heaved into the toilet, spat, and stood, desperately trying to push away the memories.

Kelton had beaten him. Reduced him to a mere assistant. A stupid, criminal assistant in the eyes of the world.

Well played, Kelton. Keep away the bad publicity of your right-hand man orchestrating a terrorist attack, yet ensure he is hunted to the ends of the earth. Anyone catching the merest glimpse of me would be on the phone immediately... all without harming your reputation.

Todd brushed his teeth and inserted his mouthpiece, which he'd grown used to. The thick beard he now had changed his appearance more than the insert. But planning and contingencies ruled his world. He had to be careful and always vigilant.

He returned to his room, dreading the next task. It was small, next to nothing compared to the way his life had changed the last six months, but he hated making his own bed. Would he ever get back to the days when he could risk being waited on, treated as he deserved?

If not, fine.

As long as I punish the people who caused my downfall.

The thought energized him, and he hurried through making the bed.

I have plans to make and people to destroy.

"Mr. Smith, good news. We've found your..." the woman on the other end of the secure communication app hesitated for an instant. "Daughter."

In his excitement, Todd nearly dropped the phone. Seated in his dining area, shaded from the morning sun, he'd barely gotten his coffee when the communication app buzzed, surprising him. Few people had his current contact information. The display showed *Shelly's Cleaning Service.*

At the start of his planning, two years before, Todd had contacted

Shelly. A contingency in case things went horribly wrong. A substantial retainer had been transferred to her account.

He'd explained the situation—or at least his version.

"I am having a party and fear some of my guests might get out of hand."

"When is your party?"

"I'm unsure. It will be a rather large party, so it will take some time to plan. But I would like to enlist your services in case I need help cleaning up."

"Of course, sir. Do you have any other details? Number of guests to clean up after, that sort of thing?"

"Not at this time, no."

Despite the vagueness, she had gladly accepted his million-dollar, non-refundable retainer with the understanding it could be years before he spoke with her again. He had money and a connection in Kelton's military-security firm who vouched for him—anonymously, of course.

A month ago, he'd finally reached out to her again.

"Shelly, this is Mr. Smith," he started. "We spoke... I guess it's been about two years. I was planning a party and gave you a retainer?"

"Of course, Mr. Smith. Long time. I trust your party was well attended." Her voice betrayed no hint that she connected him to the New York City attacks... or the bogus embezzlement stories still getting space in the newspapers occasionally.

"It was, thank you. A huge hit. But unfortunately, I have a different matter needing your attention. My daughter has cut ties with her mother and me. We thought it would be a temporary phase for her to go through, but..."

"But you'd love to be reunited. I understand. This type of thing happens a lot," Shelly had assured him. Each of them danced expertly around the truth of the matter. He'd given her the basics and let her go to work.

Now she had found pesky Haley Albright, the Central Analysis Group analyst who had ruined his plans and taken so much from him. So much.

She would pay.

Suffer.

"Mr. Smith?" Shelly repeated. He'd gotten lost in his thoughts again.

"Yes, sorry, I'm here. That is excellent news."

"You were right. She lives near Washington, D.C. Alexandria, Virginia, actually. A cute red brick house in a quiet neighborhood. And she is extremely careful with her privacy. In the end, I had to put my best man on it, and I apologize for the delay. But I have a report with the address, photos, and all the information you need to get back in touch with her."

"Yes. Well, her mother and I are afraid of her reaction if we contact or visit her. We were hoping…"

"I could arrange a visit?"

"No, more like you could bring her to us." He let the sentence dangle, wondering about her response.

Shelly paused. Todd waited, guessing she would be afraid this could be a police sting operation. Still, she'd had a million dollars of his money for years, and he'd been vouched for. Never mind that the person who had vouched for him had been killed after his men had attempted to abduct Haley.

"We're always happy to fulfill our clients' wishes. I have just the man. A former police detective."

Relieved, Todd pressed forward. Shelly had to understand how tricky the grab would be, but he wouldn't tell her about the disaster the previous time he had ordered her taken—right before the New York City operation. "I'm afraid she does not react well to authority. I believe a more surprising encounter will be required."

Shelly paused again but recovered quickly. "Not a problem, Mr. Smith. The same man can handle it."

"I would prefer a more… robust… response."

A longer pause this time, and Shelly spoke with a tone of concern in her voice. "That is not a problem, of course, but I will need to ask why. Is your daughter a fighter? On drugs? Does she carry a weapon?"

"A fighter, yes. That's a good term for it. No drugs, but I fear she may have acquired a weapon, and the skill to use it." Even with the secure app, they both were taking pains to be circumspect, but he wasn't sure how much longer they could dance around the subject.

"I understand. So a non-lethal surprise would be your recommendation?"

"Perfect. And I believe my account is sufficiently funded?"

It better damn well be.

"Yes, of course."

"If you'll indulge me, I would request at least a full team. One person—your former police detective sounds perfect—to greet her when she returns home, perhaps. With more people nearby in case they are needed."

"A team?"

"Well, yes, a team would be good. But I was actually thinking two teams if they can be nearby without arousing suspicion."

"Two teams." Shelly took a breath and Todd wondered if she was counting to ten to get ahold of herself. "Mr. Smith, we need to speak candidly. Just who exactly is your daughter, and why do you believe my very experienced, extremely competent police detective needs not only one team, but two teams as backup?"

"Well, yes. You see, my daughter works for the Central Analysis Group, a boutique intelligence division of the government. Like the CIA, only smarter. She's merely an analyst, but she has had some training and may be on alert."

Todd held his breath. Would abducting an armed intelligence officer from her home in suburban Washington, D.C. be a bridge too far for the woman? She couldn't be naïve enough to think Todd—"Mr. Smith"—was actually the target's father. If she said no, he would be stuck. After the death of the mercenaries the previous night, he doubted his military contractor contact would respond to a request for more men, especially within the United States.

After another long pause, Shelly finally spoke. "An analyst for the CAG? Yes, I believe two teams will be perfect. However, this will consume your entire retainer. Any further services will require another deposit."

Greed. Always greed. But money was no object. Nothing mattered until he had his revenge.

"I understand."

"Fine. Let's discuss the logistics and timing."

9

INITIATIVE
TUESDAY NIGHT

Thames Shooting Range
Suburban Virginia

After getting a few hours of sleep on the fishing charter, and a nap while escorting the recovered laptop to D.C. on an Air Force jet, Axe made his standing date with Haley at the shooting range, sore from the operation the previous night, but ready for more.

While rested, he still had to work to keep up with the much younger Haley. He kept his hand lightly on her shoulder, following as she hurried toward the portable plywood wall in front of her, staying low. Once there, she paused for an instant before popping up in the designated shooting area—a small opening along the top of the wall. She fired her pistol at the man-shaped target fifteen feet in front of her. Two in the chest, one in the head.

Instantly, she bent forward and moved right, hidden by the wall. Axe once again shadowed her, fingers lightly touching her back.

The range's last shooting position was to the far right, another gap along the top of the plywood wall. A second, alternate shooting position, for those interested in mixing it up, was low to the ground and further right.

Haley popped up, ready to fire, but hesitated. Axe watched her carefully as her mind processed his surprise.

After the previous shooting run, while she was in the restroom, he had substituted the normal man-shaped paper target with a larger one showing three men, all with guns pointing at her.

He dragged a plywood rectangle on a tall stand and placed it between the top shooting position and the targets. There would be no clear shot. She would have to move to the right and drop to her stomach or crouch low to take the last shots.

A full second dragged on as Haley's mind worked the problem. She stepped right and squatted. Haley lost her balance, falling ungracefully onto her butt.

To her credit, her weapon remained pointed safely downrange the entire time.

Seated, she had a clear shot at the target.

Haley hesitated again at the surprise of seeing three men instead of the expected one.

Then she fired.

Six shots rang out in rapid succession, followed by three more, fired more carefully at the men's heads on the paper targets.

Haley immediately ejected the magazine and slammed home a fresh one, taken from a holder at her side. She holstered her gun and turned, still sitting on her rear, knees up, legs spread wide. "Not fair!"

Axe shrugged, looking at her levelly. "Never assume you'll see what you expect. Be prepared for anything. Next time it might be a hostage situation, or a little old lady. We always shoot in the moment."

He offered his hand, helped her up, and they walked together to the back of the range.

"But it messed up my time. It's not a true comparison now. The previous run only had one target at the end, and from a standing position, not flat on my butt."

Axe had reserved the entire range for two hours. The owner, a fellow retired SEAL, had been happy to close early so they could have privacy. They'd worked drills both individually and carefully as a team, with Axe coaching Haley on safety and movement. Finally, they ran drills to make 'run and gun' feel natural and automatic.

"We don't shoot for time," Admiral Nalen called from near the doorway.

He'd shown up late. Haley hadn't noticed; she'd been too focused on preparing for her run. Axe noted her surprise—and her realization she had been overly focused on beating her previous time than what was going on around her.

Have to work on her situational awareness. She's competitive, which can be good and bad, but she has to learn to be more aware of her surroundings.

Haley and Axe walked to the admiral, dressed as always in spotless jeans and a white t-shirt. A black leather bomber jacket hung on a hook along the back wall. The fall air was chilly, but the indoor range was pleasant.

"We do the runs to train," Nalen continued, gently, "and keep track of our time to see where we need improvement. But this isn't a competition; the goal isn't to beat our last score. It's killing the bad guys before they kill us."

Haley nodded and wiped her arm across her forehead, taking the sweat with it. Her long golden hair was plastered to her face and neck. Running around the range with intense focus was quite the workout.

She nodded. "I get it."

She did. Axe saw it and knew Admiral Nalen did, too.

She's getting better and better. Ready for the field again, when and if it happens.

Still, something felt off. It had all night, despite her solid performance.

"How are things, Haley?" Nalen asked, leaving it open to interpretation.

She looked at Nalen, at Axe, and back to the admiral, then walked to the table along the back where they had boxes of ammo. She started reloading her empty magazines. "What do you mean? Things are fine."

Axe shared a look with Nalen behind Haley's back. Her tone suggested nonchalance, but he detected a hint of both annoyance and a warning to back off.

Axe joined her at the table to refill his own magazines. They'd put a lot of rounds downrange tonight.

The admiral leaned his back against the wall nearby, looking off into the distance. He spoke softly, remembering. "My first kill didn't bother me. An asshole firing at my Teammates. The second one didn't either. Sniper shot of a—well, never mind. Need to know. But a few months later, I started having... not nightmares, exactly. More like... sleeping memories. I was reliving the kills." He shrugged. "My mind making sense of it all, I figure. I knew I had done right. Both kills were solid. Evil men who had to die." Nalen laughed without humor. "But try telling my mind that."

Axe joined in. "Sometimes when I'm awake, I'll have a rush of adrenaline. Like if there's a loud noise behind me. PTSD, no doubt."

"What we're saying is the mind processes violence and trauma in various ways. It does it to keep us mentally healthy. Sane. So if you ever go through anything like that..."

"We're here for you."

Haley kept her eyes down as she busied herself with the bullets and magazines. "It's not a problem when I'm busy at work. Or here at the range. It's..." She trailed off.

"The downtime," both he and the admiral said at the same time.

She nodded, looking at them, relieved.

They shared a moment. Three warriors. Nalen toward the end of his career, Axe well along and running out of good years, and Haley—the next generation, just starting.

"The last run, you seemed a bit off," Axe added. "That's why we brought it up."

"You can sense that?"

Axe nodded. "When you know someone well enough, yes."

They waited for her to share. She put her pistol in its holster on her pleated khaki pants and two spare mags in another holder on the other side. "It's not nightmares. I mean, yes, I've had a few." She looked at Nalen. "Reliving the shots, as you said. Questioning whether I had to take the first one—at the warehouse, or if Axe would have handled it. The second, at the freeway, is more a dream about whether I should have fired faster or aimed better. But I'm dealing with it for the most part. That's not what is on my mind."

"Is it the Assistant?"

"No... Well, yes, but what's bothering me tonight is this weird item I came across this afternoon. The main distribution hub for the Los Angeles freshwater supply went offline very early this morning, their time. Just... poof. All their electronics stopped."

"Sabotage? Terrorism?" Nalen asked, pushing himself off the wall and resuming his ramrod-straight posture.

"Inconclusive. No explosions or infiltration. No sign of malware, ransomware, hacks, or cyber worms. Looks like all the computers, switches, everything just died. Could be a power surge, maybe bad equipment in a cascading failure. Perhaps a contractor cut corners years ago. But I have a bad feeling."

Axe had to ask. "Could this be the Assistant setting us up again? A one-two punch? Last night in Mexico to keep me busy, and a hit in LA, too?"

"I don't know. He has no connection to Los Angeles."

They contemplated it, running the angles.

"So what happens now, in LA?" Nalen wanted to know.

"They're scrambling for replacement parts and switching over to manual mode where possible. Depending on how long it takes to get it running again, it might be a big problem. Luckily, an upgrade had long been planned. They were waiting for January to do it, but they can move up the timeline."

Axe laced his fingers together and cracked his knuckles. "Looks like I'm ditching this fall weather for the California sun."

"I'll make a call to get you a plane. You have what you need?" Nalen asked.

"Always." He kept his truck—repaired since using it as a battering ram on the New Jersey Turnpike—fully stocked with his weapons and go bags.

"Wait," Haley interrupted. "It's too early. I don't have anything. Give me a day or two—"

"Haley, if you have a concern, so do we," Nalen said. "It might be another hit like NYC. I trust you. We trust you. SEALs are trained to take the initiative. We move faster and with more decisiveness than the enemy... or our fellow organizations, which tend to get bogged down in bureaucracy. We are proactive, not reactive. It sounds like you could use some eyes on the ground, so let's make that happen. If it's nothing, it's nothing."

"Worst case," Axe said, "I get a few days in the sun and some photos for my next gallery show. I think people might be tired of all my pictures of green trees and east coast wildlife. Maybe some cityscapes or shots of the ocean would jazz up the show."

Nalen walked away, dialing a number on his phone. Haley looked at him, frowning.

"It's a lot of pressure, being in your position. A lot of power. But you can handle it," Axe assured her.

"I guess…"

"On another note, did you like the present I got you from my trip?" He hoped Captain Asshole's laptop would offer a clue to Burkley's location.

"The computer nerds are still going through it. But at least it wasn't a cheap tourist t-shirt, so thanks."

"I looked high and low, but they didn't have one with, 'My friend invaded an allied country and all I got was this lousy t-shirt.'"

That made her smile.

With another glance at Nalen, still working his magic on the phone, Haley leaned forward to confide in Axe. "Gregory took me off the part-time search for Burkley today. Said there were other threats to focus on. I still have my team on him when they can spare the time, of course. They're good, and I'll stay on top of them."

Axe nodded. "He'll have to wait his turn. But you'll find him. I have absolutely no doubt. And when you do, I'll end him."

10

HOME SWEET HOME

155 Laurel Lane
Alexandria, Virginia

The streets were dark and quiet this late at night. Haley's surveillance detection route—SDR—had taken a full hour. After briefing Axe on what little she knew of the LA water plant problem, Axe went to the business airport nearby to catch a chartered jet, paid for by an eternally grateful Kelton Kellison, who was now on Admiral Nalen's speed dial.

She had left the shooting range and driven aimlessly, making U-turns at random, stopping at yellow lights, using every trick in the book to make sure no one tailed her home.

They frequently changed the shooting ranges they met at, but it paid to be careful.

Haley used the drive time to reflect on what Nalen and Axe had said about Post Traumatic Stress Disorder.

I'm fine. I am. But I admit I'm carrying around trauma. It's nice to know I'm not alone.

It felt great to be part of a team. While her group at the office worked together, she was closer to Axe after one op than she would ever be with them. She didn't yet feel a strong connection with the admiral, but it would come. For now, while Nalen led them, she and Axe were the team. A team of two, for now.

As she neared her home, she looked forward to a shower and a few more hours of sleep. She'd be out at six tomorrow morning, giving her a solid five hours of sleep if she got right to bed when she got home.

I'm twenty-one. I can handle it. Besides, less sleep means fewer dreams.

Her little two-bedroom, one-bathroom house in an older area of Alexandria delighted her. There hadn't been much time over the past few months to decorate or make improvements, but a retired SEAL friend of Axe who owned a security company had installed a state-of-the-art security system.

Burkley—"The Assistant"—was never far from their minds.

One block from her house at a stop sign inside the subdivision, she looked at her phone in its holder. She swiped to reveal the security system's status. Every window, door, and movement detector showed green. All safe.

Satisfied, she continued the rest of the way. She turned into the driveway along the left side of the house, stopping next to the side door which entered into her kitchen. She rarely used the front door and didn't have a garage. But having the car right next to the kitchen was convenient in the morning; she never forgot her coffee anymore.

The security floodlight came on automatically as it sensed the motion of Haley's car. The bright light covered the entire side yard and half the backyard, easily seen through the chain fence. No one around. Like always.

As she did every time she entered her home since spending an obscene amount of money on the security system—even after the "friends and family" discount from Axe's buddy, Haley checked her backup system.

Two tiny bits of wax, the type that surfers put on their boards, blended in perfectly with the door frame in the top right corner. In between, a strand of her hair, nearly impossible to see. An old-school redundancy that always felt unnecessary. Childish, even.

She put her key in the deadbolt and unlocked it as she glanced up, fully expecting to see the hair pulled taut like she carefully arranged it every day when she left.

After the deadbolt clicked open, she automatically pulled out the key and slid it into her pocket.

The hair dangled, pulled loose from one bit of wax.

Someone had been in her home... without setting off the sophisticated alarm.

Or they were still there.

Haley twisted the door handle as she went into autopilot, pushing open the door as she smoothly drew her 9mm.

Careful not to fall on her butt again, she dropped low.

As the door opened, her eyes swept the kitchen. To her right, a small counter, then the stove. Another small slice of counter on her right. The first corner.

Clear.

The wall with the window facing the front yard.

Clear.

The area diagonally across from the door, the corner right in front of the dishwasher...

Where a man stood in the shadows, pointing a gun at her.

She shot twice as the man fired his weapon.

Something impacted the door frame above her, chest high if she had walked through the door standing.

The man fell back against the wall.

She fired again, praying his next shot wasn't more accurate.

The spatter of brains against her white kitchen wall was obvious, even in the dark.

She pushed into the house, walking on the balls of her feet, rear nearly touching the ground, gun swinging to cover the rest of the tiny kitchen, then the small dining room.

Clear.

She aimed at the hallway leading to the bathroom, bedrooms, and living room, pushing the door closed behind her and slamming home the deadbolt. Any backup would have to use a key or try to break down the door. Either would be noisy enough for her to have a second of warning.

The hallway came next. She poked her head around the corner and immediately drew back, away from the edge, and waited in front of the refrigerator, expecting gunfire through the drywall.

Clear.

The bedroom first, on the left, or the bathroom?

I wish Axe was here.

She caught herself.

I can do this.

Haley listened as best she could with the sound of the pistol ringing in her ears. Gone were the protective shooting earmuffs she wore on the range.

Haley knew her house. It didn't feel like anyone else remained inside.

Speed over stealth now. If they're waiting, I have to overwhelm them.

Standing, she peeked into the hallway, getting an angle on the open bedroom door while staying out of view of the bathroom.

Nothing.

Except for the closet, the far side of the bed, and the part of the room she couldn't see. But moving forward would expose her to the bathroom.

She peeked around the corner nearest her to the bathroom. Nothing. The clear shower curtain didn't block the view. The glow of the nearby streetlight through the frosted glass of the window in the shower illuminated the room well enough for her to feel safe.

She stepped forward silently as Axe had shown her, heel to toe, sweeping the bedroom, tempted to put rounds both through the bed and into the closet in the name of expediency and safety, but she cleared them the old-fashioned way, leading with her pistol.

Two steps down the hall to her bedroom, the pale pink walls reflecting enough of the nightlight's glow for her to see.

Clear.

That left the living room.

Out of the bedroom to the left and a quick peek around the corner. Nothing behind the piano—an unwanted gift left behind by the elderly couple who previously owned the house. She deluded herself with the belief she would find time to learn to play.

Nothing on the far side of the couch, the only hiding space in the tiny room.

She looked out her front windows. The blinds blocked the view but allowed her to see several of her neighbors' lights coming on across the street. She lived in a quiet neighborhood. The shots would have woken and startled everyone.

She was running out of time.

A dead man slumped in her kitchen, his brains all over her wall.

She was a CAG analyst. She had a permit for the weapon, and the shooting would be ruled a clear case of self-defense.

After she was taken to the police station.

After her name and address hit the system.

After the press was on the scene and started snooping around. Eventually, it would all come out: her name, her job, probably her photo, and worst of all, quite possibly her family connection to the president.

She couldn't ruin her chances at more fieldwork by getting her photo plastered all over the news. And she wouldn't harm the president with her actions.

She ran back to the kitchen, flipped on the lights, picked up the phone, and dialed.

"9-1-1, what is your emergency?"

"I just got home and heard shots fired. Three, I think, or maybe four. They were right near me! I think the house behind me, maybe? But definitely gunshots, not firecrackers."

"We've had several reports already and police are on their way. Are you safe?"

"Yes, yes, I have the doors locked. But I want to turn on all the lights and check the house."

"That's fine, ma'am. Stay in your house with the door locked. Police will be there shortly."

"Thank you so much!"

She hung up before the woman could tell her to stay on the line. She had a lot to do.

Haley snatched a white trash bag from under the sink, getting her first look at the dead man. Older, stocky, dressed in a worker's jumpsuit with the name of a plumbing company embroidered on one side and "Sam" on the other.

That's all she took in as she threw the bag over his head, twirled the excess plastic, and tied it in a quick overhand knot.

She grabbed the man's ankles and heaved, dragging the bulk through the small kitchen, next to the tiny dining room table, almost all the way to the sliding glass door to the backyard. She stopped in front of the ancient white chest freezer, another useless item left behind by the elderly previous owners. She ate out nearly every night—why the hell did she need a full-size freezer?

She lifted the door high and turned to grab the man.

The door slammed shut, startling her.

Damn it!

She grabbed the mop from its quaint holder along the wall of the hallway. Opening the freezer door again, she wedged the mop's brittle, dry sponge into the bottom corner and the green handle against the lid.

Can I lift this guy?

She had to.

Grunting, she maneuvered his bulk into the empty freezer, pulled the mop out, and let the lid close, just as the first police car squealed to a stop in front of her house.

The blue and red flashing lights lit the kitchen.

Shit. My gun.

While the average person on the street, at the coffee shop, or in the grocery store wouldn't guess she had a weapon and spare ammunition, the pistol and magazines would be noticed by any but the most inexperienced cop.

She unclipped both holsters from her pants and opened the freezer door, dropping them on top of the dead man as a dark figure approached her side door, seen through the opaque curtains of the unbreakable glass window.

"Police! Open the door!"

Haley lowered the freezer door quietly as she called out, "Oh, thank God you're here. I heard gunshots, probably from the neighbor's house."

"Open the door, ma'am."

"Right, okay, sorry!"

She started toward the door. Out of the corner of her eye, she saw the cute plaque she'd bought years before hanging on the kitchen wall, covered in blood and brain matter. On it, a happy goat munched flowers. The saying, "Sometimes you must stop and eat the flowers," could barely be read through the gore.

The police officer hammered the door.

I can't let him in this room.

Another step toward the door, and she almost kicked an object on the floor. A yellow and black stun gun lay on the worn linoleum. Thin, silvery wires ran from it to the barbs in the door frame at chest level.

I can't open this door.

She called through the door as she scooped up the stun gun.

"That door sticks, officer, come around to the front."

She walked noisily through the kitchen, flinging the weapon under the bed as she passed the guest bedroom, turning on more lights as she went.

At the front door, she flipped on the front porch light and quickly unlocked both the deadbolt and the knob, then the large, solid bolt holding the steel door closed. There was a reason the man had come in through the side door, and it wasn't because of being more out of sight of the neighbors. The front door opened only from the inside, no matter what lock picking tricks they had.

By design. Thanks to the planning of Axe and his buddy.

Taking a breath, she steadied her nerves, then stepped outside, arms held away from her body, palms toward the officer coming around the corner. "Is everything okay?" she asked frantically. "I called in gunshots. Did you find someone yet?"

More red and blue lights flashed at the end of her block as another car approached.

The officer, a man about her age, tall and muscular, stopped as he rounded the corner of the house. He held his gun pointed downward but slightly toward her, ready if she were a threat.

He pulled up sharply, staring.

Oh, no. Do I have blood on me? Did I forget something?

The officer started to speak, stopped, and got himself together, lowering the weapon further.

"Um, no, Miss. Not yet. Several neighbors thought the gunfire came from your house."

"My house? No. I just got home and heard it. I had the kitchen door still open, and I dropped my travel mug to hustle inside. I thought it came from the next block over."

Why is he still staring at me?

"Do you need me to sweep your house or backyard, Miss?" He was all business, but there was something else there... Suspicion?

It finally dawned on her. She went through her days ignoring the obvious. After all, she'd lived with it all her life. She often forgot, especially at work, where people had gotten used to it.

She was stunningly beautiful.

He's not suspicious. He's attracted to me.

She casually brushed her long hair behind her ear with one hand and smiled at the officer. "No, thank you. You're so wonderful."

Don't lay it on too thick. Make it believable.

"I'm so grateful we have people like you dedicated to our safety. I'm fine. I checked the house, even the closets and the bathtub! No bullet holes, no bad guys. You go catch whoever did this. But maybe some other time..." She trailed off, trying to get her tone just right. She wasn't used to flirting.

He tilted his head and grabbed the radio's shoulder microphone with his free hand, not taking his eyes off her. "UNIT A15, show me clear at 155 Laurel Lane. Homeowner reports gunshots from next street over. Try Rhododendron."

"Unit A15, copy all clear. Unit A23, check out 100 block of Rhododendron."

"I have to go. If you hear more gunshots, call 9-1-1." He holstered his weapon and reached into his front shirt pocket, pulling out a white business card. "But if you are concerned about your home security, or have questions, we're always here to help. Give me a call. I'm officer Derek Johnson."

She took the card with a smile and another adjustment of her hair, promising to reach out to Officer Johnson if needed.

Haley went inside, bolted the door, and went straight for the freezer. She needed to plug it in and make sure the old thing still worked. That, and retrieve her gun. The night was far from over.

11

REVENGE

A Half-mile from 155 Laurel Lane
Alexandria, Virginia

The six-year-old panel van had a few small dents, which only added to its authenticity. Huge red and blue letters stood patriotically against the bright white paint. JOE'S 24-HOUR EMERGENCY PLUMBING REPAIRS. In smaller letters: "We come to you, day or night!" A toll-free number was on the hood, both sides, and across the rear doors.

The van could be parked on any street or in front of any business, with multiple men coming and going, 24-7, with no questions asked.

It was Shelly's go-to surveillance and assault vehicle.

Chuck, retired SWAT team leader and all-around sharp guy, sat in the driver's seat wearing loose-fitting, dark-blue coveralls. "Joe's Plumbing" was embroidered on the right. 'Joe' was embroidered in cursive on the left.

On a cheap flip phone, he dialed the number from memory and tried to look bored as the call went through. He held the phone away from his face to keep it from rubbing against his thick, 1970s era mustache.

The van was parked on the busy main road running perpendicular to all the streets of the target neighborhood, lights on, engine running, making no effort to hide. No one looked twice. They'd moved from just around the corner of the target's house as soon as they heard shots fired. A very wise move, considering the multiple police cars that rolled into the neighborhood a few minutes later.

"Shelly's Cleaning Service," Shelly answered on the first ring.

"Hi Shelly, Joe here. Having some trouble with this job." They were on unencrypted coms so would keep the conversation tight.

"What kind of trouble?"

"Sam went in to assess the leak, but I haven't heard back. Lots of banging noise from the plumbing too, and an unexpected visitor arrived to chat with the homeowner. I was already on my way to the store to get coffee, so I'm not sure what happened next."

"I understand."

Chuck silently waited as Shelly considered what he had reported. In the passenger seat, another retired SWAT member, Earl, raised his eyebrows. He'd gone soft around the middle and looked exactly like a short, frumpy, balding plumber. They'd been on jobs that had gone bad before, but not many. Shelly ran a tight ship.

"How were they on us so fast?" Earl whispered. "A few gunshots? Even though it's the suburbs, so what?"

Chuck covered the mouthpiece with his hand. "My guess is the whole neighborhood is flagged priority."

"Because of the target?"

He shrugged. "Maybe. Or a politician's kid lives nearby, or their grandkids. Somebody important."

Shelly spoke, her voice tinny coming through the cheap burner phone.

"Sam's coffee must be getting cold. Can you take it in to him?"

She wants them to go inside?

I don't think so.

"From the noises we heard, I don't think he needs any more coffee."

At least, if the three shots from the house are any indication.

"I understand. Where are you now?"

"Down the street from the job. Four blocks." She would know he had parked where he could still keep eyes on the area.

"Those pipes must be fixed, and better tonight before any more water spills. Get as close as you can in case Sam needs tools. Wait a bit, then go help him. If the homeowner isn't available,"—in other words, if the target runs—"find her so you can discuss the bill."

"Any change in how we accept payment. Cash only, right?"

Would Shelly understand his question? Did they still have to take her alive?

"Absolutely cash only. Nothing else is to be considered. Understood?"

He shared a look with Earl, who rolled his eyes, having overheard Shelly's answer.

"Fine. Cash only."

"Coordinate with the electricians to make sure you are ready."

The other team in a beat-up panel van painted "McCormack and Sons—Electricians" waited at the other end of the subdivision, watching the streets there.

"Already done."

"Okay, let me know how the repairs go."

"Will do."

He flipped the phone closed with a snap.

"What do you think?" Earl said. "Go back, or wait until she rabbits?"

"Tough either way. A moving grab without hurting her versus a forced entry when the neighborhood is already on edge."

"Plus that response time from the patrols."

"They'll send cars through all night now."

They sat in silence, comfortable together from many years in situations like this, both before they left the force and since.

"I vote for waiting to see if she runs," Earl announced. "Team Two rear-ends her at a stoplight. We're right next to her. I open the side door, we drag her out, and throw her in. Boom, done."

Chuck considered it, nodding. "If she shoots us, too?"

"With four of us? After a car accident? We've got it."

"But we'd blow the covers of the vans."

"Shelly should have changed them years ago. She'll come up with something better. Computer repair nerd van, maybe."

"Better for these days, I suppose. Okay, we wait a few minutes and move back into the neighborhood where we can have eyes on. We give her an hour or two. See if the lights go off or if she runs. Who knows, maybe Sam is fine and will pull it off in the end."

Sam had been their friend, a fellow badge from the good old days on patrol in the city. True, he'd risen through the ranks to detective, but they didn't usually hold that against him.

Though they wouldn't say it out loud, they both knew he was dead.

Haley turned off the lights to the kitchen, leaving the rest of the house lit up. She stood in the darkness, smelling the mix of blood and bleach from where she'd cleaned up the dead man's blood, hair, and brains from the wall.

She used small but powerful binoculars to scan up and down her street. She doubted there had been only one attacker.

What, he walked here? Rode his bike? No. They're out there. Waiting.

The neighbors' hedges and trees mostly blocked the view, but headlights pulled up facing her house, a full block away. The lights went out, but she didn't hear doors slam. No lights came on at the house the vehicle had parked in front of.

Could be someone coming home a bit early from second shift. Or a lover arriving for a booty call. Or a boyfriend picking up a girl sneaking out of her house.

Or the enemy preparing to abduct her.

She couldn't call Axe. He was on a plane to California.

Nalen? She didn't know exactly where he lived, but from what he said, it was a farm—which would be far away. Still, he could get help to her.

No. She'd call him with a report, but she had another idea.

She dug her phone from her pocket, the pistol once again tucked into her khakis, the extra magazines on her left side. A reassuring feeling. Her backpack with more magazines was in the trunk of her car; she'd grab it on the way if all went to plan.

She had a feeling she'd need them.

Typing with one thumb while glancing through the binoculars every few seconds, she found the contact she needed. She dialed and hoped there would be an answer.

"Hello?" The sleepy voice sounded familiar.

"Cody—wake up!"

"Hello?" He sounded confused and suspicious, but slightly more alert.

"Cody. The only easy day was yesterday."

Please remember the code phrase.

He drew in a sharp breath and paused long enough to worry her. Did he remember what Axe told him months ago?

"It… it pays to be a winner."

She let her breath out in relief.

Now, how to phrase this?

Who was listening, and if they were, did they care?

Can't be too careful.

"We've never spoken, but do you recognize my voice? We have a mutual friend."

Cody had heard her over the radio when Axe assaulted the warehouse Cody had been guarding, right before Axe threatened to torture him.

"Ummm, yeah. You're—"

"No names."

"Okay. You're… the woman in his ear. The one that…" He paused. The mercenaries he had worked with that night were going to abduct, torture, and rape her. "I'm really sorry. I hope he told you."

"He did, and no problem. You handled yourself well." Cody had gotten arrested, distracting the police long enough for her and Axe to get away. He sat in jail for days, not saying a single word aside from his name. She and Axe had gotten him out when the assault on New York was over. "I need help. From someone I can trust."

"Really? Me?" His voice rose in pitch, and he cleared his throat. "I mean, yeah, whatever you need."

"You live just outside D.C., right?" She knew exactly where he lived, having gone over his entire life carefully when she prepared his file for Axe and Nalen to review. They had discussed bringing him on board as a low-level grunt but held off to put some time between when he had been arrested and his recruitment.

"Yeah. Yeah."

"And you have a car?" Of course he did. An older, reliable subcompact parked in his assigned spot near his apartment.

"Yes."

Definitely awake now... and ready to go.

"Great. Here's the plan." She explained what she wanted from him and hung up. Then she turned from the window and started packing.

———

Haley filled her travel backpack with essentials: passport, cash, both work and operation clothes, a small toiletry bag, tablet, laptop, and the required charging cords... and all the ammo she had in the house.

Strapped to the outside, mostly covered by a thin black jacket, but ready for quick use, was a rifle—a short barrel M4. She hoped she wouldn't need it. She didn't have the range time with it she had with her pistol. Tonight, she regretted not training with it more extensively.

The chest freezer at the other end of the room hummed quietly. Hopefully, the old appliance wouldn't give out with the dead man inside. She idly wondered how long it would take for the body to freeze solid. And what she would do with the two-hundred-pound ice cube when she returned from this mess.

Focus. Deal with the body later. Adapt and overcome.

She felt ridiculous as she kept watch in the dark at the kitchen window. She had changed into black tactical pants, a black long-sleeve tactical shirt, and black technical assault boots, all gear Axe had helped her pick out. Her blond hair was tied back in a ponytail bun so it wouldn't flop around. She wore the high-grade plate carrier Axe had selected for her, complete with ceramic polyethylene level IV armor.

Aside from a med kit and various other emergency supplies, the vest's pouches were filled with ammo for both her pistol and the rifle.

A razor-sharp six-inch fixed-blade knife hung upside down from the left front chest strap. On her belt at the small of her back, mounted horizontally, was another knife. Her right front pocket held a four-inch folding tactical blade.

Her backup pistol, a smaller 9mm, could be easily reached on her right ankle.

I have three knives, three guns, and enough ammunition to wage a war. But not the skills to use it all.

She took a long, deep breath, held it, then released it slowly. She waited, then repeated the breathing exercise. It calmed her and kept her focused.

In her earbud, she heard Cody driving. He'd called minutes before, and they kept the line open. "My app says I'm ten minutes away," Cody reported, sounding excited yet trying to be cool.

"You're coming in from the east, correct?"

"From the east, copy." Haley had him approaching from the opposite direction of the large panel van parked along the street to the west, which she guessed contained a backup team waiting for another try at her.

They must be determined if they're still hanging around.

"Copy. I'll call back in a second." She hung up and dialed the number she had memorized while packing.

Plan for the worst, hope for the best.

"Officer Johnson?" She wanted to sound capable, a bit worried… and a lot interested in him. "Sorry to bother you during your shift. This is Haley Albright, 155 Laurel Lane. You were at my house earlier with—"

"Yes, I remember you, Miss Albright. Is something wrong?"

"Please, call me Haley. Well, yes, and no. First, I wanted to thank you for tonight. Perhaps I could take you—and your girlfriend or wife, of course—out for lunch to thank you, and her, too, for all the support she gives you." Nailed it. Rambling, but not too desperate.

"I would love that, Miss—"

"Haley."

"Haley. That's not necessary but thank you. Besides, I'm single."

He sounded professional, but she hoped she detected a hint of an opening in his initial denial.

Why is he single? No, I'll worry about it later. I have to play my part.

"No problem, so am I!" She toned it down, wanting to sound less like a bimbo. "I have a busy week ahead of me, but I'll call next week, if that would be okay?" She didn't want to come on too strong, but she didn't have any experience asking men out. Too many hit on her to have learned how to do it.

"Again, not necessary, but maybe we could meet for a quick cup of coffee before I start my shift."

"Done. And… there is another issue. I just wanted to let you know in case you or your fellow officers drove by. The neighborhood doesn't feel safe tonight with the gunfire earlier. I'll stay with my brother— he's coming to pick me up."

She hated sounding like a scared, delicate flower, but chalked it up to fieldcraft. It was the role expected of her, the one which would offer the biggest benefit. She tried to harden her heart, hating the idea of using him, but that was the gig.

It's because he's tall, cute, and I might enjoy a date with him.

At some point, if they went on a date, she'd confess she wasn't a damsel in distress who needed protecting. She probably owned more guns than he did, and was a better shot, too.

Wouldn't want to start a potentially good relationship on the wrong foot.

"Have you seen any suspicious activity?"

"Well…" She didn't want to be too eager.

"What did you see? Big or small, it doesn't matter."

"Some kind of van drove up in front of my neighbor's house, up the street from me. They parked, but I didn't see or hear anyone get out. I've probably seen too many movies, but I wondered if it was someone casing a house. You know, to rob it? And maybe it was the same person who fired the gunshots earlier." She laughed at herself, sounding very much like a bimbo. "I have an overactive imagination! Anyway, my brother will be here soon. Everything will be fine."

"I'm not near there, but I'll have a car drive through your neighborhood. They'll check out the van."

"If you could do that… oh my gosh, thank you!"

"Happy to help, Haley."

"I'll call next week."

"Looking forward to it."

She hung up and pressed a button to call Cody. Scanning the street, she saw no movement.

How long will it take for a police patrol?

The timing had to be right.

"Getting close," Cody answered.

Haley slung the backpack over her left shoulder and debated drawing her gun. No. The motion detection light would come on as she stepped out. With the activity of the evening, a neighbor might easily look out. No need for them to see her holding a weapon. Besides, she could draw and shoot quickly enough if necessary.

"Almost there."

"Pull up three houses down. There's a big bush near the street. Park there." It was the neighborhood go-to spot because it wasn't directly in front of anyone's house. "We have to wait for the police."

A minute passed. The street remained dark and quiet.

"Okay, I'm parked. Lights off?"

"Yes. But keep the engine running."

"Copy."

Come on. Time to serve and protect. Or, in this case, disrupt and distract.

"What do you think?" Chuck slumped low in the driver's seat, his eyes high enough to see the target house through the side window. Lights were on in the living room, but the kitchen, where Sam had planned to ambush the woman, remained dark. They should have brought night-vision goggles but didn't think they would be needed with street and house lights all lit up. A car had arrived a few houses down and sat idling.

"Probably a booty call. They're too far from the target to be for her."

"I guess." Still, he sat up straighter to better see the older, foreign subcompact. A streetlight behind the car silhouetted the driver.

"I think we should wait longer. If she got Sam, I'd rather get her on the way to work. Besides, the neighborhood is on alert." Earl slumped as well, his eyes closed. He relaxed while Chuck took the first surveillance shift, then they would switch. Neither would sleep, but rest would give them an advantage when the time came.

"Yeah, you're still right." He had a bad feeling about this. The three shots, rapid-fire, were from an experienced shooter... and hadn't come from Sam's trusty old .38 revolver. He had been a good man, capable, wearing a bulletproof vest. Chuck's imagination took over, seeing the man he'd known and worked with for two decades laying in a pool of blood on the target's kitchen floor.

In the van's side mirror, Chuck saw a car turn from the busy street a few blocks to the west.

"We're made." He sat up and started the engine. The car had passed under a streetlight as it turned. Even from a distance, he identified the distinctive shape of a police cruiser.

"Could be a follow-up patrol," Earl said, though he slid up straight and buckled his seat belt.

"This woman is skilled. That guy is her driver. Damn it! I parked too close, and she called it in."

He turned on the lights, put the van in gear and started forward, slowly. It would look suspicious to pull out as the patrol car came onto the street but would be much better than being boxed in, questioned, and eventually arrested once their bullet-proof vests and weapons were discovered. They could always try to show their private investigator licenses, drop names, and mention their time on the force, but it would be touch and go.

And there was no way either of them would shoot at a fellow cop.

"If he pulls us over..." Earl started.

"Won't happen. No probable cause now that we're driving away. The van is clean. If they call the toll-free number to check, Shelly will handle it." He sped up but stayed well below the speed limit.

"Call Team Two. Warn them and tell them to take over. Have them leave a spotter at their position and hustle west to the main street."

Earl pulled out his own burner flip phone and dialed. "You think she's going west?"

"It's what I'd do. Go toward where we were."

Earl spoke with his counterpart in the other van, not bothering to use codes. Burner phone to burner phone in one neighborhood wouldn't matter. There would be nothing to trace later on.

They passed the target's house. No movement.

Chuck checked the side mirror. The police cruiser stopped at an intersection two blocks back, not hurrying. They might make it.

He looked at the car parked a few houses down from the target. A man wearing a baseball cap, face turned away, held his middle finger up.

"Bastards!"

He watched in the mirror as the car's lights came on, trying to see the license plate, but there wasn't one. The car turned into the target's driveway. Then he was too far away to see clearly.

Earl updated Team Two quietly next to him.

"Tell them to hurry. She's rabbiting. Older subcompact, no license plates, dark color, maybe green or blue."

Earl repeated the information as they risked slowing to a complete halt for a stop sign. On impulse, Chuck signaled right and turned. He floored it, running the stop sign at the next block as he turned right again.

They won't send more than one car to the neighborhood.

"We're not out of commission yet."

———————

Haley stepped outside. The motion detector floodlight caught her. She waved at the patrol car as it passed. The man, not Officer Johnson, nodded and kept creeping down the street. The van had gotten away, but the cruiser had served her purpose.

She locked the deadbolt, checked that the knob was also locked, and expertly connected the strand of hair back to the other small blob of wax at the top of the door. Though she didn't know when she'd return, it paid to know if her house had been compromised. They had missed the backup before; they might miss it again.

The alarm would arm automatically, though they had bypassed it somehow. She'd already made a mental note to see what could be done to beef up her security.

Her car's trunk popped open as she pressed the key fob in her pocket. She grabbed her small daypack, which contained extra magazines and bullets. She slammed the trunk, opened Cody's backseat door and slid in, dumping her gear on the seat. "Ready?" she asked him. It was her first time meeting him in person, though she had seen him through Axe's rifle scope at the warehouse six months before. The paleness of his skin surprised her. A cap covered his short red hair, though she knew it was there. He had to be a few years older than her, probably mid-twenties, but he seemed young.

I've killed. He hasn't. That's why he seems like a kid.

She closed the door and uncovered her rifle, unstrapping it from the outside of the backpack, then looked up when they hadn't started moving. Cody stared at her in the mirror.

Damn. I know that look.

"Yes, I'm hot as hell, Cody. Get over it and get your head in the game."

His mouth closed and his Adam's apple moved comically as he struggled to get himself under control.

"I'm Haley. Pleasure to meet you. Axe speaks highly of you and all that. Can we go now, please?" She tried to hold in most of her impatience, but not all of it. "And roll down the windows, all of them."

He hit the buttons. The windows rolled down as he put the car in reverse and turned to look backward. "Wait." The car stopped instantly. Haley unstrapped the small pistol from her ankle, struggling in the confines of the backseat.

Cody's eyes widened when she handed the pistol to him. "You drive, I shoot. But if I get taken out, this will give you a chance. It's loaded with one in the chamber. Oh, and rack the passenger seat all the way forward. I'm going to need the room."

She debated using the rifle but decided against it. The pistol would be easier to handle in the vehicle. She drew the 9mm and got ready.

Was she overreacting? Maybe she was paranoid, and nothing would happen.

Yeah, right.

With the seat forward and Cody armed, they were finally ready. "Now, let's go. Back out, go west. I'll direct you."

Chuck pushed the van hard, flying west along the street parallel to Laurel Lane, blowing through stop signs.

Next to him, Earl kept the line open with Team Two. They were four blocks to their right, moving more slowly, hoping to avoid the police cruiser which they had both lost track of. Luckily, the other van had a lead on them, so driving slower was fine.

He pulled to the side facing Park Boulevard, the major north-south street serving the area, immediately switching off the lights. Earl was all business, sitting up straight. Were it not for his partner's baggy work jumpsuit, spare tire around his middle, and bald head, it could have been twenty years earlier, a few years out of the police academy, on patrol together.

"Two just stopped. Like us, at the stop sign, waiting," Earl relayed.

"We have her boxed in."

"Unless she doubles back."

"Shit! Didn't think of that."

He debated putting the van in gear and turning around or sending Team Two back to their original position. "Confirm with Two they left a spotter behind."

Earl spoke into the phone and nodded a moment later. "Spotter in place, hidden so the cruiser won't bother him. They have coms. He's near Laurel Lane so should see her."

The subdivision's streets ran east-west, all terminating on either Park Boulevard or Raleigh Avenue. While there were a few streets that ran north to south inside the small subdivision, they dead ended after a few blocks. No matter which way the target turned, she would be easily seen if she left the area.

"This time at night..." Earl said.

"Yes. Tactical error," Chuck agreed. Had she waited until close to rush hour, there would be many vehicles leaving the area. It would have been easier for her to blend in, and harder for them to hit her.

"Two has a possible sighting. On Laurel."

They both leaned forward and saw the subcompact car. "Got her." Earl had a better angle. "Let's hope... Yes, she's turning right."

"Roll Two!"

"Get in front of her!" Earl urged Team Two.

They waited, knowing the other van would casually turn, two blocks ahead of the target vehicle, trailing her from the front.

Chuck edged the van forward, watching the target accelerate with Two's van further ahead.

He gave her another few seconds, then flipped the lights on, signaled, and turned slowly onto Park Boulevard, trailing the car now nearly a half-mile away.

"Two has point. The first stoplight, we take her. Stun guns, mace, nightsticks, whatever. Alive and mostly unharmed is better than unharmed but in the wind. We've been made, so we're backup—we'll be right behind them. They should surprise her, but if she resists or shoots, they'll take the heat while we scoop her up."

"I like that part," Earl mumbled before relaying the orders. "They want to know what to do about the driver."

"He's expendable, but I'd rather not leave bodies lying around. So if they kill him, they chill him."

Haley kept her eye on the van ahead of them, one lane over, moving slower than them.

"Did we make it?" Cody asked as he drove along the deserted street in the left lane. He glanced at her in the mirror.

"Sorry to break this to you, but we haven't started yet. See that van? Bad guys. And back about half a mile, that other van? Bad guys."

He sat up straighter. "Okay. Now what? How do we get out of this?"

Point to Cody. Bad guys in front and behind and he's not freaking out.

"We don't have to figure it out. We only have to wait." She let him think about it. To be on their team—assuming they both made it through tonight alive—he had to be able to think. Her file on him didn't indicate subpar intelligence. Axe's contention was that the kid only lacked training, experience, and opportunity.

"They want you bad. They either have a plan or will make one. Then we'll act. Turn their plan against them."

Well done again.

"We're outnumbered, but they want you alive. Or they did, before you killed their man. Do you think it's still the same?"

"I'm betting my life on it."

"But, um, they probably don't need me alive, right?"

"That's right." Haley paused to let it sink in. "You okay?"

Cody didn't hesitate. "Yes. You're a pro."

Probably not the best time to tell him I'm only an analyst.

A block ahead, the stoplight turned from green to yellow.

"Should I run it?"

They wouldn't be at the intersection before it turned red. A car traveling from their left waited for his light to change.

The van ahead of them slowed, brake lights glowing red.

"No, stop. Let's get this over with so I can get some sleep," she said with more bravado than she felt. "Stop at the crosswalk but be ready to pull a few feet forward when they come. It will make them hesitate and give me an edge. Remember, you drive, I shoot. Focus on the road, the light, other cars, and the van behind us. Leave the bad guys to me."

Haley had a split second to decide. One of Axe's many sayings pounded in her mind. "The enemy you allow to live is the one you must fight another day."

On the other hand, leaving a trail of bodies on the streets of suburban Alexandria would be a problem.

I sure hope these guys are pros.

She scooted to the left side of the car, right behind her brave driver, and prepared to jump out.

Cody coasted to a stop next to the van, waited a few seconds, then moved two feet forward before stopping again.

"Take her now!" Chuck called as he sped up. They would be out of the fight for the first several seconds but would arrive in time for backup—or cleanup.

Earl didn't bother speaking into the flip phone. His counterpart in the other van had put his phone on speaker and must have set it on the dash. Earl did the same.

The two men heard the panel door slide open and saw two men exit the van...

At the same time, the target stepped out of the back seat on the driver's side—holding a pistol.

"Gun!" they called together, their police training kicking in.

Haley had to wait until the men came around the back of the van, an agonizing half-second that seemed to stretch for hours. From the way she'd had Cody stop the car, she had good cover.

When the first man came into view, she fired two rounds center mass into what she prayed would be a bullet-proof vest. Since the man inside her house had worn one, she hoped they all did. If not, well, she'd fall back on Axe's slogan about not leaving the enemy alive to fight another day.

The first man stumbled backward. It took all of Haley's conscious thought to not follow her training and shoot again at the man's head. "Always shoot in the moment," Axe seemed to whisper to her.

The second man barely avoided his stumbling partner, stepping to his left while aiming the stun gun at her. Again, she pulled the trigger twice as her front-sight focus converged with the center of the man's chest in the background.

An instant passed, lasting several seconds in her mind, as she watched the man topple backward, the stun gun unfired.

The driver stepped out of the van carrying a police officer's nightstick in his hand. He never got close enough to use it. Haley's rounds caught him dead center. He backed into the side of the van before sliding to the street.

Now for the original assholes.

Haley swung right and put two rounds dead center through the windshield of the rapidly approaching van, causing the driver to slam on its brakes. She unloaded three rounds into the engine block, one into each of the front tires, blowing them, and finished off by shooting both the left front and rear tires of the van next to her.

"Get ready to drive!"

She kept the pistol raised, aiming directly at the driver of the van to the rear, who raised his hands. She stepped back, slid in the backseat, slammed the door, and stuck her arms and head out the window, immediately bringing the gun to bear again on the rear van.

"Go now. Turn left. Fast, but don't overdo it."

Turning left allowed her to keep the second van covered and watch as the three men she shot picked themselves slowly off the ground.

Haley let another several seconds pass as they drove away, pistol trained on the men, before she struggled to get through the window, into the car.

"Police!" Cody yelled, panicked. Haley contorted, the unfamiliar bulk of the plate carrier slowing her, trying to get all the way into the backseat.

Red and blue lights came on.

The cruiser turned right off a side street, heading toward the intersection where she had just shot three men and two vans.

Relief flooded her. The cruiser was going to the scene, not chasing them.

The feeling lasted only until she and Officer Johnson locked eyes as he drove past.

"Drive fast. Get off this road and out of town."

Cody complied as she sat back, her mind replaying the view of the police officer's handsome face as they stared at each other.

He has my cell number.

Time to go dark. She opened the secure communication app used by Axe and Nalen and composed a quick message to them both.

House compromised. Ambush attempted. Escaped. Not injured. Not in danger. On the run with Cody. Going dark. Will communicate via non-secure comms when I can get a burner phone.

Did she need to call it in to her team? And if so, how much would she tell them?

It's the Assistant. I have to tell Gregory. Well... maybe not the whole story.

She hit the speed dial button for Gregory's emergency cell.

He answered on the second ring, sounding sleepy. "What's wrong?"

"Earlier tonight, I was ambushed when I walked into my house. I'm fine. I got away with the help of a friend. But it's the Assistant, I'm sure of it. I don't know how he found me, but I'm staying with my friend. Just wanted you to know."

"You're safe and mobile?"

"Yes."

"With your... friend?"

"Not that one, no. A different one. Just an ordinary guy."

"What do you need?"

"Nothing. But I'm going dark. I don't know if my cell is compromised. I'll be at work in the morning though."

"I'm pleased you told me. I'll send out an alert to the team and you can give me a full report at the office tomorrow. Be safe."

He handled that well, all things considered.

The phone rang as she prepared to remove the battery. She recognized the number of Officer Johnson's cell.

Sorry, buddy, can't help you.

The battery came out easily. The phone went in one pocket of her tactical pants, the battery in another.

Haley relaxed back into the seat, then heard Axe once again in her mind. "The op isn't over until everyone is safe back at base."

She moved to the right side of the car, switched out her nearly empty magazine for a fresh one, and thought for a moment. She looked around as they made yet another turn.

"Cody, you did great. We're safe now, I think. So here's what's next. We hole up for the night. Tomorrow I get a different car and go to work. You've done your part."

His disappointment showed. Such a sweet kid.

"I could help…"

"I'll let Axe know how helpful you were. And we'll all get together. How's that sound?"

Cody nodded, resigned.

The kid had potential. Maybe they could work him into the team earlier than planned.

But for now, the Assistant is definitely a danger. I have to get him before he gets us.

12

INTELLIGENCE
WEDNESDAY

Central Analysis Group Headquarters
Alexandria, Virginia

Haley took the seat Gregory offered as he finished a call. "Yes, we're on it. Thank you," Gregory said into the phone. As always, his hair was perfectly arranged. His round, tortoiseshell glasses brought out the brown in his eyes. He looked younger than his sixty years, still keeping himself in shape, but he had aged during the time Haley had worked for him.

Some of that gray hair is because of me, I'm sure.

As he hung up the phone, his gaze flicked over Haley's black tactical shirt, much more form-fitting than the usual blouses she wore to cover the pistol and magazine holsters on her hips. Today she wore a black blazer to hide them, though Gregory's practiced eye lingered on both before meeting her gaze.

He took a breath and sighed.

"Haley, before you tell me the story, how much do I need to know?"

She caught herself biting her lip. Talking to Gregory seemed to bring out all her emotional tells.

"That's what I thought."

She wondered for the thousandth time whether he knew or just suspected her secret mandate to work with Admiral Nalen and Axe as unsanctioned assets of the President of the United States.

"Summarize it—for the record. You'll write up a full report for me... later."

Later meaning, 'Keep forgetting to write it because I don't want to know.'

"A man armed with a stun gun shot at me as I entered my home. I escaped with the help of a friend and holed up at a hotel last night. I've abandoned my house, car, and cell phone until I figure out who found me and how. Here's my new phone number." She leaned forward to put a sticky note on his desk.

Gregory nodded, the smallest flicker of relief flashing across his face.

"But you suspect the Assistant?"

"Yes."

He thought for a moment. "Fine. Run it down." Gregory turned back to his computer, dismissing her.

That went better than I thought it would.

Back at her cubicle, she dove into the data. There were records of cell phone calls from her neighborhood to go through. Data from cell towers along her route—she would see if any calls stayed open from the house to the intersection where she had shot the men.

Her mind flashed to her kitchen. The slow-motion replay of killing the man had been flitting through her mind off and on since she and Cody had settled into a hotel for a few hours of sleep.

Her stomach churned at the memory of the smell of blood and bleach as she cleaned the intruder's brain matter off the kitchen wall.

Three. That makes three people I've killed. What have I become?

Haley put the memories aside the only way she knew how—by losing herself in the work. A few minutes later, focused on her computer screen, she sensed movement behind her. She spun in her chair, instinctively reaching for her pistol.

Nancy and Dave took a step back in alarm, raising their hands.

"Easy," Dave said as his eyes tracked her right hand at the holster, no longer hidden by her jacket.

Embarrassed, she took a breath and let her hand drop. "Sorry. A little jumpy. The Assistant took a run at me last night." They nodded. They had received Gregory's alert. "Abduction attempt. Obviously, I escaped," she joked.

They stared at her, silent, not smiling.

Tough crowd.

She doled out analysis assignments to each of them. "If we can find suspicious cell calls from my neighborhood last night, we may identify the team who went after me and track them down. If so, we can analyze internet traffic from their location. We won't be able to see encrypted messages, but maybe the location data will help narrow down the search for the Assistant. Questions?"

There were none. They all got back to work.

A simple search brought the police report from the previous night onto her screen. Haley read about a "road rage incident" where two vehicles had been disabled by numerous shots from a pistol.

I'm glad I didn't use the M4. A pistol is much more common. The rifle would have raised a lot more red flags.

Wayne—the head of security—had made her leave her backpack with the rifle and her cache of spare ammo at their security station.

Too much firepower for the office, my ass. He was just envious.

Reading further down the report, it stated three men had been shot, all former police officers.

Shit.

All three survived due to their bullet-proof vests.

Thank goodness for their forethought... and my time on the shooting range.

Several non-lethal weapons had been found in the vans, pointing, in the words of the report, to "an operation to apprehend a fugitive or bail jumper."

Five former police officers were being held for questioning. None had provided any details so far. Each had also been carrying a licensed pistol.

Wanted for questioning was a pale man in a baseball cap, along with a female with blond hair, seen at the time in a car near the scene. A detailed description of the car was included, but not of her.

Officer Johnson held back on my involvement, but he nailed Cody's car. Impressive eye… and interesting choice.

She texted Cody.

Do NOW. Rent large storage unit at edge of city. Park car inside. Take taxi—not ride share—to nearby mall or grocery store. Pay cash. Wait one hour. Taxi to airport. Rent car. Excuse is 'Mine's in the shop.' More soon.

A few minutes later, he replied. "On it."

He's a good kid. Well, a kid several years older than me. But still. Shows promise.

All her life she'd felt either too young or too old. When she went to college at sixteen—and graduated two years later—she had been out of place. Getting her master's degree had been the same. But she had more real-world experience than others her age, which made her feel disconnected from other twenty-one-year-olds. And while Cody had spent years in the Army, she had crammed a combat tour's worth of action into a few days while working with Axe.

Haley fought to get her mind back on track, concentrating on the shootout and its aftermath. If she could find the histories of the men she shot, it might give her a clue as to who hired them. With the employer in hand, she might convince them to give up the Assistant.

I would love to see the look on his face as the authorities swoop in.

It would be a fitting culmination to the week.

Wait—it's only Wednesday?

Refocusing, Haley put herself in Burkley's shoes. First, the ambush of Axe and the SEALs. Then the attempt to abduct her last night.

She knew the Assistant's next move.

Kellison. He's in danger.

The security around him, retooled and staffed by people Axe recommended, couldn't be breached by less than a small army. And while Burkley had pulled together a group of mercenaries in Mexico, it wasn't likely he could do it domestically. Still…

Kelton deserves a warning, but if I can capture the Assistant, any threat against Kelton becomes moot. The call can wait. He's safe.

13

DARKNESS

Despite the cool breeze off the bay, Bec had woken up earlier than usual. She tossed and turned, trying to get comfortable.

The computer system she worked on the day before had been stronger than she thought, frustrating her.

She sat up suddenly with an idea. A sneaky way to get far enough in to suggest it to Pioneer as a site with more promise. A publicly traded company would gladly switch their cybersecurity software if their systems were proven vulnerable. Another win for her.

If I'm not going to be part of their cult, I can stay in their good graces by being the best hacker they have. Maybe they'll overlook my lack of enthusiasm for worshipping Pioneer.

It was almost dawn. She would love to go in early to try her idea, but this morning had been declared a mandatory unplugged time to celebrate nature and connection.

Bec had made plans to hook up with an aging hippie couple from her side of the island. They would paddle board together, but she could excuse herself after a few hours and go into the center a bit early.

The Control Center
St. John, United States Virgin Islands
Wednesday, 11:10 a.m. Atlantic Standard Time

Stefan held his hand over the palm scanner, building the suspense. He smiled at Gunther on one side, then at the twins on the other. They had been together for years. Were he capable of such emotion, he would have loved them. Instead, he felt mild pleasure at having them near.

"This morning we take the next step in the journey. From this day forward, our success is assured. Soon, I shall assume my rightful place. You will be my high priest and priestesses, interpreting my will and freeing me to wield my full power."

He gently put his hand to the scanner.

The Hand of God.

On the huge main screen in front of them, a grainy image showed a brief flash of light as the eight-foot rocket launched from the stern of the converted fishing boat.

It was anticlimactic.

Gunther tapped on Stefan's tablet and the large main screen split into ten squares—two rows of five windows. The upper left window displayed the rocket's telemetry data. In the others, live public webcams streamed the early morning commute in and around downtown Los Angeles.

The rocket's window displayed two rows of numbers: time and distance to target.

The three of them barely moved, their eyes glued to the upper left screen.

He hadn't planned to speak, but as the moment drew near, Stefan proclaimed, "Let there be darkness."

The countdown timer and distance to target hit zero.

The telemetry data stopped.

The live webcam feeds clicked off as one.

Stefan smiled and couldn't hold back a proud and defiant shout. "Yes!" He thrust his fist into the air.

I am a god.

Stefan nodded his satisfaction at Gunther before he turned to the twins and gave each a long, slow, celebratory kiss. He would bring them into his bed tonight.

"Release the recruitment ads. Begin the disinformation campaign. And ship the second batch of missiles. I will proceed with this design."

He would never admit it to his loyal subjects, even these three, his innermost circle. But he'd had the smallest concern the device would not work as designed.

His original inventions, when he was younger, had been genius. They still made him millions of dollars a year. But the science behind the creation of the EMP had been challenging. Had he lost his touch?

No. This morning's first real-world test proved he was as brilliant as ever. Perhaps more so. Taking the design of the electromagnetic pulse from theory to practice had consumed two full years of twenty-hour days. Miniaturizing it to fit on such a small rocket had taken nearly another year.

Luckily, rocket science had been simple for him.

So had the logistics of organizing the manufacturing, shipping, and distribution of the original missiles.

But committing to the production of so many devices prior to testing had unnerved him. If he was wrong, if the device failed or didn't perform as expected, he would be seen as fallible, even with only half of them shipped.

Not a terrible outcome overall, but being seen as a failure was not an option. Even with his limited empathy, he would have disliked killing Gunther and the twins—the only three people who knew the entire plan.

He would have, though.

Gods do not fail.

The Control Center
St. John, United States Virgin Islands
Wednesday, 11:13 a.m. Atlantic Standard Time—7:13 a.m. Pacific
Standard Time

Bec's keycard wouldn't open the door. Instead of the flashing green light and self-satisfied beep, it blinked red and buzzed angrily. Her glasses slid down her nose. She pushed them back into place absently.

Weird. It shouldn't be locked. I should be able to report a little early.

And she swore she heard a faint, triumphant shout from inside.

Don't be curious. Don't be curious. Don't be curious.

For years, her dad's nickname for her had been George, after the monkey whose overly curious mind got him into predicaments. For Halloween one year when she was little, her mom made a brown fake-fur outfit for her. Her dad wore a yellow raincoat and matching hat. They had won the prize for best costume at a neighborhood party.

Bec turned away with a nonchalant shrug for the security camera mounted above the door, then walked back to her four-wheel-drive pickup in the control center's parking lot. She might be able to access the building's Wi-Fi network from her phone—the illicit, explicitly forbidden device she'd smuggled onto the island against repeated verbal and written directives.

To be sure there was absolutely no confusion, new hires, including her, had to write out, "I do not have and will not acquire any type of cellular phone or other such device without written authorization." As she turned in her promise months ago, the small cell phone sat in her sock, hidden by her jeans.

Once a hacker, always a hacker.

She'd gotten lucky. The next batch of hires had been stripped on arrival, given temporary clothing while theirs was treated to ward off mosquitos—they had been told—and their luggage carefully searched. Three people had been immediately fired and sent back on the same ferry that brought them for having electronics that could connect to the outside world.

It should have served as a warning to her—a big flashing red sign.

Instead, she ignored it, happy to believe it was merely part of the group's anti-electronics crusade.

She wasn't bothered by the Movement's stated ideals. If they wanted to build a beautiful tech-free utopia on the island, more power to them. A movement fostering greater connections between people, love for the great outdoors? She could get behind that.

She didn't need to use more tech than she had at her workstation forty hours a week. All she wanted was to enjoy this island paradise, collect her money, and wait for Conroy's magic touch to make her rich by proximity.

But no way would she give up her phone. She'd risk losing her job to be able to text Mom and Dad—always from different locations on the island—or for the fun of an occasional off-duty hack.

Bec stopped by the truck and bent to retie her shoe, casually releasing her phone from its holder hidden in the narrow gap between the cab and the bed. She swung into the driver's seat, leaned back the few inches it would go—no king cab for her—and relaxed. If anyone was watching, or reviewed security cam footage later, it would look like she'd tried to go to work early, failed, and returned to her truck for a nap.

This is a bad idea.

A tiny smile played across her face.

Bad ideas are fun.

She opened the Wi-Fi section of the phone and saw three bars from the building's network, which she'd hacked as a matter of course her first week on the job.

Leaning back, chin to chest, hands held low to keep the phone hidden, she could still easily see the screen.

She navigated to the security section of the Center's system, located the cam feed, and toggled through the cameras facing her. Perfect. The scene looked exactly as she'd hoped: a bored worker relaxing before her shift.

Next, she switched to the cameras covering the control center, just in time to see Pioneer, Gunther, and Emma and Anna, the twins, leaving the room, all smiles.

What have they gotten up to this morning?

Switching cameras as they walked, Bec followed their progress back to Pioneer's wing of the building but lost them once they entered it. The only camera allowed near his office was at the main entrance to his suite.

With them out of the way, she'd be safe and undisturbed for a while, until either a guard came to check her out or another employee arrived.

She went one level deeper in the system and returned to the control room cams, setting the display time for thirty minutes earlier.

In jerky, low-resolution video, she watched Stefan direct Gunther at a workstation. Unfortunately, the computer's screen wasn't clear on the security camera feed, and none of the cameras caught the main monitor either. The system was in place only to spy on the workers.

Or in this case, for her to spy on the management.

In fast forward, slowing down to watch brief snippets, she saw Gunther type on the keyboard, move the mouse, then sit back. They all waited, looking up at the large monitor the entire time, then Stefan jumped for joy, raised his fist in the air, and gave a long kiss to each of his bimbos.

What the hell did they do?

Bec exited the system, powered off her phone, and slipped it in the gap between her seat and the back. She'd return it to its hiding place when she exited the truck to start her shift.

In the meantime, she did what she had pretended all along: closed her eyes and relaxed. But her mind churned a mile a minute, trying to figure out what kind of scheme a billionaire genius technology playboy inventor was up to.

14

DAWN

Interstate 10
Near the Convergence of Interstate 5, Interstate 10, US Route 101, and
State Route 60
2.5 Miles East of Downtown Los Angeles, California
7:13 a.m. Pacific Standard Time

The white king-cab pickup from the rental agency lost all power in an instant. Engine, power steering, and the radio—gone.

Axe signaled to pull over, though the instinctive move did nothing. He pushed the hazard flashers button as he coasted.

Nothing.

The freeway was bumper-to-bumper traffic. He knew the roads were always crowded, but the sheer volume of cars amazed him.

Axe's maneuvered his nearly new pickup fully onto the shoulder just as he lost all forward momentum.

Every other vehicle had gone dead like his, slowing to a stop. Some drivers pulled to the shoulder, though many either didn't bother or couldn't move out of traffic in time.

All these cars losing power at the same instant? This is not a coincidence. Haley was right. Again. Something's up.

He reached for his cell phone to call her.

Dead.

Of course. If it took out all these cars, the phones are toast, too.

Axe glanced at his digital sports watch to note the time.

Duh.

Habits are hard to break.

People slowly stepped out of their cars and trucks. The streetlights were off, both the huge ones spaced every quarter mile on the freeway and the ones on the city streets.

Cars were dead down there, too.

The houses and businesses near the freeway were all dark. Moments before, many had exterior lights or signs on.

No longer.

Axe opened the door and pulled himself up, using the truck's height to get an overview. The soft hint of dawn lit the sky to the east, though the sky over the city itself was still black on this late fall day. Except for this dark oasis, the vibrant city had lights on everywhere. He estimated he was near the epicenter. To the north in Pasadena, the lights were on. Behind him and south, planes still took off from LAX.

Bizarre.

His original plan, after landing at the Van Nuys Airport north of downtown, was to take advantage of driving the opposite direction of most morning commuters to investigate the water plant east of the city.

He had underestimated the traffic. The cheerful GPS voice had rerouted him several times around various collisions and other slowdowns, until he ended up passing through a complex interchange of intersecting freeways near Boyle Heights, just east of downtown Los Angeles. He'd gone far out of his way.

What could cause this? A blackout? No, it would explain the streetlights, but not the watch, phone, or truck. Maybe a solar flare?

He didn't have the background to figure it out.

He considered the situation. With his medium backpack he'd brought on the chartered plane from D.C., he had enough water for a day and food for two. There was the pistol in his concealed carry holster, two spare magazines in a holder on his left side, and a tactical folding knife in his pocket. He also had a short-barrel M4 in his pack, along with his favorite six-inch fixed blade, his plate carrier, spare ammo, and extra clothes. Plus his camera.

Which won't work at all now, either. Damn it, I loved that camera.

He climbed into the bed of the truck and assessed the scene from the higher vantage point.

Cars haphazardly stopped on the dark freeway, blocking every lane, including the shoulders.

The glow of the rest of the city in the distance.

People milling around, checking and rechecking their cell phones for power.

He climbed back into the truck and grabbed his backpack. He could take care of himself. But how could he further the mission?

Surveying the miles of vehicles blocking the road ahead and behind him, he had a thought. Without leadership, the roads would be a disaster for days.

He could start by helping clear a path for emergency vehicles. Surely someone, somewhere, had a plan—or would quickly come up with one—to restore power. It would only help if there were lanes free. Right now, with the shoulders blocked by a few people like him who had pulled over, and the other lanes jammed with other vehicles who hadn't, no one could get through for the inevitable road rage and health issues to come.

Easier said than done. After grabbing his phone—just in case—and the folded paper map he'd requested at the rental agency counter, he shouldered his backpack.

"Hey there," he called to the nearest vehicle, a fancy sports car in the next lane over. A sharply dressed twenty-something sat, fruitlessly trying to make his phone work. "Can you help me push my truck back into the lane to clear the shoulder?"

The kid ignored him.

Axe tried with three other cars near him. None would help, though no one was rude. Just wrapped up in their own world.

Okay. What now? Stay with the truck until help arrives? Or go?

The water treatment plant was thirty miles east. He couldn't walk there, couldn't call a cab or rideshare, and couldn't get back to the airport.

Priorities: personal safety. Check.

A few people were coming together to chat and strategize. It had the feel of the start of a block party. While there could be social unrest later, right now the mood remained calm. More frustration than fear.

Next: team safety. No way to know.

The third item: comms.

Roughly three miles away in any direction were lights. Lights meant power. Convenience stores at this hour, department and electronics stores opening later this morning. A convenience store would have a cheap cell phone. If the... whatever it was—call it a solar flare for now—hadn't knocked out the entire cellular network of the city, he could buy one and call in.

If not, he could persuade a store owner to let him use their landline phone.

He could be very persuasive.

Three miles in a city at dawn with a medium pack. A phone call, then return. He could be back in an hour. Ninety minutes tops.

He stepped back into the bed of the truck. To the west there were vehicle lights as far as he could see.

This is a major thoroughfare. A natural chokepoint. With all these cars stuck, it's going to take hours to clear up. Days. Tempers will flare. There will be road rage incidents. People with health problems.

Axe faced the back of the truck and used his fingers to whistle.

"Listen up!"

There was plenty of dawn light to see. People looked, curious.

"We're all stuck. Probably a solar flare or something. But traffic back there is still building. We're going to help each other move vehicles out of the way. Right now, all six lanes are blocked, including the shoulders. Let's move the cars on the shoulders back into the lanes. We may have to move cars in the lanes over, forward, or back to make things fit. But we need the shoulders clear enough for emergency vehicles and tow trucks. Got it?"

Instead of nodding, people looked around to see what others would do. No one moved.

Axe jumped down and walked quickly to his pal in the sports car, now sitting with his door open, seat tilted back. Axe stopped by the open door. "Hey. Time to help."

"Nah, man, I'm good. Thanks, though." He closed his eyes and let out a frustrated sigh.

"You don't understand. I'm not asking you. I'm telling you. Time to help."

The ice in Axe's voice made the man open his eyes and look. Axe's military bearing and physical presence made him sit up.

He opened his mouth to protest, but Axe beat him to it. "Help. Now."

The man nodded slowly.

"Great. You push from the back. I'll steer." Axe walked to the truck, trusting his commanding tone would compel the man to follow. Another man nearby moved to help. Together, they squeezed the truck back into the space created when he pulled over.

Within a few minutes, people nearby were assisting each other and passing Axe's directives forward and back. On the other side of the four-foot concrete divider wall, drivers going west did the same.

Axe continued to help, using the time to question people about what they had seen, heard, or guessed about the situation. One woman claimed her child saw what he called "fireworks"—a small explosion in the sky to the west.

This could all be a new form of electromagnetic pulse weapon. Fired from... where?

He looked around, considering.

Safest place to launch from would be a boat on the ocean.

He'd call it in, then investigate.

It took a while, but eventually the shoulders were clearing behind and ahead.

Axe jogged back to his truck, opened the door, and tossed the keys on the seat. He slammed the door and hustled over to the man with the sports car, who was gathered behind his car, talking and laughing quietly with two other men and a woman.

"Hey, I need more help. Come with me." He walked toward the shoulder and stood in the center of the lane, knowing they would follow. The group stopped behind Axe's truck. Cars were approaching on the shoulder, not at highway speed, but not creeping along, either. Their headlights illuminated Axe where he stood.

"I'm with the military and I have to call this in," he told them while looking west at the approaching traffic. "I need a ride and one of these first cars is going to take me to a phone. They might not stop for just me. Stand in the lane. Once I'm in the car, you can step back, or ask for your own ride."

"You're crazy, dude. No one's giving out rides."

Axe turned his head slowly to stare at the sports car kid.

"Yeah, okay bro, I've got you're back." He stepped next to Axe, and the rest of the small group did the same, blocking the shoulder lane.

An older car stopped, driven by a young woman who looked terrified at the group blocking her path.

Axe approached the passenger door slowly, doing his best to look unthreatening. She opened the window a crack as he bent down to speak to her.

"I'm with the military and need to report... this." His hand gestured vaguely to the dead cars around them. "Can I get a ride to the nearest convenience store?"

"Marine?"

"Sorry. Navy."

"My dad's a Marine. I'll give you a ride. Hop in." She unlocked the door and moved several items off the seat.

He smiled his thanks, took off his backpack, and slid in. Axe waved to the group in the road, who moved out of the way. The woman started forward more slowly. "So, where to?"

15

EMP

Central Analysis Group Headquarters
Alexandria, Virginia
11:00 a.m. Eastern, 8:00 a.m. Pacific

Haley dove into her abduction attempt, uncovering several promising leads to track down, but she could always use a few more.

Would it be worth the risk of arrest to meet with Officer Johnson to pick his brain?

No.

I have to keep my head in the game. This is not the time for unnecessary risks... or romance.

She sent a few items to Nancy and Dave, then started to backtrace the movements of the two panel vans with traffic camera records for the area.

An alert from Gregory popped on her screen: ***My office, immediately.***

Uh oh. I bet he found out about the dead guy in my freezer somehow, or the shootout in the street.

She hustled to his office. Once again, he was on the phone as she entered.

"Yes, sir. Yes, sir. I have my best analyst here now. We'll look into it and get right back to you."

I'm his best analyst?

She carefully hid her surprise and pride.

At least when he chews me out both for shooting people and not telling him about it, I know where I stand.

He hung up the phone. You're completely off the Assistant as of now. I have—"

"Gregory," she interrupted, "I'm so close. He made a mistake going after me. I feel it. Let me run with this."

"This is not a discussion. I need you to—"

"You have an entire department of people like me. Let me—"

"Not like you, Haley. Not like you," Gregory repeated quietly.

I'll take that as a compliment... though I'm not sure he totally meant it that way.

"Will you please be quiet for one minute? Try to remember I'm your boss."

"Sorry."

"Have your team run it down as they have time. But I need you all elsewhere. Something's happening in Los Angeles. I'll send the preliminary file to your station. I brief in," he looked at his watch, "twenty-five minutes."

Neutral. Blank. Show nothing. Don't let on about Axe and my LA hunch.

"I'm on it." She hustled from the room, down the long hallway toward the bullpen, the cube farm that housed her desk.

Does he know I sent Axe to LA? There's no way he could, right?

Haley's eyes widened as she read the short brief on her screen. She hit the keyboard, increasing the size of the text so Nancy and Dave could read from their positions standing behind her.

Forty-five minutes earlier, a roughly three-mile circle in Los Angeles—which included two of the busiest freeway interchanges in the nation—had gone dark.

That might be why I haven't heard from Axe. Not because of me switching phones. He's either investigating, helping, or stuck in traffic.

The weather had been warm, with no storms, tornados, or lightning.

There were no fires or reports of earthquakes.

But every vehicle, cell phone, and other electronic device in the area stopped working.

Traffic—already notoriously terrible—was horrendous throughout the city. Most areas were at a standstill. Surface roads and freeways were being closed to prevent more people from adding to the problem. A stay-at-home recommendation had gone out from the mayor.

Most of downtown LA lost power as well, including all the Financial District.

An immediate curfew for the downtown areas and the dead zone was being debated.

The power company for the area claimed to have suffered no blackouts; their equipment in the area, along with every other electronic device, had simply stopped working at 7:13 a.m. local time —10:13 a.m. in D.C.

Plus, of course, one of the area's three fresh-water treatment and distribution plants remained offline, a fact lost on everyone but Haley. Luckily, a plan had been in place to upgrade the facility east of the city after the first of the year. The timeline would be moved up. In the meantime, the city worked with a national bottled water company to distribute free drinking water to those in need.

Haley stood. She much preferred doing research on her own, sifting through the collection of data, allowing her mind to roam and put connections together. Having a team still felt cumbersome, but it had its benefits, too. She could brainstorm with the others. "Ideas?"

"Could the power company be lying to cover up a major malfunction?" Nancy asked rhetorically.

"Solar flare is my best guess," Dave said, though he sounded skeptical.

"It's an EMP," Haley said quietly.

Dave looked at her with a puzzled frown. "An electromagnetic pulse follows a nuclear explosion. No destruction has been reported. No radiation alarms. We would know if Los Angeles had been nuked."

"It's the only reasonable explanation. All electronics destroyed in a specific area. No other destruction. Gregory is briefing in twenty minutes. We meet again in ten. Dave, prove me wrong. Nancy, find out what the rest of the world thinks. Go."

They hurried to their desks.

Furtively, Haley pulled out her new cell phone and sent a text to Axe. Normally they'd use the secure communications app, but the cheap phone available at six in the morning from the convenience store she had Cody stop at on the way to work didn't allow for apps that fancy.

It's H. on new burner phone. Status? LA dark. At office so text preferred.

For good measure, she sent a text to Admiral Nalen with her new number, something she had meant to do first thing after stopping at Gregory's office… before losing herself in the hunt for the Assistant.

She had barely slid the phone into her pocket when it buzzed. Nalen had replied.

Copy. Watching on news. EMP?

She replied simply: *I think so. Working on it.*

Now she had to find which countries possessed the capacity to detonate a small electromagnetic pulse device over the busiest freeway in the United States during rush hour.

"Nancy, what do you have?" Haley asked.

"Chatter is all over the place, as expected. UFOs. Seismic activity. A government plot to make people use public transit or a dozen other theories. And solar flares."

"Anything plausible?"

Dave spoke up. "A few scientists are pushing solar flares, but I checked into their backgrounds. All have rumors of being less than ethical. Basically, they can be bought to say whatever someone wants. But in reality? I don't have the science background, but it should be a larger area for solar flare. Like all of California, not a few miles, and not a circle. Of course, an EMP would cover a larger area as well."

"Can you prove me wrong?"

"No," he grudgingly admitted. "An EMP seems like the most logical explanation for now. Though there are problems with the theory."

"Yes, like no one having perfected the technology yet—for a large area, let alone a focused strike."

Haley looked at her watch and stood. "I have to brief Gregory. Keep digging."

"Our working theory is the Los Angeles incident may be a targeted, mini electromagnetic pulse." Haley stood in front of Gregory's desk.

"My first thought as well," Gregory agreed. "Any proof?"

"Not yet. But the same type of thing happened Monday night at a freshwater treatment plant to the far east of the city. All electronics, dead instantly."

"Get me the information on that. They are going to want to know if this is terrorism or an attack from a foreign nation."

"We've heard nothing, and none of our sister agencies have any intel regarding it, either."

Gregory frowned. "Is there any chance it could be the Assistant?"

Haley hesitated.

I didn't even consider it. Could he have pulled this off?

She shook her head. "Again, no indication. My sense is this is beyond him, and he has no connection to Los Angeles as far as we know."

"The Financial District is down. Could this be related?"

"Possibly, but—nothing against LA—their financial district isn't world-class. New York, despite still being rebuilt, would make a much better target. Chicago, as well."

"Who could pull off an EMP?"

"Nation-states," Haley answered immediately, grateful for her few minutes to gather the data. "The research and development costs would be tremendous. The brainpower required to develop the EMP technology alone would be incredible, let alone to miniaturize it and put it in a suitable delivery vehicle. A rocket is farfetched, as this type of technology would require at least the size of a cruise missile and probably much larger than that. Its detonation would have been noticeable."

"Which nation-states?"

"Us, for one. We've been working on it for years. My security clearance isn't enough to get the nitty-gritty, but nothing I can find indicates we are there yet. North Korea would love it, but unless they've had a tremendous breakthrough, they're decades away. China or Russia would be my best guess, but we wouldn't have missed a launch."

"A cruise missile fired from a sub in the Pacific?"

"We narrow it down to Russia. Again, no indication they are close to the technology either. Plus—"

"We would have noticed a launch and detonation," Gregory finished.

"What about state-sponsored terrorists?"

"Iran, obviously. But again, a lack of treasure, time, and talent."

"We're saying it's impossible, but it's clearly not." He picked up the phone. "Find out more. Go."

Haley suspected Dave had a higher security clearance than her. He'd been in intelligence for twenty-five years and had been vetted over and over. She was relatively new.

"Dave, find out who could have perfected an EMP. Nancy, work on the delivery vehicle. Weather balloon, detonation from a nearby mountain or building, whatever. But let's keep our minds open to alternate explanations."

"What about the Assistant? Your abduction?" Nancy didn't want to let it go, either.

"Even bad guys have to wait their turn," she said. "For now, we run with this. It could be the opening salvo of an attack. While much of our military is shielded from an EMP because of planned protection against a nuclear strike, not nearly enough of it is. And hardly any consumer electronics are safe. Gregory is going to get jumped on. My guess is that within the hour, he's going to put the whole team on it. As soon as the White House hears 'EMP attack in Los Angeles,' the shit is going to hit the fan. Let's get ahead of it so we can bring the rest of the analysts up to speed."

She turned back to the computer, her mind already racing to the many items she needed to do, trusting Nancy and Dave to get moving.

16

DOWNTOWN

Downtown Los Angeles

The Marine's daughter dropped him off at the first convenience store with lights on. He'd given her a hundred dollars. "For gas," he'd said. She tried to hand it back, but he got out of the car with his backpack, waved, and went into the store to buy a cheap pay-as-you-go cell phone.

By the time he came out, she was gone.

The new cell phone couldn't connect to a network.

I bet the towers are dead or the rest of the system overloaded. This city is going to be a mess for weeks. Why would they target the freeways? To create chaos? Or...

Axe started jogging along the city's surface streets toward downtown. *This could be a distraction. Or maybe they were off target by a few hundred yards.*

The warm air felt wonderful compared to the east coast's cold weather. He made good time, running as fast as he could without looking like a man fleeing the scene of a crime. He didn't take the time to remove his light jacket hiding the pistol at his waist, though wearing it while running warmed him up quickly. His black backpack barely bounced, held close to his back with the multiple straps fully tightened.

He had to zigzag as none of the smaller roads ran due west toward downtown. But it gave him a chance to snap a few photos with the cheap cell phone. A low-resolution camera, but perhaps his eye and the scenes of the dark, crowded freeway would compensate.

If his hunch was correct, he'd need the rifle and body armor soon, but didn't want to gear up and look like the fully armed warrior he was until the last possible moment.

The area felt like a scene from a post-apocalyptic movie. A few people were outside talking to neighbors and comparing notes. The city was quiet with no sounds from HVAC systems or traffic. It felt still, peaceful... and wrong.

Axe finally reached the Los Angeles River—a huge concrete ditch running north to south. A trickle of water sat in it, barely flowing, along with a few bushes, lots of trash, and several abandoned shopping carts. The gray concrete walls had large squares of white paint as far as he could see in both directions where the city had covered an abundance of graffiti.

He ran on the bridge over the river—and a bunch of train tracks— finally venturing into the downtown neighborhoods.

The streets here felt more eerie than the other areas he had run through. Normally bustling, even later at night due to the convention center, residences, tourist attractions, and a basketball stadium, most people were inside. He saw a few people at windows, peering out.

Cars filled the streets, some abandoned, many with people sitting inside, apparently cold with the morning temperature around fifty-eight degrees. One wore a stocking cap. It felt warm to Axe, but people here apparently found it chilly.

Closer to the financial district, he saw more people out. A few news reporters, the homeless, and the odd worker who hadn't heard their places of business weren't open all milled around in various stages of shock or confusion.

From various directions, he heard engines revving, coming closer. The sound carried in the quiet morning air and sounded strange in the stillness.

There were thuds and crashes, sounding like…

Iraq, when the Army moved vehicles out of the way by crashing into them.

A block in front of him, a police cruiser sat in the center of an intersection, lights flashing, a weary-looking officer standing near the front of the car.

Probably supposed to be off duty but was ordered to extend his shift.

The officer jumped toward the sidewalk as a large black pickup truck, equipped with a shiny black grille guard, smashed into the back of the patrol car, spinning it onto the sidewalk as the truck sailed through the intersection.

The cruiser clipped the officer, sending him flying. He landed on his side with a loud thud.

Axe sprinted to the intersection, pulling his pistol.

The truck raced ahead and turned a few blocks away.

Around him, more engines revved, but he didn't see any other vehicles.

Axe holstered his gun as he neared the officer, not wanting to be perceived as a threat and shot by accident. "Hey, buddy, you okay?" The man groaned and rolled onto his back, eyes closed.

"I'm going to call this in with your radio. I'm a friend. Hang in there."

The officer, a white man in his early forties with close-cropped dark hair, had a stocky build of mostly muscle but carried a few extra pounds around his middle. His uniform had torn along the right side, but Axe couldn't see any blood or obviously broken bones.

Axe took the handheld microphone off the officer's left shoulder strap. "Break, break, break. Alexander, Homeland Security. Officer down, corner of—" He looked for the street signs. "Eighth Street and Main. Send an ambulance."

There should have been an immediate voice response, followed by sirens a few seconds later as other nearby units responded to the "officer down" call.

But there was nothing from the radio, and no sirens.

Radio must have been damaged.

"Hold on, I'm going to use the car's radio."

He started to rise but stopped and bent down again as the man spoke. "Radios are dead. Comms are out," the officer gasped. He looked at Axe, wincing in pain. "I'm okay. Just had the wind knocked out of me." He blinked several times, looking closer at Axe. "Who are you?"

"Alexander, Homeland Security." Axe had a badge in his wallet which could confirm this due to Admiral Nalen's forethought. While the president had made their little group a legal clandestine entity after saving New York City, it was top secret. The only people who knew were the three of them, the president, and the few people needed to make it legal. But given their secret status, and complete lack of funding, the question had arisen: how could they act officially if necessary?

The solution was a pile of identification cards, badges, and documentation from various government agencies. Axe could be from the IRS, FBI, NSA, or many other entities.

For this mission, Axe had more IDs in a hidden pouch at the bottom of his backpack. But in his wallet, he carried a badge identifying him as Alex A. Alexander from the Department of Homeland Security.

The man seemed okay, so Axe offered his hand and helped him sit up. "What was that truck doing? And I heard other vehicles racing around."

"No idea."

They slowly moved to the side of the nearest building. The officer leaned heavily against it and closed his eyes. The people who had been on the street or in their cars had vanished. He'd seen the same thing before in Iraq, Afghanistan, Somalia, and other countries.

People know when danger is nearby.

"Your radios fried like all the other electronics?" Axe scanned the area, on alert for other vehicles.

"My radio is fine, but the system is mostly down. They sent me back out after my shift ended." He eyed Axe's black tactical cargo pants, thin black jacket, and large black backpack. "What are you doing here?"

"I was on my way to an op and got stuck on the I-10. Total chaos. No way to make it, and the op is off anyway, I'd guess. At least for me. But I had a thought—why would anyone crash the power on the freeways at rush hour? Just to mess things up?" He waited for the cop to ask, but he didn't. He just shook his head.

"Not my department. As long as people don't start killing each other, I'm supposed to sit here and keep the chaos to a minimum, however I can. None of the brass much care if stores get robbed or not, either. It's all insured. But we can't let people get hurt or killed."

A sound tactical decision from the top. Prioritize lives, not stores.

"Good point. My concern was if this is a potential terrorist attack, maybe whatever they did to flip the power switch was a distraction. How many banks are in the downtown area?"

"There's a huge one a few blocks over." The officer gestured with his chin in the direction the black truck had turned. "Altogether, I'd say a few dozen smaller banks, five or six large main branches."

"What else would people target here for a big score?"

"Apartments and lofts of some pretty wealthy people. A few tech companies. Government buildings, including your offices, right?"

Axe nodded, but he had no idea where the Department of Homeland Security Office was.

Change the subject, quick.

"Okay, so banks. What happens to a vault when the power goes out completely?"

"Back up power?"

"I assume it's all fried, like my cell, truck, and all the rest of it. Any electronic device in the area seems to be dead."

"Like I said, if banks get robbed, they get robbed. My orders are to keep people safe. As long as no one is in danger—"

The sound of gunfire a few blocks away interrupted him. "Well, shit." The police officer straightened and immediately swayed, almost falling over. Axe steadied him.

"You might have a concussion." Axe quickly slid off his backpack and removed his jacket. He took the M4 from the pack, loaded a round, and checked the safety.

"Whoa." The police officer stood, still woozy, one hand holding the building for support, checking out Axe's rifle. "That's a lot of firepower."

Axe took out the plate carrier next and slid it on, quickly settling it in place and securing the straps. Putting it on always felt so familiar, like coming home. "Here's the plan. I'll go check it out. You stay here, cover my six. Don't let any more trucks come through and get me from behind, got it? You can handle that?"

He nodded, which caused him to sway again. "I got it."

"Listen—if you have to go to the hospital, I understand. But make your mind up now. If you stay, you cover me. I need to know you'll be here."

"I'm staying." His voice had resolve. "I've got your back."

"Thanks. You can call me Alexander. Axe for short."

"Dan."

"Back in a bit." With that, Axe raised his M4, flicked off the safety, and hustled down the street toward where the truck had turned.

17

DATA

Snippets swirled in Haley's mind as she ingested data with incredible speed.

Threats.

Rumors.

Reports.

Confidential informants.

Moles.

Signal intelligence.

She felt like a fish in the ocean, surrounded—enveloped—by the information.

Not a fish. I'm a shark. Hunting.

Her eyes opened and she looked around, disoriented from her journey inward.

And I smell blood... but I can't find the source.

Hours of work had produced no results. Not a single hint. With all the data at her disposal—public, private, and classified—she found nothing related to EMPs, Los Angeles, or a threat against the country. Aside from the normal, everyday "death to America" that littered the databases, of course. With all the United States did right for hundreds of millions of people at home and around the world, there were always some on the left, right, and center, foreign and domestic, who found a part they hated enough to plot against the country's success.

Is the lack of evidence alone proof there is a threat? Or is that paranoia?

Haley shook her head. The lack of sleep this week could be hindering her. Then again, while stressed and exhausted before, she made magnificent intuitive leaps, connecting far-flung data points with others to produce results none of the other analysts could duplicate... or grasp. Including Gregory.

But today, nothing.

So far. It's here. Keep at it. It will come.

First though, tea. Or maybe she'd splurge and get some diet soda for the extra caffeine.

Haley walked to the small break room, leaving her headphones on. Over the months, the rest of the group had grown to accept her, especially after her change in demeanor six months ago from being in the field. Her involvement in the situation had been highly classified, though a few old-timers in the room may have been able to access the reports. Those men and women, like Nancy and Dave, however, tended to be discreet. They wouldn't be around if they couldn't keep their mouths shut, outside the office or in.

She moved automatically, her mind in the zone as her body went through the motions of preparing her pick-me-up. A tall glass from the cupboard. Ice cubes from the freezer. A single-serving diet soda from the fully stocked refrigerator. The gray twist cap. Foam filling her glass.

Waiting for the bubbles to subside so she could fill the glass to the top, she watched the TV, tuned to a news channel. A talking head switched to a vaguely familiar face. The chyron displayed his name. Stefan Conroy. She hadn't heard about him in years. He'd been one of her childhood heroes. Only about ten years older than her. Brilliant. A man who went where he wanted and let nothing stand in his way.

She filled the glass more and waited for the bubbles to subside one last time.

The words displayed in closed captioning on the muted TV spoke of technology and connection.

But his posture...

The previous month, Gregory had brought in an FBI body language expert for a lecture and demonstration for the team. They had access to countless hours of video footage of interrogations and interviews in their databases. Gregory had believed the lecture would help them analyze the raw footage when needed.

Onscreen, Conroy answered questions, looking earnest and open. But also...

He's... hiding something? That's not quite it. A secret? His eyes are almost... taunting? Daring me to...

Her body set the nearly empty soda bottle on the counter as she remained fixated on the screen.

The work of the previous hours coalesced into one striking realization.

It's him. He's behind this.

18

HOMELAND

Downtown Los Angeles

Axe peeked around the corner, then immediately pulled his head back.

A block away, the black truck sat idling on the far side of the street, all four doors open. A man stood in the back, slowly turning to scan the entire area. He wore shiny black body armor, looking like a futuristic gladiator. His head was encased in a black motorcycle-style ballistic helmet, with a black visor shielding his face. He carried a rifle—a civilian M16—and held it ready like he knew how to use it.

The truck and a long, thick chain had been used to yank the heavy doors from the building.

The walls of the old block building shook, raining dust.

There goes the vault.

Axe took another glance. The man had turned his back to Axe. He watched the doorway, attracted by the blast.

Smoothly, Axe moved forward, rifle up and ready, using a parked white van on his side of the street for concealment. His eyes watched the man's body, alert for any movement.

After a few seconds, the man's head turned to look at the nearby intersection to the south. Axe sprinted forward, timing it perfectly. He hid behind another parked car just as the man continued turning, looking in Axe's direction. He gave the man time to complete his task, but still waited to move.

Give him a few minutes in case he walks around. *He's had training. Not special forces, though. Experienced, but not expecting trouble, or he'd be in a more defensive position. He's on watch for police and a deterrent for civilians.*

After sixty seconds, Axe peered through the car's window, wishing he had his own ballistic helmet to protect his head. The man once again faced the bank's entrance.

Crouched low, Axe rushed forward. He had to pass an open area— a small, mostly empty parking lot, which he did as the guard repeated his previous pattern, looking south.

Axe stopped behind another car. One more sprint and he'd be at the truck.

A man's voice called from the open hole where the bank's doors had recently stood. "Gimme a hand!"

Peeking around the car's trunk, Axe watched the guard jump down from the truck bed and move to the bank entrance. Another man, dressed in the same full-body armor, walked backward, dragging a huge black duffel bag. The lookout joined him and together they hauled it the rest of the way. They lifted the bag into the truck bed, grunting loudly. "More coming. This is a huge score!"

While the men were distracted and their view blocked by the bulk of the truck, Axe sprinted to the front of the vehicle, bent low. He crouched by the dented grille.

"Be right back with the next one."

The second thief hurried back into the bank. Axe made his move before the lookout could hop back into the truck bed. He stalked his way along the driver's side, past the open doors.

The guard was facing south to check the intersection, leaving his back exposed.

With three silent steps, Axe came up behind the man. He planted one foot, and with his forward momentum, kicked as hard as he could between the guard's legs with the other.

Even with the armor's padding, it had the desired, devastating effect. The man dropped instantly, cupping himself, making no effort to cushion his fall.

No mercy.

Axe grabbed plastic military cuffs from the webbing at the rear of his plate carrier and zipped the man's wrists together, not attempting to pry the man's hands from his groin.

Axe slipped a larger set of zip ties over the man's ankles, then a small one to connect the wrists and ankles tightly together before he removing the man's weapon from the sling and placing it in the truck. The man lay gasping, secured in a tight ball.

Squatting, Axe heaved the guard onto the shiny black bed liner, quietly lifted and latched the gate, and ran to hop into the driver's seat.

Axe shifted into gear and peeled out, hearing a pleasant thump and moan as the man's body slid around behind him. The rest of the truck doors swung shut as he accelerated.

He had what he needed.

He turned left, leaving the bank behind. None of the other bank robbers had any idea their get-away ride had deserted them. Axe's face lit up with a huge grin.

Let them think this asshole robbed them and left them behind.

Weaving around the few dead cars in the road, he drove two blocks, turned left, and stuck his arm out the window to wave at Dan as he approached.

He hit the brakes hard as he got to the corner. The truck slammed to a stop. In back, the guard slid forward and smashed into the front of the truck bed with a grunt of pain.

"Brought you a present," he called to the officer, who looked much better than before. Dan stood tall, no longer leaning against the building.

Axe hopped into the back of the truck and handed the guard's M16 to Dan, who accepted it without swaying.

Glad he's doing better.

Axe dragged the lookout to the rear of the truck, opened the tailgate, and used his foot to push him out. He landed on the asphalt with a thud and a groan.

Next, Axe pushed the heavy duffel bag out of the truck. It landed on the guard, eliciting another groan.

"You're definitely not Homeland Security," Dan muttered, bending to shove the duffel bag off the man, then removed the guard's helmet. A dark-haired Caucasian man grimaced in pain. His nose was crooked from being broken at least once in the past, and he had the beginnings of a splotchy black beard. He looked about thirty years old.

"Recognize him?"

Dan removed a pistol from the man's leg holster and felt for other weapons as the man lay dazed on the ground. "No. Where'd you get him? And the truck?"

"They're robbing the bank on the corner."

Axe opened the duffel. It was filled with stacks of one-hundred-dollar bills, wrapped with bands indicating each was ten thousand dollars.

Dan whistled. "That's a lot of cash."

"They're getting more, but without the truck, and no working vehicles nearby, they'll only be able to take what they can carry, assuming they're brave enough to run through the city dressed in full body armor."

"It would definitely attract attention."

Axe looked back toward the bank, debating.

"What?"

"I'm trying to decide if I should go back and pick off the rest of them." He hadn't heard any more gunshots.

If people aren't in danger, my priority should be to gather intel. Getting into a gun battle in downtown Los Angeles, even without many people around, should probably be avoided.

"Hey." Axe nudged the guard's head with his toe. "Feel like talking?"

The man pressed his lips together in defiance and closed his eyes.

Leaning forward, Axe whispered in Dan's ear. "Ask what I'm going to do with him, then play along."

Axe nudged the man's head harder—a soft kick. "Talking now is much better than talking later. The bank. Did you know about the job in advance, or was it a spur-of-the-moment decision this morning when the power went out?"

The man opened his eyes, glared at Axe, and shook his head.

Dan asked with genuine curiosity. "What are you going to do with him?"

"You mean, will I leave him for you to arrest? No. Sorry, my friend. With all that's happened this morning? The power going out? We need answers quickly. No Miranda warning, lawyer, or cushy jail cell for this one."

Dan played the wide-eyed cop well. "Enhanced interrogation? Is that legal?"

"Hell yes, it's legal! Certainly in a terrorist situation like this!"

"Dude, I'm not a terrorist," the man protested in an all-American California accent.

"Shut up," Axe said with another light kick to the back of the lookout's head—not enough to hurt, but enough to remind the man how defenseless he was. "You had your chance."

Axe spoke quietly to Dan, just loud enough for the guard to hear. "We've got something better now. Have you noticed fewer drug-related crimes lately?" He nodded, giving Dan some help.

"Yeah?"

"We made a deal with the cartels. The less violence there is, the less we'll hassle them. You know the brass never cares about the drugs, right? No one does. Only about the violence."

"Right, right," Dan played along.

"Every cartel has a bunch of people like you and I. Soldiers. They follow orders, just like us. But each also has a few crazies, usually the son or nephew of the head guy. You know the type: they like to hurt people."

"I know the type."

"At first, the soldiers followed orders and the violence mostly stopped. Little stuff here and there, we could deal with. But the crazy guys..."

"They kept at it."

"Right. They like hurting people. They couldn't stop. So we

decided, why not kill two birds with one stone? Give them what they need: people they can go to town on. Hurt as much as they want."

"Wait." Dan looked at Axe, trying to gauge his seriousness. "You're going to give this guy to a drug cartel?"

The man on the ground was already shaking his head. "No, come on, man, I'll talk."

Axe laughed and gave him another light kick. "You absolutely will!"

"Isn't that illegal?" Dan was either a great actor or truly concerned Axe meant what he said.

"Nothing is illegal in the war on terror, brother, you know that. Get this," Axe said, leaning closer. In his peripheral vision, the guard struggled to hear. "This one guy, a bodybuilder? They starved him for days, gave him only water. They put him under in a hospital. Told him he needed emergency surgery, but they would take care of him. When he woke up, groggy, they brought him a perfectly cooked steak. Sizzling. He was with it just enough to devour it. Licked the plate!"

Dan looked at him, spellbound, unsure what to believe.

"As he finished, they pull the sheet back to reveal one of his legs is gone." Axe paused, disgusted at himself for making up such a horrible story, but knowing both the bank robber and Dan were buying it. "Get it? They fed him his own leg!"

"No, no, no!" The man on the ground sobbed and struggled frantically to escape the zip ties. Dan looked sick.

"Poor guy. It broke him. They got all the intel we needed and then some. Every dirty little secret the guy had. A few days later they returned him to us but…" He trailed off. "Let's just say the guy's never going to be the same. On the other hand," he added quietly with steel in his voice, "the intel saved a school in Chicago from being bombed. Kept three hundred sixty-eight kids from dying, plus their teachers."

"I'll talk!" the lookout sputtered, the words flying out of him. "We knew a few days ago about the power going out. We had blueprints, schematics. Whoever planned it hooked us up with the explosives for the vault. All we had to do was get the truck, weapons, and body armor. There are other crews around downtown doing the same as us. We compared notes. I heard it all!"

"Dude, save it for the cartel, okay?" Axe rolled his eyes, bored. "It's out of my hands now."

"The guy in charge of my crew is Carlos Antonellos. I know his house, his girlfriend's place where he'll go to hide. I can help! Don't let them torture me. I'll cooperate!"

Axe pretended to weigh the options. Finally, he let out a long sigh. "The cartel crazy guys have to be kept happy, okay? But I tell you what..." He pulled the cheap cell phone he'd bought at the convenience store from his pocket, hoping it had what he needed. With a few taps, he found the voice recorder and opened it. "The officer is going to keep watch in case any of your buddies wander this way. You tell me all you know. Quickly, but in detail. No hesitation. Got it?"

The man nodded eagerly.

Axe knelt, holding out the recorder, his finger hovering over the record button. "If you hold back, or it sounds like you are, I stop. No warning, no second chances. I don't need to do this. I'm helping you out."

As Dan stood guard, the man—Jake, he said his name was—told the whole story, speaking so fast Axe had to tell him to slow down. Names, dates, times, and locations all spilled from him. He'd paid attention during the planning of the operation and had a great memory for details.

Finally, the man fell silent, spent. "That's all I can think of."

"You did good, Jake, and you're lucky. I believe you. But..."

"No! You said—"

"Don't worry, I'm not taking you to the cartel. The officer here will arrest you and take you in. But when you get to the police station, you waive all your rights. You tell them you'd like to make a full statement immediately. You have valuable information you want to share. They'll set up recorders, video cameras, the whole deal. Detectives will come in and ask you questions. You answer them and explain all that you told me."

Axe leaned down until his face was an inch away from the man's. "If you mention our conversation, the cartel, or describe me in any detail, I will hear about it. My people will snatch you up. We won't give you to the cartel to interrogate. I already have your intel, right?

We'll drop you off to them as a present, a goodwill gesture to keep violence off our streets." His voice dropped to a whisper. "And, my friend, I don't want to think about what they will do to someone they know we didn't need back."

Axe backed away as the man's bladder let go.

People were appearing on the streets again, emerging from high-end condo buildings and a few stores. Axe moved to the patrol car and flipped a button to open the trunk. He manhandled the heavy duffel bag full of money into it, then called to Dan. "You want him in here with the bag, or your back seat?"

Dan looked at him in disbelief. Axe shrugged and slammed the trunk.

He returned to the prisoner and cut the zip ties as Dan handcuffed the man's hands behind his back. They helped Jake up and put him in the back of the patrol car.

Sorry for whoever has to clean off the seat.

"Take him back to the station. Get the confession on tape, get all the details into the system. I'll work it from my end. Let others work it from theirs."

Dan hesitated, uncomfortable.

Axe leaned in so Jake couldn't hear. "I made all that up about the cartel. I—we—would never do that. The idea is to present a plausible reason for the subject to confess without actually harming them. It's an enhanced interrogation technique, but psychological, not physical. Thanks for playing along. You did great."

"What are you?" Dan asked.

"I'm a good guy. Truly. Some assholes took out three miles of an American city, got criminals to launch robberies, and who knows what else is coming. If I can get operational details by making up a scary story, I will. Much better than letting more attacks happen. And I did it within the rules. Your detectives are no different, promising to 'help out' a suspect if he confesses."

He turned the tables on the officer. "Now let me ask you a question. There are a few million dollars in the trunk of your cruiser. Are you, the money, and the prisoner all making it back to your station? Do I have to worry about you, Dan?"

Axe saw the answer on Dan's face and nodded, pleased. He was also a good guy who would do the right thing.

"And if I could ask a favor? It would mean a lot if your description of me was pretty vague. After all, you suffered trauma when your head got thumped. I'm some guy who said he was from Homeland Security. The less said about my involvement today, the better. I'm supposed to be incognito. What do you think?"

This is it. Is he with me?

"Can't keep you out of my report."

"True, but you had a concussion. Maybe you can't remember exactly what I look like, or what my name was. Allito, Alonzo, Antonio, something like that."

The officer eyed him. "You're definitely not Homeland, are you?"

"I have a badge in my wallet that says I am."

A brief smile twitched on Dan's face. "My kid has a badge saying he's a sheriff in the Space Force."

"I gotta get me one of those." He paused, judging the man. Then he nodded and turned toward the big black truck. "See ya, Dan."

"See you…" He paused. "Homeland."

Axe hopped into the truck and drove. They wouldn't need it as evidence; they had a full confession, a bag full of money, a hero cop, and a city in chaos, filled with electronic devices that would never work again.

19

SUSPICIONS

Bec hadn't seen Pioneer yet, though Gunther popped into the Control Center twice. She spent the morning on the hacking ideas she woke up with, which worked better than she had hoped.

She also had to carefully snoop out what the inner circle had been up to earlier. With their interest in security, Bec suspected all the workstations had keystroke loggers, tiny programs that kept track of each mouse click and computer key typed. These weren't likely to be monitored in real-time but could be used to review any activity on her machine, so she needed to cover her tracks.

First, she pulled up her top twenty-five target spreadsheet. This morning's hack would take the place of one item on the list. For the moment, she added it to the bottom as number twenty-seven. One of the other techs had been busy and added her latest target as number twenty-six.

The two recent additions gave Bec a good excuse to reevaluate the status of the top choices.

Nothing jumped out at her until she got to the Los Angeles Water Treatment Facility, which had already been grayed out by Tina, but not removed completely, which was Bec's job. Investigating the reason for potential removal would be well within her purview. A quick search online revealed why the target showed as no longer active.

The facility is completely offline? How?

A more expansive search showed many problems in Los Angeles, a place she disliked.

It's a city full of hustlers. No soul.

Besides the water plant being offline, they had a blackout downtown. People blamed UFOs or the government, but the most likely causes, according to experts quoted in the news, were seismic activity or solar flares.

Probably what happened to the water plant. Just bad luck it went dead before we could hack it.

An online article mentioned how the power failure affected the financial district, which made her wonder if she could exploit the situation. As the power came back on, systems would reboot. Perhaps she could find a way in. Two big hacks in one week would help keep her position secure, even if people guessed she wasn't falling for the cult's bullshit.

Had she not dug deeper trying to find a decent-sized system to target, she would have missed it. An article listing the top companies offline mentioned the estimated time of the power outage.

7:13 a.m. in California. That's 11:13 a.m. here. Weird. It's when I stood at the door and heard a shout. It has to be a coincidence, right?

Her insatiable curiosity couldn't let it go.

Maybe I should check the tapes again to see if the time matches Pioneer's yell.

She spent a half-hour researching LA targets, taking copious digital notes, adding her theory of using the crisis to hack the systems.

The notes would show her diligence and—hopefully—hide her concern.

Could Pioneer somehow be responsible for both the water plant and the power going out near downtown Los Angeles?

She didn't know how or why and wasn't sure she wanted to.

This is very, very bad.

Bec hadn't brought her workout clothes to the office, but it didn't matter. She would go for a walk in the comfortable, loose-fitting tomboy clothes she wore every day. A short walk during her afternoon break wouldn't be suspicious given the back-to-nature edict of the Movement.

Act normal.

She felt paranoid. No one watched her any more than usual, but the knowledge she had—or rather, suspicion—made her worry people suspected her. But she couldn't contain her curiosity. She had to find out whether it was a strange coincidence or if she had gotten involved with something much worse than a mere hippie nature cult.

Which meant a speed walk on the steep narrow roads near the center, fast enough to get sweaty.

Ending right next to her truck.

The cell phone came out of its hiding place easily as she finished stretching her legs and sat inside to rest.

Damn glasses.

She slid them back up her nose as she powered up the phone, holding it low.

Please catch the Wi-Fi signal... Yes!

She navigated her way into the building's security system and re-watched the clip from the morning.

There. Pioneer's body tenses, then it looks like he shouts. He raises his fist in the air. 11:13 a.m. That's 7:13 a.m. in LA.

It wasn't concrete proof. But it showed he knew about the event beforehand and watched it happen—and was happy about it.

A fist in the air? That's not just happy. It's proud. Defiant.

It wasn't enough.

Even if it was, what the hell could I do about it?

She should quit the job and leave the island.

Would they let me leave?

The question made her shiver despite the warm, humid day.

I need to get back inside before they start to wonder where I am.

She quickly considered her options. The local authorities were likely bought and paid for. Or worse—members of the Movement.

The CIA? No, she was inside the United States. NSA? They do electronic spying. The FBI?

She navigated to their website. Right on the main page was a button to submit tips. She tapped it. A webform loaded.

A quick look at her watch showed she was out of time. She composed a brief note and submitted it. Then she powered off the phone, faked a yawn, and got out of the truck.

One more stretch got the phone back in its hiding place. She hurried back inside the building, trying with every step to remember how to act normal.

20

BILLIONS

Onboard *Mine, All Mine*
Isla Mujeres Yacht Club
Isla Mujeres, Mexico
Wednesday afternoon

Todd sat on the stern deck, shaded from the afternoon sun, smiling gleefully. On his tablet, the stock price of Kelton's company, Cottswoth-Goldentech, plummeted, then dropped more. It had fallen thirty-six percent already, and the market had plenty of time to beat it up more before closing for the day. There were more rumors and details to come, he knew.

'Assistant'? I'll show you 'assistant!'

Watching Kelton go down in flames almost made up for the apologetic phone call first thing that morning from Shelly of Shelly's Cleaning Services.

He held up his hand to check on the drying blood. After the bad news of Haley escaping both teams of men, he had…

—Freaked out.

No.

—Needed to focus.

Yes. Better.

He had fished out the broken piece of brandy glass from the trash.

Anything to make the pain stop.

He'd pressed the sharp edge against the healing skin of his hand, slowly driving it into the wound. Blood gushed.

The physical pain distracted from the frustration and emotional anguish at seeing another one of his plans—

Fail.

No. Not work out because of the incompetence of others.

He hadn't bothered with a bandage afterward.

The stock price dropped another two, then five, then twelve percent.

The bet he had made against the stock would net him millions of dollars.

Kelton had lost several billion dollars of personal net worth. So far.

Could an assistant do that to you, Kelton? I don't think so. I hope you have rainy-day money set aside. If you're leveraged, you'll be bankrupt by this time next week.

He got up. The time for the long-awaited cigar had come.

21

VENICE

Venice, California

Axe found a parking place for the truck a few blocks from the beach. He could smell the Pacific, so much different than the Atlantic. It felt like coming home, since he'd done his SEAL training in San Diego, only a few hundred miles south.

Traffic had been fine driving west. There was power and little indication of the chaos downtown. He had stopped at a big-box electronics store and bought a top-of-the-line cell phone to replace his fried main phone and the cheap burner he'd purchased earlier. With the miracle of cloud backup, he was back in business in half an hour.

He walked toward the water, enjoying the vibe. The area was filled with a variety of interesting people. Venice Beach was busy even on a Wednesday.

His first glimpse of the ocean took his breath away. As he soaked in the stunning blue of the water, the warmth of the sun, and the area teaming with a mix of interesting people, he heard a voice from behind him.

"Hey, Frogman. Spare ten bucks for a veteran?"

Axe snapped his head around. What he thought were trash bags against the wall of a building had spoken to him. Upon closer inspection, he made out two eyes in the pile.

"Losing your edge there, Frogman?"

"Why did you call me that?"

"Nobody moves like you boys do."

Axe stepped closer as the newspapers and bag fell aside to reveal a man with a big, bushy beard gone full gray. He also noticed what most people would miss: the shopping bags filled with the man's belongings were neatly organized along the building. None of them overflowed. And while the gray hair and beard hadn't seen a brush or scissors in years, they weren't greasy. He didn't smell, either.

Despite living on the street, the man had his life squared away.

Squatting, Axe pulled out his wallet. He removed a bill and offered it. "Sorry, I only have a twenty."

The man cackled with delight, revealing clean, straight teeth, and took the offered money. "Pull up a chair, Frogman."

Axe took off his pack and joined the homeless man on the ground in the shade of the building. He removed two bottles of water from his pack and handed one over. He did the same with an energy bar.

"Sure beats MRE's!"

Homeless, yet clean and taking care of himself. Interesting.

"Where did you serve?"

"Where didn't I serve—that's the question!"

"Navy?"

"Why do you say that?" the man asked, testing him.

"You don't like being inside, and in fact, can't stand sleeping indoors. Too many years in a tin can is my guess."

The man took a pull of his water. "Smart one, are you? Not a 'tin can,' but I know what you mean. Go on."

"You also can't be out of sight or smell of the ocean."

"Bah!" Despite his denial, Axe saw through the act.

"You were at least mid-level, too. All squared away," he gestured at the neatly arranged shopping bags. "So it's habit now. You could have dropped the bullshit right after discharge." The man frowned and narrowed his eyes.

"If I'm hitting too close to home, tell me. I'll shut up," Axe said.

"Nah. Longest anyone talked to me in a year, not counting the ones trying to save my soul. Go on, if you got more."

"You recognized how I walk, so you spent time around SEALs. We haven't been stationed on ships much in the last decade or two, so you were in a while ago—or you played in the sandbox. I can't figure out how old you are, so I'm going to play it safe. Call you navy military intelligence. How'd I do?"

The man mumbled, "Damn SEALs always think they got it all figured out." But he smiled and added, "Not bad for a trigger puller."

"I won't try to save your soul but, brother to brother, what do you need? If anything?"

"Ha. The twenty will be enough to last me for days. Don't eat much. No bills, no hassles. I'm the only free one around here. I do what I want, go where I go."

"Family? I got a phone. Internet too, if it's working. Got anyone you want to call and say hi to, tell them you're okay?"

They watched a pair of older teens walk by with their noses, lips, and eyebrows pierced, wearing designer clothes.

"No, they got their own lives. I call collect first of every month to check in, let them know I'm still alive."

"Good." Axe finished his water bottle. "As long as you're where you want to be, doing what you want to. You do have more freedom than most."

"I am all set, trigger puller. Thanks, though. It's nice to talk, especially to a guy who understands and don't try to fix me. But," the man added with a devilish smile, "I think it's about my turn now."

"Your turn for what?"

A barefoot surfer walked by, wetsuit stripped off to his waist. He waved and smiled at the homeless man, who waved back. They obviously knew each other.

"You did me, I get to do you. Let's see," he trailed off, peering at Axe closely. "You got a bit long in the tooth, didn't you, Frogman? Don't see no Team buddies around, so you're all on your own." He shook his head and frowned. "A Team guy shouldn't be all on his own. Means you lost a step, didn't you?" He shook his head. "Happens to the best of us. But when your job is running and gunning, you lose the step, you're either dead, or you're out."

Axe sat silently, reassessing the man again.

The man chuckled and quoted Axe mockingly, "'If I'm hitting too close to home, tell me and I'll shut up!'"

This guy's sharp.

"No, no. Go on, old-timer. Let's see what else you got."

"So since you ain't dead, you lost a step and got out. But," the man paused, looking Axe up and down, "you stayed in shape because it's habit, as you said earlier. But you couldn't quite get your head around not saving the planet. Kicking down doors and blowing shit up. Could you, Frogman?"

Axe gave the briefest of nods.

The truth hurts.

"Now you're out on your own, or maybe you got a distant team for back up somewhere. And here you are, still trying to save the world. But now, all by your lonesome." The man sounded sad. He stared at Axe and winked. "And trying to figure out how the hell someone shot an EMP at downtown Los Angeles."

Axe's eyes widened in surprise.

"Boy, you should see your face!" the old man said, laughing with delight. "You ain't the only one with a brain, trigger puller. And I got the radio, don't I?" He reached in the nearest bag and brought out a small battery-powered radio.

Axe recovered quickly. "Right on all accounts, chief. They're saying on the radio it's an EMP?"

"Nah, but what else could do that damage with no other impact? They're saying solar flare. Please. With an almost perfect three-mile radius? No. Sky-detonated EMP. Launched from a boat." He gestured toward the ocean. "Flies straight inland, climbing quick, blows up over the freeway, creates a mess. You think you know it all, Frogman. But I forgot more than you've ever learned." He tipped his head back and roared with laughter.

Axe put the pieces together. "You saw the launch?"

"I like to look out at the ocean at night. Sneak out to the end of the pier. There's a cop who's a former Marine. Not half bad. Patrols the area, doesn't hassle me because I keep my eyes open and help out now and then. Tips and such."

"Tell me what you saw."

"A launch. Twenty, maybe thirty-degree angle. Not big. Hell of a lot smaller than anything we had." He meant during his time in the Navy. "Seemed almost like a toy, like something a high school science club would shoot off. Would've missed it but was looking at the right place at the right time. Got lucky."

"What did the boat look like?"

"Too far out. Couldn't see the boat. Just saw the flash."

Axe waited for more, but the man just looked at the ocean, done talking.

"Very helpful. I'm Axe, by the way. What do I call you?"

"I like 'Chief.' That's a good one."

Pulling his wallet from his pocket, Axe took out several bills, folded them, then removed an old business card from a gun range back east he'd been carrying around. He found a pen in his backpack and wrote his cell number on the back of the card, then handed the bills and the card to the man.

"This will hold you for a while, Chief, or maybe treat yourself to something nice. And if you ever want to talk, you call. I'd love to hear your stories, and I have a bunch of friends who would, too. Bet you've got some amazing ones."

The man hesitated for only a moment before he accepted the money.

Axe got out his new phone. "Amateur photographer. Trying to find my way in the world, like you said. Do something other than pull a trigger. Can I get a shot of you?"

Chief hesitated, but Axe saw he was intrigued. "Sure, but only once I'm set. Clear?"

"You got it."

The homeless man rearranged his blankets, bags, and other items carefully until Axe could barely see him. "You step back now and take your shot."

It worked perfectly. Axe snapped a few frames, changing angles and adjusting the settings, until he had one he liked. He held the phone to the man, displaying the picture.

"Nice one, Frogman." With his face still hidden, his eyes left the camera and locked onto Axe. "You can handle yourself all alone, shooter? You armed and dangerous?"

"I can take care of myself."

"Good!" The man laughed. "I'm way too old to be your backup."

Axe shook his head. "I bet you could hold your own."

"Ha!" Then he continued, under his breath, staring at surfers sitting in the water, rising and falling on the swells, waiting for waves. "Maybe once upon a time." He stuck out a clean hand from beneath the pile. "Good luck."

Axe took it, impressed by the firm grip.

"Stay frosty, brother."

"Stay frosty, brother," the man repeated.

22

KING

Central Analysis Group Headquarters
Alexandria, Virginia
3:19 p.m.

The glass of soda bubbled, forgotten on the counter as Haley stalked from the small kitchen. She stopped at the edge of the cube farm, thinking.

Marcus.

In a moment, she arrived at Marcus's cube. They hadn't worked closely together and barely knew each other.

She knocked on the metal support and stepped into his cube. He spun in his chair. He looked unhappy to see her, especially so close. Office culture dictated a person's cube was their castle—only the invited should come into the tiny space.

"I need help." He looked surprised, and she realized she had never asked for help at the office before. "You do workups. Did you do one on Stefan Conroy?"

"Yes. But I'm in the middle of—"

A dismissive wave of her hand cut him off. "Summarize it for me. Threat? Nut job?"

This isn't scoring me any points, but so what. And I'm in his space.

She stepped back, which seemed to mollify him. He absently tightened his tie, as if preparing for a presentation. He dressed up every day. Today's combination was a gray, skinny tie against a perfectly pressed white shirt and charcoal-gray vest. He looked sharp.

"A little of both, probably. Too brilliant to not be considered a threat of some sort, if he ever put his mind to it. Rich, as you know. Patent income, mostly. His wealth hasn't grown much, especially compared to the rest of the tech world, because he hadn't come up with anything new in years. But about a year ago he started a small company, gathered a team, and moved from the Silicon Valley area to St. Thomas, then St. John, US Virgin Islands. He's developed a robust —some say revolutionary—cyber security product using AI to protect systems. Very clever. A lot of companies worldwide, even some governmental agencies, have switched to it. Rave reviews. The man hasn't lost his touch."

"That's it? After ten years, he's back in the game? Why?"

"Unknown. There are rumors, but little proof. But it's clear he—or entities controlled by him—have bought up every house, business, and piece of land he can get his hands on in St. John, and to a lesser extent in St. Thomas, as well. At this point, he is basically the king of those two places. He has employees hoping to make it rich when his company goes public. Followers and admirers who love the idea of getting away from technology and back to nature and who have relocated there. He's very careful to call it a movement, but in some ways, it looks like a cult. Seems benign, though. Doesn't ask for money, doesn't lobby the government, doesn't make people leave their families. On the contrary, he wants them to stay in touch, become closer."

It rang a bell now. She'd heard of the movement to get away from it all, use a minimal amount of technology, stay off social media. She was too security conscious to have any social media presence, and no time for it, so she hadn't paid attention. But Marcus sounded enthusiastic, which made her wonder how much appeal the movement had for him.

Marcus continued, quieter. "There may be a dark side, though it also might be detractors making stuff up. The most salacious rumors include a harem... dozens of kids with many women. But no reports or even whispers of coercion. The FBI had someone on the inside for a while. It was all free love, like the '60s. People—the women, in this case—are free to come and go as they please, stay in touch with family. No laws broken."

"You said he's a king? Is that his deal?"

Marcus shrugged. "Who knows? Our psych people say he's on the sociopathic spectrum. 'Lacks empathy' is their term if I recall correctly. It's all in the report. You have access."

A king.

"Haley?"

What happens when being a king isn't enough?

"Haley, you with me?"

"What? Oh, sorry, lost in thought."

He looked at her strangely. Her budding reputation for being weird wouldn't be helped by this conversation.

She forced herself to look him in the eye, smile, and speak sincerely. "Thanks, Marcus, I'll check out the full report." She had to wait while he said words she didn't hear.

Eventually, Marcus stopped talking, allowing her to turn and walk away. It was time to dig deeper. She needed to be sure before she once again put her reputation, career, and life on the line.

23

BLONDIE

Central Analysis Group Headquarters
Alexandria, Virginia

Instead of going straight to her cubicle, Haley hurried back to the break room, desperate for the diet soda she vaguely remembered pouring and leaving someplace. She found it on the counter.

She chugged it, letting out an unladylike belch after. Now she could get to work.

At her desk, she cracked her knuckles. The hunt always went more smoothly with a place to start—a theory or specific target. She paused, willing the caffeine to kick in. She still felt exhausted. Only a few hours of sleep early Tuesday morning after the Mexico op, then four hours of tossing and turning with Cody on the far side of the king-sized hotel bed the night before.

Haley took a deep breath and let it out slowly, focusing her mind. She would look into Mr. Stefan Conroy. Let the data flow over her. Test her hypothesis.

Another cleansing breath and she began.

She started with a huge funnel, inputting Stefan's name. It would produce an incredible volume of data, including Marcus's profile workup. Much of it she could skim, speed reading the public information while focusing on any raw intelligence in the databases of local law enforcement, FBI, Interpol, and others. She didn't expect much criminal activity, but with a person as rich and famous as Conroy, you never knew.

As usual, she would start with the most recent information and work her way backward. It would take hours, maybe days, reading report after report, looking through rumors, half-truths, and lies, weighing each nugget. Trying to tell fact from fiction. Considering the angle each informant might come from, why they would offer a tidbit for their handler.

Haley blinked in surprise.

Or maybe it won't take long at all.

A recent entry, right there at the top. An FBI web form submission dated… today. Internet traffic location disguised.

The message was brief and to the point.

On St. John. Work for Stefan Conroy. Suspect he caused LA 'solar flare' affecting freeways. Unsure of method. Also believe he is behind the LA water plant shut down. More to follow. Reply: WhiteKnight@privatemail.com Will check when able. ~ White Knight

Whether it was the nickname 'White Knight,' reminding her of the hours of chess played with Uncle Jimmy long before he was President Heringten, or the wording of the message, she wasn't sure, but this was real. She knew it in her gut.

And it connected to the feeling she had in the break room, watching the body language of the so-called "Pioneer."

Haley would continue her research. Gregory would have a fit if she told him she based everything on her instincts and a form submission on the FBI website signed by "White Knight."

But first, she had to put a contingency in place in case she couldn't find more proof. Gregory would veto any action against such a well-known figure. Best-case scenario, he would turn it over to the FBI. They would sit on it, unwilling to stick their necks out.

The world didn't have time to waste. It was up to her and Axe now.

She hurried back to the conference room for privacy.

Time to make the call.

Kelton wouldn't answer his phone.

Of course. My new burner phone is an unknown number to him.

Haley jogged from the conference room back to her desk, getting looks from everyone, like meerkats popping up to see the commotion.

Have to risk using my regular phone. It should be okay. If the location is being tracked, they already know I spend most of my time here.

The battery went back in and she powered up the phone while jogging back to the conference room. Most of the analysts ignored her this time.

Three calls from Officer Johnson, but only one voicemail.

No time for him now.

The secure messaging app had one note from Axe, left much earlier. He had arrived in LA and would go to the water plant to poke around.

Not bothering to pull up his contact, she dialed Kelton's private cell phone number from memory.

He answered on the third ring, sounding rushed and worried. "Haley. Not a good time, sorry. Call you back." He hung up.

She hit redial.

"What?" he screamed. She'd never heard him so stressed.

"Make the time."

She and Axe had saved his life and kept his secrets. She didn't want to say it, but he owed them.

He took a breath. "Hurry. I'm in trouble here."

"What's going on?"

"Don't you watch the news? My company—well, all my companies—are under attack. Cyber, ransomware of my vendors, denial of service, everything. Customer data leaked—old data, from a hack years ago that hit half the industry that we were instrumental in fixing for everyone, but try explaining it to people, especially the media. Hold on." He barked orders to people near him. "So, yeah, not a good time."

"Sixty seconds, and a favor."

"Go."

"Our friend tried to abduct me last night. I escaped, but it was a professional crew." They were on an insecure cellular line—who knew how many people were listening, but it was probably many.

"Glad you're safe. But there's no way he can get to me. Unless…"

"Yes. I suspect he's behind whatever is happening there now. Also, I can't get into details, but your buddy got ambushed—he's fine. Then me. Now you."

"It would explain a lot. What else?"

"A serious question. What happens to a rich man turned king when being king is no longer enough?"

"Our friend is rich, but not rich enough for what you're asking."

"Not our friend. Another person."

There was silence followed by more yelling before he came back.

"First," Kelton explained, "you get rich more for the challenge than the money. After about fifty million a year income, the money means nothing until around a billion. But it still doesn't mean much. A bigger superyacht, faster planes. Eventually, it's about control," he said bluntly. "You end up wanting more power over people. Wilder experiences. A bigger and better empire. Stardom."

"And once you have all that? You're a king, you have loyal subjects. You lack for nothing, no luxury or experience is out of reach. Then what?"

"You become a god."

The word hung in the air.

A god. He wants to be a god.

"I'll let you go. Good luck fighting off our friend."

"Now that I know it's him, it might be easier, thank you."

"Oh—the favor."

"Name it."

"It's big."

"I'll give you whatever you want just to get you off the phone, Haley."

"I'm happy to hear that. Where is your yacht?"

Haley sat in the conference room, holding her phone. The comms app waited for her to make up her mind.

Can I do this? I'm a twenty-one-year-old junior analyst. Who am I to make these decisions?

She tapped the icon to place the secure call to Admiral Nalen.

"What do you have?" Nalen was all business. It sounded like he had been expecting her.

"We believe it's an EMP."

"Who is behind it?"

"That's the problem. I have nothing."

"If you had nothing you wouldn't have called."

He was sharp. "You're right. I have a hunch."

"What do you need?"

"Permission to investigate."

"You do not need my permission."

"In the field."

"Same answer."

The implications made her catch her breath. She didn't know where to go from here.

Nalen continued. "Your uncle and I both support you, one hundred percent. My role is oversight. Guidance and support. You have an asset. Use him."

Now she felt on more solid ground. "Well, that's it. I have a plan, but it involves more than just the asset."

"Continue."

"Our friend from the warehouse."

Damn it, we need code names. With his red hair... Lucky? No, it would tempt fate. Cherry? He'd hate it. Ember. Oh, yeah.

"Ember." Would Nalen get it?

He did. "Nice. Is he ready?"

"For what I have in mind? Yes. Probably."

"Approved. Not that you need it."

"The plan requires one more person."

Silence from the admiral as he thought it through. "Your uncle would kill me if something happened to you. And it would destroy him, too."

"I know."

The silence stretched for several seconds.

I haven't convinced him.

"I'll be careful. Axe will be right beside me the entire time. And it's low risk. Relatively."

A sigh. "You proved yourself last time and you're excellent on the range. I only wish you had more hand-to-hand combat training."

"That's why Axe—Papa—is there."

"Approved, but take it slow. Let Papa do the heavy lifting. Now, fill me in on the details, Blondie."

Blondie?

She wasn't sure she liked that. Then again, Axe hated his new "Papa" call sign, and she couldn't get used to it, either. Axe was Axe.

What about him? He needs a name. A Navy reference?

She had it. "Yes, sir, Pirate."

The admiral chuckled for a second and listened as she detailed her plan.

24

WATERFRONT

Santa Monica Waterfront

Axe spent a fruitless day chatting with people in and around marinas, searching for a clue to a boat that may have fired an EMP missile. So far, he'd found nothing.

The large audio file of the bank robber's confession had finally finished uploading to Haley from his burner phone, along with a summary of what he knew so far, but he'd only gotten a quick thumbs up emoji in reply.

Must be a busy day on her end, trying to get to the bottom of this.

He felt useless, wandering around, trying to gather intelligence. Plus, he hadn't slept and was slowing down.

He considered getting a hotel room, but in the end, frustrated with his lack of success at further intelligence gathering, he returned to the truck, cracked the windows, tipped the seat back, and slept.

25

VACATION

"Yes, come in," Gregory called. Haley pushed open his office door.

Haley hadn't reached his desk before Gregory shook his head. "I can tell I'm not going to like what you have to say."

She smiled tiredly. "You're right."

Gregory sighed, took off his glasses, and polished them with a cloth he took from his top desk drawer. He didn't invite her to sit, but it didn't surprise her. He often preferred to hear his updates that way. It made people think better—and get to the point faster. "Tell me."

"No real leads on the EMP—and we're confident it was an electromagnetic pulse device detonated in the sky east of downtown LA." She had finally received a report from Axe which mentioned an eyewitness viewing a single, small explosion in the sky at the exact moment the power quit.

"No chatter, no one claiming responsibility?"

"Oh, there are people claiming to have done it. Laughably so. One group said they used a death ray. Another guessed the cause correctly but—I kid you not—misspelled EMP in their press release."

Gregory looked baffled. "How did they spell it?"

"ENP."

He dismissed it with a shake of his head. "Typo. Merely careless."

"They spelled it the same three different places on one page."

Gregory shook his head at the stupidity.

"I found a preliminary report of bank robberies throughout downtown LA." Haley avoided mentioning her unsanctioned asset's enhanced interrogation, and the recording of it he had sent her. "A patrol officer caught a thief in the act and he's waived his rights. Singing like a canary. His crew knew about the event days in advance. Not the exact minute, but that it would happen this morning. They and other crews were also given detailed plans and specific assignments of which banks to hit."

"So this was pre-planned. Maybe the freeway was a distraction?"

"Maybe. Or the device went slightly off target."

"Conclusions?"

"If it was an advance attack, more would have happened by now. No posturing from any of our adversaries, either nation-states or known terrorist organizations. If it was for money, it may have been successful; we won't know for hours, if not days, when people can get into the banks and count."

"A one-off?"

She shook her head. "No indication either way. But if you had advanced EMP technology, had created a way to miniaturize it, and a mastery of rocket science, would you stop at knocking out three miles of freeway and downtown Los Angeles, just to rob a few banks? I wouldn't."

"If they could only produce one device?"

"I'd bluff. Blackmail the country, specific industries, even a particular technology company, claiming I would rain down hell from above unless I got what I wanted."

"Sure glad we have you on our side. But I cannot report that we don't know what's going on. Keep digging—there's no such thing as secrets anymore."

Gregory turned back to his computer, paused, then looked over at her. She hadn't budged.

"You're not leaving. Do you have more?"

"Yes, and no."

His head slumped. "Haley, you can't do this to me again."

She waited silently.

Make him ask.

"Fine. What do you have?"

"Only a hunch."

"Not another one of your hunches. I can't take hunches to the other intelligence agencies, let alone the president."

Haley ignored his exasperation.

"I've put several tiny pieces together but have a gut feeling I know what the overall puzzle picture looks like."

"Any proof? Something that I would be happy to share with…" He nodded his head to the left, toward the White House far in the distance.

"Well… actually, yes. Maybe."

"You've lost me. Give me what you have or get back to it."

She hesitated for a second, on purpose, to prepare him for the shock. "I believe Stefan Conroy is involved. My hunch directed me there. Then, when—"

"Hold on." He thought for a second. "Stefan Conroy, the genius inventor from years ago? Billionaire Stefan Conroy?"

"Yes. When I started—"

"What the hell do you have against rich men? What is the problem?"

She didn't take his bait and smiled instead. "No problem. But the FBI got a tip on their web form saying the exact thing I thought: he's involved in the freeway EMP and the water plant hit the day before. Which, looking at it with fresh eyes, could have been the first test of an EMP."

Gregory slowly pushed back his chair and walked around the desk. She turned to face him. They were about the same height: her five foot ten would have been taller had she worn her normal heels and not the sensible, lightweight black combat boots.

He stared at her for several seconds. She didn't hide her feelings. No poker face. She let it all hang out.

"I'm going to ask this, Haley. Straight up, because it's that important. As good as you've gotten at not letting your face betray you, I'm better at reading you than you are at hiding things. Especially when I put my mind to it. Like now."

She felt uncertain and nervous and knew it showed. Which made her more nervous and uncertain. A vicious feedback loop.

"Did you plant an anonymous tip on the FBI website, or have anyone else do it, to back up your hunch?"

She didn't know what to expect, but she hadn't expected that. Not even close.

"What? No!"

How dare he! I may not play by all the rules, but I don't cheat!

"I would never—" she started, but he'd already turned away.

"I believe you." He sat down and leaned forward, his forearms on the desk. "You have consistently been right. I have to at least take this seriously, though you don't have a shred of evidence aside from the anonymous tip, right?"

"Correct."

Get back under control. I have to sell this to him.

"A hunch."

She nodded, her lips in a tight, apologetic smile.

"Can you explain it to me?"

Haley shook her head. "It makes sense in my mind, but I rehearsed it on the walk to your office and it sounds completely crazy out loud. So I'd rather not burden you with it."

To his credit, he leaned back and appeared to seriously consider the problem.

"You've obviously got a plan. Tell me."

"If it's him—"

"A very big if."

"Yes. But if it is, there's no time to get the FBI involved. If we tell them my suspicion—"

"Raw hunch," Gregory corrected.

She acknowledged the correction, giving him the point. "My hunch, they'll debate it and, in the end, decide it is too great a risk to infiltrate his organization. And it would never happen in time."

"Why such a big hurry?"

"Conroy, or whoever it is," she said, beating him to the punch, "wouldn't fire one—let alone two—EMPs at Los Angeles if they weren't close to their end game. My guess—and yes, this is pure conjecture—is the water plant and freeway were both tests of the device and delivery system. They succeeded, so he—or whoever—" she added quickly again, "will proceed with their plan."

"Which is?"

"Unknown. The logical inference is many more EMPs hitting the United States. Possibly the world. Or, if he has only manufactured a limited number of devices, a massive bluff and blackmail push."

"For what end?"

"The usual. Greed, control, power, revenge, or he's just plain crazy." She wouldn't tell him her true belief—that Stefan Conroy wanted to be a god among men.

"And what do you propose to do about it? You're an analyst—" He held up his hand before she could interrupt him. "With some impressive success in the field. But we do not conduct field operations."

Can I tell him about the president's secret directive for Axe, Nalen, and I? Has he already been read in? No.

"I… um…"

"Tell you what. Why don't you take a vacation? Sort out your feelings about being an analyst or consider changing organizations and moving toward field ops. If that's the direction you want to go, I'll of course put in a good word for you."

She fumed, not sure what to say as he spun in his chair, his back to her, and bent forward, fiddling with the lower cabinet of the bureau behind his desk.

He's benching me? At a time like this? He said I was his best analyst! He's a coward, that's it. Too afraid to take risks. Too long spent behind a desk.

It wasn't like her to be speechless, but did she dare speak her mind? He held her career in his hands. No matter how connected she was to Uncle Jimmy—President Heringten—she didn't want him pulling strings to get her a cushy job. She needed to make it on her own merits. She bit the inside of her lip until she tasted blood.

Gregory turned back to her, holding a large manilla envelope. "Here. You deserve a vacation, Haley." She took it automatically, then tore at the flap when he nodded at it. "You've done great work. Come back refreshed with a better idea of your future."

She spilled the contents into her hand. A passport, driver's license, credit cards, gym membership card, a few dog-eared business cards from various places. A frozen yogurt loyalty card with nine of the ten little ice cream cones hole punched. One more purchase and she'd get a free sundae.

All were in the name of Holly Schoharie. With her picture.

The IDs were great, but Admiral Nalen could handle fake identification. What he didn't have access to yet was the ability to create background legends.

Going into the field as an undercover operator required more than a driver's license in a new name. These days, it required a long history of social media posts, credit card purchases, tax returns, and all the other data needed to support an identity.

On several pieces of paper from the envelope were the names and logins of two social media accounts, plus a full dossier covering her background, family, childhood, and more recent experiences.

The envelope contained a complete life for a person to step into, all carefully created, backdated, and documented.

The sudden realization of what she held, along with the work which had gone into creating it, floored her. After a second, she shut her mouth, which was gaping open, and licked her lips in embarrassment.

"Speechless is an unusual look on you, Haley, and I'm not sure I like it. Have a wonderful vacation. Get some sun."

With that, he turned to his computer and ignored her. After a few seconds, she took the hint and left, unsure what had happened, but thrilled with the prospect of going back into the field.

Clutching the packet, she knew she had the tools needed to complete the mission but was left uncertain about her standing. She was officially on vacation, but had a full false identity and history provided by Gregory Addison, director of the Central Analysis Group.

I think I'm now Gregory's unsanctioned asset.

26

PLANS

THURSDAY

Dulles International Airport
Dulles, Virginia

"Are you guys sure about this?" Cody shivered in the cold predawn darkness. He had only a sweatshirt to keep warm. He wouldn't need a coat in a few hours.

"Absolutely. You've got this," Axe said, hiding his doubts. He had flown in an hour before from Los Angeles via another private jet, arranged by Admiral Nalen and paid for by Kelton Kellison as ongoing thanks for saving his life. Why not—the man had plenty of money. "Say it back again."

"First rule: Don't mess up and die," Cody recited. "Second rule: if caught, don't confess." He paused. "Wait. You never explained why."

"Because as soon as you confess, they kill you." The quiet truth hung in the air between them.

"Don't worry about that," Haley said. "We'll be nearby and won't let anything happen to you. I promise."

"Did I let you down in D.C. six months ago?" Axe asked.

"No," Cody said, his voice gaining strength from the memory. He had given Axe and Haley valuable intelligence… albeit at the threat of torture from Axe. He had switched to their side when he realized they were the good guys. He ended up in jail because of it, where he sat for several days. Haley had Kellison hire hotshot attorneys to get him out and the charges were eventually dropped. "You told me to stay quiet and you'd get me out. And you did." He looked at the ground, then back up at Axe. "But I'm not great at making stuff up."

"We know, and you won't have to," Haley explained for the third time. "You're going to tell the truth every time. If you're not certain, you say you don't know. Be yourself. The only thing you never, ever mention is Axe or me, either from six months ago or now."

"If they press, I say I met a woman who I liked, but who didn't share my feelings," he said, warming up to the cover story and blushing when he looked at Haley.

"And that was the final straw. Enough of the cold weather, enough of the aimlessness, enough of the loneliness. I'm ready for the next thing. Maybe I can help with their boats. I'm good with boats. Or I could be a guard because of my military background. Whatever, I want to help and live a quieter life, but with, like, purpose."

"Exactly. You've got it." Haley held up her fist, and they bumped —Haley enthusiastically, Cody less so.

"I guess. I just do better when I have orders to follow."

Axe put the command tone into his voice. "You want orders? Fine. Here they are. Infiltrate the organization. Get close to Stefan Conroy, though not as his right-hand man or anything. Keep your eyes and ears open. Be yourself: helpful, kind, hardworking. Tell the truth. Don't mention Haley or me or being on assignment with us. That part is off limits. This was all your idea, your own doing." Cody nodded happily, standing straight, responding well to the directions. "Gather information and wait for me to make contact. If I don't, wait a few weeks or a month, then do what feels right. Call Haley at the number you memorized and ask her if she's changed her feelings about you. If she says yes, come home if you want to. We could be wrong and he's not a bad guy. So if you like it there, stay. Leave if you want to leave. But if Haley says no, stay undercover. Maybe the investigation takes longer than we think. That's it. Except…?"

"Don't mess up and die," he said with more confidence.

"You got it. Now go." Haley already had the kid's cell phone and had helped him craft his online application to join the movement. They hadn't heard back but figured he wouldn't be the first person to apply, then eagerly fly straight to the island.

He took one last look at both of them before walking into the departure terminal for his flight to St. Thomas, setting in motion the first step of Haley's plan.

"I hope he's ready," Haley told Axe as they walked to the separate chartered jet terminal. She didn't feel completely convinced.

"He can do it," Axe replied. "The Army trained him well, and he's smarter than he thinks. All he needs now is a chance to spread his wings. Learn to not only follow, but lead."

The stress of leadership weighed on her. While she had contributed intel used to send SEAL Teams and other forces into danger, deciding to put Cody's life on the line again shook her. She stopped, then turned to go after Cody. She had to call it off. He was too good of a kid for this.

"Haley, wait." Axe caught her arm. "It's the smart move. He's perfect: there's no guile in him. They'll gladly scoop him up. I bet he finds a place in their inner circle in no time. All we have to do is go get him out."

"I... the responsibility is overwhelming. What if something happens to him?"

I couldn't live with myself.

"It's possible," Axe admitted quietly. As hard as it was to hear, she liked he didn't BS her. "But it's his choice. He's serving his country, the same way he volunteered for the Army and risked his life in the Middle East."

"He's doing it because he has a crush on me. And a man-crush, or whatever you call it, on you. He wants your approval. I'm the girlfriend he would love to have, and you're the father figure."

Axe's face turned blank for an instant, which was as much of a tell as if he frowned or narrowed his eyes.

That's right, he's sensitive about his age.

"Sorry."

"No, you're right. But we all have our motivations. If you had picked a random kid off the street, I wouldn't go along with it. But Cody went through basic training, has been in a few firefights, and is a patriot. He seems sweet, but he's tougher than he looks. He'll do his duty. Let's do ours."

Haley hesitated another second, then they turned and continued toward the private plane that would take them to Miami.

They had avoided discussing Conroy or the overall plan around Cody, figuring the less he knew, the better. Now they had time.

She summarized the attempted abduction and ambush, but Axe interrupted her before she got too far.

"Wait. What happened to the guy in your house?"

"He's dead. In my chest freezer."

He examined her face as they walked. She didn't hide her mixed emotions. She had killed another person, though it had been absolutely necessary. But it still bothered her.

Axe didn't say anything. He didn't need to. She knew he'd been there and done that.

She finished the tale quickly, including how helpful and steady under pressure Cody had been in the getaway car. Then she shut up and waited.

"You handled yourself well," Axe said. "Good shooting. We'll get the admiral's help with the ice cube when I get back from this op. Now, what's going on, and where am I going?"

Haley provided the key points as they entered the private charter terminal, checking to make sure no one could overhear. "Stefan Conroy, the billionaire genius inventor, may be behind what are believed to be two EMP strikes in Los Angeles."

"Proof?"

"None. A hunch is all." She waited for him to hesitate or question her decision to launch a mission based on her hunch, but he didn't.

"Good enough for me." He meant it, which strengthened her.

"I'm not going to find proof online. He's too smart and too careful."

They walked through the quiet building where it was still much too early for the usual executives, VIPs, and the wealthy to be flying. They settled in a darkened corner, with Axe setting his backpack on the chair beside him. Haley did the same with hers.

The flight was reserved for later just in case the departure time was traced back. Haley was unsure how carefully their movements would be tracked. It didn't hurt to be cautious.

"How am I going to get in? They'd suspect me from the start. A retired Navy SEAL would never join that type of movement."

"Exactly. Which is why I'm going with you."

Axe didn't seem surprised.

"You know I'm happy to be on your team again in the field," he started. "But—I'm going to be blunt here because I know you can handle hearing it—you're too beautiful to be incognito. You stick out like a sore thumb and don't realize it because you're used to the attention. You don't notice how people turn to look at you wherever we go. How men keep you in view and try to come up with an excuse to talk to you. Women too—they think you're a famous model and debate getting a selfie with you. You don't blend in."

I notice. I've just gotten good at pretending.

"True. Which is why I'm going to hide in plain sight."

Axe smiled. "Brilliant. Run it down for me."

Haley explained her plan, then waited for Axe to pick it apart.

"A great start." He added a few missing pieces in the way he'd been trained, including exfiltration options, contingency plans, and safeties. She retrieved her phone, opened the secure comms app, and sent notes to Admiral Nalen, asking him to put Axe's added ideas into play.

When they had the plan ironed out, Axe asked about Conroy. "So what's his deal? If he's the one behind this, what's his motivation?"

"His public talks are a mishmash of anarchism, self-determination, and returning to a time when we were all tribal people looking out for ourselves, primarily, and our small groups. But I believe his true motive is more along the lines of autocracy."

"Autocracy? Sorry, I guess I'm not as well versed in the various forms of government as I should be."

"Think of a monarchy, like Saudi Arabia, or dictatorship, like North Korea. One person in charge with no oversight—no courts, no elections. Nothing to keep them in check aside from the threat of being overthrown. But if I'm right, he's taking it a step further."

Axe barked a laugh. "What's a step further than how North Korea runs things?"

"I don't think he wants the headaches of ruling—the management of it—hence the 'self-government' angle in his public talks. Basically, he wants to be a god."

Axe's eyes widened, and he nodded slowly. "All the benefits of power and being a ruler, but with none of the drawbacks."

"Exactly. Whatever goes right, he takes credit for. If something goes wrong, it's the fault of the people. They either didn't manage themselves correctly or, for the devout, they are suffering his wrath."

"Hold on. This is a con, right? He can't believe it will ever work. Billions of people worldwide are suddenly going to worship him? Governments dissolve without a fight and turn to him for guidance?"

"Seems like a reach, but he is a certifiable genius, and he may be behind the EMPs, both of which make him dangerous and worthy of our focus."

Axe nodded. "I agree. We're in the same position as last time: we have a conviction of an imminent attack, but no proof at all. We're ahead of the curve. Understandably, no one else wants to stick their neck out on our hunch. We're on our own. Either we get more intel backing up our theory so we can call in the troops, or we stop it ourselves."

"The question in my mind is whether he's just a delusional, power-hungry madman, or a delusional, power-hungry madman with the means to topple governments and rule the world as a god among men."

"We'll soon find out. We have a good plan."

But she knew another one of Axe's favorite sayings and saw it on his face. He was thinking the same thing.

No plan survives first contact with the enemy.

27

RANSOMWARE

"Report." Despite the early hour, Stefan dressed impeccably in his form-fitting black t-shirt tucked into lightweight black slacks. His black beard was freshly trimmed. He stood, legs spread wide, hands clasped behind his back.

In front and to his left on the control room's command platform, Gunther sat at the computer terminal.

"Thirty minutes ago, I received an alert from one of our teams in Rotterdam."

Not the containers. I need those for Europe.

"Continue."

"Eighteen of the twenty containers have been cleared and have left the port."

"And the other two?"

"They have been flagged for inspection."

Damn it! How were they caught? If they are inspected...

"We cannot have that."

"Yes, Pioneer."

With all his precautions, a thorough inspection could reveal the missiles hidden in the shipping containers. If discovered, an investigation would quickly follow. In short order, the devices would be revealed for what they were: dangerous, revolutionary technology.

They'll connect the two containers to the other eighteen.

First the port authorities, then the government of the Netherlands, would put all their efforts into tracking the other containers. He had layers of defenses in place, but eventually they would find who had designed, manufactured, and shipped them. It would take time, and he could speed up his plans, but it would cause undesirable ripple effects.

Also, other ports worldwide would be notified. His plan would be constrained. He had enough other devices in place, ready to go, but the result would be diminished.

He wouldn't have that.

"Is the hack ready to deploy?"

"Yes, Pioneer. Awaiting your input."

"Well done, Gunther."

We work together like a well-oiled machine. My high priest has done well. He shall be rewarded.

The twins were still asleep in Stefan's bed, tangled in the sheets after he had enjoyed them again earlier, before being alerted by Gunther.

I shall rethink Gunther being my high priest and the twins my priestesses. Perhaps I shall make them demigods and allow them to indoctrinate their own priests. After all, in a few weeks, there will be plenty of worshippers to go around.

Stefan stepped forward and placed his palm flat on the scanner. The screen glowed green for a second and beeped a confirmation. He removed his hand with a satisfied smile. Stefan closed his eyes, imagining the scene and savoring the moment. Once again, he thrust his fist into the air, celebrating his victory. The chaos about to unfold would immediately stop any investigation into his two containers.

It was a sound strategy and was already proving effective in Los Angeles.

And if an inquisitive individual kept at it, the search would end there. No records could be accessed to track the other eighteen containers. By the time any alarms were raised, it would be too late.

Four thousand miles away in Rotterdam, at 12:26 p.m. local time, the computers of the Port of Rotterdam froze.

On every monitor, a message appeared in Dutch, English, French, Mandarin, Cantonese, Spanish, Arabic, and Italian.

This computer system has been temporarily locked. Please contact your IT department.

Across the facility, the port's many automated cranes, robot arms, and unmanned vehicles halted mid-cycle.

Huge cargo containers dangled in the afternoon sunshine, stuck halfway between ships and shore.

Europe's biggest seaport—the largest outside of Asia—ground to a halt.

In the office of the IT department of the Port of Rotterdam Authority, the scene was chaos. All the computer monitors showed the same message as at the port, except for the IT director's screen. On hers, in eight different languages, the message read:

We have hacked your system. All your files are encrypted. Please consider a suitable offer, commensurate to the amount you stand to lose each day—to be paid to us in cryptocurrency—for us to release your files. We will be in touch with instructions.

Stefan opened his eyes, reluctantly ending his enjoyment of the pandemonium. But he had to catch a speedboat, then a plane.

"Come, Gunther. Time for my trip. Let them flail for a solution. It will be amusing to watch them grow progressively more desperate."

It's good to be the king... but it's better to be a god.

28

GOVERNMENTS

Worldwide News/Entertainment Group
Studio B
Miami, Florida

A voice from behind the camera counted down. "We're back in five, four, three…" The man went silent, but his hand remained visible below the camera lens. Two fingers, one, then a sharp gesture, pointing at the gorgeous blond sitting in a short dress and high heels, legs pressed tightly together and demurely angled away from the camera. A red light appeared above the large studio television camera.

"And we're back to continue our fascinating discussion with Stefan Conroy, genius inventor, billionaire patent holder, and, most recently, founder of a start-up company specializing in AI-equipped cybersecurity. We've covered all that, and now," she turned toward Stefan sitting in a plush chair next to her. "I'd like to cover some of your more… shall we say, 'interesting' social ideas. Your main one, it could be argued, is controversial. That is…"

Stefan smiled, radiating charm. His gray slacks, tight black t-shirt, and black sport coat fit him perfectly, showing off his powerful body. With a smile and a twinkle in his eye showing he knew how wild the idea sounded, he said forcefully, "Governments shouldn't provide for people."

Tabitha Steward, former much-loved meteorologist from a competing station, lured away with the promise of her own interview show, drew back with a surprised look. She was the quintessential girl next door, if the girl next door was the most intelligent woman in the city, had incredible instincts for drama and story, and was in better shape than a professional athlete.

"That's a bold statement. Governments came about to both protect and provide for groups of people."

"Yes, but they have grown bloated, inefficient. America's democracy, Sweden's socialism, China's communism. The style of government doesn't matter! Government itself is the problem."

"You're suggesting we... what? Abolish governments? That sounds absurd." She smiled with a skeptical tilt of her head.

"Of course it does. And I'm not suggesting we do it all at once, of course." He leaned toward Tabitha, speaking with his hands as he warmed up. "But a good starting point would be for people to care for each other, instead of looking to their government for help. We must go back to our roots. People looking out for their next-door neighbor, the people across the hallway or street. Spreading the care, with more and more people coming together."

"Sounds lovely. But how do you propose we do this? A government mandate?" Tabitha laughed at her own quip, an intoxicatingly throaty chuckle that—along with her brains and beauty—had made her an international star.

Stefan joined her, slapping his leg lightly in delight. "You're too much!" He sighed with pleasure at her wit, then said seriously, "No, no, of course not. We do it bit by bit, family by family."

"I hope we get there. Now, your movement has another tenet, right?"

"Yes. I recommend living closer to the land, getting back to nature however much one can. Not walking through our lives with our faces turned toward screens, ignorant of the real world surrounding us. Each city has parks. Why not visit one?"

"Why not indeed? So far though, it sounds like what you're

suggesting can work in perfect harmony with how the world currently functions. Why not get closer to nature, as you say, while looking out for one another, yet keep our governments intact, exactly the way they've successfully worked for hundreds of years? In our case, that is. In other countries, much longer than that."

"Excellent question, Tabitha. The latest challenges facing governments, along with the many issues in the past, all prove my point. How can we trust the government—no matter which country you live in—when they cannot manage the primary tasks assigned to them: caring for their people? Protecting them from harm? Providing for them? If any publicly traded company was run like the United States, or the UK, Russia—it doesn't matter, pick a country—the shareholders would revolt! The CEO would be gone in days, and the board of directors shortly thereafter if they didn't right the ship."

"You present interesting points, Mr. Conroy."

"I believe we must join together like our ancient ancestors. Care for one another. Detach from computers wherever possible, and certainly when not using the tools as appropriate: for improved work efficiency. I hope your viewers will consider what I've said. If it resonates with them, perhaps they will join me in rising up."

Tabitha's face hardened. "You're not suggesting violence, are you Mr. Conroy?"

Stefan's eyes widened in surprise. "Oh my goodness, not at all! I'm sorry if I wasn't clear. I merely suggest people commit in their own hearts to look away from their government and so-called leaders. Instead, Tabitha, let's look toward ourselves. Let's each find a genuine leader in the community; a person with wisdom who offers smart solutions. People we feel we can trust. Let's follow them instead."

"Thank you for this eye-opening discussion tonight. I'm sure you've given people much food for thought."

"And take more time away from electronics!" Stefan added in a rush with a smile, realizing the interview was over. "They will be the ruin of us if we continue to let them rule our lives. But after, of course, watching the rest of Miss Steward's program! Priorities!"

Stefan smiled at Tabitha, and she smiled back, delighted with his last statement. "And definitely not until after watching these messages from our sponsors."

They both smiled directly at the camera until the red light went off.

"Thank you, Tabitha, for the opportunity," Stefan said in a quiet voice. "A true pleasure to speak with you. I hope the program proves to be a highly rated crowd pleaser."

"I'm sure it will, Stefan." She stood and waited while an assistant unclipped her microphone, pulled the cord from under her dress while unhooking a small transmitter pack from her bra strap, then zipped her dress up, all while preventing people nearby from glimpsing Tabitha's anatomy.

Stefan averted his eyes, giving her privacy. He stood still while another assistant unclipped his mic, slid it down the front of his shirt, and removed the transmitter from the back of his waist.

Once the mics were gone, and the aides out of earshot, Tabitha whispered, "You're lucky I didn't ask about the harem or the children. Forty-six is it, now?"

"Baseless rumors," he whispered back, a fake smile plastered on his face for any of the crew watching. "And luck has nothing to do with it. The hundred thousand shares of my company will be worth a fortune when I go public in a few months, won't they, Tabby?"

"I told you not to call me that!" The smile remained, but her eyes told the story of her anger.

"When you're ready to return to the island, we await you with open arms."

"That'll be the day," she mumbled as her producer came over, all smiles.

"Mr. Conroy, thank you for flying in for the interview. Great to have you," she said.

Stefan shook hands all around, signed an autograph for a nerdy cameraman who wouldn't shut up about how great it was to meet him, and made his way out the studio door. He had one night in Miami before returning to the island, and he planned to make the most of it. A time for fun and a business opportunity that had fallen into his lap.

29

SECURITY

Miami, Florida

Axe stood with his arms folded just inside the entrance of the small, exclusive boutique shop. Outside the thick glass doors, the rich and famous strolled past in the open-air mall. Their assistants trailed them, laden with purchases from high-end shops.

He saw several security details discretely tailing their charges. Two men who moved, dressed, and scanned the area exactly as he was doing, were loaded with shopping bags gripped awkwardly in their left hands. At least they kept one hand free to reach for a weapon or fend off an attacker.

Bad operational security. Protective units shouldn't be sherpas.

Haley laughed cheerily and took Kelton Kellison's credit card back from the saleswoman who had just had a great day of commissioned sales.

Axe had told Haley he'd rather not go from store to store to store; she should purchase her needed items from as few locations as possible.

"If we're going to play the role, let's do it right," he told her.

"Which means following my protocols and taking security seriously, even if there's no actual need."

He marveled at Haley as she turned, holding five large shopping bags. She smiled as she walked toward him, seeming in her element.

"Here you go, Alexander," she said loudly enough for the saleswoman at the register to hear. She held out the bags.

He gave her a drop-dead glare. They had discussed this. Real security didn't carry bags.

"Alexander," she said in a warning tone.

Axe reluctantly took the bags, sliding them on his left wrist.

"Thank you. You're such a sweetheart. One more stop. Come along."

They exited the shop without looking back, though the saleswoman called out, thanking them.

The bright sun and warm air hit them, welcome after the chill of the shop's air conditioning. Once the door shut behind them, Axe whispered through gritted teeth, "This isn't part of the plan."

Haley walked a step in front of him, which was part of the plan. She whispered back, "If anyone checks, they'll see me acting exactly as they would expect Kelton Kellison's newest 'friend' to act. And you reacted perfectly. The next time she's bored, the woman will mention our little scene to her friends. It's all part of the cover. And remember, there's no real danger."

He had to concede the point. He looked exactly like the other professional security, reluctantly carrying the shopping bags, reduced to an assistant, taken down several notches by his employer—because she was in charge. She held the power. He was merely an employee, bought and paid for.

Haley moved ahead, expertly walking on the new high heels like she still wore her technical assault combat boots. The thin fabric of Haley's yellow sundress was momentarily back-lit, allowing Axe—and several other men who glanced over—a view of her lean yet shapely physique.

She walked directly to another store. Axe slowed, noticing the scantily clad mannequins in the window.

"Holly," he hissed, using her new alias.

Haley ignored him, swung open the door, and swayed inside, letting the door swing shut. Axe caught it with his free hand, glanced around automatically to note any potential threats, then hurried in behind her.

A smiling woman about Haley's age had already greeted her.

This is going to be hell.

He immediately noted the rear exit, potential places to take cover, security cameras, and four other women—two customers and two saleswomen.

With her blond hair loose and flowing, a minimum of makeup applied in the jet as they approached Miami's executive airport, the wispy sundress, and high heels, Haley's beauty outshone the other women's. Which, if Axe's senses were correct, was instantly noted by all present.

In the months they'd known each other, he had come to take her beauty for granted. He mostly saw her at various gun ranges with her hair tied back in a ponytail or bun, wearing no makeup. While he acknowledged her model-quality looks, it was her brain he appreciated more. Besides, he was technically old enough to be her father. He thought of her as a colleague. If he dwelled on it further, she was a niece or a younger sister, not a potential romantic partner.

"Alexander? What do you think about this?" Haley smiled devilishly, relishing his immediate discomfort as she held a see-through lace teddy in front of her and turned her shoulders from side to side.

For a moment, Axe could only stare. He quickly regained his composure. "Very nice, Miss." His face flushed red as he blushed.

The staff and other customers noticed the interplay between them.

I'm sure this is exactly how she planned it. If we had discussed it, I wouldn't have reacted right. Well played, Haley.

The next forty-five minutes included more of the same, as Haley selected every type of lacy, skimpy, and exotic lingerie available.

As Axe once again surveyed the store, taking his security detail role seriously, he overheard the saleswoman tell Haley the total bill. He turned his head in shock to see if this was yet another of Haley's teases, but the amount seemed accurate. Haley didn't hesitate to hand over Kelton's credit card yet again.

That's more than my first car cost!

He tried to wrap his head around having so much money. What would life be like, being able to spend thousands of dollars on frivolous purchases?

The items filled three more bags, which Haley handed to him as she breezed by on the way to the exit. He had to carry them in his right hand, completely against every operational security rule in the book.

At least now they could return to Kelton's house—or rather, his Miami house, to be exact, since he had several around the world—and prepare for the dinner party later when they would set a trap for Stefan Conroy.

30

DATE

"Well, how do I look?" Haley asked as she stepped from the master bedroom into the hallway, carefully walking on the highest heels she'd ever worn.

Axe's face said it all. His lips parted and he drew in a sharp breath, his eyes scanning her quickly up and down. He gulped as his eyes made their way back up to meet hers.

"It'll do," he croaked. She laughed. Though they were in the middle of an operation, it felt good to get dressed up. She did it far too little, focusing instead on proving herself with her mental abilities while actively downplaying her physical attributes. Her entire wardrobe, aside from the form-fitting tactical clothes, was chosen to hide her supermodel body.

But tonight she had a job to do and a role to play. It would be a big change from her normal life. Instead of minimizing her beauty, she had to downplay her brains… at least slightly. She wanted to appear stunningly beautiful, yet also reasonably intelligent—without revealing how smart she truly was.

Haley took a breath and slipped into the role she, Axe, and Kelton had come up with. She would be Kelton's date, a woman he had met months ago but who had only recently agreed to see him. Tonight would be, in reality and in the fiction they would create, their first date.

"One couple is already here," Axe informed her.

"The ones Kelton said always come early and stay late?" she whispered as they walked down the long hallway to the living room.

"Yes." A door chime sounded in the distance. "That will be another group," Axe said, walking a few steps behind her.

Dinner would be served at 8p.m. The guests had been asked to arrive around 7:30. The first couple had arrived at 7 sharp.

The initial part of the plan looked like it would work. When they first approached Kelton, he had agreed but admitted his clout had diminished. "I'm not sure I can get people to dinner at my house with the situation my businesses are in. I might be toxic."

"People will want to attend exactly because of that," Haley had explained. "They'll be able to tell their friends they had dinner with you as your life went down the drain. It's like not being able to look away from a car crash."

He'd sagged at her words but cheered up when she continued. "Besides, if we're right, you'll be saving the world."

"What if Conroy says no? Do I still have to throw the party?"

"He won't say no. He'll smell blood in the water and come to feed."

"It'll work? You'll be able to get what you want out of him?"

"If he's the type of man I think, it will work like a charm."

"And you'll be my date?"

"For the duration," she'd said, which is what clinched the deal.

The voices and laughter of several people carried through the living room as Haley entered. A man, around sixty-five, and his wife in her mid-twenties, a few years older than Haley, stood holding drinks. They looked awkward at having been abandoned by Kelton, who greeted his newest arrivals near the front door.

Kelton claimed she's his wife, though he wondered if they have an arrangement of some sort.

Haley walked straight to them. "Good evening. Pardon me for

arriving late. I'm Holly, Kelton's…" She hesitated slightly, by design. "Date."

The man stepped forward, offering his hand while his eyes devoured her body. The tight black dress, purchased earlier that day for an obscene amount of money, was enticing, sexy, and elegant at the same time. It was by far the nicest outfit she'd ever worn. The thin black spaghetti straps and plunging neck revealed much more of her breasts than she felt comfortable with, and the thin fabric clung to her hips, ending halfway to her knees.

He can tell the dress is too thin to allow any sort of underwear.

"So nice to meet you, Holly. Any friend of Kelton's is a friend of ours. I am David Ollevenson and this is my wife, Della."

Della is less than thrilled with me… or rather, hubby's reaction to me.

David lightly kissed Haley's offered fingers. Once he finally let her hand go, she turned and leaned forward a few inches to air kiss in Della's direction.

Della's dress was longer than hers but had a slit up the side, showing her left leg nearly to the hip. Her hair was a dirty blond, in contrast to Haley's bright yellow. It fell in small ringlets to her shoulders, brushing against the tied straps holding up her dress and large breasts.

"Oh my God, I love your outfit!" Haley exclaimed, in her best imitation of some of the women she had known in high school and college. She stepped toward her, smiled a bit dismissively at David, and got Della a few steps away from her husband. "Do I dare beg you to tell me where you got it?"

I need to break the ice with the women. The men will ogle me, but I need the women on my side or the night will be a drag. The quickest way to do it is to focus on the ladies.

With a few questions and a ton of wide-eyed flattery, Della quickly warmed to her. Haley leaned closer. "Can I confide in you, Della? I'm so nervous! This is my first date with Kelton. We have a mutual friend who introduced us, but… this isn't my scene at all! I work in an office, though I've always wanted to be a model like you."

Whether she's a model or not, she's going to love that.

Della broke out in a huge smile, revealing perfect white teeth, and took a step back to look Haley up and down. "You're not already a model?"

"Wait—do you really think I could be? Don't play with me!"

"Of course you could be! I could introduce you to my agent and—"

"Holly!" Kelton's voice boomed across the room as he strode confidently toward them. "You came! I'm so happy!" He wore black jeans and a white button-down dress shirt on his tall, wiry frame, ignoring his own party's elegant dress code. But it was his signature look, the outfit he wore nearly every day, shown in countless magazine articles as he expanded his empire. His perfectly styled longer dark hair had hints of gray despite his thirty-something age. He looked every inch the successful young tech billionaire and empire builder he was.

Kelton stopped before her and smiled charmingly. "I am so happy to finally spend time together." To Della, he said, "Della, so nice to see you! How's the tennis game?"

"You play tennis, too?" Haley said, surprising herself with how sincere she sounded. "I should have known," she added, looking over Della's figure. The woman soaked up the attention.

"Do you mind if I steal her for a moment?" Kelton leaned toward Della conspiratorially. "This is our first date. Don't tell anyone, though, okay?"

"Of course not, Kelton. My lips are sealed!"

"Thank you." Kelton offered his arm to Haley. "Holly, if you please? I'd like to introduce you to the rest of the guests."

Haley took his arm, and they walked across the spacious living room to the small group chatting in the front entry hall. "'My lips are sealed,'" he muttered in a whisper to Haley. "That'll be the day. It'll be all over town by dawn, if not by midnight." They reached the group of three men and four women. "Everyone, please, your attention. I'll introduce you properly in a moment once we get drinks, but first please meet my friend Holly Schoharie."

She was greeted heartily by the men, along with fake but plausibly sincere words from the women, every one of them a shade of blond.

Haley smiled pleasantly, allowing her nervousness to show through.

Let them see my fear.

They moved as a group toward the full bar on the far edge of the room, where a bartender stood in his impeccable white servers jacket, a welcoming smile on his face. Della and David had already congregated there, having refreshed their glasses.

"Miss Holly, your vodka tonic," the bartender said, handing her a tall glass with both a lemon and lime wedge in it. She immediately took a sip.

Just enough vodka to make it seem realistic—perfect.

One plan for the evening was for her to pretend to get tipsy. Several drinks, none with much alcohol, would allow her to fake the level of drunkenness necessary.

Kelton introduced her one by one as the others chatted, leaning against the bar. The timing worked out perfectly, as their mark had settled at the far end with his dates, two stunningly beautiful twins. "And finally, this is a man I know only by reputation, though I'm thrilled to have you here, Stefan. Holly, this is Stefan Conroy and his friends Ella and Anna."

She looked at Kelton and back to Stefan, without another glance at the twins. "Wait. Stefan Conroy? Pioneer? I thought you looked familiar!" She let her mouth drop open. "Oh, my, God. Is it really you? I downloaded your speech from the other night to listen to again on the flight this morning. I can't believe I'm meeting you. Oh, this is incredible! I love your message—oh my God, I'm so sorry, now I'm babbling!" She felt her cheeks redden with honest embarrassment at how she sounded.

Nailed it.

Haley grabbed Kelton's hand in hers and kissed him hard on the cheek. "I can't believe you did this—did you invite him because of what I mentioned Tuesday?"

Kelton's panicked surprise was genuine. This wasn't at all how they had planned the meeting between her and Conroy. His wide eyes sought hers, then flicked to Conroy, who did exactly as Haley expected —he stepped in to save his fellow billionaire playboy.

"Miss Holly, it is my pleasure. Kelton did invite me because he mentioned how much of an impact my little speech had on you."

Perfect. An instant bond formed between them based on a mutual lie.

"And, oh, I can't believe it. Ella and Anna the supermodels?"

Haley laid it on thick, but she was pulling it off. The two blonds smiled at her, pleased to be recognized for the right reason, given their history. It had been a long time since they'd been referred to as models instead of "murderers," or worse, "former models turned convicted killers." And no one had ever called them supermodels.

Haley dropped Kelton's hand and fanned her face. Under her breath, just loud enough to be heard by the men and women near her, she sighed, "This is the best day of my life!" She drained her glass in a few gulps, turned to the bartender, and said, "I'm going to need another drink to help pull myself together!"

31

DINNER

Axe waited in the front entryway at parade rest in the nicest suit he'd ever worn, from their last stop at the fancy mall. He stood close enough to the door to be perceived as guarding it, yet able to see the dining room and hear most of the conversation around the large table. He would have liked to be closer, but he couldn't pull off the role of a server. And security wasn't needed in the same room as the guests inside the locked and well-guarded home.

Haley played her role to perfection. Stunningly beautiful—and a bit self-conscious. Like she knew she didn't quite fit in with the mega-rich enjoying dinner. It worked well with her cover as an office worker at a business consulting firm.

She also found the balance between seeming too interested in Stefan Conroy and not interested enough. She played his ego well without alienating his two dates, who sat in silence, smiling pleasantly without uttering a word. When required, Stefan spoke for them. They nodded or shook their heads if necessary.

The conversation flitted from one subject to the next with the practiced ease of people used to making small talk with others of their kind. For several minutes, the latest ultra-fast luxury jet was discussed, including its cost and whether it would be worth the money to upgrade.

I can't believe any of them would worry about the money... but then again, maybe that's why they have so much, because they always think about it.

David, the first guest to arrive, was by far the oldest. He seemed out of his depth with the younger Kelton, in his thirties, Conroy, in his early thirties, and the other men, none of whom were over forty.

He's old money, not new. Wonder if he feels lucky to be invited.

The women were all well under thirty, and Haley looked like the youngest.

"All stations, report." The voice of Kelton's security team leader and a distant acquaintance of Axe's—Doug, aka "Mad Dog"—came through the tiny high-tech wireless speaker in his ear. It was several generations nicer than the equipment used by the SEALS.

"One. All clear."

"Two. All clear."

"Three. All clear."

The calls came through until it was Axe's turn as position ten, one more than usual for the house detail. He had been accepted with open arms by the team, as he had been instrumental in them being hired once Kelton realized how slip-shod his previous security had been when filled with men dishonorably discharged from military service. Axe's exact role had been kept close to the vest; they had been told he served as personal security for Miss Holly Schoharie. He trusted the loyalty of every member of the detail as far as physical protection went. None of them would allow their charge to be harmed. But with all the money available to Kelton's competitors and enemies, all it took was a guy tired of working for a living to pass along gossip or intelligence.

Trust only goes so far.

"Ten, all clear."

"Dessert will be served in five. Things break up quickly after that but be prepared to stage a phone call for K to get him out of the clutches of D&D." David and Della were apparently a fixture at

Kelton's parties and the security team had standing instructions to extricate Kelton from their conversation when signaled. They planned the operations with care, going to extremes to ensure they were realistic, so David wouldn't suspect he had overstayed his welcome. Tonight, an emergency phone call about his business' ongoing cybersecurity problems would tear Kelton away from the last remaining guests, who would be escorted out because Kelton would be quite a while.

The security detail hadn't been told about the change of plans. This evening, Kelton would refuse all calls. The evening would last as long as Haley needed to reel in Stefan Conroy.

32

HOOK

Kelton Kellison's Miami House
Miami, Florida
9:43 p.m.

They sat around the living room, tongues loosened by exquisite food and expensive liquor.

Haley snuggled up against Kelton on one part of the large sectional sofa, acting tipsy. She kicked off her high heels and tucked her feet under her, the already short dress sliding higher. She tugged it down half an inch, then turned to laugh at a comment from David who, though older than the rest by twenty or thirty years, proved himself witty and engaging.

After that, she ignored the dress, though she felt it creep up. Out of the corner of her eye, she saw the men watch and hope it went higher.

Her role as the overwhelmed date to a billionaire, new to the clothes, liquor, food, and five-star service, had come easy to her.

Harder had been keeping her mouth shut and her opinions to herself. The role of a submissive woman who worshipped her rich man was not a good fit for her. Still, she'd held her tongue, laughed delightedly at the jokes, mostly lame but with a few good quips thrown in by David and Kelton, and had bided her time.

On the sofa, the topics switched between food, travel, and expensive toys. Without an obvious agenda, each man was given time to discuss their businesses briefly—none of the women worked except Haley. Each of the men had his time to shine and brag.

Conroy mentioned the many new contracts his cybersecurity company had landed.

"Perhaps Cottswoth-Goldentech would consider using us," he said.

Kelton nodded immediately. "Yes, I wanted to discuss that with you." Kelton had used an immediate need for better cybersecurity to get Conroy to the dinner party, claiming to be losing the battles his company fought and in need of a consultation.

"Of course. If I can help, I'll get my best team on it."

"Thank you, Stefan, I may take you up on that," Kelton said quietly, acknowledging his difficulties.

There was a short, uncomfortable silence. All knew about Kelton's recent troubles and the excruciatingly large market loss he'd taken the day before.

Haley took her chance. "Excuse me, if you don't mind, Mr. Conroy—"

"Please, Miss Holly, call me Stefan."

Haley stammered, "Th-thank you, mister—darn it, I mean Stefan," she laughed nervously. "Will you be sharing another message this coming Monday? I... I would like to be prepared to watch it live this time instead of streaming it later." She turned to Kelton. "Maybe you could fly up to D.C. and we could watch it together?"

Kelton pulled her closer to him and whispered in her ear.

She laughed and said, "Oh, you're bad!" Turning to Stefan, she looked expectantly at him.

Finally!

Stefan had suffered through the inane conversation before the dinner and barely made it through the meal. Imagining the many things he could do to young Holly kept him going, while he paid just enough attention to the conversation to contribute from time to time and appear interested.

Don't blow it. Getting Kelton Kellison into the fold would be a coup. I might even make him a priest. With his contacts and reach...

A rumor persisted of Kellison's close connection to the current President of the United States of America. While Stefan had nothing but contempt for any of the so-called leaders of the world, having a line to the president during the coming weeks as he transitioned from tech billionaire to god of the world might come in handy.

"Why not come watch it live, in person, Miss Holly? You and Kelton are welcome anytime. The ladies and I would delight in giving you a personal tour. Our home really is the Paradise Found we call it."

Holly's eyes widened delightfully for a moment before her face fell. "I would love that," she said, and he didn't doubt it for an instant. He had an image of her walking slowly across his bedroom toward him as he lay on the bed, waiting. "But I have to get back to work Sunday night, and Kelton promised to show me his yacht."

It looked like she belatedly realized the reaction her disappointment might have on Kelton because she turned and offered him an apologetic, embarrassed smile and snuggled closer.

Her skirt inched up. One more movement...

"The yacht is here in Miami?" It would complicate matters, but perhaps he could convince them to sail to St. John. Or at least send the ship ahead and join next week. He couldn't let Holly—or Kelton—get away.

"Actually, it's in San Juan. I had it in Curaçao for hurricane season and it's just arrived. We were planning on flying down tomorrow."

"Perfect! It's only a hop, skip, and jump from San Juan to St. John. Please, Kelton, say you'll both come. Holly, today I recorded an in-depth interview with Tabatha Steward from Worldwide News and Entertainment Group. It will air tomorrow night. You can watch it with my followers and me and have a nice discussion afterward. Plus, Kelton, while you're there, I can introduce you to my team. I'm sure they could consult with your top people to help immediately. No charge."

Kelton's eyes flashed with desperation first, then greed.

There's nothing the rich enjoy more than receiving something free.

He had Kelton in the palm of his hand. He'd already helped him lie to his new girlfriend, and it looked like Kelton's company might be in worse shape than known.

"I suppose we could do that. Sounds like fun, actually."

Holly squealed in delight and wiggled excitedly, like she was running in place. For an instant, the dress slid up higher before she pulled it down an inch.

I must have her.

Out of the corner of her eye, Haley caught Stefan looking. A hungry look flashed on his face. She hugged Kelton, surprising him yet again. She pulled her dress down to a more respectable position, pretending to be embarrassed.

Got you, you pervert. You fell for it all. Hook, line, and sinker.

33

INTERVIEW

Cody slumped in the uncomfortable white plastic chair at the end of one of the many rows of empty seats. The Center's intake building—an unused terminal wing of the airport—had teemed with new recruits when he landed many hours ago. Now, however, only he remained. An older man with a mop and yellow bucket of water cleaned the floors at the other end of the large room. He'd already done the area where Cody sat. Cody had raised his feet off the ground so he didn't miss a spot.

What have I gotten myself into?

Cody was exhausted and unsure of himself. He'd been up since long before dawn at the airport with Haley and Axe. At first, working with them seemed glamorous and exciting. A chance to do something important, be all he could be. It's what he'd wanted from the Army, but guarding supply convoys hadn't exactly done it. Sitting in an airport, forgotten, didn't feel like living his best life, either.

After his briefing from Haley and Axe, he'd flown from D.C. to Miami, then from Miami to St. Thomas. Finally, he had been directed to the arrival area for pilgrims, as they called people who joined the Movement.

He'd been scolded for arriving without being invited, told to fill out forms, then have a seat and wait to be called.

That had been hours ago. He was hungry and thirsty, but he'd stick with the plan. Axe and Haley needed him. He could never let them down.

Besides, this is more comfortable than most of my time in the Army. At least I'm indoors and no one's shooting at me.

Cody's eyes closed and head dropped as he fell asleep. A few minutes later, he sensed a presence in front of him. He sat up straight, rubbing his eyes. A stocky woman with a pretty face smiled at him. She had long dark hair that flowed around her shoulders.

"Cody?"

He nodded.

"Sorry to keep you waiting. Can you come with me, please?"

He followed her past the long rows of chairs to a door with a numbered keypad lock. She blocked his view of the keypad and punched in a code, opened the door, and held it for him. "Come on in."

The room was tiny, like a small walk-in closet. The bright overhead fluorescent lights shone on a bare white table with a large gray plastic tub, similar to the ones from security lines at the airport. There was a door to the left and a door to the right. On a hook on the wall to his left was a short white robe, made of thin paper material, like something you'd put on at the doctor's office, except a robe instead of those gowns that left your entire backside showing.

"My name is Kim and I'll be doing your interview today. Please strip off all your clothes. Put your watch, phone, backpack, and clothing—everything you have—in the bin. Then put on the robe and come through this door when you're ready." He could tell she'd given the same speech over and over.

She left through the door on the left. He followed her instructions, leaving all his belongings in the well-used but clean plastic tub.

Wearing the too thin, too short robe, he walked on the cold tile floor through the door into what looked like a section of the airport terminal. It had walls with unfinished, unpainted drywall, no windows, and no furniture except for a plain white table near the center of the room, used as a desk by Kim. She sat in an expensive-looking black mesh chair with his paperwork in one hand and a tablet on a small plastic stand to her right.

He stopped in front of the table. Kim gestured at two pieces of tape, worn and curling up on the corners, that formed an X on the floor four feet in front of her.

"Okay Cody, tell me why you're here." Her voice was pleasant, but tired… and bored.

This is it. My live interview. I can't blow it.

"I heard Mr. Conroy—Pioneer—Monday night. He really inspired me. Since I left the Army I've felt… aimless, I guess. When I heard him talk, it did something for me." He hesitated, trying to put into words what he felt when Haley played him the recording—and how to convince the woman to accept him so he could continue his mission.

They said to always tell the truth.

Cody shrugged and spoke from the heart. "I… Well, when he said to make plans to detach from technology on Wednesday morning and socialize with friends or family," he swallowed hard, looked down, then shyly back at Kim. "I didn't really have anybody to socialize with. That was really depressing. I liked being in the Army, but it wasn't a great fit. I think I'm more sensitive than most of the others were. But I enjoyed the camaraderie. There was always someone around. And I thought…" He looked down again. "Pioneer made it sound like maybe there were other people like me. I've never been into technology, and I like the idea of living a simpler life, being close to nature, and spending time with other people who feel the same, I guess."

I'm blabbering. I think I blew it.

As he finished speaking, Kim took an electronic pencil from the table and made a few notes on the tablet. "So you just decide to fly here?" There was skepticism in her voice.

"I thought about it for a few days. My car had broken down, and I'd rented a car to get around, but I didn't have anywhere to go. It all seems so… pointless. I've been feeling aimless since I left the Army. I guess I just wanted a purpose again. So I booked my flight and flew down here. I guess I decided to take a chance. Is that okay? With my military background, I hoped I could help out. I'm also good with boats. I grew up on a lake and, this is an island, so…"

Did I lose her?

He panicked and tried to backpedal. The operation could probably wait a few weeks, right? "I have money saved from the Army. If you need me to fly home and come back in a couple of weeks when you have an opening, I can do that. I kinda just want to help and… Maybe see if I fit into your community."

Kim made a few more notes on her tablet, then shuffled the papers of his application. "Tell me about your time in the Army. What did you do?"

Okay, I haven't blown it yet.

This was safer ground. "Almost always guard duty. From the start, they said I was reliable. I never tried to snooze on duty or work it so I could stand around with other people and talk. I'm good at staying awake and alert. The Army finds out what your skills are and puts them to good use." He shrugged with a smile. "I was a good guard. Mostly I sat in trucks, calling out alerts if I saw anything suspicious as we rolled in convoys."

Kim leaned forward, interested. "And did you see suspicious things?"

Cody nodded, happy to talk about his successes. "I stopped us from getting ambushed once, and a bunch of times called in suspicious individuals. Some of them were bad people that we had to shoot when they shot at us."

"Did you shoot anybody?"

"I shot my weapon several times, covering fire, but I don't think I killed anybody." He knew he sounded disappointed because he was. Six years in the Army, many of them riding shotgun for convoys, and while he could say he saw combat, he didn't think he'd come close to hitting the enemy.

Kim made a few more notes. "We don't have many guns here, Cody. We are mostly a pacifist movement. Have you had any hand-to-hand training?"

"Yes, ma'am, at basic training, but in all honesty, I've never had to use it in the real world."

I hope this is working. Axe and Haley said to be honest.

"Now," Kim said with an edge to her voice. "You mentioned this briefly in your application, and when we did an investigation into your background, as we do with all applicants, we discovered a situation from six months ago. Tell me more about it."

Cody looked at the floor in front of him and used his toe to get the curling black tape to stick to the floor. Haley had said they would ask about this. He thought he was ready, but the humiliation of that night still bothered him.

I bet my face is beet red.

"Yes, ma'am. I worked hard to get in with a company. I wanted to do military contracting for a good firm, kind of continue what I did in the Army, only freelance. They finally let me in. They had a last-minute mission and needed one more person." He paused, swallowed hard, and began again. "At the last minute, they said I wasn't qualified to go on the mission and made me stay at the warehouse with the leader of the group, the captain. I would help guard the warehouse until the other guys returned."

He flashed back to when the captain had been killed right in front of him—by Haley, he now knew.

"They had a former operator with a grudge. He targeted the warehouse that night. I don't know all the details. Anyway, he killed the captain and overpowered me." He felt the heat spread further across his face and knew exactly how red he looked when he blushed like this.

"The police responded to the gunshots that killed the captain. The attacker escaped. I felt like an idiot. I failed in my first real mission. All I had to do was guard the building, and I blew it."

Cody took a deep breath to pull himself together, surprised at how much the memories affected him. "Anyway, the police arrested me because of the captain's dead body. I wasn't sure what to do, but they told me I had the right to remain silent, and that seems smart. Eventually, the police let me go because it was clear I hadn't shot anyone—they did this test on my hands. And the gun the company had given me wasn't the same gun that shot my captain. I think the owner of the company might've paid for a big shot attorney or something—

this smart guy came to the jail and got me out. The charges were dropped. At least, that's what the lawyer told me."

He finally looked up at Kim, who seemed sympathetic. "I chose the wrong company, and it turned me off to that type of work." He shrugged helplessly. "But guarding is what I'm good at, aside from that one night, I mean. And the lawyer told me the operator was like some super-soldier or something, and if he could kill the captain, it wasn't my fault that I couldn't stand up to him."

Bring it back around now. Don't blabber.

"When I saw Pioneer on the internet, it clicked. Why not get away from it all, see if I can help here, either guarding or like I said, I'm good with boats." He smiled eagerly. "I'd actually prefer boats if that's an option. I can even fix them a little."

"But you're good at staying awake on guard duty? Observing things? Following orders?"

Cody stood up straighter. "Yes, ma'am."

"Good. We need men like you." She used the pencil to scribble something, maybe her signature, on the tablet. She set the pencil down and waited a few seconds, staring at him. "Cody, would you like to join us?"

He smiled eagerly and nodded. "Yes, very much so. I just want to start over with better people—people more interested in nature and saving the world than blowing it up."

"You'll love it here. Welcome to the Movement, Cody."

I did it. I'm in!

34

STRATEGY

FRIDAY

Aboard *The Kellison*
Approaching St. Thomas, Unites States Virgin Islands

Kelton and Haley entered the ship's massive master suite laughing quietly and holding hands. As soon as they closed the door, they let go, both of them looking relieved.

Axe stepped out of the master bathroom with a raised eyebrow. "How's the act coming?" he asked.

"It's exhausting!" Kelton said with a sigh. He walked over and flopped onto his enormous bed of two king-size mattresses pushed together.

Haley put her fists on her hips. "Kelton, darling, how dare you!" she said with a laugh.

"Sorry Haley, nothing against you, but my business right now is swirling down the toilet, and I'm out here on the ocean playing superspy," he said. "Besides, I never thought we'd make it this far. But you reeled Conroy in. I hope you know what you're doing."

Haley, chastened, said, "Sorry, Kelton. I know this is a sacrifice for you. How's the attack on your company? Are you able to keep in touch and manage it from here?"

Axe had seen Kelton's lavish office. With modern communications, Kelton was likely exaggerating his inability to stay in touch.

"Truth be told, there's very little I can do here or there. But I would just rather be back in my office, surrounded by my minions, so I could have people to yell at," Kelton said, half-joking.

Axe chimed in. "As soon as the chopper returns, you go back to San Juan, and from there, you can fly straight back to New York."

"I thought you needed me on the island."

"From what I saw of Conroy last night, I'm even more inclined to believe in Haley's hunch. You might as well go back. It could make things easier for Haley and me." They hadn't told Kelton much, just that they needed him so they could get close to Conroy, but not why or what they suspected.

"What about the cybersecurity demo? I could use all the help I can get, and besides, if his software is as good as I'm hearing, I might want to invest in his company. Get in on the ground floor. Assuming I have any money left after this week," he sighed.

His companies were being continuously hit by effective cyber attacks. Gossipy rumors had spread like wildfire throughout the tabloids, ranging from obvious falsehoods to stories that rang true to the casual reader. Outlandish behaviors, philandering, drunken sex parties, drug use, and other excesses. All had contributed to a rapid decline in his company's stock price, as well as many large, important clients canceling contracts for every one of the many businesses in his empire.

Already, Kelton had lost $26 billion of his net worth, according to a story Axe had read that morning as they flew by helicopter to the ship, already en route to St. Thomas.

"Kelton, please," Haley said as she walked to the bed and sat down on the edge next to his sprawled body. "Trust us. My prediction is that Stefan wants you more than you need him. In fact, I think it's likely that if you go to the island, he won't let you leave. At least, not for several days. It would only make your situation worse to be completely out of touch. Use your team to fight off the attacks. You know how the Assistant thinks. You can do better than any artificial intelligence software."

Kelton nodded reluctantly. "I guess. But what the hell is Conroy up to? Why are you pushing so hard to go in?"

"We can't tell you right now," Axe said. "But you shouldn't set foot on the island. Besides, you have a great excuse to return to New York and," Axe smiled, "yell at your minions."

"Haley," Kelton said, "you may not be my type, but you and Axe still saved my life. I care about you both. If it's that dangerous to go to the island, why not fly back with me? Send in the Marines or something instead."

Haley glanced at Axe, shushing him with a look before he could brag about Navy SEALs assaulting the island instead of Marines. "We think Conroy is even worse than Todd Burkley, and the further you are from him, the better. You've had enough excitement for one life."

"Fine, fine. So what's the plan?"

Kelton left the master suite, closing the door quietly behind him, leaving Haley and Axe alone to strategize. The plan called for Kelton to fly back to New York City with half of his security force so he could better manage his businesses. He would tell the staff that Ms. Holly, as she was known, since they were keeping everyone on board in the dark about her real name and the true purpose of her presence, would continue to St. Thomas.

The yacht would dock. Haley and Axe would take a private speedboat, furnished by the Movement, to St. John for a tour to watch Conroy's TV interview in the presence of the man himself, and spend at least one night.

They would apologize for Kelton's sudden departure and inability to take part in the activities, but Haley and Axe were convinced Conroy wouldn't mind. In fact, they suspected he would be delighted Haley was being left on her own, abandoned by her brand-new boyfriend, with only one security guard to protect her.

Axe moved to the plush chairs facing the extravagant gas fireplace in the middle of the master bedroom suite and swiveled them to face each other.

"What's your take on the situation?" Axe asked.

"Like we told Kelton, I'm convinced he's up to something, probably exactly what we suspect him of."

"I agree. There's something off about him... I mean, more than just the usual billionaire playboy genius deal. And did you see the blond guy in his entourage? He seemed to be more than security, but he waited outside, standing next to the car the entire time. That man is a stone-cold killer."

"That's Gunther, his right-hand man. We don't know much about him, just that he's been with Conroy for years and was born in Germany."

"Jake, the bank robber I caught, said his boss made fun of their contact, saying his English was perfect, but he still had a slight German accent. He called him 'The Nazi.'"

"Exactly. It's another clue Conroy is the man we're looking for."

"I agree, but again, circumstantial evidence. Nothing we can use against him or give to your boss to take to the president. But Conroy certainly is interested in you..." Axe said, leaving an implication in the air that he hoped Haley would pick up.

Haley looked surprised. She tilted her head and said with a small smile, "You disapprove of my... methods?"

Axe shook his head firmly. "Not my call. I leave the spy shit to you. Just—I hope you know what you're doing." He paused, concerned, but trying not to be a prude. "Since we're on the topic, what are you doing?"

Haley shrugged. "How better to infiltrate than to appeal to what truly motivates the man? I mean, come on, who shows up for a dinner party with two dates? A playboy. A player. There are rumors he has more than forty children from that many women. I'm using what I have to my advantage."

"Isn't that... I don't know, it seems... exploitive."

"It's only exploitive if others do it to me, or make me do it, not if I'm choosing to do it myself."

Haley sounded defensive. He didn't want to push, but this was a talk they had to have. "So, what's your plan in that regard?" He wasn't her father figure, but perhaps he could be a mentor. They were in this together, and they only had each other. This talk was important.

Haley hesitated, and Axe thought he caught her cheeks flush with embarrassment. "I'm not sure. I could seduce him?" It came out as a question.

"You won't have to seduce him. He already wants you. But that's not what we do."

Haley frowned. "Isn't it like shaking the tree? Move forward, see what happens."

Axe nodded. "True, that's exactly what I say. But what you're proposing has problems. The biggest is that it won't work. Sleeping with Conroy isn't suddenly going to make him spill his secrets to you in bed. And I doubt he leaves his plan for conquering the universe lying around on his nightstand. So unless you plan on spending the next year as his concubine, and probably having a child by him, I doubt you're going to get into the inner circle that way. So while it's your decision, I can't advocate seduction as a realistic method of achieving our goal."

Haley sighed. "I know, I know." She bit her lip. "But remember, this is my first real field assignment, aside from the New York situation. I'm a little out of my depth here."

Axe sat forward. "You're doing a great job. You figured all this out by yourself. You hooked Conroy. We're in. My gut tells me we're on the right track. Let's come up with some plans and contingencies for our time on the island. We'll have to play a lot by ear, but having the basics of communications, some codewords, and strategies in place will carry us through well."

Haley took a deep breath and nodded.

Axe hesitated, then dove in. "Before we do though, you need to think about the big picture. You're going to have to decide who and what you are."

He leaned forward to explain. "I'm an operator, a trigger puller. It's what I do. This spy shit is new to me. You've been an analyst—one of the most gifted I've ever seen. But you want to work in the field. You need to decide if you're a trigger puller," he pointed at himself. "A spy.

Or a spy handler—like what you've got going with Cody and me. Or, of course, an analyst. What you decide dictates your actions."

"Or my actions dictate what I am."

"Another approach, yes. But remember, many people can do what I do. Me, my former Teammates. The people that went before us, and the newer guys coming up. All of them are ten times better than you on offense." He assessed how she was taking his words. She didn't look upset.

"But all of us put together," Axe said quietly, "couldn't come close to matching you in the analysis department. Don't let your talents go to waste. But make sure you reach for your dreams. You want to be a small fish out here in the ocean of operators, fine. But in the sea of analysts, you're a shark."

Haley stared at the ocean gliding serenely by outside the suite's vast windows. "Food for thought. For now, keep your analyst hat on and plan the rest of this operation. With your favorite trigger puller's input, we can figure out what this lunatic is up to and put a stop to him together." He waited until she looked at him. "I trust you with my life, in and out of the field. And I'm both happy and proud to be a team of two with you. Good enough?"

She nodded, a look of resolve on her face. "Good enough. Now let's figure out how to nail this guy."

<hr />

After an hour of talking, they had a better plan for the next stage, and it was nearly time for Kelton to be off. The helicopter would arrive shortly. A knock at the door interrupted them. Axe gestured for Haley to put her feet up on his chair and pretend to read one of the pricy oversize books on the small coffee table in front of her.

He hustled to the door, his footsteps silent on the thick carpet. He opened it, making sure whoever it was could see Haley relaxing while he stood guard.

Kelton's chief of security, Doug, held out a satellite phone. His muscular frame filled the doorway. His short dark hair and nicely groomed beard made him look more like a professional rugby player than a security chief.

"Phone call for Miss Holly."

"Great, thanks, I'll take it."

"Man on the line says for Miss Holly's ears only."

Haley stood and walked to the door, in character as the new, wide-eyed girlfriend. "For me? Who would call me here? My parents, maybe?"

"Must be, Miss Holly. An older man's voice, maybe around sixty though—not too old."

"Thank you… Doug, right?"

Doug nodded, impressed she had remembered his name.

"I'll take it in here," she said as she accepted the phone. "Would you gentlemen excuse me?"

Axe and Doug stepped out of the room into the small open landing at the top of the grand staircase. Axe flashed back to six months before, when he had been chased up these stairs by Devlin, a former SEAL gone rogue, before later shooting him in the master bedroom closet. Down the stairs, Axe could see where he had been shot at by Todd Burkley, the Assistant, who was still out there, after them.

We'll get to you next, Todd.

He couldn't see any bullet holes and hadn't noticed blood stains or other signs of the violence on the ship.

Axe strained to hear Haley's call, but the door—the whole ship—had been designed to be as quiet and soundproof as possible.

Mad Dog shook his head disapprovingly. "You're running an op."

Axe hid his surprise. He had been expecting a dressing down, guessing the security team figured he and Haley were an item. "What makes you say that?"

"Come on, man."

"How do you know we're not sleeping together behind Kelton's back?"

"Seriously? You're old enough to be her father." His tone made clear he thought the idea ludicrous. The man stood, muscular arms crossed, waiting.

Axe debated what to say, staring the man down, hoping he'd back off without an answer. Mad Dog had a great reputation in the warrior community. That, and a few close friends' recommendations, had made Axe recommend the man and his firm to Kelton. Kelton's former guys had to go; they were loose cannons, less than honorable. Besides, Axe had killed four of them the night he assaulted the compound and superyacht.

I'm not going to lie to him. But it's not time to let him in on the details, either.

Axe gave a tiny nod of acknowledgment. "It's need-to-know only. You can handle that?"

"Hell, yeah. Just don't like being treated like a child. Or a private. That shit ended a long, long time ago. Can you tell me the objective?"

"Specifically, no. In general? Save the world as we know it."

He offered Axe a grim smile. "Always down with that. Let me know if you need me and my team."

"We might. For now, all we need is what you're already doing: keeping Kelton, Miss Holly, and the ship safe."

"Hooyah."

"How's your vacation?" Gregory asked Haley.

Did they have to be so circumspect on the satellite phone, or could they speak plainly? She'd let Gregory take the lead. "Fine, so far. On my way to St. John with my friend."

"Just wanted to let you know we're doing fine back home. But we are so glad you chose the Caribbean and not the Netherlands as you considered. Have you seen what's happening over there?"

"No, I've been out of touch."

"The Port of Rotterdam has been hacked. Can you believe that? A ransomware event, from what Nancy and Dave tell me. I doubt it would affect people on vacation, but still, glad you're safe and having fun. I'll let you go. Send us a postcard or call anytime."

"Thanks, bye for now."

After passing the phone off to Doug, who accepted it without a word, Haley retreated into the master suite, followed by Axe. She paced the gorgeous room slowly, thinking.

"What was that?" Axe asked.

"My boss, Gregory, with a veiled update from my team. The Port of Rotterdam has been hit with a cyberattack."

"And they suspect Conroy?"

"No, I only told Gregory about my hunch. But I told them to keep an eye out for any large, important targets being hit. When they reported to Gregory, he suspected Conroy."

"Gregory believes in you more and more."

"Then I guess we better sort this out."

"Any ideas why he would target a busy shipping port in the Netherlands?"

"None."

Which frustrates me to no end.

"But I wonder what else he has. We're playing catch up, which I hate."

They headed out. The helicopter would arrive soon, taking Kelton back to New York, and she had a show to put on—goodbye kisses and promises to see each other soon. The illusion had to be maintained... just in case.

In a few hours, the ship would arrive in St. Thomas.

That's when their true test would begin.

35

DREAMS

Todd celebrated the afternoon with another cigar on the rear deck of the yacht. Kelton's Cottswoth-Goldentech stock had dropped another eighteen percent.

The Chinese were playing hardball. They had released what could only be doctored photos of Kelton at a nightclub, doing drugs and groping multiple women. Several tabloids claimed to have proof of Kelton's unacknowledged children, who he wouldn't support financially.

And some of the lesser quality business newspapers had reported "rumors, so far unsubstantiated," of Kelton's companies skirting the rules against child labor in multiple countries.

The first two stories were false but would be difficult to disprove. The last was true. Todd had provided all the proof Happastology—the Chinese firm—needed.

They took the "proof" of Kelton's culpability in the attack on their company and the death of their employees and ran with it.

Still, Kelton deserves it. That he didn't know about the violence, and in fact condemned it and me when I told him, means nothing. He's a greedy bastard that used me up and spit me out. He called me his—

Todd took a deep breath and let it out slowly. He needed to keep calm and not let his rage get out of control as it had in the past.

It looked like Happastology wouldn't stop until Kelton was destroyed.

Already the man had lost billions of his personal fortune. His name was becoming synonymous with cheating, excess, greed, and exploitation.

And finally, there were rumors he was off sailing his yacht as his business went down the drain. To everyone, he would be a person to avoid, personally and professionally.

How does it feel to run it all yourself, Kelton? A bit harder than you realized, isn't it?

Todd wished he could speak with his former friend. He daydreamed for a moment, savoring the cigar. Kelton's superyacht sailing into the marina. How he would wait for the perfect moment, perhaps when the man went for a walk on the dock with no security detail. He could stab him this time. No gun. Just twist the knife and watch the man's life drain from him. He puffed at the cigar and smiled, eyes closed, picturing the blood and the cries of anguish in vivid detail.

No. He opened his eyes. *Better the way it's going now. An even longer, slower death. It will be a joy to watch him try to rebuild his business without me doing it all for him. He'll finally see the truth— that it was me all along.*

Todd suspected Kelton would be booted from his position as CEO of the company, and chairman of the board, by Monday morning.

I bet the board of directors gave him a week to see if he could turn it around. And when the end of the week is worse than the beginning, what recourse will they have? The company is greater than one person.

Once they fired Kelton, the company would no longer pay the huge annual bill for his protection. And if Kelton ended up broke, which Todd suspected would be the case, he wouldn't have much extra for a large security detail.

At some point, you'll be vulnerable. Then, my old friend, we'll have some fun. Or rather, I will.

First, he'd use Kelton as bait to lure the analyst to him. He would take his time with each of them. Perhaps play them off each other.

Would you sacrifice an eye for her, Kelton? Would you for him, Haley? Or would you each beg me to harm the other instead?

What would it do to a person's soul to know another suffered because you wouldn't? The question thrilled him.

He closed his eyes again, lost in thoughts of revenge and violence, delighting in Kelton and Haley's screams of terror. Their pleas for him to stop echoed through his mind.

I will leave the bodyguard for last. Let the regret eat him alive when he realizes he couldn't protect either of them.

His cigar lay forgotten in the crystal ashtray as he sat back, eyes closed, daydreaming.

36

DIG

FRIDAY NIGHT

The Control Center
St. John, United States Virgin Islands

Bec continued working on her latest hack, hoping to make more progress. There would be yet another Pioneer speech tonight in the soccer stadium, with mandatory attendance. They would all be kicked out of the control room at 5 p.m., and she had a lot of work to do.

A New York City headquarters of a bank in Saudi Arabia had been assigned to her by Tina, who over the last few days had taken on a more active role in handing out projects. While she hadn't officially been promoted, she'd started acting like a manager.

I guess sleeping with the boss lets you throw your weight around.

Thankfully, Bec's inbox remained free of more orders for conducting background checks. Dozens of new pilgrims continued to arrive every day. Someone had to look at their lives so they could keep out criminals and anyone with a history of violence. It mostly fell to others, but a larger volume of pilgrims than usual had arrived Thursday, pulling Bec away from her normal duties.

One background check assignment had come to her late yesterday. Something about the man had caught her eye. From his driver's license to other photos she found online, Cody looked... different. She liked different. Short, shockingly red hair. A pleasant smile on his pale face. She had a good feeling about him, though she doubted they'd ever come into contact.

Romance? Now? No, it's not the time for dating. I'm half caught up in a cult and suspect the leader of... what? Terrorism?

Besides, would a man like him want a tomboy like her?

No. And I have to get my mind back on figuring out what Pioneer is up to. All while acting like a good little worker bee, so they don't suspect me.

She hadn't had an opportunity to check her quickly created anonymous email account since she had submitted the form on the FBI's webpage.

Do they take those seriously? Or did it disappear into a black hole?

If she could just get a bit more information, she'd contact them again with further details.

After that, she could either leave paradise for good. Or stay, knowing Pioneer wasn't actually behind the problems in Los Angeles.

She'd spent much of the day avoiding the bank assignment. Instead, she researched the hit list of targets for hacking attempts. The top twenty-five list had new additions, including the Saudi bank. But the complete list targeted the computer systems of over two-hundred-fifty governments, corporations, and other entities worldwide.

Many had been grayed out over the past few days, meaning they were no longer active high-value targets.

"Five minutes," Tina called cheerfully yet with an edge, sounding like a grade school teacher bossing around her young students.

The time call jolted Bec back to the present. She hadn't accomplished much today. Perhaps she could come in and work a few hours on Saturday. Though technically frowned on, since the Movement recommended two full days of rest without technology, her department worked when needed. Systems were often easier to penetrate on the weekend, and management had long conceded hackers often worked best when most inspired. They were given wide latitude.

Another reason the lockout Wednesday morning felt so weird.

She made a few final notes of promising angles of attack on the bank system, logged out, and left the room with everyone else.

Everyone except for Pioneer, Gunther, and the twins, who remained behind.

What are they up to now?

Against her better judgment, she vowed to return early for work in the morning, check the security camera footage, and see if the timing matched any unusual events, like the electrical issue in Los Angeles.

37

DOCK

The Docks
Cruz Bay
St. John, United States Virgin Islands

Cody watched the approaching luxury speed boat from his guard shack on the dock. His face hurt from smiling so much. He had never been happier. It was nearing the end of his day, and he couldn't wait to do it all again tomorrow.

Late the previous night, he had been assigned a bunk in a building on St. Thomas, across the bay. It had formerly been a dorm of a university that had been shut down and taken over by the Movement. He'd get a permanent bunk assignment tonight on the Movement's main island of St. John.

In the morning, he had ridden the first ferry from the port in Red Hook, where a few cruise ships still docked to expose tourists to the island and the Movement's message. It had deep enough water for them and any luxury yachts interested in visiting the island.

He'd been assigned this guard shack in Cruz Bay, the main city—large town, really—on the western half of the island. He had also received a mentor, a pleasant, skinny, gray-haired man who explained the job. "Help any boats coming or going. No unauthorized visitors but be pleasant. There's little crime here, but look for people—mostly locals—'borrowing' things from other people's boats. And if anything big happens, pick up this red phone." He showed Cody the phone on the wall of the little shack. It had no dials or buttons. "It connects straight to the Center. Our main HQ. If anyone arrives who isn't on the pre-approved list, you politely ask them to stay in their craft until you check in. Then you do what the people on the end of this line tell you, without question. Can you do that?"

Of course he could. Being around boats all day beat any guard duty he had in the Army. The sun and air were pleasantly warm, people were invariably in a great mood, and no one had arrived who wasn't on the list.

Haley and Axe could be wrong. This could be the real deal. Maybe I could stay here. Like, forever.

Cody stepped out of the shack and walked to the main arrival dock as the speed boat slowed in the no-wake zone of the bay. He stood at parade rest, his smile only briefly marred as a thought hit him. His pale skin had turned light red from the day in and out of the guard shack, though he had tried to stay in the shade as much as possible.

I'm going to need a large hat and sunscreen.

Then he was all smiles again.

They might have some for me at my bunk. They're super smart here. I bet they've thought of everything.

His breath caught for a moment, and he glanced around nervously to see if Theodore, his mentor, was close enough to notice. He didn't see the aging hippie, which was good. The man had eagle eyes and might notice the change in Cody.

Haley said to be myself. I can do this.

The boat slowed, drifting to a stop expertly at the edge of the dock. The crewman in the bow threw Cody the line, which he tied to a cleat, then hurried to the stern of the boat to do the same with the other line.

I would naturally look, so why not?

He smiled at Haley, her magnificent long blond hair ruffled by the light breeze off the water, her skin already darker than it had been a few days before in D.C. He had noticed her perfect skin when she emerged from the bathroom in the hotel room they shared after her ambush. Right before she had made it clear—gently—that he wasn't her type, and they would keep their relationship professional... though she appreciated being rescued by him that night.

"Welcome to St. John. Paradise Found," he said as he took her hand to help her off the lightly swaying boat.

"Thank you!" she said with a smile, then promptly ignored him, stepping onto the dock.

He repeated the greeting for Axe with almost the same smile, though Axe refused his helping hand and didn't say a word to him. In fact, he looked pissed.

I bet they strip-searched him and confiscated any weapons he tried to smuggle in.

Last came Kim, his interviewer from the previous night who had done his intake. His eyes lit up. As he took her hand and helped her onto the dock, he whispered, "Thank you so much, Kim. This is a dream come true!" He was sure she had put in a word for him about working around the boats.

She merely smiled and nodded, racing to catch up with Haley and Axe. "Pioneer should be with us shortly," Kim said to Axe and Haley. "He was called into an unexpected meeting. As I was saying, there are two towns on the island," she started, leading them inland. He listened as he was handed a large, expensive-looking roller suitcase and a much smaller, beat-up duffel bag that could be slung like a backpack. Haley and Axe's luggage.

He followed the instructions from the deckhand and took it to the black four-door SUV idling at the nearby curb. As soon as the bags were loaded, the driver nodded and pulled away, slowly driving along the street, shadowing the group of tour guide Kim, VIP Haley, and her bodyguard.

They did it. They infiltrated the Movement. But I really, really hope they're wrong about this place.

38

IRAN

This was Stefan's favorite part. The touch of his hand to the screen would unleash destruction and mayhem somewhere in the world.

The Hand of God.

He turned to Gunther sitting as usual at the computer terminal to the left. "The Israelis have been tipped off?"

"Yes, Pioneer," the man said in perfect English, with only a hint of his German upbringing coming through. "Your follower, who has consistently supplied them with reliable information in the past, informed them many of the Iranian defenses would be offline tonight, and to be ready."

"Do we have any confirmation they have received the message or have taken action?"

Gunther frowned. "No, Pioneer. That is beyond even us."

"No matter. Israel cannot resist a vulnerable Iran. They will launch missiles and drop bombs. Iran will retaliate as they are able."

My words are prophecies now.

Of course, it helped that the few followers he had recruited in the

Middle East were intelligent and resourceful. They had planted suitcase EMPs, a modification of the missile, in and near many of Iran's critical command-and-control facilities. Given the country's ideology and political situation, a lack of command would cripple their response. Few average Iranian soldiers would dare fire without the direct order of their higher officers.

Orders which wouldn't come.

Not all locations had been targeted however, due to both the difficulty of smuggling the devices into the country and the lack of enough true followers.

This would allow the Iranians to absorb the initial blows from Israel and counterattack later. In the end, it would work to his advantage.

Tonight, Stefan would start a war in the Middle East.

The next step of his carefully crafted plan to rule the world. First, the Middle East. In three days, when the world was properly fixated and the United States distracted helping its allies, he would destroy South Korea, allowing North Korea to invade. Then, every few days, a new conflict. India and Pakistan. Russia and Ukraine. China and Taiwan.

After that, he would hit the internet access points. Communication would end.

The real fun would begin then. The main barrage of EMPs would be unleashed, hitting all major technology left unscathed by his earlier attacks.

In a few weeks, there would be millions at war. Electronics all over the world would be destroyed, along with all ability to manufacture new ones.

Amid the chaos and killing, he would offer his solutions.

At first, governments of the world would resist. But at war with their enemies, they would be powerless when their citizens rebelled and demanded Pioneer's help.

He smiled. At last, his ten-year plan was beginning.

"Are the devices online?"

"Yes, Pioneer." Gunther pressed a few keys. The jumbo main screen on the wall at the front of the room displayed two windows. In one, a map of Iran, filled with red blinking lights. While they mainly centered on Tehran, several flashed along the border, and a few in the middle of nowhere: communication nodes.

"And the satellite view?"

Even as he said it, Gunther sent the live feed from the commercial satellite, easily rented via an online portal and streamed anywhere in the world.

Gunther, usually unemotional to the point of being comatose, shared the smallest of smiles, and his eyes shone with excitement before he recomposed his face to a more neutral expression. "The satellite is locked on. Now is the time, Pioneer."

Stefan winked at the twins standing by his side, then pressed his palm to the scanner, his eyes locked onto the main screen.

The result delighted them all.

One second, the tiny lights of the country were on.

The next, the lights winked off.

He could imagine the confusion.

The chaos.

The fear as they realized their precious country was exposed to attack from their hated enemy.

Surely not all the country's people were fanatics. But it seemed their leaders were.

Tonight, many of those leaders would die, struck by bombs and missiles from Israel.

Other fanatics would rise up and demand justice.

Many would die in the coming days.

Whoever was left would be much more receptive to his message.

He alone would be able to pick up the pieces.

He alone would offer them hope of a better future.

Security.

Peace.

Harmony.

And all they needed was to worship him.

Not as their God, for few would forsake their deep-seated beliefs.

No, merely as their savior.

He could live with that.

For now.

Starting tonight, and for the next few weeks, countries would fall. The world would burn. And afterward, he would be there to lead his people into the next world.

His world.

39

ISRAEL

Gregory picked up his phone but before he could speak, he heard Nancy finishing a sentence in the background. "Ask him to hurry."

Dave spoke quickly. "It's Dave and Nancy. You need to see this. Something is happening in the Middle East—Iran and Israel. Can you come to us? We want to stay at our desks to monitor this if you don't mind. And Nancy says—"

"Yes, I heard. I'll be right there."

He hurried out of his office, trying to remember if they'd ever shown him real-time analysis before.

No. This is a first. This is because they've been working with Haley, I'm sure.

Gregory arrived at Nancy and Dave's double-sized cubicle. They had removed the divider wall between their two cubes years ago, making one large workspace. He looked over their shoulders at their screens—Dave on the left, Nancy on the right. "What are we seeing?" It looked like a satellite feed of a dark landmass. He wracked his brain trying to think of an area so large with so few lights. A desert, perhaps.

"Iran. It went mostly dark a few minutes ago. We suspect they've been hit by Haley's EMP."

While it wasn't Haley's electromagnetic pulse, he knew what Nancy meant.

Dave spoke up, rolling his desk chair to the side. "And this is Saudi Arabia." His screen showed a radar image tracking several dozen aircraft, split among three groups flying within Saudi airspace along the Persian Gulf. "These planes took off from Israel. F-15s, we believe."

"Training mission?"

"Yes, a multi-country training mission announced yesterday and planned for tonight. All players in the area notified—the usual," Nancy said. "Fuel topped off by airborne tankers."

The three groups of aircraft turned east and crossed over the Persian Gulf. One group kept turning to head northeast. They would be in Iran's airspace shortly.

"This is real-time," Gregory confirmed.

"Yes."

Nancy switched her screen to show what Dave's displayed, then Dave clicked his mouse and reworked his screen as Nancy spoke.

"Sir, this is not a training mission. This is a first strike. Our analysis is, given this many aircraft, most likely configured with air-to-surface missiles or bombs, they are about to hit Iran's known and suspected nuclear research facilities."

A low, quiet whistle from Dave's side of the cube. His screen now displayed an enlarged radar shot of Israel's airspace. Dozens more aircraft were taking off.

"They are going to bomb a lot more than the nuclear facilities."

Gregory had a horrible thought. "Is there any sign Israel is behind the EMP strikes in Los Angeles?"

Dave answered, eyes still on his screen. "No, sir. We haven't been able to find any information about the EMPs. No chatter, hints, nothing."

"Well…" Nancy said slowly.

"What?"

"The Port of Rotterdam ransomware hack," Dave said with a frown at Nancy.

"When it hit," Nancy said, picking up the story, "I guessed it was about the EMPs.'"

"What evidence is there?"

"None."

"But we both thought it."

"No," Dave corrected. "I agreed when you said Haley would tie it to the EMPs."

"Until a few minutes ago, we had no data suggesting EMPs could or would be used any place besides the hits in Los Angeles. But with this..." Nancy gestured toward the screens. "How are they getting the EMPs around the world? Too risky to fly them in. Has to be in container vessels. There are hundreds of thousands of containers going through ports each day. Only a tiny percentage are manually inspected. But what if Rotterdam had a concern and was about to inspect the wrong container?"

"You're saying Rotterdam was hacked to prevent an inspection of a container with EMPs inside?"

"No, I'm only saying, 'What if?' It's what Haley would do," Nancy added, with a touch of defiance unusual in the older woman. "And not because of the inspection of one container, but because finding one would lead to others."

"The hack happened yesterday. Whatever happened in Iran tonight didn't go through Rotterdam."

"No, it would have been Port of Jebel Ali in Dubai. Just across the Gulf from Iran. Look, Gregory," she said while looking pointedly at Dave, "I'm trying to think like Haley. If she weren't on vacation," her tone making it clear how she felt about Haley's sudden disappearance, "she'd probably figure a way to either connect it all or rule it out. I've seen her leaps of logic. They're both exciting and terrifying. I can't follow them and would never feel comfortable going out on a limb as she does. But she's been encouraging us to follow our guts, and mine tells me this: Iran has been hit by EMPs, like the ones used in LA. Most likely by the same group or person, though there is no obvious connection. Iran and LA both have busy ports nearby—Long Beach in

California, Jebel Ali in Dubai. And with Rotterdam going offline, my hunch tells me Europe is next."

Gregory considered the possibilities. Nancy sounded sure of herself despite the complete lack of the merest hint of evidence.

What would Haley do?

"I want a deep dive into the major shipping ports of the world. Look for any unusual activity. Pretend you're Haley and put outliers together."

How much should I tell them?

He leaned closer, crouching slightly to be at the level of their ears. "And this part goes no further than the three of us. Haley is not on vacation. She is running a special research project and is away from her computer for the time being. Before she left, she suspected the billionaire genius Stefan Conroy might be involved in at least the design of the EMP. Possibly the firing of them as well. So figure out if he has any connection to shipping. It may be hard to find, but this is well within your capabilities. Get to it."

How long would Haley need? A day?

"I know it's already late, but I want a full briefing at 4:45 a.m.."

Nancy gasped, and Dave swallowed hard. They focused on their screens as he turned back to his office.

I'm going to have to tell the president about Haley and her suspicions soon.

40

WW3

James Heringten, President of the United States of America, stood near the Resolute desk, waiting to be connected to his call.

It was taking much longer than usual.

He started pacing, a habit he'd picked up only recently. It helped him think. He crossed in front of the desk, reached the far wall, and spun to walk back.

Iran had gone dark a short time before.

He had been given a flash briefing within five minutes—only the facts: one minute, Iran had been operating as usual. The next, much of the country had lost power.

No backup systems had come online.

His briefer, a younger officer, had been unwilling to draw conclusions, but James knew it had to be EMPs, like in Los Angeles, only on a much larger scale.

He'd immediately told his staff to call Israel's Prime Minister.

If I were in his shoes, I would launch a full-scale attack. There has never been an opening like this.

With Iran's defenses offline, Israel could wipe out the known and suspected nuclear weapon research sites.

It wouldn't take much more to target the entire hardline government, all the religious leaders, and the many others who had vowed to wipe Israel off the face of the Earth. Rhetoric, most in the west believed, but dangerous and terrifying, nonetheless.

A large attack would most likely draw others into the fight. Saudi Arabia would assist Israel, at least to grant fly-over permission for Israeli fighter bombers. Jordan would, as well.

Iraq would come to the aid of Iran. The Houthi rebels in control of western Yemen would launch raids into Saudi Arabia. Syria would attack Jordan.

It would be a free-for-all. Decades of built-up animosity would be released.

All the players would seize the opportunity for payback, to flex their military might, and to appear strong in the eyes of their people.

If the conflict ended there, it would be a miracle.

But if others got involved, it could be the start of World War Three.

Russia would back Syria. Thankfully, China had been cautiously cultivating connections with several of the countries of the region for years, so would most likely avoid taking sides.

But the United States would stand by its long-term allies Israel and Saudi Arabia.

I don't want the men and women under my command fighting and dying yet again for the chaos of the Middle East.

He'd learned from the presidents who had come before him, who had sat at the desk he passed as he paced.

He would do his damnedest to keep the United States out of it. But, if he had to, he would go all in. Full wartime footing. A mandatory draft of all eligible young men and women. All possible civilian factories converted to producing guns, tanks, planes, and other items for an active-duty military of three million fighters, ready to work with America's allies to remake the Middle East.

In the meantime, he would play peacemaker and hope to head off a worldwide conflict.

There was a sharp knock on the door. A small group of aides

entered. His Chief of Staff, Chad David, brought up the rear and closed the door, nodding once to James.

"Sir, the Prime Minister is about to answer," one aide said. He picked up the phone on the desk, pressed a button, and handed the receiver to him.

"Radar shows ninety-six aircraft in Saudi Arabia airspace, about to cross the Persian Gulf toward Iran," another aide added. "They took off from Israel, sir."

The group gathered around two phones on the far side of the room, which would be muted so the staff could listen, take notes, and offer analysis later.

James waited for a few seconds, then heard a click. A female voice announced, "Mr. President, Mr. Prime Minister, you are connected."

James jumped right in. "Mr. Prime Minister, please. Don't do this. I understand your—"

"Mr. President," the Prime Minister cut him off. "This is an opportunity like no other. We have no choice."

"I understand, but—"

"Mr. President, I took your call out of friendship and the strong relationship our countries share. But this is our path. If Mexico continually called for your country's destruction, and frequently launched attacks into your territory, perhaps you would appreciate our position better. As always, we welcome the support of the United States but do not require it. Good evening, Mr. President."

The line went dead.

What the hell?

"He hung up on you, sir," an aide said, stating the obvious.

The rest of the people in the room remained silent, unsure what to do.

"I want a full briefing as soon as possible," James said quietly as he hung up the phone.

"Sir, nearly everyone is gathered in the situation room. They'll be ready for you in a few minutes."

"Thank you." He glanced at Chad, who ushered the aides out, remaining behind after closing the door.

"'The only easy day was yesterday,'" his right-hand man and former SEAL quoted, citing a SEAL core saying.

"And we don't have to like it, we just have to do it. So let's get on with it."

They left the office and headed to the Situation Room to see what could be done to prevent the next world war.

41

INFILTRATION

Pioneer Park Soccer Stadium
St. John, United States Virgin Islands

Axe and Haley watched, spellbound, as Conroy stood onstage in the middle of the football field, smiling as the full stadium chanted for him.

Clap-Clap-Clap "Pioneer!" *Clap-Clap-Clap* "Pioneer!" Over and over.

They sat in comfortable, padded seats in a skybox off the top concourse of the stadium. Below were at least ten thousand people yelling at the top of their lungs. Several were crying with joy at the sight of their leader.

Axe fixed a neutral expression on his face and continually scanned the area for threats. Kim, their tour guide, sat next to Haley, giving her a running commentary. He couldn't hear much over the chanting, but it sounded like propaganda—the wonderful works Pioneer had done for the community, his genius for starting the movement, and how people enjoyed their lives in Paradise Found, as they called the island.

This is crazy. How are people buying this?

Haley smiled and played along. She seemed enraptured.

I hope she's strong enough to resist the cult of personality. If not, I'm in a load of trouble.

Upon arriving in St. Thomas, they had been welcomed by Kim, who had introduced herself as their hostess. She would take them to St. John for a tour before watching the TV interview on the stadium's jumbo screen. Next, they had stripped—in separate rooms—while their luggage and clothes were inspected. "No weapons or electronic devices are allowed on the islands. It's for the good of everyone."

Thankfully, they had been informed of the rule before they arrived, so Axe had not brought his usual arsenal of pistols and knives. He hated it. Not having weapons felt foreign. Wrong.

I feel naked.

He could handle himself without a knife or gun, but it had been decades since he'd gone more than a few minutes—usually in the shower—without at least one weapon.

After their tour, they arrived at the impressive, newly built stadium. In the stands, people sat quietly, chatting happily with one another, a sense of anticipation in the air. Pioneer was running late and hadn't come to see them. No explanation was given.

A few minutes ago, a group of thirty fit men and women dressed in black tactical clothes surrounded the stage, facing out. Legs planted wide, arms folded. Instead of pistols at their waists, they had long, fixed-blade knives. They looked strong and focused.

Conroy's personal security detail.

Finally, Pioneer himself appeared, bounding onto the stage. The audience surged to their feet, and the chanting volume increased.

After a minute, Conroy nodded slowly. The audience stopped chanting and became silent immediately.

"My friends." From their room at the top of the stadium, Axe could hear and feel the sigh of pleasure from the audience. Everyone remained standing.

Conroy gestured to the many cameras. "Once again, our friends, our fellow brothers and sisters, join us live online. Many others will view the replay over the next days and weeks. To you all, I say: welcome. You are home."

Several women near the field screamed in pleasure, which made

Conroy smile in their direction. Kim and Haley were engrossed, leaning forward to get closer to Conroy.

"The world is an unusual place. Technology reigns supreme, robbing us of our serenity and connection. When it works, that is. When it doesn't, it harms us more. We have grown so dependent on it, not having it even for a few minutes leaves us feeling lost. We have forgotten and strayed from the old ways of teamwork, togetherness, and community."

Axe knew this refrain from analyzing the man's previous speeches with Haley. He listened but kept his eyes roaming. Haley and Kim. The audience—still standing, hanging on Conroy's every word. The stadium. And the man's private guard.

Their eyes moved like his, searching for threats.

They have training, but how much? Are they doing a job? Or are they true believers?

Zealots don't give up when confronted with a situation they will surely lose. They keep fighting, willing to die for their cause, making them extremely dangerous.

But they won't think tactically. They stick with their orders without looking at the bigger picture.

They could be outmaneuvered and outthought. But they fought to the death. Surrender and failure were both unfeasible to them. They would rather die.

Which I've used to my advantage several times.

Axe tuned back in as Conroy continued. "The time is near when each of us must make a choice. Do we choose to accept the tyranny of technology controlling our lives? Or do we renounce our over-reliance on it? Reconnect with one another? Which side will you be on?"

The lines were similar to the previous speech.

What do people see in this guy? You want to unplug? Unplug! You don't need a guru to tell you how. And you certainly don't need to worship him for telling you.

Conroy continued along the same lines for forty-five minutes. The audience ate it up.

42

OPTIONS

The White House Situation Room
Washington, D.C.

James leaned back in his chair at the head of the long table. His National Security Team had started the briefing on Iran. It had taken longer than he wanted to gather the intel. Every department had been surprised by the events of the evening.

"Mr. President, as you know, in the middle of the night local time, Iran went offline. Much of its power generation is gone, and many, though not all, of its defenses have been shut down."

"An EMP?" In their effort to ensure he was thoroughly informed, it took his people forever to get to the meat of the sandwich.

"Nothing conclusive, but yes, sir, it seems to be the only reasonable explanation."

"What connection is there between Iran and the possible EMPs deployed in Los Angeles earlier this week?"

"We have been looking into it, but—"

"You have no idea, correct?"

"Yes, Mr. President," the CIA director said with an embarrassed look downward as she shuffled her notes.

"Sir," the Chairman of the Joint Chiefs of Staff chimed in, "we would have seen any missile launches, even small ones like what may have been used in LA. We saw nothing, so we suspect a different type of device."

"Could it be Israel coordinating a first strike? Their special forces taking out the Iranian defenses?"

People looked pointedly at the Secretary of State, who cleared his throat. "Mr. President, if that were the case, we would assume the Israelis would have informed us." James felt the elephant in the room; all knew of his conversation with Israel's prime minister, along with its abrupt ending.

"Sir, they could not have pulled it off without us having at least an inkling," Ms. Hill, the director of the CIA, added.

"We'll get back to that."

The view on the large screen changed. A graphic appeared showing aircraft icons with the paths they had taken from Israel, through Saudi Arabia, and into Iran.

Other icons denoting explosions dotted the map of Iran. An aide spoke from his laptop. "The Israeli planes first hit Iran's air defenses." The explosion icons along the coast of the Persian Gulf brightened. "Then they targeted all suspected nuclear weapon sites." Several icons around the country glowed. "From satellite imagery, it appears they were successful."

"Just those targets?"

"No sir, that was the first wave. More planes hit crucial military infrastructure, from command and control to military equipment factories."

James could feel they were leading up to a delicate subject. "Come on, whatever you're dancing around, get to it!"

"Sir, yes, sir. The last group of planes destroyed the residences, offices, and other locations where both the Supreme Leader and the President of Iran would be. We suspect both are dead but have not confirmed this yet."

Come on, why not lead with the good stuff? I have to shake things up after this crisis.

"Any signs other countries are retaliating?"

"None so far, but the night, as they say, is still young," Hartman, the Chairman of the Joint Chiefs said, his bald head shiny in the bright lights of the room.

James contemplated the situation. "Recommendations?"

"Stay out of the way and hope it doesn't escalate, sir," Hartman quickly said. "The last thing we need is to be involved in a regional war we have no way of winning."

The men and women around the table nodded in agreement.

"If Israel needs our support?"

"Slow walk them, which should be easy to do, given their statement to you earlier," Hartman continued.

James nodded. "What about big picture? Who is behind this, and why?"

No one spoke.

"Ms. Young, why do we not know more?"

"Intelligence gathering in the area is difficult. We rely on our allies—Israel and Saudi Arabia. If they knew about this, it makes sense they would keep it to themselves, knowing we would counsel peace."

"Yes, I get that. But any leads? Hunches, gut feelings? I understand your reluctance to present me with rumors or guesswork, and normally I appreciate it. But right now, I could use more."

His team shuffled papers, made notes on yellow pads, and avoided his gaze.

In the silence, a voice came from the speakerphone in the center of the table.

"Mr. President, Gregory Addison here." Because of the remoteness of the Central Analysis Group campus, and their mandate to provide an overview of the nation's intelligence picture, Addison rarely came to the White House. But James had been impressed with him at an Oval Office meeting after the New York crisis, as well as his calm demeanor during the Mexico incursion earlier in the week.

"Go ahead, Mr. Addison."

Maybe Haley's come up with something.

"I may shed some light on that, sir, from a best guess standpoint. But could I have a word... privately?"

"Just spit it out, please, Mr. Addison. No one will think less of you for voicing your hunches."

There was silence from the speakerphone.

Why the hell would he need to speak with me privately? Unless... if it's about Haley...

James cleared his throat. "Fine." To the room, he said, "I'll be back shortly. I want all embassies in the Middle East to go on alert. Evacuate all non-essential personnel. I don't want to wait until this goes south and play catch up. And I want concrete ideas for a variety of scenarios. First, if Israel requests our military help. Next, what our options are if the conflict spreads, and how we can prevent that from happening—militarily and diplomatically."

Voices called out, "Yes, Mr. President," and all stood as he left for his private office.

The president's smaller, less formal workspace is located off the Oval Office. Once inside, his Chief of Staff connected Gregory's call. "Go ahead, Gregory. You're on speaker in my private office with only my Chief of Staff."

"Yes, sir."

The man seemed reluctant to continue. "Gregory, Chad knows all about Haley, so please, get on with it."

"Yes, sir. Your assumption is correct. It is about Haley. She had a hunch, which we have been pursuing. She believes a man named Stefan Conroy may be behind the EMPs in Los Angeles. We suspect the same technology may have been used on Iran."

"Stefan Conroy—the genius tech guy from years ago? Now he runs..."

James glanced at Chad, who filled him in. "A cybersecurity start-up using AI to stop hacks before they start."

"Exactly, sir. Based in the Virgin Islands. Specifically, St. John—and St. Thomas to a lesser extent."

"Why don't you and Haley give me a full briefing of her hunch and your recommendations in fifteen minutes?"

"Well, sir, that's why I wanted to speak with you privately. She had no proof, but she had a plan to... develop more information. I took that to mean her... friend... who she worked with in New York six months ago."

"And?"

"Haley needed a vacation, so I gave her time off."

He exchanged a glance with Chad.

He covered his ass by giving her comp time to pursue the lead. Officially, she's on her own. But he also made sure I wouldn't be mad at him for hindering her. Smart. I'll play along.

"Has she sent a postcard?"

"No, sir."

"Any idea where she's staying?"

"My guess is somewhere on St. John at the moment, sir. I spoke with her earlier today, but we were on an open line. She's doing her thing, Mr. President. Like six months ago."

"Thank you for your discretion, Mr. Addison. I'll see if I can reach her through a backchannel."

"Yes, sir. I have my other analysts working a lead, based on her initial assessment. I hope to have more for you soon. If it is Conroy, he's covered his tracks well. But my people will find it if it's there."

"Call back when you have something, day or night."

He hung up and paged his secretary. "Mary Beth, see if you can reach Admiral Nalen. I could use a workout partner today, I think."

"Any specific time, Mr. President?"

"Now would be good."

I hope to God Haley has figured this out. If not... we may be screwed.

43

CORRELATION

Pioneer Park Soccer Stadium
St. John, United States Virgin Islands

From her usual place in the stadium, Bec listened as Pioneer captivated his audience. While she clapped and cheered at the right times, her mind was elsewhere, making plans.

On Saturday mornings, the faithful joined Pioneer for yet another celebration service.

As if Monday and Friday nights aren't enough.

Attendance Saturday was recommended, but not mandatory.

She debated sitting in her truck to review more security footage to find other times Pioneer, Gunther, and the twins had been alone in the Center during off-hours. She could check on a correlation.

That will take too much time. Sitting in the truck so long would be suspicious.

Thinking of the layout of the Center, she wondered how far the Wi-Fi extended. Could she pick up the signal from the jungle at the closest point to the building?

It's a risk, but I'll get up early, take my phone, and go for a hike.

I'll sneak close to the Center and do my research. I can also check my email and reply or send another report to the FBI if I figure out what this nut job is up to.

With her plan in place, she tuned back into the speech, just in time to watch the TV interview of Pioneer broadcast on the jumbo screen.

44

PRETEND

While watching the mind-numbing speech from Conroy, followed by the TV interview of softball questions lobbed at him, Haley considered her options.

I may not be cut out for life as an undercover spy.

She followed the spectacle in front of her and occasionally shared wide-eyed, ecstatic nods with Kim. But Axe's talk earlier was on her mind.

As much as Haley loved the thrill and challenge of this type of operation, faking interest in the man's message for hours was difficult.

No, I have to pretend to be enraptured.

And to think she had considered sleeping with Conroy to gather intel.

Ugh.

She watched him on stage. He had a certain charisma, and his message made sense. Connect with each other more? Get our faces out of our screens? Live our lives?

Yes, please!

But not like this. The appeal, she suspected, was the man himself. Conroy had the looks, the moves, a charming smile, beautiful eyes, great teeth. His obvious intelligence showed, but he never spoke down to his audience. He had a gift—a way of connecting with the crowd that made each person feel he spoke directly to him or her. There was also a subtext. Conroy left something unsaid.

If you're part of his group, you're special.

Could that be it?

She watched him on stage, wondering what he was capable of.

45

HANDS

The Center
Private Residence Wing of Stefan "Pioneer" Conroy
St. John, United States Virgin Islands

Haley glanced over her shoulder at Axe standing against the wall behind where she and Conroy sat. She appreciated Axe tremendously. Without him, Conroy would have jumped her an hour ago, forcing her to sleep with him or turn him down, jeopardizing the mission.

Conroy had glared at Axe several times. He had offered dinner—to be eaten in the next room with the other staff. Axe had refused.

Haley played the young bimbo to perfection, not noticing Conroy's unsubtle looks to send her bodyguard away.

Axe hadn't used the restroom, asked for water, or sat down. His determination and willpower amazed her.

Conroy was getting restless. He might enjoy a challenge, but he wasn't used to being denied. Soon, he would either order Axe out or ask her to do it.

Neither she nor Axe could allow that to happen. They had agreed on the yacht—they stuck together. Any effort to separate them would end the operation immediately. Haley would demand to return to the yacht and go on a tirade if denied, making such a scene they would be happy to get rid of her.

Time to seize the initiative.

Haley glanced again at Axe, then leaned forward to whisper in Conroy's ear.

"Stefan, you know I'm Kelton's girlfriend. And I'm a good girl. Well," she giggled, barely believing how she sounded, "not all the time…" She smiled and bit her lip suggestively. "But with my bodyguard around…"

Conroy's hand slipped onto her thigh, pushing the thin fabric of her sundress. Her body blocked the move from Axe's watchful glare. "I could order him away. We could be alone."

"Kelton would hear about it."

"Only if you go back to the yacht… and to him."

"Oh!" She giggled, quieting herself with a hand over her mouth. "Now who's bad?"

"Doesn't my message resonate with you?"

"So much!"

She wanted to roll her eyes at the character she was playing, but Conroy was buying the whole act.

"Then stay. You could be an integral part of what is coming."

There. That's why I thought I could get intelligence out of him.

With wide eyes, she asked, "What's coming?"

"You'll have to stick around to see." He seemed over the moon for her, his eyes attentively focused on hers, making her feel like nothing else in his world mattered.

If I actually was who I'm pretending to be, I would fall for it.

"I would love that. But… I have to think. Kelton…"

"Kelton is a big boy. He can take care of himself."

She bit her lip again—he seemed to love it—as she pretended to consider his offer.

"What if I stay another night?" She leaned closer, lowering her voice to a whisper. "Maybe you could… I don't know how to say this…" She thought of the first time she kissed a boy, hoping to make herself blush at the memory, and felt her cheeks flush. "Maybe if my bodyguard was distracted? By a woman, I mean," she said, though she thought the point had been made. "Tomorrow at dinner, maybe a female security guard could..." she giggled again, "offer to show him the perimeter?"

She put her hand on Stefan's and slid it higher on her thigh. "What do you think?"

He practically drooled as he whispered, "I'll take care of it."

His hand slid further, but she stood abruptly. "Pioneer, thank you for the invitation. This has been one of the best days of my life!" She held her hand out for him to take, praying he wouldn't kiss her fingers. He bowed his head toward them, but she drew her hand back.

Turning, Haley gestured to Axe. "Come. I need my beauty sleep!" They had rooms next to each other at a private villa a few miles down the steep, winding road on the way to Cruise Bay, and their boxy orange SUV would be outside waiting, along with a driver.

I wonder if I'm the first woman to reject him. It will either drive him crazy with desire, or he'll turn on me.

From the reactions of the many men who hit on her, she suspected he would be even more interested, though in the past it had gone either way. Some became enraged, used to getting all they desired. If the same happened with Conroy, they were in trouble. A dozen of his black-clad private security filled the Center building.

"I look forward to seeing you in the morning, Holly. I have a brief event to attend at the stadium if you would care to join me. If not, we can catch up over brunch."

She smiled and waved as Axe held the door for her. Gunther escorted them out past the layers of security, and into their waiting SUV.

She and Axe would return to the villa, get some sleep, and implement the next stage of their plan in the early morning hours.

46

CONTINGENCIES
SATURDAY

The White House
The President's Private Residence
Washington, D.C.

James sat in his comfortable leather chair, not enjoying a glass of sparkling water. Though he would love to have a double Scotch, he elected to keep his mind sharp during an international crisis and potentially the start of World War Three. Even at one in the morning, he might be summoned to the Situation Room. He couldn't show up drunk and make decisions affecting the world.

His old friend and former SEAL Teammate, retired Admiral William "Hammer" Nalen, sat across from him, also sipping sparkling water with obvious distaste.

The admiral had arrived moments before, taken the offered drink, and sat down in the living room of the residence.

"You've heard the news?" James began.

"Iran dark and Israel launched an attack is what they're saying on the news."

"They have about as much as we do." He tried to cover his

unhappiness with the lack of information from his so-called intelligence services.

"And by now you've heard about Haley, I bet."

"Her boss and I spoke privately, yes," James said.

"You know," Nalen said, "any time you want to be read into what Haley and Axe do, we can set up comms and code words. Or I can come by every day to hit the gym together if they're on an op. But I figured you'd rather stay at arm's length. Plausible deniability."

"Yes, that would be my preference. When this is over, let's work out a system so I don't have to get you over here in the middle of the night to find out what Haley is up to."

"Blondie."

James looked at him blankly.

"Haley's new code name."

He nodded. "Kind of obvious, but simple." He leaned toward his old friend, pleasantries over. "What has she gotten herself into now?"

"Haley has infiltrated Stefan Conroy's organization using a legend created by Gregory Addison. On his own, as I have limited resources for creating background material. He went out on a limb."

"And why did he do that?"

Nalen smiled slightly and took a sip of the water. "I may have bumped into him. Unofficially."

"Interesting conversation?"

"Yes, especially given what Haley had mentioned about..." He tipped his head in the general direction of the East Wing of the building, where the vice president had his office. Or rather, the former VP, before his unfortunate "suicide." The new vice president had elected to not work there while the rooms underwent "long-planned refurbishing."

"What did you say?"

"Only that entire books could be written about what he didn't know. I mentioned his rising star needed room to grow and might, eventually, need to stretch her wings. Venture forth from the nest. He would be wise to plan for such an eventuality. Then I gave him my dead-eyed stare," he gave it to James, who had to hold back a shiver, "and I left. He did the right thing."

"Fine job, as long as she's safe. So what's the situation, and the plan?"

"She's undercover as a stunningly beautiful D.C. business consultant who caught the eye of Kelton Kellison and is now his new girlfriend. He got her in with Conroy. Axe, the retired Navy SEAL, is her bodyguard. They're on the island. She's doing the work. It takes time."

"I need more. Is this an opening salvo? Are we next?"

"No idea. You know how this works. It's an op into enemy territory. We let them do their jobs like we were allowed to do back in the day."

"Except now I understand the frustrations of our higher-ups who wanted more done, faster. Ideally yesterday."

Nalen's gaze drifted off into the distance. "I remember." His eyes snapped back to James. "But we don't want to blow her cover by positioning assets near the islands. Haley is incredibly smart and talented. And Axe is a one-man wrecking machine if necessary, or a scalpel when needed. They'll get you what you need."

"We're putting all our chips on two people, Hammer. My niece, who's a gifted analyst and wanna-be field agent. And a retired Navy SEAL who is past his prime and not afraid to admit it. Versus one of the most brilliant minds on the planet. And that's if she's right. What if she's on the wrong track?"

"I wouldn't bet against her, sir."

"When is her next check-in?"

"Saturday—today, I guess," Hammer added, checking his hefty diver's watch. "Twenty-four hours after leaving Kellison's superyacht, they will check in. If not, it's a sign either they're in danger or blown."

"See if you can get a message to them. They have my authorization to take out Conroy by any means necessary if they deem him a threat. No need for proof or 'beyond a reasonable doubt.' Her hunch is enough. I'd rather have the blood of one potentially innocent man on my hands than the death of billions. If he has more of these weapons, it's the end of civilization as we know it. As it is, he's working on starting World War Three."

"If it's him."

"Yes. What happens if you can't get in touch with Haley, or she misses her check-in?"

"I have a contingency in place. Do you remember Doug 'Mad Dog' McBellin?"

"Just the name."

"He's the chief of security for Kellison and is on the yacht in St. Thomas."

"He has a team?"

"Yes, but the contingency is for him to go to the island and find Haley and Axe. Just in case their cover isn't blown, but they're in deep and can't report. Mad Dog will get it done."

"One guy?"

"No, my friend. One former SEAL."

"Fine. Get him on his way right now. Don't wait until later today."

"Rules of engagement?"

"Shoot anything that stands in the way of Haley and Axe fulfilling their mission."

Nalen left after their discussion, with a date to return for an after-lunch workout, when he could report on Haley's situation.

James strode into the Situation Room, feeling out of place in jeans, running shoes, and a sweatshirt. At this time of night, the room held junior staffers, though every man or woman competent enough to work here could handle any request he had.

"Good evening, or rather, good morning," he said as the surprised staff stood. Normally, people assembled in the room, then reported to the president's secretary that they were ready for him. Rarely did he show up unannounced.

"Based on recent intelligence, I need some contingencies put into place immediately."

"Yes, Mr. President," the assistant to the Joint Chiefs said. "May I ask, sir, to what intelligence report you are referring?"

"You may not."

The man blinked in surprise but recovered rapidly. "Of course, Mr. President. What do you need?"

Work the problem…

"I need a contingency to carpet bomb St. John and St. Thomas, US Virgin Islands. Also, a separate plan to take out specific targets. Plan on up to four, most likely concrete buildings built to withstand hurricanes. One may be a bunker-type facility."

"Yes, Mr. President," the assistant said, struggling to hide his surprise and concern.

"Get them planned. Brief me on them at zero six hundred. But besides the briefing, I want to hear the planes are on standby and rapid-ready. Understood?"

"Yes, sir." He still didn't understand the situation, but his Commander in Chief was giving him orders. James had no doubt they would be carried out… after the man checked with the Chairman.

"Last, I want a SEAL Team activated and on alert. Same target: St. John and-or St. Thomas. Spin them up, get them staged and ready to go."

"What type of target, sir?"

"Prepare for a high altitude, low opening insertion, either onto the islands or into the surrounding water. Ready for anything in enemy territory."

"Yes, sir. I'll make it happen."

"Good man. I'm going to get a few hours of sleep."

"Thank you, Mr. President," the men and women called out as he left.

I hate playing defense.

The solution? Go on the offense.

Even if it meant putting the life of his niece, and a few thousand other people, in danger.

If I bomb St. John and St. Thomas to take out Conroy, and it's not him behind all this… may God have mercy on my soul.

47

SHIPPING

Central Analysis Group Headquarters
Alexandria, Virginia

Gregory didn't bother to leave the building. He ate in the staff break room while his team worked, took a nap on the sofa in his office, and stood in Nancy and Dave's shared cubicle at 4:44 a.m.

They looked as bad as he felt. Both had fresh, steaming mugs of coffee next to them as they spun their chairs to look at him.

"What did you find?"

"First, sir, let me say this continues to be circumstantial. There could be a multitude of legitimate reasons for what you are about to see," Nancy cautioned.

"I understand. Proceed."

"With your directive to target Stefan Conroy and his 'Movement,' we discovered carefully hidden shell companies controlled by him and his followers. All were multi-layered and created an extremely tangled web."

"There are no valid business reasons to structure an organization in such a complicated manner," Dave added.

"These businesses all had one primary purpose: shipping.

Specifically, standard shipping containers. The bills of lading universally claimed they carried Movement literature, toys for kids, or food for the underprivileged," Nancy continued.

"What did they carry?"

"Unknown, sir. However, we have been able to track many of them," Dave said, turning to his computer. "But only as far as the ports. As they left the ports, the transponders were deactivated."

"Show me."

With a click of the mouse, a map filled Dave's large monitor. On it, the major ports of the world were represented with blue dots, from Los Angeles to the Port of Busan in South Korea, Shanghai to Rotterdam.

Dave tapped at his keyboard. "These are the last known locations we have for the containers we linked to Conroy's shell companies." He pressed the return key. An overlay appeared. Hundreds of red dots cluttered the map at the shipping facilities.

Gregory blinked repeatedly, taking in the magnitude of the situation. "How many?" He managed to ask.

"362," Nancy answered in a voice barely above a whisper.

"How many missiles could each container hold?"

Nancy and Dave shared a glance. "Hundreds, sir, depending on how they are packed. It would depend on whether he attempted to hide the devices beneath legitimate cargo, paid bribes, or trusted the sheer volume of containers passing through the ports to protect him from discovery."

Gregory's eyes were still glued to the red dots on Dave's screen. "Rotterdam?"

"Yes, sir. The ransomware shutdown at the Port of Rotterdam may have been to protect Conroy's cargo. We accessed records from right before their systems went offline—a lucky break, as a technician had disconnected a computer from the system for maintenance. It shows two of Conroy's containers still in port, marked for random inspection. Eighteen of his containers had already departed the facility."

"There are at least eighteen of his shipping containers in Northern Europe?"

"As of Thursday, yes. They could be anywhere by now."

The financial center in London. Banking in Zurich. Ukraine is far away but would be ripe for invasion by Russia if hit.

"How did Conroy—or whoever—pull this off under our noses?"

He meant it as a rhetorical question, but Nancy answered. "He's a genius, sir. And, if it is him, the most probable answer is he spent the past ten years working on the devices, manufacturing, and planning."

"But we've only recently heard about him."

"He has increased his public presence, but as we look into it more, we can see how his recruitment has been growing over the past few years. Private chat groups, word of mouth, members recruiting like-minded people. It's a brilliant cross between a cult and a terrorist organization. All well hidden behind a 'peace and love' story."

"If it's him," Dave said.

"Still no proof?"

Haley would have found it by now. Why does she feel the need to get out in the field? She should be here where she can work her magic. If I had a team of people with her talents...

He hadn't gotten enough sleep. His mind was veering off into tangents.

"We can definitively connect him to the shipping containers. We wouldn't have found it without your instruction to follow Haley's hunch and do a deep dive on him. Even then, it was difficult to piece together. He's quite good," Nancy said with admiration.

Dave picked up the brief. "Again, there may well be a reasonable explanation for the shipping containers. Considering how well he's planned, I suspect he has a cover story in place. Perhaps they really are filled with what he claims. My guess is at least some are."

Gregory had to call the president. "Get me more," he told them, turning to leave.

"Sir, it's not there."

Which is exactly what Haley surmised, and the reason she went into the field: to get more proof so action could be taken.

"Find the shipping containers. Use traffic cameras. Trucking weigh stations. Also, if they truly contain EMP devices, what are the most likely targets in each of those areas, given Conroy's anti-technology and anti-government views? Get the entire team on it."

He looked at the map on Dave's screen as Nancy typed out a group message. The United States had dozens of red dots on the screen showing shipping containers. Los Angeles. Newark. Savannah. Houston. Seattle. Miami.

And Norfolk, Virginia, less than two hundred miles from Washington, D.C.

48

RECON

It took bushwhacking through the thick jungle behind their villas, but they eventually made it to the hiking trail. Axe led the way, speed hiking uphill in the humid morning air, already warm as the sky lightened. The sun would rise in about twenty minutes, and with it, the day would become hotter. They had timed it perfectly—the jungle was just light enough for them to find their way.

Haley followed, easily keeping pace. As planned on the yacht, they had stayed in character last night. He pretended to be the stoic bodyguard, disapproving of Haley's friendliness toward Conroy, yet attempting to hide it. She acted the part of the beautiful new girlfriend of a billionaire who was being courted by yet another billionaire... and letting it all go to her head.

This morning, twenty minutes ago, she had knocked on Axe's villa door next to hers, and demanded they go for an early morning trail run.

Now they were on their way to recon the Center. They would be picked up at the villas at 7:30 for breakfast, followed by a trip back to the soccer stadium to see the Saturday morning service for Conroy's ultra-faithful. Until then, they would see what they could.

Shake the tree.

Axe wanted to find a landing zone for a helicopter in the hilly terrain for SEALs, in case they needed to assault the Center. If they were right about Conroy, it would be nice to call in reinforcements instead of handling his extensive security detail by themselves. They marched on, quickly approaching the Center buildings.

Outside the Main Center Building
St. John, United States Virgin Islands

Bec lay flat on the ground, mostly concealed by foliage at the edge of the jungle. It would be dawn soon. She wanted to finish by then and begin the long trek back to her apartment.

Unfortunately, the Wi-Fi wasn't cooperating. The signal would be strong long enough for her to log in, then would fade, interrupting her work. It would be strong again for several minutes before cutting off abruptly. It frustrated her, but she kept at it.

In the past hour, she had found two instances of Stefan putting his hand to the scanner. She'd noted the exact moments in a text file on her phone. The latest had been early the previous evening, right before the Friday night celebration. As usual, Gunther ran the workstation several feet from the hand scanner. Pioneer proudly placed his hand on it as the twins watched silently next to him.

A few more minutes of work would allow her to scan the rest of the security camera footage to see if Pioneer got up to more mischief overnight.

If she could get the Wi-Fi to hold steady.

Her arms and part of her head stuck out of the thick undergrowth and onto a scraped dirt track keeping the jungle at bay. She scanned the area, looking for threats, and risked inching forward another foot. Her hands extended, willing the phone and the Wi-Fi to play nicely together. The connection display showed one bar for a few seconds before it flicked off, then back again.

Closer. Then an internet search, another FBI tip, and I'm out of here.

If the results were bad, she'd return to her apartment, shower, pack, and get on the next ferry to St. Thomas. She would think of an excuse to quit and leave immediately.

Another few inches forward left only her feet in the foliage.

I'm wearing all black against the dark ground. I'm fine here.

The Wi-Fi signal indicator showed one bar... and it held steady. Another bar flicked on, off, then on and held strong.

Yes!

Her fingers flew, navigating the sign-in screens again. The system had logged her off when she lost connection.

Almost there...

"Hey!"

A guard stared at her from thirty yards away. He looked surprised at finding an intruder. He wore the khaki shorts and shirt of a typical Movement guard, not the black pants and tight t-shirts Pioneer's personal security wore.

They locked eyes. "What are you doing there?" He started toward her, more inquisitive than angry.

Run!

She scrambled back through the thick underbrush. In her haste, her glasses slipped off. She didn't need them to see—they were only to make herself look smarter. But leaving them behind would be a clue to her identity.

No time.

She'd rather avoid the immediate threat of getting caught and risk the guard finding the glasses.

Ditch the phone.

The gnarled roots of a large tree formed an opening. She shoved the phone into it. If they caught her with it... She didn't know what they'd do, but it would be worse than the trouble she was already in.

The man's footsteps pounded on the other side of the wall of plants. "I said stop!"

She rushed along a tiny path through the thick jungle. The hiking trail passed nearby… if she could find it again with the man on her tail.

The guard crashed into the jungle, fighting the plants instead of getting low and using the opening she had found.

Doesn't want to get dirty. Good. It will slow him down.

She took a wrong turn and lost the thin trail.

Behind her, the man grunted with relief. He had made it through the thick barrier at the edge of the cleared zone.

There!

Two steps brought her back onto the narrow trail. Several more brought her to the wider main trail.

All downhill from here.

With the Center at the top of the hill, she could speed down the trail. She'd run it many times before. The guard looked fit, but more like a bodybuilder, not a runner. She had a small lead, plus the advantage in speed and agility.

Bec took off at a fast but careful pace along the still-dark trail. A slip now would be disastrous.

What the guard lacked in trail running experience he made up with determination. Somehow, he was gaining on her.

She used her right hand on a narrow tree along the trail, grabbing it and swinging around the tight switchback. The move allowed her to keep her pace and not slow down.

Behind her, the man cursed as he fell with a thud.

Mom always said my curiosity would get me into trouble. If I get out of this, Mom, I promise I'll do better next time.

Axe figured the middle of the jungle would be the safest place for them to compare notes. As the jungle continued to lighten, they began jogging—slowly enough to move quietly up the zigzagging trail. "How are you feeling about our progress?"

"Relieved he's buying it," Haley said. "I guessed right—his weakness is blonds."

"Or women in general."

"Either way, it's working. He thinks of me as a sex object, not a threat. A potential conquest, not an adversary."

"Perfect. But if we don't get a lead this morning, we might have to go to Plan B."

Their backup plan called for Axe to leave in a huff because of Haley's flirtatiousness with Conroy. He would use the speedboat from the yacht to return for a snatch and grab mission, abducting someone from the inner circle, preferably the blond twins or another highly placed figure. With an offer of immunity from prosecution—and sparing them from his enhanced interrogation methods—they would hopefully tell what they knew.

"Let's wait until—"

They heard a muffled curse from up the trail.

And running feet coming their way.

Axe looked around. On their left, the trail dropped off at a steep angle, falling ten feet into a small ravine. There were only small ferns at the bottom, so the cover offered would be limited.

To the right, two feet of high grass and ferns, then thick trees. Also not ideal.

"Down!" Axe whispered, pointing to the grass. Maybe she would blend in enough. If not...

He fought his way through the jungle, trading stealth for speed, hoping whoever approached them would be too focused on their own drama to hear.

There.

He hefted a small branch, the thickness of his wrist and four feet long. One end broke away as he lifted it. While it wasn't as solid as he'd like, it might do the trick.

Axe thought of the many times he had chased a terrorist or other high-value target.

The pursuer isn't always the bad guy.

He'd have to make a split-second decision.

What else is new?

Bec pushed herself as dawn made the trail easier to see. The guard's determination and the risks he took to keep up with her proved how bad it would be to get caught.

She practically flew down the trail, gaining a short lead. She risked a quick glance back, didn't see him, and surged forward on a straightaway.

A young man dressed all in black.

No. A woman with short hair. Baggy clothes. A tomboy. Scared, but keeping it together.

Axe stood two feet off the trail, barely hidden by thin trees, the broken, partly rotten branch in his hand.

She ran right by him.

His gut told him she wasn't the bad guy in this drama.

A man dressed in a guard uniform came into view, his red face angry and determined. He ran faster than his muscular physique suggested he could.

Bad guy.

Axe waited another second, wanting to time it perfectly.

When the guard was nearly parallel to him, Axe calmly took a step forward, brought up the branch, and swung at the man's head.

The guard stopped abruptly, landing flat on his back in the damp dirt of the trail, out cold.

He never saw what hit him.

Axe turned in time to see the woman glance back at the commotion. Her eyes widened as she saw Axe. She slowed for a few steps before she took off.

Bec met the man's eyes.

Who the hell is that?

It didn't matter. This was life and death. She had to get back to her apartment, get her things, and get off the island, even if she had to swim for it.

She turned and picked up her pace.

Haley leaped to her feet, barely glancing at the man on the ground next to her. Axe would handle him.

With her face pressed to the grass, she had seen the woman run by her out of the corner of her eye.

Now she watched the baggy black t-shirt swing around another of the trail's many switchbacks.

Follow your gut.

"White Knight!" Haley called after the woman.

Bec heard a woman's voice.

Where did she come from?

She had yelled something, obviously directed at her.

The pounding of her heart in her ears and the adrenaline coursing through her body slowed her processing time.

Did she say…

Bec slowed, giving herself a chance to think.

White Knight.

A weird phrase to yell at a trail runner.

She could keep running. Who cared if they were probably good guys who had read her message to the FBI? It could be a trap. She should save her own skin.

Bec slowed more, still undecided.

Her mother's voice came to her. *"Curiosity killed the cat…"*

Her father's voice, playfully adding the ending to the idiom often quoted in their house, *"But satisfaction brought it back."*

Bec stopped and turned, looking at the stunning blond in tight-fitting running shorts and top approaching her.

Sorry, Mom. Guess 'I'll do better next time' will have to wait.

49

COGCON

"As you were," James announced to the people standing as he swept into the Situation Room. He'd gotten a few hours of sleep despite the stress of the ongoing crisis. Armed with a to-go mug of coffee, he was ready to tackle the day.

"What do you have for me?"

"Mr. President, Gregory Addison from Central Analysis Group has requested he go first," an aide said.

This will be interesting. He better keep Haley's name out of it.

"Mr. Addison, are you with us?"

Gregory's face appeared on the large screen on the far wall. "Good morning, Mr. President. If I may dive right in. Over the past several hours, we have compiled intelligence you need to see. However, I must caution that, while the information is potentially alarming, we have no clear proof. At best, this is circumstantial evidence. But yesterday you asked for hunches. This is ours."

"Circumstantial? In a court of law, what would happen?"

"Sir, they would dismiss the case immediately."

The man doesn't pull any punches—I like it.

"Fine. We'll take it with more than a grain of salt. But you're right, I asked for hunches, so give me what you have."

"Sir, my team and I believe technology billionaire Stefan Conroy may be behind the suspected EMPs in Los Angeles and what we think are EMPs with a different delivery vehicle in Iran."

Disbelieving whispered conversations broke out around the table.

"People," James said, addressing the men and women in the room with him, "listen up. You'll get your chance to speak." To the man on the screen in front of him, he said, "You mentioned potentially alarming information."

"Yes, sir. Based on our analysis, Conroy has been shipping what he says are books and pamphlets about the Movement, toys for kids, and food for the underprivileged worldwide. We believe this a ruse to hide shipments of EMP missiles and another unknown delivery vehicle— our best guess is a suitcase EMP, similar to a suitcase nuclear device."

He couldn't identify who did it, but one person at his table—or perhaps an aide in the chairs along the wall—gasped.

James thought fast. "How many devices?"

"No way to know, Mr. President. It would depend on whether the shipping containers were filled with legitimate items, with only a few devices carefully hidden in each. This is what I would call the best-case scenario. We found 362 containers linked to Conroy and his movement, so approximately 724 devices."

James' heart pounded faster, and he struggled to present a calm exterior. "And if each of the what—362 containers—was packed with EMPs?"

"Upwards of 100,000 devices, Mr. President. While each is relatively low yield, if that is the correct term, with that many missiles or suitcase EMPs…"

The implication was clear. The world as they knew it could be destroyed.

"Here is a map of the ports where the containers were shipped." Addison's face was replaced by a graphic showing many of the world's busiest shipping ports marked by blue dots. "And this shows the location of the containers when their transponders were switched off."

An overlay appeared, showing hundreds of blinking red dots, several at every port around the world.

A shocked silence filled the room.

"Mr. President," Addison said, his face appearing in a small window at the upper right of the screen, "once again, we could be wrong. But I do not believe we are. My entire team is tracking the containers. They are also compiling a list of potential targets in each area. But I recommend you immediately implement the Continuity of Government evacuation. While we don't believe missiles are currently inbound, and much of our government electronics and comms are shielded against an EMP strike, we must protect your ability to lead the country, sir."

I didn't see this coming when I woke up.

They had war-gamed a scenario over the summer after the New York City crisis, working on their response in the event of an attack on Washington. A key aspect involved protecting the ability of the government to function. One tool at his disposal was the COGCON systems, or the Continuity of Government Readiness Condition, which set readiness levels for the executive branch. He didn't need approval from Congress or any other entity to change it.

"Set COGCON 3. Immediately prepare the alternate sites. I want them up and running. Track down the leaders of agencies. Let them know I'll be setting COGCON 2 at some point this morning." It would send at least half of the essential staff to alternate locations to preserve the most important functions of their agencies.

"COGCON 1 can wait until we see what happens in the Middle East and if any other countries get hit." Full deployment of staff and leadership would be called for only with more data... or another strike. He didn't want to be overly cautious—nor too cavalier—with his responsibility to maintain the government of the United States.

And while Air Force One would be safe from an EMP, he didn't want to escape to it unless absolutely necessary.

Suddenly announcing a change to COGCON 3, then COGCON 2 in rapid succession, would cause a stir. He needed a cover story.

Calm is contagious. And there's no school like the old school.

A drill wouldn't survive much scrutiny, but it would buy him a day.

Maybe two.

"People, I know some of you enjoy a close relationship with the press." He met the eyes of one person after another. No one at the table dared look away, lest they appear guilty. "You know how much I hate it. But in this case, use it. Present this to your contacts as a pain in the ass, surprise readiness drill to test our systems from an overly cautious president. I want to hear how annoying I am," he said with a small, tight smile. "But if there is the merest hint the COGCON alerts are the real deal, I swear I will replace every one of you, just to make sure I got the leaker. No investigations, no BS, no exceptions. One word and you all go. Got it?"

There were murmurs of assent. Had he scared the blabbers straight?

"Mr. Addison, do you have any other information?"

"Some of the containers are still in transit. They are included in the list. Other than that, I will have more for you in a few hours."

"Thank you. Share your findings with the rest of our intelligence community, if you haven't already."

James looked around the room at America's best and brightest—or at least, the ones committed to government service. "I want the full resources of the United States of America at work tracking down every one of those containers. Prepare all our special forces, Military Police, Marines guarding embassies, and diplomats. Get small groups of men and women with weapons and bags of cash ready. As we discover the location of a shipping container, I want the nearest group to go to the location and bribe or kill whoever is in control of the EMPs. Any that can't be taken or bought get shot. The devices are a clear and present danger. They cannot be allowed to stay in the hands of Conroy's followers, nor fall into the hands of our enemies... or our allies. Made in the USA by a United States citizen, it's US property being seized by the United States government. No exceptions, no excuses, no quarter given."

The briefing continued, with news of the conflict in the Middle East escalating overnight. More countries were pulled in. The Middle East was at war, and it would spill over to the superpowers if the situation wasn't handled perfectly.

'May you live in interesting times,' indeed.

50

RUN

The Jungle
St. John, United States Virgin Islands

Axe knelt over the guard, confirming the man was knocked out and not dead. "We only have a minute before he regains consciousness, so talk fast. Unless…"

Haley knew exactly what he meant. "I don't think killing him is warranted."

"I agree, but if he comes to and we're still around, it may be necessary."

"Did the guard get a good look at you?" she asked the young woman who they had saved.

"I don't know. It was dark, but maybe."

Haley bit her lip, deciding, then shook her head at Axe. They'd have to risk it. A dead guard would be more of a liability than a guard with a story of chasing a suspected spy.

She turned to the woman. "I read your tip to the FBI. That was you, right?"

The woman, still catching her breath, nodded. "Who are you guys?"

"Not now. What other data do you have?"

The woman still wasn't sure about trusting them, so Haley continued. "I suspected Conroy was behind the EMPs in LA, too. We're here to find out what else he's up to, but we're at a dead end. Please. We're the good guys."

With a nod, the woman decided. "I hacked the security cameras. On Thursday at 6:26 p.m. local time, Pioneer pressed his palm to a scanner and celebrated afterward, the same way he did when the power went out in Los Angeles—both times."

Haley exchanged a glance with Axe. This was the proof they needed.

"Last night at 5 p.m., same thing. But I haven't been able to research what he did."

"How are you doing this?"

"I had a smartphone. The Center's Wi-Fi extends just far enough to connect in the parking lot from my truck, or on the back of the building near the jungle line. I left it there."

"Where, exactly?" Axe asked.

The woman explained in detail and gave him the passcode to unlock it.

The guard groaned, coming around.

"Can I use the phone to call out?" Axe asked.

"Yes, cellular works, but they might track it, so be careful. Don't stay on long. And don't get caught with a phone. Also..." She hesitated, embarrassed.

"What?"

"I lost my glasses at the edge of the jungle. Big black nerd frames, very distinctive. If they find them, they'll know it's me." She described where they had fallen off her face as she scrambled through the vegetation.

"I'll find them. You two," Axe told them, "go. I'll get the phone— and glasses—and call it in. If I'm not back soon, dump my pack in the jungle and go with Plan B."

Haley turned to the woman. "Go. We can talk while we run."

They ran. Haley waited several minutes, hearing nothing from behind them, before speaking again.

"By the way, I'm known as Holly here, but my name is Haley. And my partner is Axe."

"Bec."

"What else can you tell me?"

"I was hired as a hacker. A white hat, you know what that is?"

"Yes. One of the good guys who hacks to discover security holes but doesn't exploit them."

"Exactly."

Both women ran easily, as if it were a pleasant morning for a trail run. A chance to discuss the latest happenings in their lives, instead of a madman's plans for the end of the world.

"I hacked all types of companies, banks to tech firms—and some governments—looking for initial openings. When I found them—and I found a lot—I'd put them into a spreadsheet. We all did it. There are a bunch of us. Pioneer would look at the list, quiz us, then tell us which ones to target. Once we found a way into the systems, we'd report. The sales department contacts the company or whoever and tells them about our hack. They use it to sell the cybersecurity software suite Pioneer invented."

Haley considered the idea. It sounded plausible. But was it an actual business, or a front for something else?

"How many systems?"

"I don't know. A lot. Hundreds over the past year. But lately, someone is taking my scouting work and continuing without me. Breaking in and shutting me out. I don't know who it could be."

"Conroy?"

"He makes the big decisions, but I don't know who advises him, if anyone. Not me, that's for sure."

"Gunther—the blond guy with the dead eyes?"

"No, he's a right-hand man. He operates the workstation, but he's no hacker or techie. More of a meathead than a brainiac. Maybe Tina. She's another hacker. Plain, but ambitious. She's Pioneer's lover. Or one of them, actually. I get the impression he has many."

Oh, I know all about that.

51

TRAIL

The Jungle
St. John, United States Virgin Islands

"Hey, buddy, you okay?" Axe spoke quietly from behind the guard. The man's eyes were closed, but he had moaned a few times as Axe approached.

"Hang in there. I'm here to help."

Help me, I mean, but you don't need the details.

The poor guy groaned. His forehead had a cut and an egg-sized bump where Axe hit him with the branch.

Axe had an idea and squatted so he could pick the man up in a firefighter's carry.

"Just relax. I've got you."

He hefted the man and adjusted his grip until he was holding him upside down around the waist. Axe staggered forward toward the trees along the trail.

Two trees had branches that split off the main trunk about nine feet off the ground. The limbs formed narrow triangles.

"Almost there," Axe grunted, struggling to carry the man.

"What?" the man asked groggily.

"Trust me. A few more seconds. Help me out—straighten your legs."

Axe muscled the man up and angled one ankle toward the first tree. With a heave, he got the guard's foot through the narrow opening, then lowered him until the ankle wedged tight.

"Hey!"

Axe wiggled and nudged the other leg as the guard fought to process the situation, directing the second foot through the other tree's opening. Once in the right spot, he lowered the man, letting both ankles become firmly wedged. Axe let go, ready to grab the guard if the trees didn't hold.

"What the hell?" Still groggy, the man hung upside down, legs spread wide, facing the jungle with his back to Axe, both feet stuck in the crooks of trees.

Axe scrounged until he found a vine. It was green and hard to break off, but by bending a section back and forth several times, he got it started. His teeth finished it off.

He made quick work of binding the man's hands behind his back before tying the vine to another nearby tree. The man's arms, tied together behind him, extended out from his body. There would be no way to jackknife himself up so he could untangle himself from his position.

"You have a concussion," Axe told the man. "Looks like you ran into a low-hanging tree branch. This will keep your back stable while I go get help."

Utter bullshit, but if he's out of it enough, it will make him wonder for a while.

"What?" The man struggled, pulling his tied arms.

"Don't fight it. You don't want to make it worse, right? I'll be back with help soon."

Wonder how long until he figures out I'm not coming back?

After relieving the man of his radio—and a small pocketknife— Axe ran up the trail, grinning. It was a well-used trail, so eventually someone would come along and find the man. Or he would wiggle out of the vines holding his arms and heave himself out of the trees. Either way, Axe would have enough time to find the phone and report to

Nalen what they had learned. He could bushwhack back to the apartment or, if time was tight, stay in the jungle and watch the Center for more intel.

Not a bad morning, so far.

Axe slowed as he neared the top of the hill. The Center would be ahead and to the left.

He heard the scuff of a shoe on dirt and barely had time to step off the trail. There was no time to silently work his way into the thick jungle, so he crouched low as a guard came into view around a switchback.

The man, in his mid-twenties with a blond crew cut, moved slowly, looking to his right where the trail fell off steeply.

Trying to find his missing buddy.

The man had skill. He moved carefully, stepping quietly.

Listening for his colleague moaning in the ravine?

A few more steps forward brought the man next to Axe, barely hidden in thin cover at the edge of the jungle.

Keep walking. If you don't...

This close to the Center, Axe couldn't risk discovery.

Haley is right. Stefan is behind this, which means all the people working for him are fair game.

His personal rules of engagement allowed for deadly force against the enemy.

The guard stepped away from Axe, close to the far edge of the trail. He leaned over to check the steep downslope and the mucky wet area fifteen feet below.

An animal moved in the jungle behind Axe, scampering away.

Axe tensed, preparing himself.

The guard spun and looked right at Axe.

Axe sprang forward, the daily squats, box jumps, and running giving him extreme speed and force.

Instead of raising his arms to defend himself, the guard reached for his radio.

Big mistake.

Axe led with his forearm, slamming it into the man's mouth. He felt teeth give way, then he and the man flew off the trail. With the force of Axe's lunge, momentum carried them clear of the steep hillside. They plunged toward the wetlands below.

With a splat, the guard landed in the flora and mud. Axe landed on top of him an instant later, knocking the air out of the man.

Axe grabbed the guard and rolled him face down. With his broken teeth and lack of oxygen, much of the fight had temporarily left him.

Sorry, brother. You chose the wrong side.

Axe held the man's face to the ground, submerged in a few inches of muddy water.

When his body allowed him to breathe again, his nose and injured mouth took in a thick mixture of water and mud.

Being close to death ignited his fighting spirit. He thrashed with all his might, but Axe's superior training, strength, and positioning kept the guard's face submerged.

It didn't take long for him to stop moving.

Axe felt the life leave the guard.

Would they buy a second guard disappearing in one morning?

Doubtful. But an accident? Maybe.

Choosing his foot placement carefully, he stood and walked on rocks, roots, and grass to conceal his steps. He moved to a section of the hill he could climb, stepping carefully to avoid leaving footprints.

Looking down at the dead guard, it appeared at first glance the man had fallen face-first fifteen feet into the ravine and drowned.

Suspicious, but it might buy some time.

Axe resumed his hunt for the small opening off the main trail the hacker woman had described.

There.

He could hear indistinct voices and guessed they came from the clearing outside the Center building.

Get the phone and report in.

He stalked silently along the thin game trail, considering his options.

The guard he had killed would be found within the hour, possibly sooner. Some would want to believe he tripped and fell into the ravine —a freak accident.

But no officer would accept the coincidence of one guard missing and one dead in a single morning. More guards would be sent down the trail. The one Axe had left hanging in the tree would be found and questioned.

He would report seeing and chasing the woman. But Axe hoped that with her speed and his blow to the head, the guard wouldn't be able to describe her well. Given her appearance, he could easily have mistaken her for a dark-haired young man.

The guard might shade the truth to make himself look better, creating multiple attackers out of thin air, as well as the ass-kicking he handed out before eventually succumbing to their superior numbers.

Axe had seen it before in troops around the world. No one wants to be thought of as weak or incompetent.

Their mission hinged on what the guard saw and could report.

I should have just killed him.

Axe held perfectly still as men moved on the other side of the hedgerow, patrolling slowly.

They stopped. One poked at the thick jungle trees.

Axe lowered to the ground. If caught now, there would be too many people to fight. Given his skill, he could successfully hide in the jungle for hours, but it would close off avenues of investigation for himself—and Haley.

No, he couldn't be seen. He took a slow breath and went into stealth mode.

In sniper school, Axe had discovered and perfected the technique. With a conscious decision, he could somehow shut down and make himself invisible. Instructors had nearly stepped on him and been shocked when he eventually showed himself.

He used the skill now, calming himself, drawing his energy within, and flattening against the dark earth. He could wait until they passed.

A few feet in front of him, clearly visible on the ground just inside of the jungle, lay the hacker's oversized black glasses.

The more thorough guard took another step closer to him. The toe of his black boot stopped inches from the glasses.

If he moves, he'll crunch the glasses and come fully through the hedgerow.

Axe crept his arm forward.

Almost...

He couldn't quite reach.

Moving his body the tiniest amount allowed his fingers to graze the glasses.

"Shh! Did you hear something?" the closest guard whispered to his partner.

Axe went back into stealth mode, his hand extended and exposed, fingertips resting on the glasses.

"One of those huge freaking lizards, I bet. Those things creep me out."

Axe didn't move. Didn't think. Didn't feel. He was a black hole. Empty.

"Yeah, probably right. Still..."

Axe felt the man prepare to lean forward and step further into the jungle.

In a flash, he pulled his hand back, the glasses tenuously held between two fingers. He brought his arm close to his body and returned to stealth mode.

52

LOCKDOWN

Stefan entered the lobby of the Center where Gunther stood, looking concerned.

I've never seen him look like this.

Gunther dismissed two nearby guards and greeted him.

"We have a problem."

Stefan glanced around. Normally early on a Saturday morning, the Center would be quiet. Not today. There were many more of his personal security detail than usual, armed with their knives. Khaki-clad regular security guards stood both inside and outside the glass doors at the entrance. And a lone member of his personal guard stood at the entrance to the Control room, looking alert and ready for action.

If there is trouble, I may have to break open the armory and issue the guns.

He hated the idea. History was filled with examples of rulers destroyed by their followers. An uprising from his people was unlikely, but he feared guns in the hands of an unhappy populace more than an attack from outside.

"A guard is missing," Gunther said.

"That's it?" All this activity seemed like an overreaction, especially given they were nearing the end game. His extensive plans had remained undetected.

The world governments have no idea what's coming.

He smiled, lost in thought, then frowned. Not all his plans were working out. He had resorted to having the mousy hacker woman in his bed last night... Tina, he thought her name might be. While enthusiastic and eager to please, she was no beauty like Holly, who had turned him down.

No one rejects a God.

It just wasn't done. His anger flared again.

Still, tonight, she would be his. He had explained his plan to Tina, and would enlist the help of Ella and Anna, as well. One of them—or all three, he didn't care—would seduce Holly's annoying guard.

Or the bodyguard may have an unfortunate accident. The island can be a deadly place. Accidents happen all the time.

"Pioneer?" Gunther looked at him with concern.

He hadn't been listening, lost in thought of what an evening with Holly would be like.

"Say the last part again."

"The missing guard is reliable. A true believer. He was due for a promotion to your personal guard detail next week. It is alarming he is missing and not answering his radio. In addition..." Gunther's German accent was stronger than usual.

"Yes? Say it."

"We checked our security camera footage. The cameras show him running toward the jungle line, but he went out of sight. But in accessing the cameras, we discovered an unauthorized user reviewed footage of the control room this morning."

The truth dawned on him. "From Thursday morning and Friday night?"

"Yes, Pioneer. Someone knows about the Hand of God."

Stefan closed his eyes, bringing the full scope of his considerable brainpower to bear on the problem.

Who could it be?

He could think of no one. "Have we been infiltrated?"

"Doubtful," Gunther said. "We have purposefully allowed no one new at the Center for the last six weeks, specifically to avoid this situation."

"New people to the island?"

"For St. John, only one, a security guard. Carefully vetted, working at the docks, and bunked in Cruise Bay with three others. He has a solid alibi—two of the men in his room vouched for him being there all night."

Gunther looked at him strangely.

"What is it? What do you have to say?"

That's just it. He doesn't want to tell me.

Something he should be able to figure out on his own.

He glared at Gunther, willing him to explain himself.

"We have boats patrolling the water and men watching the coastline twenty-four hours a day," Gunther explained, his accent stronger than ever. "No unauthorized boats are allowed close to the island. No planes or helicopters have overflown or approached. We are in lockdown except for the one guard." He looked at Stefan expectantly.

I don't get what he's—oh no.

"Holly?" He regretted saying her name the moment he spoke. The single word revealed his feelings. "No!" He sounded like a petulant child. Gunther looked away, embarrassed.

Not her. I haven't had her yet!

"It could be her bodyguard. Or any of the hackers or other people on the island."

"Yes, Pioneer."

The look on Gunther's face...

He's humoring me. Me! His god!

It enraged Stefan back to his senses. He had a decision to make. He wouldn't allow his personal desires to interfere with the plan. "Lockdown all communication systems on the island. No cellular, no landlines. Cut off the cell towers on the nearby islands, as well. Close the library and disable the internet everywhere on the island except for the control room of the Center. Ethernet only. The only access will be from workstations we monitor."

Gunther looked relieved at his orders and commanding tone. He nodded at every instruction and gestured for the guard at the control room door to come over to them.

"Close everything down. No arrivals or departures. I declare a special, mandatory relaxation day. Absolutely no technology except inside the control room."

Gunther relayed his orders to the guard, who transmitted them through a walkie-talkie.

What else?

If they are on to me, choices must be made.

"I will move up the timeline. It all happens now."

"It will take time to prepare," Gunther said. "And what about the Saturday service?"

His most faithful and devout would already be streaming into the stadium. He could use them as additional guards. More eyes and ears would be helpful if the authorities arrived.

They will also make effective human shields, if it comes to that.

"I will attend as always."

He would give a speech preparing them for what would happen over the next few days. The time had come.

"I will require more than just your expertise to prepare. Bring in the woman—Tina. And another tech." He thought for a moment. "The one who looks like a boy."

"She is not part of the inner circle, Pioneer."

"But she's always here, I've noticed. She's a hard worker and obviously believes in the cause. Get her by the time I return."

He had one more thought. "And get more guards. We must hold this facility until the endgame is reached."

Gunther nodded once, then hesitated again. "What about the woman and the bodyguard, Pioneer?"

"I will ask them for the truth."

And I'll get it, one way or another.

53

PHONE

The Jungle
Outside the Center Building
St. John, United States Virgin Islands

The guard poked around the foliage, making a racket, before giving up. "Nothing could get through this mess," he declared. On the other side of the hedgerow, the guards moved away, continuing their patrol without making it through the thick jungle growth near where Axe lay in stealth mode.

As they walked away, Axe spotted a tree that could be the one the woman mentioned. It had large, exposed roots.

After slipping the hacker's glasses into his pocket, he silently moved forward until he could reach between the two largest roots.

A radio call blared from nearby, less than five feet away. The only thing separating Axe from the man with it was a thick row of vegetation. One guard hadn't moved on. Axe cursed himself for being in too much of a hurry. He should have realized only one man had left the position.

"Attention all units," the man's radio blared. "Evans missed his check-in. Report if you've seen him."

The volume got turned down halfway through the call, but Axe used the noise to slip his hand into the opening. He found the phone, pulled it out, and unlocked it. Only two bars of cell service, and no Wi-Fi.

On the other side of the trees, the guard hadn't moved.

I'm running out of time.

He'd have to settle for a text.

He entered Admiral Nalen's number from memory and typed. The phone made a tiny *click* with each letter.

Axe stopped typing and froze. The noise wasn't common in the jungle. Had it been heard?

The guard didn't move closer, but Axe couldn't see him. Was he on alert?

Axe carefully backed away from the thick row of trees and the guard on the other side.

Slow is smooth and smooth is fast.

He stopped a few feet from the main trail, shielded from view behind several small trees. He bent forward to dampen the noise from the phone with his bulk and continued the text.

A. on borrowed phone. Safe.

They still had no evidence Stefan was behind the EMP attacks, but Axe had assaulted one guard and killed another. If they were wrong, they were wrong big.

1 EKIA. One enemy killed.

Time short. Conroy behind EMP. No new proof but high conviction. Send Team.

Now, how to prove it was really him?

TOEDWY

The only easy day was yesterday. He'll figure it out and know it's me.

It would have to be enough for now. When more men were on station, they could get to the bottom of the mess. If he and Haley had it wrong and Conroy wasn't behind the EMPs, they would apologize and move on. At worst, they would be embarrassed and have wasted the resources of a SEAL Team.

And killed an innocent man.

Best case, they'd have the men and weapons to stop Conroy from further destruction.

He pressed the send button.

Instead of an immediate "Message Sent" confirmation, the phone hesitated, working at sending the message. He checked the bars along the top. None.

Instead, after several seconds, the display read: "No Service."

54

PREPARE

Haley and Axe had been upgraded to Conroy's private seats, an area of three rows, center field, for Pioneer's die-hard faithful. Mostly women, mostly blond.

Haley fit right in.

The other women smiled happily at her, but she could tell they compared her looks to theirs. They all played nice, but she'd experienced more than her share of jealousy and hatred because of her beauty. She recognized the underlying vibe.

The women perceived her as competition for their god's attention.

Axe sat directly behind her on the other side of the plush maroon velour rope strung between stanchions behind her row of seats, separating her VIP section from the rest by an empty row—aside from Axe.

He'd appeared at the Villas as she finished her shower, knocking on the wall separating their bathrooms. Minutes later, showered and dressed in an outfit of black tactical cargo pants and a tight gray t-shirt, he had knocked on her door.

They didn't dare risk updating each other, still not knowing how much surveillance they were under, but she read the frustration in his eyes. The tiny shake of his head indicated he either hadn't found the phone or the call hadn't gone through.

Standing in the crushed stone parking area of the villas, waiting for tour guide Kim, he stood behind her and quietly gave her the news.

"Phone couldn't connect. We're on our own. One guard killed. I'm sure they've found the other by now. We're the logical infiltrators. Probably blown, but we may have a bit more time before they figure it out. Depends on command and control—their level of training and how willing they are to report bad news. I suggest we play it out, but it doesn't look good."

"Could we make a run for it?" She barely moved her lips, still facing the incredible view of Cruz Bay below them and St. Thomas in the distance.

"We'd have to swim. In daylight, they'd find us."

They had already considered a long nighttime swim from the north side of the island to Tortola in the British Virgin Islands, where the Movement presence was slightly less than in St. Thomas.

"What about our twenty-four-hour check-in?"

She had made it clear she had to call Kelton in the afternoon or he'd be upset, which would mean he'd send the security crew to retrieve her.

"I doubt we have that much time." As scary as the words were, Axe didn't sound upset or worried.

"So, we're stuck?"

"No. We're undercover and in deep. Time to play it out and hope for the best."

His saying popped into her mind.

Hope for the best, plan for the worst.

Sometimes his calm exasperated her.

I just don't have his experience in the field yet.

She hated to ask because she suspected the answer. "If we're not running and about to get caught, what's the plan?"

Kim's boxy bright orange SUV, so common on the island, turned into their small parking area. Over the crunch of the tires on the gravel, Haley could still hear Axe's response.

"Violence of action."

Now, after a breakfast buffet with Kim, they sat in the stadium to endure yet another of Conroy's speeches. Around her, the crowd started its familiar chant.

Clap-Clap-Clap "Pioneer."

Haley joined in, smiling in anticipation, playing her role.

The only way out is through.

They would adapt and overcome. For now, the safest play was to continue as before, a blond bombshell torn between two mega-rich suitors.

The stadium was about half full, so she estimated five thousand people stood and chanted with her. From this part of the stands, the energy felt much stronger than up in the private skybox.

It felt like the best concert she had ever attended, only ten times more powerful.

Haley barely had to fake her enthusiasm.

I can see how people fall for this. It's intoxicating.

Instead of preceding Conroy onto the field and standing at attention around the stage, ten of his private guard surrounded him as he jogged from the stadium's tunnel, across the field, and ran up the stairs.

That's different from last night. Is it always this way on Saturdays?

She felt Axe stiffen behind her.

I think we're blown.

Axe knew the minute he saw Conroy's private security team. The night before, they had been professional and alert.

Now they were on edge.

They surrounded their protectee and ran with him to the stage. A change in security posture meant a suspected threat.

Whether they know we are the danger or not though, remains to be seen.

It could simply be the two missing guards from the Center.

But he knew better.

I hope I made the right call.

He hadn't liked their chances of escaping the island, let alone swimming three to five nautical miles to Tortuga, depending on what part of St. John they left from. A very long swim—in daylight—with patrol boats looking for them. No, running would have gotten them caught and made them look guilty.

He'd played the odds, but it looked like he had lost.

Stefan stood on stage, smiling at his adoring followers. Once again, his message would be streamed worldwide. And it might be the last one seen… at least until he assumed the mantle of leader of the world.

And God of the Earth.

He kept the pleasant smile on his face as he found Holly sitting in his house seats instead of the private skybox. He had a question for her. Having her and the bodyguard close would make the part after the question easier, whichever way it went.

Logic told him one of them, or both, was responsible for this morning's hacking and the missing guards.

He hoped, for Holly's sake, the bodyguard was solely to blame.

His heart—or more honestly, his body—desperately wanted her to be innocent.

But he would do the right thing, no matter what. There was too much at stake to let a woman interfere, even a woman as spectacular as she.

"My friends," he began as always. The audience fell completely silent as soon as he opened his mouth to speak. Today's message would be different. He couldn't wait any longer to prepare them, and the world, for what was to come. He gestured for them to sit, a departure from normal which would get their attention.

"Today's message is different. More important than ever. It is finally time to address it." His seriousness had people on the edge of their seats.

"Governments of the world are universally corrupt. Nowhere are the so-called leaders out for anything but their own self-interests. Whether those interests are financial, the accumulation of power, or merely staying in office to keep their jobs, the common people suffer."

The audience soaked in the truth of his words.

"For the past ten years, I have worked to overcome this. Our Movement has grown slowly but steadily."

The words flowed from him. He felt the power. This was his moment.

"Now it is time to rise up. To do away with the political class holding us under their thumbs. To take power from them and place it securely into our own hands."

A few people in the stadium shouted with joy and he nodded, giving the rest of them permission to join in. They did, and for several seconds the stadium shook with the sounds of their approval.

He held up a hand, and his people fell silent. "Will this be easy? No. Having power takes responsibility, and with responsibility comes pressure. Stress. Effort. Work."

He loved the feeling of every eye on him, soaking up his message.

"But will it be worth it? Yes. To control our own destinies? To have communities? Closer connections to our fellow brothers and sisters? Yes. All worth the struggle."

"Yes! Yes! Yes!" the audience shouted. A few stood, which caused the rest to stand and yell.

"Oh, but I can guess what some of you are thinking. 'Pioneer, how can we have change? We have voted... to no avail. One party to another, nothing changes. We have moved from one system of government to another. Nothing changes.' Have I guessed correctly?"

A few of the people in the stands were brave enough to nod.

"Others of you wonder, 'Change? How? I am no revolutionary. I have a wife, a husband. Children. A car, a home, a job, a life. I am not the type to march, to storm the halls of power.'"

More nodded. He knew his people, both here and the ones watching and listening around the world. He wondered how many millions he reached this morning.

"To all of you, I say this: only prepare. Change is coming. You do not need to be revolutionaries. Only commit in your heart. Be ready for change. When the time comes, band together. Join with your friends and neighbors. You will not need to demand change. You will be the change!"

"Pioneer!" people called out. A woman in his private section fainted... but she did it every time he spoke. A security guard nearby caught her—as usual—and helped her sit, fanning her face.

"Lead each other in small groups. Those small groups will be part of larger groups. Together, you shall rule from a position of strength with other true believers. Reject the old and embrace the new."

He lowered his voice to a whisper. "You will know the time when it comes. I will see you on the other side and will happily guide you further."

He bowed modestly as his people clapped and chanted his name.

Stefan counted to ten, then lifted his head.

The live video feed would be turned off by now. For confirmation, he looked at a technician in front of the stage. He nodded and mouthed, "Offline."

All he had to do was raise his hand to silence the crowd, though he could tell they would have rather kept clapping and chanting. "I have a special message for you, my most loyal followers. Over the next few days, you will be my eyes and ears. You will report immediately to the nearest security officer or your community leader if you see any unusual activity. Specifically, people you don't know or who look like they don't fit in. You will prepare to defend this, our island paradise, as well as our larger mission. Some of you may be called on for special assignments. I know you will accept them with enthusiasm and do your best. This is our time. The world will soon know that you are the chosen ones." He let them take it all in. They stood in awe of him and their upcoming duties.

"You are the right hand of God."

Bec stood, shocked by what she heard.

Whatever he's doing, it's happening now.

She clapped and chanted on autopilot as Pioneer left the stage and crossed the field at a jog, surrounded once again by his security detail.

On the trail run back toward her apartment, Haley had convinced her to attend the Saturday service. It made sense: if she hadn't been identified by the guard, appearing to be devout wouldn't hurt.

And if she had been seen, staying away from her apartment for as long as possible would be best. It would give Haley and her bodyguard time to enact their plan, whatever it was.

With Pioneer's speech, though, she didn't know what to do.

Time to get the hell off this island.

But how? Movement to and from the island was always tightly controlled. If intruders were expected—or if Haley and Axe were already in trouble—it would be impossible to leave.

After Pioneer was out of sight, the chanting died down. People filed up the stairs and out of the stadium.

As she exited with the hundreds of others from her section, a guard standing by the door waved her to him. "You are Rebecca Dodgeson, tech at the Center?"

She fought to keep her voice steady. "Yes?"

"You have been summoned to duty by Pioneer himself. I will take you."

The man didn't wait for Bec's acknowledgment but turned and led the way toward his SUV.

There was nowhere to run. What else could she do? She followed him, despite her heart pounding and legs feeling weak.

Is this how it ends?

55

QUESTIONS

Pioneer Park Soccer Stadium
St. John, United States Virgin Islands

"Pioneer wishes to speak with you and will join us momentarily," Kim said cheerily.

It doesn't sound like she's suspicious or nervous.

Haley watched the rest of the audience leave, buzzing with excitement and discussing what Conroy's speech meant for their future. Only she, Axe, Kim, and four khaki-clad guards remained. They stood at their seats in the middle of the row, with Axe in his row behind them.

As soon as the last spectators exited, Conroy appeared, hurrying toward them across the field. Once again, the guards surrounded him.

Without being too obvious, Haley checked the position of the regular guards in their khaki shorts and shirts. They had moved closer on some imperceptible signal and now guarded the end of her row, blocking them from leaving.

A guard opened a small gate to the field. Conroy jogged up the stairs to the end of her row. Several of his guards joined him on the stairs. Gunther stood behind Conroy, his dead eyes looking at her without expression.

This is bad.

Kim's excitement at being near her leader made her quiver. Conroy looked at her and smiled benevolently. "You have done well, my friend. I accept responsibility for our guests. You may return to your normal duties."

Kim's face glowed at the compliment but fell at the dismissal. Yet she bowed her head and said, "Yes, Pioneer." She hurried up the stairs toward the main concourse exit.

"Holly. I have much to do today. But first, a question. Where were you this morning?"

She couldn't lie. There were likely security cameras at the villa that had recorded her exit earlier. "I went for a run this morning through your beautiful jungle, which I hope to see more of with you today. If you have time, I mean." She batted her eyes at him, still clinging to the hope he found her irresistible... or at least that she could influence him and buy some time.

"A run you say? Interesting." His eyes bored into hers. "Another question. Would you rather sleep with me or Kelton?"

The change in direction caught her off guard. She had steeled herself for a question about the run, the jungle, or missing guards, not about her relationship with Kelton. With her eyes locked onto his, she hesitated.

"Kelton," she blurted out. Given a choice, she would choose neither. But if it was one or the other, Kelton would win every time. He wasn't her type either, but at least he wasn't insane and bent on destroying the world.

"Ah, the truth hurts, as they say," he said with a frown of sadness. "And why are you here, Miss Holly?"

"I find your Movement fascinating and want to learn as much as I can about it," she said truthfully.

Conroy stared at her. She got the feeling he was torn. Had she won him over?

He looked at Axe, standing a step behind her as always. "And you, Mr. Bodyguard. Why are you here?"

"To keep her safe," Axe said.

If Conroy fancies himself a god, he might think he can spot lies. So far, we've only told the truth. But if he asks the right question, we're in trouble. How smart is he?

Beside Conroy, Gunther stiffened and put a hand to his ear. He whispered in Conroy's ear. They shared a look, with Gunther nodding encouragingly.

"I have just been informed we found a guard in a ravine—dead. And earlier we had a guard go missing. I don't believe either of you is lying, yet logic says only you could be responsible. There are no other reasonable explanations. But just in case, Miss Holly, I shall spare you. Later tonight, we will have ample time to discuss the Movement and your lack of interest in sleeping with me."

He turned to Gunther. "The men need real-life practice. Give the bodyguard to them. Kill him. Make her watch. It may help her attitude. Keep her safe. I have plans for her." He turned back to Haley. "The end of the world is coming, but I have time to have fun, whether or not you are willing."

Looking at Axe, he added, "For you, Mr. Bodyguard, it will be over in a few minutes. For the rest of the world, a new era will begin forty-eight hours from now. I was going to take my time and do it right. But just in case you're not alone, I will move up the timeline. Unless you have backup already here, or on the way, you will lose. I win. By Monday morning, I will be worshipped by all. And you, Miss Holly, will be the last woman to enjoy my bed before I transition from a mere man to a god among men."

"Ha!" Axe snorted from behind her.

"What a joke," Axe continued. He imitated Conroy's voice, but made it higher-pitched, sounding like a child. "'I will be a god among men, worshipped by all.' That'll be the day! You think we don't know all about your precious little EMPs?"

Haley's mouth dropped in shock.

What is he doing? This isn't part of the plan!

Conroy noticed. "Miss Holly, you're surprised. Perhaps you are what you claim to be. No one could fake it so well. I can't tell you how relieved I am!" He turned to Axe. "So you figured out the EMPs? Big deal. There's no defense. It's much too late. By tomorrow afternoon, the world will have limited electricity, no communication, and few working electronics. It will revert to a simpler time. And while some governments have shielding in place for their crucial electronics, not all do. Besides, there are other ways to bring down systems than electromagnetic pulses."

"'The world will revert to a simpler time,'" Axe repeated mockingly in the childlike voice. "You don't have a clue." He shook his head, then looked at Haley. "And neither do you! You think Kellison has fallen for you? It was all a ploy to get me here. This guy may be an idiot," he nodded to Conroy, "but he would never let me in otherwise. You're all morons."

"An idiot? Morons?" Conroy chuckled while Haley watched the interaction, unsure what to do. "But you're the one about to die, bodyguard. So who is actually the stupid one, after all?"

Haley stared at Axe, stunned by his tactical choice.

He's trying to save me, but we should have held out. Conroy couldn't know for sure we were the infiltrators!

Axe's eyes burned with anger. "Fine, you may be right. But you would burn down the world so you can pretend to be a god? Please." He shook his head scornfully. "You're pitiful."

"I am not!" Conroy's outburst caught them all by surprise. He got himself under control immediately. "I am helping the world. People will rise up and manage themselves. They will turn to the one man who has vast storehouses of computers, microchips, food... and a plan for a better world. A way forward! They will follow me. I understand my limitations, small that they are. I will be a god to them, not to myself. 'In the land of the blind, the one-eyed man is king.'"

Axe chuckled with delight. "Is that how you say it? I heard it differently. 'In the land of the blind, the one-eyed man is considered insane.' And hey, if the shoe fits..."

Conroy's eyes narrowed in hatred. He took a deep breath, fighting for control, before turning to Gunther. "Tell your men to make it hurt. Kill him slowly. Stop and question him when he's gotten a taste of the pain. If he answers truthfully and is helpful, they can be merciful and end it quickly."

He stepped back. Gunther whispered orders to the nearest personal guard, taller than the rest and blond like Gunther. The man was likely an officer.

Conroy leered at Haley, his lust obvious. "Now, I have World War Three to start. But Miss Holly, I will see you later so we can discuss this further. Whether you are actually surprised by your bodyguard or not, I promise we will have many hours of fun together."

Conroy started up the stairs, surrounded by four of the personal guards. "And as for you, Mr. Bodyguard," he called over his shoulder, "Have fun dying!"

56

DEFEAT

Pioneer Park Soccer Stadium
St. John, United States Virgin Islands

Gunther whispered more orders to the guard officer, then hurried up the stairs after Conroy.

Axe considered the ten guards—plus the officer and the four regular guards at the end of Haley's row. He could kill a few, but not all of them. At least Gunther had left. It would have been much worse to suffer while the younger man gloated.

He leaned forward to mutter in Haley's ear. "At least now we know we were right."

She didn't seem to appreciate the humor at all.

So this is how it ends.

The tall guard—the officer—drew a pistol from the small of his back and pointed it at Axe. "Onto the field," he said, with a thicker German accent than Gunther's. "You will fight with honor, answer our questions truthfully, and we will make the end as painless as possible. A bullet in the head if you prefer."

Axe stood still for a moment, meeting the man's gaze, and nodded his acceptance. "Warrior to warrior—I will die with honor."

"If not, you will still die, and she will suffer," he said, nodding to Haley.

"You were ordered to not harm her."

"I was told to keep her safe," he corrected. The man moved two steps up the stairs and gestured with the pistol.

As soon as Axe started forward, the man leveled the gun at Haley.

This complicates matters.

Axe let his shoulders slump in defeat, his hands naturally falling to near his pockets... and the small knife he'd taken from the guard in the jungle.

Two guards waited at the end of the row of seats, their knives not yet drawn. They seemed confident they could handle him without weapons, and that he would go to the field quietly as ordered.

The men need training, all right.

The officer stepped over the rows of chairs until he stood next to Haley. Axe stopped and looked at him. He needed the man to believe he would do anything to save Haley.

"You won't harm her?"

"If you tell what we ask."

"Why don't you ask now, instead of when I'm injured? I may have nothing to lose at that point."

The man nodded in agreement but said, "You might lie."

Axe shrugged. "Ask."

The guard grabbed the back of Haley's neck in his strong hand and squeezed. Haley gasped but didn't cry out. "Are there reinforcements on the way?"

"No," he answered, willing the man to see the truth.

"Who else knows about Pioneer's connection to the EMPs?"

Axe had to think about it for a second. He held up one finger. "The director of a small intelligence analyst group in the United States government, but he demanded proof before passing the information along. Proof I haven't provided yet." He ticked another finger. "Kelton Kellison knows I suspected Conroy, but he is a civilian. He owed me a favor and set this up with his new girlfriend for me. That's it—well, no. My handler, a retired admiral, knows I came here and why. Again, he demanded proof which I didn't have. I convinced Kellison to host a party, invite Pioneer, and the rest fell into place naturally. And I have had no contact with anyone since I arrived."

That's all true. Not the whole truth, but this isn't a court of law.

"Fine. I believe you. But you still have to die."

Axe let himself slump again and nodded, acting resigned to his fate. "Sorry, Miss Holly," he said quietly, turning slowly and walking the final steps toward the two guards.

Haley watched Axe's posture change. He looked defeated, like he'd already given up.

'Sorry, Miss Holly?' What the hell? That's it?

She looked around, frantic to find a way out.

It can't be the end.

But they were unarmed and outnumbered eight to one.

Conroy would win, and the world would burn. As absurd as his plan sounded, the genius had spent years planning it. There would be much more coming than he had revealed. Unless they escaped and put a stop to it, all was lost.

People everywhere would rebel when their governments couldn't protect and care for them. When Conroy offered a way forward, replacements for essential technology, and—most importantly—food and electricity, people would flock to him.

Eventually, Conroy would rule the world.

Haley would either be a forced concubine or would die. If she got lucky, the end would be quick and painless. She shuddered, considering what would happen if Conroy enjoyed her beauty and companionship.

I should have stayed in the office. What was I thinking, trying to be an operator?

She had failed at her first actual mission.

I did my best.

Sometimes our best isn't good enough.

I tried. At least I went for it. Without me, no one would suspect Conroy.

Later in the afternoon, when she and Axe didn't report, wheels would be set in motion. Others would be sent to investigate. Maybe they would succeed where she failed.

Lost in thought, she almost missed her opportunity.

One second, Axe walked down the stairs to the soccer field and his fate. The next, the guard next to him sagged. Axe whirled, his arm a blur. Blood splattered her face. The chief guard next to her flailed at the knife buried to the hilt in his larynx.

It took her only an instant to react.

The gun.

She wrenched the pistol from the man's other hand. He put up little resistance. The knife in his throat meant he'd be dead in a few seconds.

The hours on the range paid off. The gun came up automatically. Her eyes swept the scene. One of the two guards near Axe lay on the ground. The other fell forward, blood spurting from his throat, cut lengthwise with his own knife.

One guard on the step above Axe reacted fast. His knife cleared its sheath as he stepped toward Axe, coming in from his blind spot.

Her eyes focused on the front sight, as Axe had taught her, and squeezed the trigger as the man's mass appeared behind it. A shot to the body pushed him back, and she let him fall without the second body shot or bullet to the head. She had to conserve ammunition, and none of the guards wore body armor.

Axe had breathing room, though more men rushed toward him, knives drawn, both up the stairs and down. He'd be fighting on two fronts.

Haley shot the lead man coming down the stairs as Axe stabbed a man coming up.

Sensing movement behind her, she remembered the two regular guards. Acting on instinct, she dropped to the ground, just in time for one man to miss his attempted flying tackle. He sailed over her. She spun and shot him in the back of the head as he landed. She turned again, still low, and shot his partner in the heart two steps from her.

She lunged backward to keep from being crushed as he fell, stepping on his partner lying dead behind her. The second guard landed on the dead officer.

Four shots.

She didn't know how many rounds the gun held. She hadn't seen more magazines on the officer. It felt like her slimline, concealed-carry pistol at home, but she hadn't time to check the model or the magazine.

Make them count.

She couldn't see the other two regular guards. Standing and leaning left, she saw one crawling along the row behind her, hidden by the chairs. She shot him in the head as his panicked eyes met hers.

That's what you get for sneaking up on me.

There was no time for remorse.

This is life and death, them or me.

She leaned to the right and saw his partner attempting the same approach. He struggled backward as she shot him in the face.

Haley turned, looking for high-value targets. Axe slashed and stabbed at the end of the row of seats, holding his own, spinning to keep the guard on the steps above him at bay before quickly turning back to slash at the one below. The narrow aisle prevented more than one man from each side attacking at a time, but Axe had his hands full.

I can make it easier.

She shot the last man on the stairs above him as Axe finished the one below. "Clear up the stairs," she yelled.

Haley assessed the situation, counting the remaining enemy. She had shot all four regular guards but four men of the personal guard were left. One fought in the aisle below Axe. They traded slashes and thrusts.

Either Axe is tired, or the guard is good. It's taking all Axe has to hold him off.

The last three men were flanking him, climbing over the seats on the far side.

She stepped onto the back of the seat behind her, careful to not slip with the blood from the dead officer coating the bottom of her shoes. She took long steps up, from chair back to chair back, angling for a better shot at the men flanking her partner.

Now she had the angle, but a precarious stance. She fired at the closest man flanking Axe, coming along the row of seats, dropping him with a lucky shot to his chest as she fought for balance.

The next guard leaped over his dead comrade and rushed forward, intent on stabbing Axe.

He's too close.

If she missed now, she'd kill Axe.

If she didn't fire, the man would kill him while he focused on the worthy adversary below him on the stairs. Haley took the shot.

The bullet nearly skimmed Axe's shoulder.

The man staggered, hit in the arm, but didn't stop his charge.

She fired again. Blood spurted from the guard's head and he dropped heavily to the ground.

Peace through superior firepower.

She turned the weapon at the next nearest man moving toward Axe, steadied herself for the difficult shot, and squeezed the trigger.

Click.

The gun was empty.

Do they know?

The man looked at her with a sneer and changed directions, racing toward her.

"Axe!"

She turned and hurried back to her original position, carefully stepping on the seat backs, hoping for a second magazine. The gun had been a game-changer, and with more bullets, they would be free and clear in no time.

Haley slipped and fell, her shoulder hitting a seat hard.

The guard who had sneered continued toward her.

Axe wouldn't be able to get to him in time, even if he hadn't been in his own life-and-death fight.

She had a few seconds. Diving, she flung herself onto the dead guard who lay on top of the officer. She pushed his body to the side enough to feel the front pockets of the dead officer.

Nothing.

Her hands searched frantically for more ammo.

Nothing.

The cargo pockets!

She didn't risk a look at the man coming down the aisle above her. He had to be almost here.

The cargo pockets were empty.

I'm going to die.

In desperation, she grabbed the handle of the knife protruding from the officer's throat and rolled onto her side, both hands thrusting blindly upwards.

Her attacker fell on her, his knife swiping her stomach as she buried hers into his mouth.

He fell on top of her, crushing her beneath his bulk.

57

ATTACK

Pioneer Park Soccer Stadium
St. John, United States Virgin Islands

Axe slashed the forehead of the guard in front of him. Blood gushed into the man's eyes, blinding him for a second.

It was the opening Axe needed. He stepped forward, blocked the man's knife arm with his forearm, and thrust his own knife up, under the ribs, and into the man's heart. Stepping back, he pulled out the knife as the man fell to the ground and died.

Haley yelled his name. Axe turned in time to see a guard land on top of her.

"Haley!"

He ran toward her, fearing the worst.

Axe rolled the man off her, expecting to see her dead.

Free of the crushing weight, Haley sucked in a deep, gasping breath.

"Are you hurt?"

Haley shook her head, looking at her stomach. Her shirt was ripped and a small amount of blood seeped through. "I don't think it's deep."

Axe tore the shirt more, careful to not hurt her, and confirmed her hunch. The man's blade must have been moving to the side as he dove onto her, because the wound was only superficial, little more than a deep scratch.

"Your shooting saved my ass," Axe said as he offered her a hand up.

"Our asses. And I wouldn't have gotten the gun without the knife to the throat of the officer. Nice job, by the way. You're going to have to show me how to do that."

"Once we get out of this, you've got yourself a deal." Turning to practical matters, he asked, "No more ammunition?"

Haley looked at the dead officer as she stood, brushing herself off.

"None. Why only one ten-round magazine?"

"My guess is the same reason prison guards aren't issued weapons: too easy to be overpowered and have them used by the inmates. Conroy would be concerned about a revolt."

"But the people on the island want to be here."

"Even more reason not to have guns around. But I guarantee they have weapons. My guess is they are unlocking the armory right now."

They both looked toward the players' entrance tunnel on the field level. Ten more black-clad guards, knives drawn, ran toward them.

"Grab an extra knife, put it in your waistband. You never know."

They armed themselves with two knives each, then stepped over the bodies around them to get to the stairs.

The group of guards was only fifty yards away and closing fast.

"We can't take on ten more with knives, not even with the coaching you gave me last month."

Axe started up the stairs, vaulting three steps at a time. Haley kept up, her long legs matching Axe's leaps.

"I've got a plan."

The guards reached the bottom of the stairs he and Haley were climbing and started up after them. Axe slowed down, taking the stairs one at a time.

"Hurry!" Haley hissed.

"No, we need to let them close the distance."

The bright sun glared around them, reflecting off the blue metal seats of the stadium.

They reached the concourse level and Axe glanced back.

Perfect.

He gestured for Haley to run next to him and took off toward the dark tunnel leading back to the concession area.

The guards—all men, all angry at the death of their comrades—were gaining on them.

"As soon as we're through the tunnel, break left. I'll go right. Our eyes will adjust to the darkness, but they won't have time. When they come through, run at them, slashing. Just like I taught you. After that, follow me along the upper walkway. Hit and run, got it?"

Then they were into the darkness. Axe broke right, watching Haley go left around the corner. He caught his breath, grateful for the momentary pause.

His eyes adjusted quickly. He drew the second knife, showing it to Haley, hidden behind her corner. She followed his lead and held both knives, ready.

The slap of shoes along the stairs changed tone as the guards moved onto the concourse and rushed toward them unsuspectingly.

He locked eyes with Haley, gauging the perfect time.

Wait... wait...

He nodded at her and launched himself around the corner.

His right hand slashed at the face of the first guard, connecting on his right cheek. Blood spurted, but Axe didn't slow down. He swung his left arm, connecting with the throat of the next man, then he slashed the third guard with his right hand, missing vital areas but cutting deeply into his upper arm.

Axe moved forward, a silent, deadly machine. The fourth guard tried to slow down, sensing or seeing what had happened to the three in front of him. He tripped, falling backward. His quick reaction and clumsiness allowed him to slip under Axe's slash, though the crack of his head on the concrete sounded worse than the damage Axe would have done with a knife.

The guards had formed into two groups—as Axe had hoped. The first five, quickest up the stairs, had come Axe's direction, but the next were on Haley's side of the large hallway.

The last guard on Axe's side got a special treat: Axe had time to stab him in the stomach, then slash his throat. He collapsed in a heap.

Haley had reached the end of her group and was running toward him. He led the way back through the opening into the dazzling sunshine, and onto the landing that ran around the stadium at the top of the seats.

"Hurry!" Axe sprinted as fast as he could. Haley fell a few steps behind. "We're going back around to ambush them again," he whispered, hoping only Haley would hear. "They'll now turn to follow us, but they'll be more cautious. We hit and run again, but slower. Do more damage as long as you're not at risk. Remember the best parts of the body to slash and stab. Then run back down the interior hallway."

They turned into the next dark hallway to the interior concourse. Axe slowed. He put a finger to his lips and advanced quietly, gesturing for Haley to move behind him.

They wouldn't get caught in an ambush.

At the corner of the hallway and concourse, Axe paused, ready. Blood dripped from both knives.

He crouched low and stuck his head slowly around the corner, allowing only one eye to poke out before ducking smoothly back. The corridor was empty, but he heard cries of pain one hundred feet away in the next hallway.

He hurried silently down the concourse, keeping close to the wall, Haley on his heels. This was the most dangerous time. If one of the wounded guards dragged himself around the corner to safety, or took the concourse to flank them, they would be in another head-to-head battle. Even wounded, ten men—or nine, if the one Axe stabbed was out of the fight—would overwhelm them.

They either weren't well trained or well led, however. None had thought to put a man on rearguard or send a few to flank them down the concourse.

Once more, Axe gathered intel by crouching low and slowly glancing around the corner, careful to make no sudden movements that would draw the eye.

In the darkness of the tunnel, he saw one man flat on the ground, blood pooling around him.

The one I stabbed.

Another sat against the near wall, knees up, head in his hands.

The one who fell.

Two from Haley's group sat against the far wall, their shirts off, tearing them into bandages to stop the flow of blood from deep slashes on their stomachs.

Excellent work. One dead, three mostly out of the fight.

The other seven were stacked up along the same wall Axe leaned around, facing the field, preparing for a charge.

Axe pulled his head back and put his mouth next to Haley's ear to whisper. "Take care of the three who are down—along the far wall— when I start on the line. Slow and quiet. We'll pick them off until they notice, then run back this way."

He didn't wait for a reply. He knew she'd hold her own.

They moved silently around the corner. The two along the wall were too busy with their wounds to look up, and the man with his head in his hands didn't budge as they crept past him.

Axe snaked his arm around the seventh man—at the back of the stack—and slashed his throat. After lowering him gently to the ground, he moved to the next man and stabbed him in the back of the neck, severing his spine.

The fifth man turned at the noise, just in time for Axe to stab him in the throat.

The fourth man turned at the commotion and yelled in surprise. Axe stabbed him through the stomach, under the ribs, and into his heart.

The remaining three turned as one. It took only an instant for them to assess the situation. They charged.

"Run!"

Axe turned back toward the darkened inner concourse, noting two dead men on the opposite wall.

The man who had his head in his hands now slumped. Blood spurted from the gaping wound in his neck.

Haley was nowhere to be seen.

In an instant, Axe knew her plan. He ran down the middle of the hall, then swung wide right, taking the turn back the way he and Haley had come.

A third ambush. I should have thought of it.

The three men pursued him, driven—and reassured—they could see him in the gloom.

As he turned the corner, he saw Haley out of the corner of his eye, hidden against the wall, ready to leap out.

"Come on, you cowards," Axe yelled. He spun and crouched low, waving both knives. As they rounded the corner, all three guards slowed, focused solely on him. They separated, forming a line in front of him.

Haley calmly stalked from behind, stepping close to the two men on her right, and stabbed them both at the same time in the kidneys. She pulled the knives out, ready for the next move.

The guards grunted in surprise and turned right into Haley's slashes to their throats. They stood, blood spurting, dropping their knives as they grabbed their throats, trying to stop the blood.

Well done!

The last man was too distracted by the fate of his friends to see Axe's knife as it penetrated his heart.

Haley was covered in the blood of several guards and had a thin red cut visible on her stomach. "You did an amazing job with little training. You okay?" He wondered if she would lose it now that the danger had passed.

She wiped blood from her face, smearing it more than cleaning herself. "Fine. What about you?"

A few shallow slashes had found their mark. "No problem, nothing critical." He looked around, thinking. "Next moves? We're obviously blown—both of us now, I'd guess, unless they didn't report in."

"And no hope of help."

"None. Since the cell phone had no service, we have to continue to assume we're on our own."

"We have to stop Conroy… but just the two of us?"

"What about…" He was reluctant to use Cody's name, just in case they were under surveillance or civilians were hiding nearby.

"Ember?"

Axe thought for a second and got the reference to Cody's fire-red hair.

Perfect name.

"Last I saw him was at the dock."

"No worries. On our own, as usual. Let's go. We can figure out a plan on the way."

Axe led the way toward the stairs, which would take them to the parking lot, where they'd have to steal an SUV. Out of habit, he pushed open the heavy metal door all the way to the wall to block any potential enemy hiding behind it, waiting to ambush him.

"They'll know we're coming," Haley said. "We can't outrun radio. Could—"

A grunt of pain interrupted Haley as the door stopped well short of the back wall.

Axe spun as it swung back toward him, revealing Kim, their tour guide. Her face was a mask of fury. "You traitor!" She screamed, pushing past Axe to get at Haley, who had come through the door behind him.

Axe tackled her as she went past him, taking her down an instant before her hands, flexed into claws, could rake Haley's face.

She landed hard but immediately twisted and scratched Axe.

"How could you betray him?" she screamed with a glance at Haley, spittle flying from her mouth.

She fought with the strength of four men, hitting Axe repeatedly as he wrestled her.

Finally, Axe had enough. He grabbed her arm, twisted it behind her back with her fingers pointed toward her head, pinning her to the ground. The pressure on her arm and shoulder would be intense and knock the fight out of her.

She stopped for a second, then screamed, a combination of rage and anguish, as she snapped her own shoulder so she could roll over.

Axe had never heard of anyone—from warrior to the most fanatical terrorist—taking the extreme pain to get out of the position.

The woman got to her feet before Axe could, shocking him. She rushed Haley, one arm dangling uselessly.

Kim ran straight into Haley's knife.

Kim's mouth gaped like a fish, the realization of the situation clear in her eyes.

"I love him," she whispered as she fell back, sliding off the knife. She tumbled down the stairs. Her body came to rest on the first landing, back against the wall, neck at an unusual angle. Blood seeped from her stomach, saturating her shirt, and dripped onto the floor.

"Haley?" Axe looked at her as she stared at the body below them.

She's losing it.

"Haley, come on. Let's go. Put whatever you're feeling in a box."

Her right hand still gripped the knife with white knuckles, so he gently took her left hand and led her down the stairs. "Don't look," he said as they got to the landing, turned, and went down the next flight.

He let her go ahead, risking another ambush, to step back and dip into Kim's right pants pocket, coming out with the key fob for the orange SUV. He hurried to catch up to Haley, mindlessly walking down the flights of stairs.

He got to her and took her hand again. She didn't resist.

"Stay with me, Haley. Self-defense. She was a zealot. We need to focus on saving the world now, right?"

The parking lot was deserted, the audience having departed for a day of leisure, as ordered by their guru. Their SUV was the only vehicle in the parking lot.

Axe opened the door for Haley. She got in, still clenching the knife. He had to pull the second knife from her belt before she sat and risked cutting herself.

He hurried around to the driver's side, got in, and started the engine.

Should I drop her off at the villa? I can't take her with me in this state—she's a liability.

"Haley. Haley!"

Ice from the cooler.

Kim had offered them cold bottled water or sodas from a cooler in the rear of the vehicle each time she drove. Axe hopped out and ran to the back, got two bottles of water and two candy bars from a small shelf in the large cooler, and scooped up a handful of ice from the bottom.

Back in the front, he put the water and candy bars in the center console and gently worked the knife out of Haley's hand, replacing it with ice cubes. "Hold this, Haley."

Her body jolted as she gripped the ice tightly. Her eyes flicked to her hands. She opened them and looked at the ice, perplexed. "What?"

"It's ice. How does it feel?"

She hesitated a second, struggling to find the word. "Cold." One hand dumped the ice into the other, then she wiped the empty hand on her pants, leaving a smear of blood behind. She repeated the process, cleaning and drying the other hand. Finally, she looked up at him, her eyes confused. "What happened?"

"Nothing, you checked out for a minute or two."

"Why? Oh…"

Her eyes rolled back in her head.

"Stay with me! Feel the ice. It's cold. How else could you describe it?"

She blinked several times, looking at her hands holding the melting ice cubes. She took a breath, fighting for focus. "Wet."

"Good. Exactly right."

Haley looked at him, and he nodded. "That's it, stay with me. Listen carefully." He leaned forward and whispered so quietly she would struggle to hear him. "Are you listening?"

She nodded slowly, concentrating on him instead of fading back into shock.

Haley's mind floated, threatening to take her away again.

"Focus on my voice," Axe said from far away. She could barely hear him.

"I'm here." Haley felt weightless. All she wanted to do was close her eyes and check out. Away from here, away from the pain of… what? She struggled to remember.

Why am I in this SUV, holding ice?

Axe was saying something to her, but she tuned him out.

What happened?

The memory slammed into her conscious mind again. Holding the knife as it penetrated the woman's body...

Kim. Sweet, friendly Kim.

Locking eyes with her as she died. The loss of not only life, but of love.

Her love for Conroy.

The woman's grotesquely twisted body on the landing, spilling blood, her sightless eyes staring into the distance.

Haley dropped the ice and clawed at the door as Axe said more words she didn't understand. She leaned out, vomiting onto the hot asphalt of the parking lot. After a few moments, she felt Axe's hand on her shoulder, holding her steady as she dry heaved.

She pulled herself together, wiping her mouth with the back of her hand. She sat up and stared out the SUV's front window at the empty parking lot and the stunningly beautiful blue sky.

Axe handed her a bottle of water, already open, and she sipped. Sparingly at first, then thirstily.

Next to her, Axe opened his own water and drank before tearing the end off a candy bar wrapper and handing it to her. "You back?"

"Yes, sorry. What happened?"

"You went into shock. Your brain couldn't process what happened, so it shut down to protect you."

"My hands are cold."

"Ice from the cooler. I put it in your hands. The unexpected sensation brought you back."

"And I threw up..."

"Your brain reacted to the experience. Don't worry about it. Happens a lot. With warriors, stressors are piled on little by little starting in basic training. The mind and body learn to deal with them over time until most people are ready when they're eventually thrust into a combat role. You've been dropped into the deep end of the pool a couple of times now. But you've learned to swim well."

Haley nibbled at the candy bar, afraid it would come back up, but her body knew how much it needed a kick. She wolfed the rest of it down in a few bites.

"Hey, you did good back there. You saved my life. Both of our lives. Never forget that. Now, put the memories and feelings in a box. Seriously, take whatever images and thoughts you just had. Imagine boxing them up. You can think about it later, once we're out of danger."

She put her hand to her forehead.

There's also a dead guy in my house.

"Try it. It works."

"I will. I just remembered I have the dead body of a guy in my chest freezer back home."

She laughed and cried at the same time, releasing the stress. Her life had gone in a bizarre direction in the past year. Finally, she got control of herself. "Sorry, not very funny."

"No. But however you deal with the stress, go for it. Some guys punch things. Others try to hide their tears. A lot get very drunk, relive the event, bragging about their exploits. They either bullshit about how brave they were or tell the truth about how terrifying it was. They wake up in the morning, hungover, feeling like shit physically but mentally and emotionally much better. Stronger. There are many ways of dealing with the feelings."

"Let's add a few of them to the list of must-dos once we make it through this."

"You got it."

"What now?"

"Now we attack." Axe put the SUV in gear and drove toward the parking lot exit.

Attack? Haley took a long, steadying breath.

I just had to be a field agent, didn't I?

58

VIRUS

When the security guard picked up Bec leaving the stadium, she knew her life was over. The guard at the Center must have recognized her and reported in before chasing her.

And with Pioneer's speech this morning, the time had come for the next step in his crazy plan. He wouldn't allow a traitor in his midst to go unpunished.

But she had been politely escorted through security, into the Center building. She carefully hid her relief.

Maybe I'm not going to die yet.

Many guards in and out of the Center had guns, which surprised her. She didn't even know there were guns on the island.

I bet they've caught Haley and Axe and think reinforcements could arrive any minute.

Two guards stood at the main door to the command center room. One from Pioneer's personal guard team held his finger near the trigger of his rifle and eyed her coldly.

The other she recognized. He stood at parade rest in brand new brown khaki shorts and a button-up short-sleeve shirt, a neutral look on his sunburned face. The color competed with his short red hair.

Cody. Who made a mistake and allowed a new guy up here?

Bec stopped as the guard escorting her told the black-clad guard that she was the hacker requested by Pioneer.

Take a chance. If this is the end, at least I'll go out on a bang. Maybe he'll think of me and wonder what happened.

"Cody, right?"

The poor guy looked at her in surprise but nodded.

"I did your background check. Welcome to the island."

He nodded and was about to speak when the door clicked open. She smiled at him and walked inside.

He's cute.

Gunther and the twins sat at workstations, typing fervently. It came to her in an instant.

The twins. They're the hackers building on my work.

She should have known. All these years of people judging her by her androgynous look, making assumptions, and she went and did the same.

I thought they were dumb models. My bad.

Pioneer, as always, stood on his platform. But this morning he paced. She couldn't tell if he was worried or excited.

Tina hurried toward her, smiling happily, her eyes wide with excitement. She wore one of the long, loose, frumpy dresses she favored. "Get in here! The world is about to change—and we're part of it!"

Bec could guess what her words meant.

Good news: I'm not going to die. Bad news: everyone else is, apparently.

Pioneer saw her coming into the room and nodded at her. He glanced at the closing door. "Send in a guard, as well."

The personal guard with the rifle stood his post and nodded for Cody to come into the room.

"Approach—both of you," he said. Bec walked toward the raised platform, less certain she was in the clear. Cody walked behind her.

Tina started forward with her, then—with a disappointed glance at Bec and Cody—realized Pioneer wasn't speaking to her. She returned to her workstation.

"Names." Pioneer stood directly in front of them, legs spread, arms crossed across his thick chest, staring intently at them.

"Bec. Rebecca, actually, but I go by Bec." She tried hard not to sound nervous but didn't think she pulled it off.

"Cody, sir."

"Bec." He said the name slowly, staring at her. "You're a hard worker. Are you prepared to go above and beyond? To help usher in a new era?"

Tell the truth. I am prepared to go above and beyond.

"Yes, Pioneer."

Though my version of a new era is different from his, I bet.

It's easy for a lie to sound like the truth if you can interpret the question in your own way.

Conroy nodded with a small smile. "And Cody. Will you follow my orders to the letter?"

"With pleasure, Pioneer."

"Excellent," Conroy said, clapping his hands. "Bec, go to your workstation and follow Tina's orders. Cody, guard Tina and Bec. Make sure no harm comes to them as they do their important work."

"Yes, Pioneer," they said at the same time, and she walked to her workstation. Cody took up a position behind her, to the right, between her and Tina's desks, facing the large screen on the front wall, which displayed a map of the world.

There has to be a way to stop Conroy... or at least slow him down long enough for Haley and Axe to do something.

She'd have to play it by ear and figure it out, all under the watchful gaze of Tina, Cody, and Pioneer.

Tina turned and explained her assignment, leaving Bec with a sinking feeling.

I should have left the island months ago.

Stefan paced the small raised platform, ignoring the throne-like chair, clenching his tablet in his hands, unopened. He gazed longingly at the hand scanner each time he passed it.

"What is taking so long?"

At the left edge of the platform, Gunther clicked and typed.

"Pioneer, I am confirming the reports coming from South Korea. All assets are not in place yet."

"What percentage are ready?" Now that Stefan had moved up the timetable, he wanted to get on with it. He needed to watch the world burn—the sooner, the better. If the authorities were actually on their way, doing the most damage in the least amount of time would be the only way to come out on top. He could have easily checked the numbers and reports on his tablet, but hearing updates made him feel the power of his position.

"Sixty-five percent."

Stefan ran calculations in his head that would make a computer stumble.

Not enough.

"Continue."

He turned to the twins, side by side at workstations on the main floor. They normally did their hacking work from a small private office in his residence wing, but he had ordered them to work preparing the next round of attacks. "Report."

Anna turned and shook her head slightly. They could speak—he had overheard a whispered conversation between them one night when they thought he was asleep. But they had spoken to him only a handful of times in the years they had been with him. The only time they made noise was in his bed.

He turned next to the mousy woman who had shared his bed many times, yet never given him a child. What was her name? Tina.

"Tina, report."

She looked at him with an adoring smile from her workstation on the left side of the room. She seemed excited to be part of the unfolding adventure. While she had long known of his overall plans for world domination, the exact methods had come as a pleasant surprise to her, as had his order to come into the Center and help this morning.

"The assets in Taiwan are reporting. Most are unprepared and need time to get into position. One questioned the timeline, Pioneer. He said he could not be ready until next week as originally instructed." She paused, eyes flicking away nervously at reporting bad news. "He is on vacation with his family. 'One last time,' he said."

"Tell him to return from his vacation immediately and pray he avoids my wrath."

"Yes, Pioneer."

"Estimated timeline for..." he did more mental calculations, "eighty-two percent readiness?" He needed the EMPs to destroy all the semiconductor fabrication plants and all the chips already manufactured. A world without hope for electronics would be his for the taking, given his stockpile of chips and the machinery to make them.

Tina clicked on her screen and took several seconds to think about the answer. "Several hours, Pioneer. A large group is unprepared but moving quickly. A small group is ready. They have the most important targets. But I estimate," she leaned toward the screen, concentrating intently, "thirty-seven percent in an hour. However, at only thirty-seven percent preparedness, the small group would take out sixty-one percent of the highest value targets."

Interesting. A very intelligent young woman. I have chosen well to bring her close to me.

"Understood."

Stefan focused on the hacker with short, messy dark hair, a baggy black t-shirt, and the muscular arms of a swimmer or paddler. He only knew she was a woman from the way she moved—she had a grace that few men had. When he first spoke with her, she seemed relieved.

She must be happy to finally be admitted into the inner circle.

"You. Bec," he remembered.

My people are ready for the next step. All they need is to be led.

"The computer viruses on the top twenty-five list are nearly all activated, Pioneer," Bec reported. "I only have a few more to go. After that, as instructed, I will work on the next batch. In a few minutes, the first group will be ready for your approval."

"My approval comes from my hand. The Hand of God." He held his hand up to her and gestured to the scanner in front of him.

"Yes, Pioneer." She nodded obediently and returned to her workstation.

Bec almost gagged.

'The Hand of God.' What a load of crap.

She did the job assigned to her, but not as fast as she could have. To ensure the virus would not be discovered, it was hidden deep within the security software installed on their clients' computers. Tina had shown her how to manually unpack and enable it. Next, a final coded instruction was sent to launch the virus.

Each system had to be done manually. According to the instructions on the master spreadsheet in a hidden tab Tina unlocked for her, two inner circle hackers would have spent a full day preparing them before Pioneer initialized the attacks. Instead, today it was her job alone.

Tina's screen showed activation messages being sent to what must be terrorist cells around the world. And the twins... Bec couldn't see their screens across the room.

What are they up to?

She leaned closer to her screen, the picture of a dedicated, hard worker. But she worked as slowly as she could without being obvious.

Her mind spun, considering and discarding ways she could disrupt the operation.

The computer viruses don't matter. They won't end the world.

The EMPs, on the other hand, needed her attention.

Unfortunately, Tina called up the assets and prepared the EMPs, not her.

It makes sense. I'm not inner circle, and I'm more of a hacker than a manager. Plus, I've never slept with Pioneer. If I had only known... I still wouldn't have done it.

Was there anything she could do?

Bec drilled into a computer from the first batch of twenty-five targets, a non-military system of the government of India. She had done the initial hacking herself. Once she had found a way in, months ago, the sales team had converted the governmental department into a client of the cybersecurity software.

The results inside the system were the same as the others she'd done so far. A small kernel of the cybersecurity software had a hidden area containing a cleverly designed virus. Once unleashed, it would automatically hack its way into every other computer attached to it, whether physically or over a network. It would keep going, endlessly searching out weaknesses to exploit. Along the way, it would encrypt all data and prevent access to it.

It was the ultimate Trojan horse. The virus already had full access as a part of the security suite.

There would be no stopping it.

In minutes, thousands of computers would be held hostage by the virus.

The computers would be piles of useless junk without an unlock code supplied by the Movement.

Bec flashed to a news report she'd seen from Friday about the Port of Rotterdam falling to a sophisticated ransomware hack.

That was us. We did it for some reason. And now I'm about to do the same all over the world.

As she finished the Indian government system, she looked at her spreadsheet. There were two hundred twenty-five systems on her list, split into groups of twenty-five. Each connected to thousands of other computers.

The networked world as we know it is about to end.

She had two choices: figure out an approach in the digital realm, her specialty, or do something physical.

Could I shut down the power in here? Or...

Bec glanced at Pioneer, still pacing impatiently.

Could I kill him?

She'd be willing to try, to save the world, but between Cody, Gunther, and Pioneer himself, she would never succeed.

How dedicated is Cody? He's new...

She clicked into the next system. The going was slower as she had to follow the navigation instructions to find the hidden area containing the Trojan horse virus.

As she typed, her mind focused on her work, and her subconscious clicked in.

Cody. The only new person allowed on St. John lately. The rest of the new pilgrims were stuck across the bay on St. Thomas.

He looked sweet and innocent, but he'd been in the Army. He came from the Washington, D.C. area.

Could it be?

If Pioneer knew how recently Cody had arrived, he wouldn't have allowed the guard to enter. In the morning's chaos, someone had dropped the ball and allowed a brand new recruit to enter the inner sanctum.

Instead of typing in the instructions to launch the virus, she entered two names, hoping her luck held.

"Haley and Axe."

She stretched and looked back, smiling as she caught Cody's eye, and made the tiniest motion with her head, indicating her screen. Cody looked. His eyes widened, then looked at her in surprise, which he quickly hid behind a stoic look. He nodded.

I was right! He's with them.

Bec had an ally, though she still didn't have a plan.

Turning back to her screen, she typed again.

"What can we do?"

She erased it after a second and entered the proper command to launch the ransomware virus on yet another unsuspecting security client.

After pulling up the next target, she risked another glance back. Cody caught her eye immediately and mouthed one word. "Wait."

He seemed confident in the abilities of his friends.

We have no weapons and we're outnumbered. I hope Haley and Axe can figure something out, because I'm going as slowly as I can here.

An idea hit her. She scrolled up the spreadsheet to the third line, the computer system of the United States Department of Education. The summary next to it claimed it was the smallest of the cabinet-level departments. Its system connected to most of the other non-military computers of the USA's government. Tina had successfully hacked it months ago, and the department had become a client.

Working quickly, she first cut the listing and pasted it to position number twenty-six.

Next, she worked her way into the system and deleted the instructions she'd inserted earlier. She backed out, leaving no trace she'd been inside.

It will ensure the USA is hit in the second wave. Maybe that'll buy us some time.

There wouldn't be an easy way to explain how the high-priority United States system mysteriously moved from position three to twenty-six, but she could plead ignorance. They might suspect her, but in the hustle and bustle of destroying the world, it might be overlooked.

Cody stood behind Bec, watching her screen for other clandestine communications.

She's on our side!

He looked around the room. No one had noticed their exchange.

But what should he do now? Called to guard the main building, then invited into the inner sanctum. For a few moments, Pioneer stood directly in front of him. Cody could have taken him down, maybe broken his neck. The Army had trained him in hand-to-hand combat. He'd never had the opportunity to use it, but he knew the technique.

The opportunity had slipped past. He was definitely not undercover material.

So he just went along to get along, followed orders, and kept his mouth shut as much as possible.

Axe and Haley will come. Waiting makes the most sense, right?

Could he make a move? Clearly, Pioneer had to be stopped.

Gunther would kick my butt. With him here, I can't do a thing.

Weren't Haley and Axe the professionals? They'd told him to get in—and he'd done it. He was here and ready for orders.

If they don't come soon, I'll make a move on my own. It's time I stepped up.

59

PATROLS

The double doors to the Center were thick glass. The rest of the building was solid concrete, a nod to the hurricanes which hit the island every few years.

Two alert guards with rifles in hand stood outside the doors. Four more patrolled the front parking lot, fingers near the triggers of their guns.

All wore the black tactical pants and t-shirts of the well-trained personal guard detail.

Axe lay in deep cover two feet into the jungle. Haley lay next to him. They faced the right corner of the building, allowing them to see the front, including the parking lot, and the side. The spot was safest in terms of cover, but riskiest because the enemy might realize what a great observation spot it was. Would they patrol the inner jungle here, or merely focus on the perimeter?

Axe and Haley froze as yet another guard—this time in the khaki uniform of shorts and button-down shirt—passed them. It looked like ten or twelve men walked the area next to the jungle, constantly going around the cleared, bare area circling the building in a never-ending patrol. Without moving his head, Axe could see the man who just passed them, one further ahead, and another following behind.

Too bad the regular guards are unarmed.

One M4 would remove all obstacles.

Instead, Axe reviewed his options. Time was of the essence. Who knew what hell Conroy was unleashing on the world as they tried to figure out a way in?

Doug and the security crew on the boat wouldn't worry about them until Haley failed to check in at the agreed-upon twenty-four-hour mark this afternoon. Neither would Nalen. Help would arrive too late to save the world.

And by now, word would have reached Conroy that he and Haley had escaped, leaving dozens of dead guards behind, along with one of Conroy's lovers.

A stealth approach?

He could grab a guard, quickly change into his uniform, and resume his patrol. But what then? Walk to the door? The guards most likely knew each other. In daylight, it wouldn't work.

I need a distraction.

He could use Haley. They hadn't had time to clean up as they rushed the SUV up the steep roads to a pullout near a hiking path. He expected roadblocks and hadn't dared drive any closer to the Center building.

Bushwhacking through the thick jungle left them both sweaty, dirty, and covered with scratches. Combined with the blood of the guards, both he and Haley looked like they'd been to hell and back.

If Conroy doesn't yet know she's with me, Haley could stagger out of the jungle toward the front door.

With all the blood, the guards wouldn't see her as a threat right away. Besides, Conroy wanted her alive, whether she was a traitor or not.

Then what? I play super soldier and attack the building armed with only two knives?

He thought of brave men in World War Two who rushed machine-gun nests with no hope of surviving to give their brothers a chance to continue the mission.

He slowly turned his head to meet Haley's eye. She looked at him expectantly, believing in his ability to formulate a working plan.

I'm out, kid. I've got nothing.

Axe looked once again at the layout of the guards, hoping a plan of attack would come to him. Another guard approached slowly to their right, looking more carefully at the jungle than the previous ones. He stopped fifteen feet from them and turned to fully face the trees and undergrowth.

A red dot blinked for an instant on the guard's right arm, easily seen against the brown khaki shirt.

The red light blinked several more times.

That's Morse code!

Axe had learned it years before and never used it. He concentrated on deciphering the flashes as the guard walked closer.

D—O—U—G.

What the hell is Doug doing here?

He must have decided to provide backup and infiltrated the island during the night.

He saw us as we crept through the jungle but couldn't risk getting our attention. He must have tracked us during our approach or guessed where we'd be.

Doug would be up a tree, far enough back to be invisible from the guards, but with a clear angle to shoot through the jungle. Facing the front—and only—door, but able to also cover one side.

This changes everything.

The guard gave up his search and turned back to his patrol, coming quickly closer to where Haley and he lay.

Axe froze again, his gaze focused down so the guard wouldn't see his eyes, and went into stealth mode.

The guard slowed more, two feet to Axe's right, and poked into the underbrush. Axe and Haley were far enough back to not be stepped on, hiding in the thicker bushes and trees past where the man directed his focus. But if they caught his eye, the opportunity for stealth would be gone.

At least Mad Dog will take him out and give me a chance to rush the doors.

For thirty tense seconds, the man swept his feet back and forth in the grass.

Satisfied, or at least having proved he took his job seriously, the man walked on.

Approaching on foot is suicide.

Could he hook up with Doug in the jungle and get a weapon?

No. Mad Dog had found an ideal spot, likely before dawn. Getting to him in daylight would be too risky for them both.

An idea came to Axe in a flash. It would be unexpected and cause confusion.

And might get Haley killed, followed quickly by me.

But it would be their best shot at gaining entry into the building.

He slid his hand forward through the thick jungle hedgerow and as far into the open as he dared. Within seconds, the red aiming dot flashed on the back of his hand.

Perfect.

Using hand gestures Doug would easily understand, Axe communicated the basics of his plan. When done, the red dot flashed on his hand.

Message understood.

With that, Axe carefully pulled his arm back and nodded to Haley for them both to move further into the jungle. He would explain once they were away from the patrolling guards.

She's not going to like it.

They would need a lot of luck, a clean vehicle, and guts to pull off his audacious plan.

60

KOREA

Bec couldn't delay any longer. She could have finished fifteen minutes earlier but stalled, faking confusion about activating the virus in a few of the systems. But even Tina could have done the work by now, so her time was up.

"Pioneer, excuse me, but the top twenty-five systems are ready to execute. How do I transmit it to your station?"

Tina popped up and came to her computer, leaning next to Bec to access the keyboard. "I'll give her access, Pioneer."

She input a string of digits Bec couldn't follow into a command line.

Administrator rights. She has full access.

A window appeared, showing an active connection to various other terminals in the room. "If you leave your desk, or don't use it for two minutes, it will automatically log you out and I'll have to get you back in," Tina whispered. "Security. He's brilliant, isn't he?"

"Absolutely," Bec smiled, faking enthusiasm.

Tina supervised as Bec sent command and control of the prepared hacks to Pioneer's hand scanner.

Without the hand scan, nothing would happen. *Clever. Only he can launch the attack. He's in complete control.*

Gunther grunted at his workstation and nodded to Pioneer. "It is ready." He changed the display on the giant screen on the front wall to a map of the world.

"My friends," Pioneer began, as he did all his speeches. He looked at the twins, Gunther, Tina, Cody, and Bec. "This launch will be the first strike against the tyranny of governments. These initial computer systems will infect other government systems connected to them, radiating out in a glorious wave. In a few days, every major government will beg me for relief, which I will gladly provide, as long as they give me what I desire."

He ceremoniously raised his hand and brought it slowly to the scanner. Its light flashed green.

On the world map, twenty-five points flashed yellow, then turned green. Immediately, several of the points grew larger.

India, Pakistan, Afghanistan, Spain, Italy, then more, each growing as the virus infiltrated other systems.

Will they notice the United States isn't being hit?

Pioneer beamed with pleasure and pumped his fist into the air.

"Now the next twenty-five, please, Bec," Tina whispered before returning to her station. Tina, too, was excited by the display.

No one noticed Bec's surprise at how quickly the virus spread.

"Of course," she said, turning to her screen and scrolling down the spreadsheet.

She had spared the USA from the first strike. Did she dare risk moving the Department of Education again, from twenty-six to fifty-one?

Haley and Axe, if you're out there, please hurry.

Stefan reveled in the historic moment. He was reshaping the world.

Gunther turned to him with another of his thin, humorless smiles. "Pioneer, the next stage is ready for you. South Korea."

"Finally!" Should he make another speech?

The faithful deserve to know what is happening. They will tell the story of today. It will be legendary.

"My friends," he began. "With my next directive, much of South Korea will lose all its power and electronics. Some of their more secure military equipment will remain online, of course. But the civilians will be in the dark, and the North Koreans will easily overrun what military units remain capable of fighting. This, in addition to shutting down Iran yesterday, opens the world to war."

Paving the way to my ascension.

Stefan stepped forward once again and pressed his hand to the scanner. The light flashed green. He felt the thrill of achievement course through him. Because of his action, thousands would die and millions would suffer. And days from now, the survivors would turn to him and his leadership.

I will show them the way.

He thrust his fist into the air once again.

I am the way.

61

ATTACK

The White House Situation Room
Washington, D.C.

"Mr. President," an aide called, unable to contain his concern. "We're getting reports of mass cyber attacks against computers throughout the world."

"Anything against us?" James asked, fighting off exhaustion. He'd barely slept the night before. Strategizing about the conflict in the Middle East had occupied every waking second since his early morning briefing about Conroy, his Movement, and the thousands of EMP devices scattered around the world.

"Not that we can see, sir. But the attack appears to be spread by a computer virus."

Lucky break?

He had a terrible thought. "Do any of our systems use Conroy's AI cybersecurity services?"

The aide looked thoughtful for a moment, then shook his head. "None of the major ones, sir, but maybe..." He picked up a phone in front of him, his face showing all that James needed to know.

We could be next.

The man hung up and turned back to him. "Sir, a relatively small system run by the Department of Education signed up for the company's service. They report no unusual activity. Apparently the software is doing its job well."

I might get burned for this, but I trust Haley's judgment.

"Take it offline immediately."

"Sir?"

"Do whatever it takes, including unplugging the damn computers, or network, or pulling out hard drives, but take the Department of Education system offline. If it's literally impossible, not just inconvenient or difficult, then disconnect it from every other government computer network."

"Mr. President, I... I don't know if it's even possible."

"You heard me. Get it done, even it means sending Marines in to rip power cords out of walls. I believe Conroy's software may be a Trojan horse."

"Yes, sir." The man reached for his phone again to handle it.

James didn't know all the ins and outs of computers, but he'd studied the Trojan War and knew to distrust Conroy. If Conroy had his hands on a government system, no matter how small, he might be able to access much more than allowed.

Not on my watch.

"Sir!" an aide of the Secretary of Defense shouted. The Secretary had excused himself a few minutes before to use the restroom, leaving the man to stand in for him. He wouldn't be in the room if not an accomplished professional, but the Secretary would have been able to speak without betraying so much emotion. "You wanted real-time intelligence. We're seeing movement along the DMZ in North Korea. Heat blooms from hundreds of engines all at once. It could be any number of things. They do this from time to time to train and test their people, and to keep us on edge."

"Do you think it's—"

"Sir," the man said, "sorry to interrupt, but South Korea has just gone dark."

"Put it up on the screen."

The display changed from the Middle East to a real-time satellite display of the Korean Peninsula. An overlay displayed the border between North and South.

It was night there. In the North, few lights glowed. They had electricity, of course, but they could barely be considered a third-world country, at least technologically. Pyongyang was lit, and the rest of the country was dark, as usual.

The view of South Korea shocked him. Normally, the entire peninsula would be well lit. The country was one of the most high-tech in the world.

Seoul—only thirty-five miles from the border with the North—should have been glowing brightly, with the rest of the country filled with thousands of points of light.

It was all dark. Well, he corrected himself, mostly dark. Lights were visible here and there, including at Yongsan, the United States military base near Seoul.

"It's another round of EMPs, isn't it, Hartman?" he asked the Chairman of the Joint Chiefs of Staff.

"It appears so, Mr. President. We're gathering intelligence." The seventy-something bald man looked frayed and exhausted, though his uniform was pressed and impeccable.

James stood, which instinctively made the rest of the men and women in the room start to stand, but he waved them back to their seats. He needed to think, and as a warrior, he did his best thinking on his feet. While he'd rather be a younger man, on the ground in Korea and moving toward the enemy, his role now forced him to look at the big picture and make the tough calls.

"If we have any comms at all with Yongsan or any of our other forces in South Korea, order them to engage the enemy immediately."

"But, sir," Hartman said. "We're unsure about what exactly is happening."

"You may be, but I'm not. Pass along the order. If they aren't already engaged, which I suspect all the front-line troops are or soon will be, authorize them to start shooting. Hold the DMZ until it becomes untenable, then execute pre-planned maneuvers. The North is going to hit us with all they have, but we've prepared for this. We stand firm. Whatever else we have in the area, I want a workup in ten minutes. Stay calm, do your jobs, but dust off the war plans, ladies and gentlemen. We're in it now."

The flurry of activity increased to an even higher level as every phone was put into use, passing orders and receiving updated reports.

What else do you have planned? What would I do with this technology?

It would depend on Conroy's end game. But reading between the lines of the man's recent internet broadcasts, he wanted to rule the world.

"Hartman," James said, his quiet, commanding tone cutting through the noise. "Assume we're next. Plan on losing all electronics, including communication, computers, and security. Unless it's already hardened and protected, assume it's going to be worthless."

"Yes, sir." The men and women in the room couldn't imagine it happening to the United States, but in effect, it had. South Korea was their ally. What was happening there meant the USA had already been attacked.

"Put all our military bases on full alert. Prepare for immediate attack. Protect all the electronics we can but balance it with current safety and readiness. No sense opening the door to an attack and losing before it happens. But it also doesn't make sense to be protected now only to lose it when we get hit by EMPs."

He turned his attention to the rest of the room and waited. Within a few seconds, all calls were put on hold and the room quieted, waiting for his next orders.

"Everyone—the order of the day is for local control. All posts are to secure their own facilities in preparation for our command and control going offline."

A few faces looked at him in shock, still not grasping the magnitude of the situation.

He turned to the Secretary of State. "All embassies are to use their best judgment. If it's safer to bring everyone in, do it. If it makes more sense to keep most or all personnel in their homes, do it on a case-by-case basis. People can also go to ground if they need to."

To the rest of the room, he concluded, "The United States of America is at war with an unknown enemy. We are a big, fat, juicy target. Too big to ignore. Assume what happened to Iran and South Korea will happen to us. I want general suggestions in fifteen minutes, and specific plans in one hour. In the meantime, in the event of centralized communication failure, all posts are to protect our citizens. Get everyone armed and ready."

The Chairman of the Joint Chiefs asked, "Rules of engagement, sir?"

"If attacked, defend with extreme violence of action. Take no prisoners. No one messes with the United States of America."

He spoke to the officer in charge of his personal security detail. "Get the Vice President and staff to Air Force Two immediately. I'll stay here for the time being."

62

CONTACT

Lieutenant Enrique Zapata held on tight as his driver raced the Humvee toward the fighting. The beast of a machine had been their workhorse for the past several months of deployment as they learned the area and trained constantly. It and the others like it still ran, while the more sophisticated vehicles were dead heaps of metal going nowhere, their impressive technology rendered useless minutes earlier. How, he didn't know.

Neither he nor his men ever thought they'd be in a shooting war. They had expected the South Korea posting to be a cushy assignment. A well-established base in a friendly, civilized part of the world, with welcoming civilians who—mostly—appreciated them being around, meant the rotation should have been a casual and fun "day job."

"Slow it down, Manny," he called to his driver. "I think we're getting close." Behind him, the other vehicles of his small unit slowed as well, maintaining their distance. He couldn't see much, due to his night-vision goggles also being rendered useless, just like most other electronics around him. In one moment, they had lost much of their advantage: night vision goggles, sophisticated communications, GPS, and pinpoint accurate firing solutions for smart missiles.

Ahead lay the official border. But on the drive to the front, they'd seen tracer rounds indicating the long-threatened invasion by the North Koreans had finally begun.

"Slow to a stop," Zapata ordered. The rest of the unit would also stop in a strike formation if all went to plan.

Despite the loss of their fancy, cherished tools, they could still rely on what made them a fierce fighting group: superior training, dedication, and plenty of ammunition.

Plus, every man in the unit had dreamed of the day when he could rise to the occasion and put a stop to the North once and for all. This would be their night.

The enemy had been ready and used the shock of the power going out to launch their attack. They had rolled through the fences and made quick work of the minefields with their—working—heavy equipment.

The United States and South Korean units had been hesitant to shoot, not wanting to start an international incident over a feint, giving the North a reason to escalate.

But when the North's tanks and aircraft fired on their positions, they returned fire.

With massive firepower and working electronics, the North had overrun the primary defenses. Now it would be up to the men and women rushing to the front to stop—or at least slow down—the North's advance.

Zapata glanced at the now-dead GPS map display mounted to the dash, expecting to see his position, as well as the location of other friendly units and the enemy.

Instead, the dead unit sat dark.

Old habits die hard.

His gunner, Williams, yelled, "Contact front!" He immediately started firing the MK-19 mounted on top of the Humvee, the gun sending 40mm grenades downrange at the rate of forty per minute.

Tracers flew by them. Some bullets pinged off the metal of their lightly armored vehicle.

"Out. Take cover, return fire."

He opened his door and jumped out, staying low.

Behind him, the unit's other heavy weapons joined in, though Zapata couldn't see exactly what they fired at. But the tracer fire had to come from somewhere, and he'd be damned if he'd miss out on the shooting.

Seconds later, crouched next to the Humvee's engine block, the gunfire directed at them stopped, followed a moment later by a secondary explosion. Their advanced training had paid off. One of the gunners must have hit either an ammo or fuel store of a moving vehicle.

While nothing with sophisticated electronics worked, their heavy guns, M4s, and SAWs still did. If it came down to it, their pistols and —eventually—bayonets would, too.

In the sudden quiet, he called out loud enough to be heard by his men, taking the time to give a last update before the shit really hit the fan.

"Pick your targets. The one we got isn't alone. Far from it. You know the situation. They're coming. Resupply is iffy. Electronics and comms are gone. It's us against them. We hit them here, then we fall back. We do whatever it takes to keep them from breaking through. Got it?"

"Hoorah!" the men called softly. Their enthusiasm made him proud. While they were all professionals who had trained hard, none had ever expected to be fighting in a shooting war. The consensus was that it would either never happen or be a mopping up exercise after a president—either Heringten or one to follow—eventually got sick and tired of the North's bullshit and took them out with bombs and missiles.

But here they were, in the dark, with nothing but their guns, each other, and the rest of the units up and down the line, ready to defend the homes and way of life of fifty-two million South Koreans.

63

REPORT

The Center Control Room
St. John, United States Virgin Islands

Stefan paused his pacing when Gunther brought his hand to his ear, holding the tiny earbud in place, then spoke quietly into a microphone by his left wrist. He was proud to have secured for his people the exact equipment used by the United States Secret Service to protect the President of the United States.

Or at least, his personal guards. The regular units received radios with much more limited functionality. No sense in making it easy for them to stage a revolt, after all.

Gunther glanced back at him. He looked worried.

I've never seen the man's face pale like that.

"What is it?"

"Pioneer, a report from the stadium."

They better not have harmed Holly. If they did, they'll pay dearly.

"Continue."

Gunther looked around, shook his head slightly, and left his workstation to join him. "All the guards are dead. Miss Holly and the bodyguard are missing," he whispered near Stefan's ear.

"What do you mean, all the guards?"

There had to be a mistake.

"The twenty you left to deal with the bodyguard are dead in the seats. Another ten were called in for reinforcement. They are dead on the concourse level. And…"

He didn't want to say the next part.

What could be worse than thirty—thirty!—of my personal guard dead? No. Oh no.

"Not Holly. Tell me she is unharmed."

"As far as I know, yes, Pioneer. But one of your special followers is dead, as well."

"What? Who?"

"Kim."

He didn't know the names of most of the women. Why should he? They served at his pleasure, not the other way around. "Describe her."

Gunther spoke into his radio, waited for an answer, and relayed the news. "Round face, long dark hair. Cute dimples. Stocky. Beautiful."

He knew her. Sweet and a pleasure to be with. She had given him a son a year ago.

Rage filled him.

No one kills my women!

"Find them! They must have fled the island. Lock down their yacht in St. Thomas and send out more patrol boats. Attempt to capture them alive, if at all possible."

"What if they are on their way here, Pioneer? To stop you?"

"Ridiculous. The logical move is to escape and call for reinforcements."

"The bodyguard escaped the stadium and appears extremely capable." Gunther hesitated yet again. "Permission to cue up the full series of triggers so you can launch all with one order, instead of piece by piece?"

No! The Hand of God is my favorite part. The attacks must be done one by one.

"No," Stefan said. "Not yet. He is one man. My forces will hold him off easily."

Gunther said nothing, just stared with the cold, dead look back on his face.

"He's one man!"

Gunther didn't blink or turn away. Instead, he said in a reasonable tone, "They wouldn't send only one man."

Stefan struggled with his desire to set each part of his plan in motion region by region according to the plan he had carefully crafted over ten years.

What Gunther says made sense.

"Fine. I will consider it. For now, we continue as planned. We will have plenty of notice if the island comes under attack by reinforcements."

"Yes, Pioneer."

Gunther spoke into his radio and turned back to his workstation. Stefan caught a trace of fear on his normally impassive face.

64

OPPORTUNITIES

Along Pioneer Road
St. John, United States Virgin Islands

Axe waited ten minutes, but no cars came through the roadblock set up by the guards along the main east-west road across the island. They would have to go with the more dangerous Plan B.

"Ready?" he asked Haley. Fifty yards below them, out of sight on the other side of a hairpin turn, the guards would be standing near the SUV pulled perpendicular across the road, blocking it.

"You sure this will work?" She looked horrible with dried blood on her arms and face. Her clothes, too, were caked with dried dark red blood and wet mud from scurrying through a ravine. He didn't look any better, which would help in the coming assault.

"No," he replied honestly. "But, 'Opportunities multiply as they are seized.'"

"Sun Tzu?"

"He's the man." He squatted. "Let's go." She lay over his left shoulder. He grunted theatrically as he lifted her into a firefighter's carry.

"I haven't gained a single pound since the last time you carried me."

"Could have fooled me," he mumbled, sure she could tell he was joking.

He easily walked down the steep road. As he neared the tight turn, he started breathing heavily with fake exertion. "We're about to go around the bend. Just like we discussed," he said quietly.

Haley tapped his back twice in confirmation.

He stumbled around the corner, head down, and only glanced up when he heard movement. Both guards had turned from looking down the hill to check out the situation approaching them.

"Friends, help! I found her in the jungle. I think she's hurt!"

Both men immediately rushed toward him, neither reaching for his radio to call it in.

Suckers.

"Thank you, my friends. I'm so lucky. I thought I'd have to carry her all the way to Coral Bay! Do you have a first aid kit? She's bleeding. Here." He squatted again and gently leaned Haley's limp form toward the men. Each took an arm to support her.

"What happened?" the one on the left asked, trying to figure out the situation, more suspicious than his partner.

Axe slammed his fist into the man's solar plexus. He dropped Haley's weight as he fell to the ground, trying to catch his breath.

She immediately fell into the guard, who instinctively grabbed her with both hands. This left him wide open for Axe, who rushed forward with a forearm blow to his face, breaking the man's nose and knocking him out.

Axe focused on the first guard, relieving him of his radio, while Haley ran to the back of the guards' SUV. She removed several pieces of webbing used to secure larger items in the trunk and brought them to Axe.

He quickly threaded the end of one of the black straps through its buckle, then removed the man's floppy uniform hat and looped the strap around his neck. With a tug, he pulled it tight, nearly cutting off the man's air supply.

"Why?" the guard gasped, clawing at the tight loop. Axe waited while Haley unbuttoned his shirt and slid it off his arms, then used the rest of the strap to tie the man's elbows together. Any wiggling would tighten the strap around the man's throat, choking off his air and the blood flow to his brain.

"Long story," Axe said, moving to face the man. "You'll be fine if you cooperate. Fight, though, and I'll break your neck."

The man tried to nod but couldn't with the tight strap around his neck. Instead, he said, "I'll cooperate."

"All units," the radio squawked. "Be alert for a male, age forty-five to fifty, fit build, short, dark hair, dark eyes, wearing black pants and gray shirt. Possibly with a young blond female described as beautiful. The male is extremely dangerous and has already killed many of Pioneer's faithful guards. Apprehend the male alive, if possible. If not, execute him any way necessary. The blond is to be unharmed. Out."

Fifty? Bastards. I don't look a day over forty.

"That's you!" the guard croaked.

"If they had been quicker on the radio, we would have been in trouble," Haley said as she pocketed the second guard's radio and stripped the shirt off his unconscious form.

Axe put his guard's shirt on, buttoning it over his t-shirt, and added the floppy khaki-colored hat. He looked in the SUV's side mirror. The shirt was too tight, but he might pass for a regular guard at first glance.

It'll have to do.

"Good thing we hurried through the jungle. Let's keep it up." Haley quickly re-wrapped her long blond ponytail, capturing strands of hair that had come loose. She moved the ponytail from the back of her neck higher on her head. When she put on the other guard's hat, it concealed the hair perfectly.

The small shirt couldn't be buttoned over her breasts, which was a cause for concern. "I'm not sure we're going to get through with that," Axe said, trying to delicately dance around the subject.

She's just too voluptuous and beautiful for this to work.

"Change of plan. Get this one dressed." Axe untied the knots at the first guard's elbows but held the strap tight as Haley handed him the other guard's shirt.

"You want to live or die?" Axe asked him quietly.

"Live," he said earnestly as he put the shirt on. It fit him fine. Haley handed him the hat and went to work on the second guard, tying his arms and legs together in a hogtie. He moaned as she worked on him, coming around.

Axe retied the first man's elbows together behind him.

I should kill the second one.

He hated the idea of executing a prisoner. The man's only crime was joining a cult-like movement and manning a roadblock. He more than likely wasn't one of the inner circle, die-hard zealots.

I can't do it. Tied up and without a radio, he won't be a problem. This will all be over, one way or another, before he escapes or gets found.

"Guard this one," Axe told Haley, handing her the strap. "Knife out." He showed how he wanted her to stand.

Haley grabbed the strap running from the back of the man's neck down to his elbows, then pressed the knife firmly against the man's rear end.

Axe whispered in his ear. "Move, and she stabs you in a place no one should be stabbed. Understand?"

"No worries," the man squeaked, standing rigidly upright.

Axe grabbed the waking guard and carried him to the side of the road, where he walked a few feet into the jungle and left him face down, head tilted to the side, able to breathe.

Once back at the SUV, Axe guarded their prisoner while Haley got into the small back seat on the passenger side. She crouched on the floor behind the front seat. Axe put the guard onto the seat in front of her. Haley snaked her long arm around the seat so her knife, covered with dried blood, rested high along the inside of the guard's leg under the hem of his shorts. The man held as still as a statue. Axe clicked his seatbelt on.

Axe jumped into the driver's side and started the engine. "You move, look panicked, or sound the alarm, you understand what happens to you? Her knife cuts it all off. You might live, but you'll suffer the rest of your miserable life."

"I won't do a thing," the guard said, and Axe believed him.

65

DOORS

Axe concentrated on driving on the left side of the road. It felt wrong. As they approached the Center, he slowed to a stop before a hairpin turn. He put the tip of his knife under the strap around the guard's neck and cut it. He did the same with the strap connecting the man's elbows.

Crouched low behind his seat, Haley moved her arm to bring the knife point into contact with the guard's flesh. He sat rigid against the seat. She eased off just enough to let him sit normally.

"You get us in. You have sensitive information about the blond woman but you'll share it only with Pioneer, not over the radio."

The professional guards close to Pioneer would never allow this, but the man didn't need to know the actual plan.

If I give him a way out, he'll go along.

If he knew what they were going to attempt, he'd panic.

"No problem," the man said. "Just don't cut me there, please."

"Play along and she won't. Let's go." Axe eased off the brake and reminded himself to drive left as he guided the orange SUV up the steep incline and around the corner.

The Center building lay ahead on the left at the top of the island's highest hill. A parking lot held a few other boxy SUVs, the four-wheel-drive vehicles which worked best for the island's steep, rough roads.

Luckily, no additional roadblock stood in their way.

They figured blocking the road to the east and west would be enough.

Axe didn't look at his passenger. Haley and her knife would take care of him. He eased the truck forward, not too fast or slow. Just another pair of guards reporting for duty.

They drove past a solitary khaki-clad guard patrolling. Axe nodded to him, and he nodded back, unsuspecting. Driving slowly, Axe approached the circular drop-off area closest to the sidewalk leading to the front doors.

I hope Doug has eyes on and can tell it's me.

To be extra sure, Axe turned his head fully toward where he guessed Mad Dog would be hiding. He exaggerated the movement of his mouth, counting, "Five..." He accelerated, not fast enough to be alarming, but picking up speed as he neared the natural stopping point in the circle. "Four..." he mouthed, turning his focus on the guards nearest him, all with weapons. He nodded at the closest one. "Three." The man dropped suddenly, shot from the jungle by Doug's suppressed rifle.

Axe floored the accelerator and twisted the wheel toward the building.

The next nearest guard's head whipped toward them before he too fell lifeless to the ground.

Nice shooting, Doug.

"Two."

A third guard shouted as Axe sped up the sidewalk, the truck filling the walkway. The man hesitated, assuming there was some kind of mistake, and tried to get Axe to stop, holding his arm out commandingly.

Axe ran him over at full speed, the truck's tight suspension bouncing as the wheels crushed him. Axe kept the accelerator pedal pressed to the floor.

At the front door, both guards had their rifles coming around to bear on Axe. First one fell, then the other, without firing a single shot.

The SUV picked up speed, heading straight to the large, modern glass doors of the entrance to the center.

"One," he counted.

I'll leave the mopping up out here to you, Doug. See you on the other side.

"Hold on!"

He hoped Haley had the good sense to ease up on the knife, or the guard next to him was about to have an even worse day.

At the last possible second, Axe put his arms in front of his face and prepared for impact.

With a crash of broken glass and the scream of bent metal, the doors to the building shattered, disintegrating as the front grill crashed into them. The sides of the SUV struck the thick concrete of the building. The nose of the vehicle wedged into the gap, unable to continue forward, though the tires spun, and the engine raced.

The explosion of the airbags was expected. In seconds, Axe had drawn his knife and stabbed his, released his seat belt, and opened the door.

Bullets hit the truck from inside the building.

Great reaction time.

The guard in the passenger seat would be shot without Axe's help, but Haley would be protected by her position down low in the back.

Instead of ducking to safety, Axe grabbed the man's shoulder and hauled him out, dumping the guard safely on the ground, groggy from the accident and impact of the airbag. Haley would find her own way out on the other side.

Now, all I need is… there!

A black-clad guard's rifle lay right where the man had been killed by Doug firing from the jungle. Axe scooped it up, checked for a loaded round, and also took a spare magazine from the guard's pocket.

Haley would do the same on the other side.

Now, for the truly dangerous part.

66

TWISTER

The next twenty-five systems were ready. Bec didn't dare move the USA Department of Education computers a second time. It would only jeopardize her chance to slow-walk the rest of the list.

I'm sorry, I bought you as much time as I could.

"Pioneer, the next set of computer systems is ready for… the Hand of God."

If that doesn't endear me to him, nothing will.

Pioneer beamed at her and nodded. She sent the release to the scanner so his handprint would launch the next round of computer viruses.

Thankfully, he didn't make another big speech, only paused momentarily, as if in prayer, then reverently pressed his palm to the reader. The screen flashed green.

She had just consigned more computer systems to the virus and the ransomware demands that went with it.

Bec scanned the next group, which contained large Chinese and

Russian businesses, as well as a few government websites. These she could do faster if she chose.

Is it better for my country, and the world, to take these countries' systems out quickly? Or is it wrong for me to think like that?

She'd go the same slow pace she had so far, to keep up appearances and buy Haley and Axe more time. But with the effectiveness of the computer virus, and the number of systems she could infect, it wouldn't be long until the majority of the world's computers were at a standstill.

"Pioneer," Tina called out. "Washington is enacting COGCON 1, though they are calling it a surprise readiness drill."

"Thank you. They are afraid D.C. will be hit. I expected this."

Pioneer stopped pacing to examine the jumbo screen.

Busted!

"The entire Washington, D.C. area should be glowing with indications the computer virus is taking over their systems. Why is it completely blank? Why hasn't the virus spread through the US government's computers?"

"I handled it myself," Bec said, her fingers flying over the keyboard. "Let me check." Pioneer's Hand of God had released the virus for the system in the second round, not the first, as originally intended. Still, it should already be showing on the screen and infecting others. Except… it wasn't.

"Pioneer, somehow the Department of Education system is completely offline!" Somebody had figured out the situation and pulled the plug—literally. "Perhaps… it is down for maintenance? It is Saturday…"

A great crash came from outside the command center. Seconds later, gunfire started.

That's right outside!

Could it be Haley and Axe? Or other authorities?

Bec looked at Cody standing behind her. He looked as surprised as she felt.

"What is going on?" Pioneer roared.

"Reports of an assault on the door," Gunther said, his voice dead calm. He stood to walk to the door, but the twins got his attention and he detoured to their workstations.

They'll pull up the security cam feeds. What can I do while they're all distracted?

Bec's fingers flew, searching for what she wanted. She found it and hid the window behind the spreadsheet. Now all she needed was the right moment.

Haley stuck the rifle around the corner, keeping her body well back. She fired blindly, but slowly, as if she had targets to aim for, giving Axe cover to do his part.

Rounds flew back in her direction, impacting the front of the SUV and the concrete near her arms.

They can see me better than I can see them. But only my gun and arms...

Would it be enough? They'd soon find out.

Axe had to be almost there. A few more seconds is all he needed.

"Here! Over here!" The guard—formerly their prisoner, who Axe had saved at the last second—had his hands up, waving at his comrades inside. He leaned over the wrecked hood of the truck to yell more clearly into the building. "He's—"

Bullets chewed into his head and chest, propelling his body backward.

The guard trying to alert his buddies gave Axe the distraction he needed. He squirmed the rest of the way under the front of the truck, its steaming engine providing a bit of cover. He hadn't been shot at yet. Haley and the stupid guard had the defenders' attention.

"Send all guards to the Center immediately!" A guard down the hall to Axe's left spoke loudly, calling for help on his radio. "Send every able-bodied male, too. Pioneer is under attack!"

Axe revealed only his left eye and saw the careless man's exposed knee sticking out an inch around the corner. Before he could shoot, Haley fired, sending bullets that way.

"Now, Haley," he called, and she kept up the volume of fire, spraying the large lobby, keeping the defenders' heads down.

Axe fast crawled right toward a reception desk area as Haley's bullets tore overhead.

Made it.

He rolled onto his side and led with his gun, shooting three guards who crouched low behind the relative safety of the thick wooden reception counter. He took their place as Haley's gun ran dry.

Shots from surviving guards started immediately as they realized she was changing magazines. It gave Axe a picture of where they were. When their rate of fire eased as they neared the end of their own magazines, Axe prepared. They didn't realize an enemy had made it into the building. If he stood, he'd have an angle on them down the left side hallway.

Wait for it...

The sound of an empty magazine hitting the floor gave him the reassurance he needed. He stood and shot two black-clad guards as they reloaded in the hallway, safe from Haley's shots—but not his.

How many more are in here?

He wouldn't have time to clear the facility before attacking the control room. Bec had described it to Haley. Its door was in the center of the wall, directly across from the front doors, closed and presumably locked.

Too bad the truck didn't fit through the entrance. We could ram that door, too.

"Haley, give me a minute to clear."

"Got it!"

He'd prefer secure comms over yelling his plans for the enemy to hear.

It is what it is.

He stalked forward, crouched low, wondering if any enemy remained. And if so, how many and where they'd attack from.

Haley pivoted to cover the exterior of the building, trusting Axe to take care of himself. She'd rather be with him, but they didn't know what type of response to expect from outside, nor how quickly it would come. It made sense to guard their rear, at least until it was time to assault the control room.

She sensed a presence near her and frantically looked around, her rifle pointing left and right, trying to find the target.

From her left, around the corner of the building, a quiet voice called, "It's Doug. Don't shoot me. I'm coming to you."

"Got it, come ahead."

Mad Dog slipped silently toward her.

I have to learn how to move like that.

He was decked out in a khaki floppy-brimmed hat, black pants, a dark green long sleeve shirt, and a dark brown plate carrier. His face and close-trimmed beard were covered with camouflage face paint. "Hey, Holly, how's it going?" He seemed alert, but relaxed and happy.

"Thanks for the assist. We never would have gotten this far without you. And it's Haley, actually; Holly's just the cover, which is blown now anyway. How long have you been in the jungle?"

"Since before dawn. Nalen advanced the timeline." He smiled. "It was a nice night for a swim." He turned serious. "What's the plan?"

"Axe is sweeping the front of the building. Next, we gain entry into the control room and stop Conroy. Capture or kill."

"Good plan. According to Nalen, you have presidential authorization to take out Conroy by any means necessary if you think he's a threat."

"Excellent, because we were going to do it anyway. Axe wanted me to ask if you had any breaching tools—crowbar or, ideally, explosives."

He laughed. "The man's a dreamer. No, sorry. As it was, I had to tap into a hidden compartment in the yacht to access my rifle and armor."

"Any more backup on the way?"

"Nope."

The man seemed entirely too chipper.

I've spent enough time with Axe—I should be used to this mentality by now.

"The admiral decided to keep up appearances, leaving the other guys at the boat, just in case you hadn't been burned."

"Too late."

"Yeah, I see that." He chuckled, eyeing the mangled truck stuck in the doorway. "How about this—you go help Axe. I've got your back."

"You should be the one to go in. You're the pro."

"No, you two are a team. You know each other's rhythms and moves. I'll hold off any attackers."

"They radioed for backup—not only every guard, but every man on the island is coming. How many bullets do you have left?"

He checked his plate carrier, estimating the magazines. "About a hundred fifty. You?"

"Almost out. And there are about five thousand men on the island."

"Go. I'll be fine. And take this."

Doug handed his pistol to her with two magazines, which she shoved in her pockets. In exchange, she gave up the enemy's rifle with its few remaining bullets. He leaned it against the wall within easy reach. The pistol felt good in her hands, but she was reluctant to leave him without it. "What about you?"

"No worries," he beamed. "I brought my knife!"

Navy SEALs are crazy... but in a good way.

"Me too," she said, patting her back, feeling the knife stuck in her belt.

No enemy popped out, but Axe couldn't believe they weren't around.

Hiding? Waiting for reinforcements?

Axe didn't have time to hunt them down, if they were even in the building. He would have to deal with it when—if—they attacked.

Hurrying back to the main lobby, he called for Haley. "Haley, clear for now, come in."

"Coming low."

He turned to cover both hallways while she wiggled under the truck.

She quickly joined him, kneeling on the tile floor next to him, holding a pistol. "Doug," she explained in reply to his raised eyebrows. "He's watching our six."

"We'll need it. Did you hear the radio call?"

"Yes. We need to make this happen sooner rather than later. Is that the door Bec described?" He nodded at the metal door with a keypad next to it, a small, bright red light on top.

"Yes. And sorry, Doug didn't have any explosives or a pry bar."

"Damn. Ideas?"

"Waiting until someone comes out isn't an option." She smiled slightly. "I suppose we could always knock."

He looked at her, nodded, and walked to the door.

"I was joking!" she said, following him.

The mood in the room had darkened quickly with the sound of gunfire in the lobby right outside the door. Luckily, the lack of computer activity in Washington, D.C. had been forgotten for the moment.

Since Bec hadn't gotten any orders to the contrary, she kept logging into the computer systems of their paid cybersecurity clients, burrowing into the hidden area of the defense program, and activating the virus. She highlighted each finished network on the spreadsheet before moving on to the next, as slowly as she thought she could get away with.

While she worked, several of the systems on her list were highlighted as finished. The twins were at work. She couldn't stall much longer.

All I need is a signal. Come on, guys.

Cody struggled to display the correct emotion for the moment. He settled on resolve. In the Army, when in doubt, he narrowed his eyes and looked serious. It worked every time.

It's going to be soon. Somehow Axe and Haley will get in here—or I'll let them in.

He checked the door, which had a card reader and keypad on the wall next to it. It wouldn't be as simple as unlocking a deadbolt and turning a knob.

Whatever it takes, I'll do it. Even if I have to die, I'm going to help Haley and Axe.

He glanced at the dark-haired hacker in front of him.

And Bec.

"Pioneer, we are out of time," Gunther whispered. "Soon they will be at the door. You must take control of as much as possible. It will be the only bargaining tool you have."

"The men will retake the Center. We are safe here," he said. His usual bravado sounded hollow to him.

I am a god among men. I cannot be defeated.

"Yes, Pioneer. But I have prepped Taiwan. The assets are not fully in place but will be released as they come online. The missiles will fly toward China first, guaranteeing their immediate response. All computer chip manufacturing will be hit with EMPs and offline within five hours. The twins have finished prepping the rest of China, Russia, and Ukraine, focusing on the priority targets. They too will be set to detonate as they are available, once you put your hand to the scanner. The twins also finished with China and Russia's computer networks. They will be in your control."

"What about Europe? The United States? I need them dark."

"The hacker has done much of the government systems." He gestured to the map on the big screen. It showed an extensive network of pulsing red lines indicating computer systems all over Europe being offline, held hostage by his ransomware attack.

Another large section filled in. The entire area would be red soon.

Life as people knew it was already grinding to a halt. No internet or social media. No banking. No government services that relied on computers... which was basically everything.

Traffic lights and all public transit would have stopped working already. The power grid would soon be his, as well.

"The United States?" It looked unscathed.

"The full set of EMPs will be ready for all major cities and targets in two hours, but five percent are ready now. When you authorize it, those will go immediately. The rest as they come online, as I mentioned. But only if you authorize me to set it up the way I suggest."

Stefan stood, contemplating his options. On the large map, icons prepared by one of the twins indicated North Korea was making progress in their invasion, described more fully in the report on his tablet. The United States and South Koreans were doing their best to stop the onslaught, but with any luck would soon be overrun.

More icons showed the Middle East in flames. Iran had already launched a counterattack at Israel by air and was preparing its ground forces. Iraq had sided with Iran and was assaulting Saudi Arabia. Kuwait had come to the aid of the Saudis, along with Jordan. Turkey was playing peacemaker, but EMP missiles launched by his followers in the next wave would change that.

Success was assured if the plan was carefully followed.

He would claim his place as the first King of the World. A short time after that, he would distribute food, aid, and the electronics he had protected from his own EMPs. The people of the world would express their gratitude.

He would ascend to his true status of a god.

But what would happen if he gave up control and allowed his forces to continue the attack as they were able, instead of as he had meticulously planned?

Could the piecemeal approach work? It was far from guaranteed. He had spent years on the original strategy, which was a masterpiece of logistics and tactics. This approach could fail.

If I'm not successful, I will be... what? Not a god. Merely a man. A criminal.

But a criminal with millions of militant followers and the keys to every important computer system in the world, from business to banking, power grids to telecommunications. Governments would beg him for mercy.

He would have a great deal of leverage.

Another blast of gunfire came from outside the door. Gunther waited, his face less placid than usual. Expectant, tense, and afraid.

He nodded to Gunther. "Prepare everything possible for the next Hand of God."

"Yes, Pioneer." Gunther rushed back to his workstation and started typing before sitting down.

It will either work, or it won't.

He could still pull it off. He was truly a god. No man could stop him.

This time, the words rang true. It wasn't too late.

Was it?

Bec had overheard some of what Gunther said and could interpret the screen in front of the room easily enough. The world would soon be destroyed or under Pioneer's control.

Gunther frantically clicked on his keyboard. On the other side of the room, the twins did the same. Pioneer walked to his throne-like chair and sat, lost in thought.

"Send completed systems to my terminal immediately," Gunther called out.

Bec complied as slowly as possible, then switched windows. Gunther had to be preparing for a final, last-ditch effort to do as much damage as possible before it was too late.

She thought of her parents in Nebraska. She'd been gone too long, kept away by the lure of making easy money in paradise. What would their lives be like if Pioneer succeeded?

What would hers be like? She would be part of the inner circle. A trusted resource. They'd provide her with all she needed.

But all I want is to enjoy the island and maybe do a little hacking on the side. Who in their right mind would want to run the world? Or be a maniac's computer geek?

And what would they do to her if she took action and failed?

There was no question in her mind. She wouldn't be able to live with herself if she didn't try to defeat the man. She had to do it.

Today is a good day to die.

"Pioneer," Gunther announced from his workstation, "it is ready for you."

Time is up.

"Cody," she said softly, warning him as she pressed the Enter key.

The door behind them unlocked with a loud *click*.

———

Axe had raised his arm to knock on the door when the lock clicked, surprising the hell out of him.

A trap?

He hesitated only long enough to push Haley to the side, where she would be protected from gunfire. Entering a room with the element of surprise was dangerous. Going in when expected could be suicidal.

He pulled on the door with his left hand, keeping his right ready on the rifle, finger on the trigger. He only had a few rounds left, but how many would he really need?

———

Gunther moved faster than Bec thought possible. One second he sat in his chair, hunched forward, his face close to the screen. The next, he had launched himself toward the door.

The twins were right behind him, determination on their faces.

Pioneer merely watched them, not grasping the situation.

Tina stared at Bec's monitor. The electronic door control window filled the screen.

She knows what I did.

———

Cody heard the *click* of the door behind him, loud in the quiet control room. He stood still, uncertain of what to do. Gunther rushed the doorway. Cody hesitated, not wanting to blow his cover—or take on Gunther.

Is this it?

He'd watched as Bec slow-walked her process. Seeing how quickly she navigated some screens, he suspected she could have done the work much faster.

She's delaying the destruction. Shouldn't I protect her?

His indecision cost him the moment.

The door swung toward Axe, slowing his entry. He half expected to get shot as soon as the door cleared his body, but nothing happened. Instead, he surged forward, bringing up the gun. He took in the scene in an instant. A smaller room than he had imagined, a large screen taking up the full wall along the front. On his right, out of the corner of his eye, he caught movement and spun.

He was too slow.

A body slammed into him, taking his breath away and sending him to the ground.

Gunther.

Haley rushed in behind Axe, seeing Gunther take him down. They rolled on the floor, entangled.

No shot.

One of the blond twins was nearly to the door, her face twisted in a snarl.

Haley put two rounds into her chest, but the woman's momentum carried her forward, taking Haley to the ground.

Haley lost her grip on the pistol when the second twin kicked her wrist.

Bec had time to stand and get her arms up as Tina launched herself from her chair past a surprised and immobile Cody. Tina tackled her, clawing at her face, screaming, "You traitor!"

Bec twisted her head from side to side, avoiding the worst of the crazed woman's scratches, and caught first one wrist, then the other.

I'm in better shape. I can take her.

Cody moved into her line of sight, reaching to pull Tina off her.

"Cody, no! Get to Pioneer. Don't let him—"

Tina wrenched her right hand free and slammed her fist into Bec's mouth.

Bec's eyes watered but met Cody's. "Pioneer," she mumbled through her cut lip, hoping he'd understand.

Cody stood frozen with indecision, staring into the most beautiful, dark, intense eyes he'd ever seen. Bec wanted him to get Pioneer and keep him from doing… something. He fought his overwhelming desire to protect her and his hesitancy over doing the wrong thing.

I have orders.

He turned, leaving her to fight with the other tech.

Pioneer rose from his throne. Cody followed orders, as always, and ran toward him.

Stefan tried to process the chaos. Somehow, the door had opened. The damn bodyguard entered. Gunther took him down with a flying tackle.

Then Holly came through the door. For a moment he was distracted by her beauty, undiminished by the blood and dirt coating her.

She had been injured. His heart pounded in rage. Whoever had done this would pay.

The truth hit him like a speeding truck.

The blood is from my people. Holly and the bodyguard are together against me.

She shot Emma.

"No!"

My love.

The murderer fell when Emma's weight hit her. Anna kicked her hand, and a pistol slid across the floor.

The pistol.

He regretted not allowing weapons inside the control room. If his people had them, this would be over already. Instead, his loyal subjects fought to protect him and his plan.

What did Gunther say before running to the door?

Tina, who had shared his bed on many occasions, crouched over the hacker, hitting her.

Gunther. He had to focus on what Gunther had said, not on the fighting around him.

It's ready for me. The final Hand of God.

He stood and made eye contact with the redhead security guard, moving forward to protect him from harm.

Axe fought Gunther, who moved faster than him. Every move he made, Gunther was there, countering it. Axe was on the defensive, a place he hadn't been in years.

He's younger, stronger, and faster.

Gunther almost had him once, then again. Axe narrowly escaped a hold, which he turned into a rear mount. Gunther easily avoided the heel hooks he attempted and nearly escaped. Without thinking, Axe rolled them onto their sides, scooting his hips lower on the other man's body, still controlling his arms—barely.

With one leg between Gunther's, he swung his right arm near his left. Gunther's left arm went behind Axe's body, giving the man an opening. He took it and immediately rolled toward Axe. Axe dropped the hammer, perfectly executing a move illegal in tournaments and rarely trained due to how easily a partner could be horribly injured if taken too far.

Axe took it much too far. With his right arm behind the man's head, he grabbed his right fingers with his left, locking Gunther's head between his wrists.

He pulled, executing the perfect Twister, never giving the blond man a chance to submit.

Gunther screamed in agony as the move twisted his neck and spine, pulling muscles up and down his body in ways they weren't designed to move.

Laying in agony, Gunther still attempted to move out of Axe's grip, but the pain from the injury made his movements slow.

Axe simply changed the position of his arms and snapped the younger man's neck. In the room's commotion, the noise went unheard.

For the second time that morning, Haley fought to extricate herself from underneath a dead body. Her wrist hurt from being kicked, but her pride hurt worse at losing the weapon.

Get up!

She heaved the dead twin off her body in time to see the other sister's foot coming toward her head. She rolled away and brought her arm up, taking the force on her forearm. Still rolling, she didn't see the second kick. It connected, slamming hard into her kidney.

Haley screamed in pain.

With the twin standing above her, she was at a huge disadvantage.

Fighting her momentum, Haley rolled back toward the enraged woman, taking another kick in the process, but reducing its effectiveness by getting close before it gained full force.

Now the offending foot was in range. She latched onto it and reversed her roll again, hanging on to the foot with all her strength.

The move caught the sister off guard. She fell hard.

Haley felt the thud when the body hit the floor. And even over the screaming of the tech woman attacking Bec a few feet away, she heard the ghastly sound Anna's head made as it cracked open on the tile floor.

Letting go of the foot, she sprung up, prepared to pummel the woman into submission or kill her. Instead, Anna lay flat on her back, mouth open slightly, eyes closed, either out cold or dead.

A trickle of blood snaked from under her head, bright red against the broken white floor tile.

Cody rushed Conroy, gaining an extra step or two because the man obviously thought Cody was coming to help him. But with one step remaining before they collided, Pioneer's expression changed. He realized where Cody's loyalty lay, and it wasn't with him.

Cody didn't slow. He just lowered his shoulder and continued forward.

I can do this. It's my time.

It dawned on Stefan too late that the red-haired guard running to protect him was actually attacking him.

I'm surrounded by traitors.

Then the kid slammed into him.

Cody collided with Pioneer hard, but they didn't go down. Pioneer kept his feet. He was sturdier, stronger, and weighed fifty pounds more than Cody. They only staggered a few steps closer to the edge of the platform.

Cody tried to swing the man to the ground but couldn't. A standard Basic Combat Training move had no effect on the stronger, heavier man.

I'm probably not doing this right.

Cody struggled, trying to muscle the guru closer to the edge of the platform.

If I can push him off...

The man moved like a bear standing on two legs, stepping forward slowly, waddling from side to side with Cody clinging to him futilely. Cody kept trying heel and leg hooks, but the man avoided them. Step by step, they moved away from the edge and closer to the middle of the platform.

Cody took a risk and let go just as the man leaned to the side to take another ponderous step, sending him off balance. They didn't teach a lot of striking at basic training, but he'd done his share of sparring. Cody knew the basics. He slammed a palm heel strike to Conroy's nose, off-target a bit from having to use his left hand and coming from the side, but the effect was more devastating than Cody thought it would be.

Conroy stopped moving to cup his bleeding nose in shock.

"You hit me!"

What am I supposed to do? Kill him?

They stared at each other for an instant. Cody hit him again, this time aiming for his throat.

Pioneer made a choking noise and moved his hands from his bleeding nose to his throat, eyes wide once more as he struggled to breathe.

He looked over Cody's shoulder and narrowed his eyes. With surprising speed, Conroy swung sideways and flung his arm out toward the scanner.

Cody grabbed his other arm, but the man slipped through his grasp.

Stefan's shock at being struck by a mere mortal—twice—was short-lived. His nose bled and he couldn't breathe, but the bigger problem wasn't the red-haired traitor in front of him. It was the bodyguard coming toward him, knife in hand.

He lunged for the scanner. His plan would continue, and the world would burn, even if he wouldn't be around to see it happen.

Then again, gods don't die.

Axe dove for Conroy, desperate to end the maniac's life and protect Cody. He extended his arm, aiming for the aorta. The knife slid deep into Conroy's back, right on target. Axe pulled it out and stepped back, knowing the man was near death.

The guru landed on one knee, dying. With a last, superhuman effort, Conroy reached forward and pressed his hand to a flat panel on a stand. It glowed green for a second. Conroy collapsed, his hand sliding off the panel and dropping onto the ground.

Bec had never been in a fight before, but instinct took over. After the punch, she protected her face as undisciplined blows fell on her from both of the crazed woman's fists.

With a lurch, Bec sat up, taking punches to both eyes. She pulled her body close to Tina's, burying her head in the woman's chest, and rolled.

As they fell together to the floor, Bec let go with one arm and dropped her forearm on Tina's face, forcing the woman's head against the floor harder than it would have hit normally, her neck twisting awkwardly.

Tina went limp. Bec held herself ready, prepared to continue the fight. It took a few seconds, but eventually she noticed Tina's broken neck and glassy eyes. When she felt for a pulse, there wasn't one. She had killed Tina.

There's no time to deal with one death with the world at stake.

Bec looked up in time to see Axe pull his knife out of Pioneer's back.

"No! We need him alive!"

Pioneer's hand hit the scanner and he fell to the ground.

67

DROP

Powerful men and women, who reported to the most powerful man in the world, the President of the United States, were spiraling out of control.

The lack of sleep, too little information, plus the incredible pressure on them, were finally taking their toll.

James took a mental step back and surveyed the scene. His top minds, yelling into phones, trying to make sense of a world going down the drain.

This has gone on long enough.

"People!"

Even his command voice couldn't cut through the chaos.

He turned to the Marine guarding the door and mouthed what he wanted. In a booming voice, the former drill instructor yelled the only words James figured would cut through the fear, uncertainty, and dread threatening to overwhelm the room.

"Attention!" It came out of the man's mouth as a loud drawl, sounding more like, "Tennshun!" than the proper word.

Instantly, all sound stopped. Every military member in the room snapped to their feet, standing tall and straight. The few civilians in the room did the same, though with less rigid posture.

"People, get yourselves under control and calm the hell down," James said. "Yes, the situation is a cluster. Yes, the world is on fire. But we're not going to solve it by losing our minds. Finish the calls you're on and give me a report of what you have in thirty seconds. At ease."

After a much quieter half minute, phones were returned to their cradles and the men and women of his national security team turned their attention to him, still standing at the head of the table. He gave no one permission to sit. They'd focus better on their feet.

"First, what's the security of our country?"

Hartman spoke up. "The Department of Education system is offline as ordered, sir. No attack is possible. We shut it down completely."

"Excellent. Have there been attacks directly on our soil?"

"No, sir."

James spoke in a calm, commanding tone. "That's great news, but it will likely change soon. People, crises will keep coming. Our focus has to be on the big picture and protecting our country and citizens, not merely gathering a list of all that is going wrong. I'll hear the reports from Korea and the Middle East in a moment. First, can anyone help me get ahead of this?"

"Mr. President," Hartman continued, "the planes you ordered are approaching St. John. If you believe the intel," he said the word with distaste, "that control of the attacks is coming from the island, they will need a go order from you. Or, if you need more time, they can also remain on station indefinitely, as we have air refueling capacity on the way."

The idea of attacking United States soil—and citizens—with no more proof than the Central Analysis Group's hunch wasn't going over well.

"The satellite feed of St. John is online now. We only have it for a few minutes, sir, before it passes out of range. We'll be dark."

James had coordinated the planes and satellite so he could make a decision while watching a live feed. Hopefully, the view would give him—and his reluctant military and intelligence leaders—all they needed to go ahead with his last-ditch plan to stop Stefan Conroy.

Heaven help me if Haley is wrong.

The view of the Virgin Islands appeared on the screen. The view zoomed in to St. John as one of the people in the room controlled the satellite camera.

The island looked peaceful from space. But as the camera continued to zoom in, it revealed the details of the center of the island, where it looked like the main east-west road connecting the two towns seemed to somehow be alive.

"Zoom in there, the middle of the island. What's wrong with that road?"

As the picture became clearer, it revealed hundreds of people, perhaps thousands, hurrying toward the top of the mountain from both sides.

"What are all those people doing? That's the Movement building, correct?"

"Yes, sir. We believe it houses the main offices of the Movement. It appears the people are converging on that location."

"Would Stefan Conroy be there?"

"I… it's hard to say, sir."

"Closer. Get in closer to the building."

The camera moved in as Hartman tried to stall—and cover his ass. "I'm sorry, sir, this is real-time, and we don't have any analysis prepared for you. If you could give us a few minutes to—"

"The planes can stay on station?"

"Yes, sir. If we need to refuel, we can."

Should he go now, or wait?

"Mr. President, sorry to interrupt, but you need to hear this," an aide spoke up. "Much of Europe just went offline, and we have reports of missiles being fired from Taiwan to China. Not a lot, but we expect the Chinese reaction to be swift and overpowering."

"Europe—were there EMPs over their cities?"

"No, sir, at least not yet. It appears to be communication and internet related only. They still have power. And it's happening sporadically, unlike Iran and South Korea. It appears less coordinated."

"Excuse me sir, but I…" The aide controlling the satellite camera had zoomed in further. "If you look at the front door of the building, Mr. President."

James peered at the screen. The resolution from the spy satellite astounded him. "Is that an SUV wedged in the doorway?"

"It appears so, yes, sir."

Only a SEAL would assault a building by ramming it with an SUV.

He didn't hesitate. "Give the planes the order to drop immediately. Target the concrete building."

Several faces looked at him, mouths open.

They don't know whether to follow the order or not.

"People, this is on me. I have all the proof I need. This worldwide operation is being controlled from that building, and we must stop it right now. Trust me."

After an agonizing second, his order was repeated into the phone. "The operation is approved. Drop, drop, drop."

I gave you all the time I could, Axe and Haley.

35,000 feet above the island of St. John, the United States Air Force planes dropped their lethal cargo. It fell silently toward the Center building far below.

The entire room watched the view of St. John suddenly go dark. "We've lost satellite coverage, Mr. President. But the planes dropped and were on target. They are returning to base."

An aide sitting along the wall gasped and rushed forward with a laptop. "Oh my God," she mumbled, showing the screen to her boss, the Secretary of Defense.

"What is it?" James asked.

The aide touched the trackpad and her display extended to the main screen on the wall. On it, a talking-head news reporter cupped her hand against an ear. The closed captioning ran below.

"We are receiving multiple reports of power going out in cities across the country. Los Angeles, Chicago, Miami—"

In the situation room, the report stopped.

People tapped computer keyboards, and others looked at telephone handsets in confusion.

Finally, after conferring with his counterparts, Hartman said the obvious. "Mr. President, it appears that Washington has been hit. Civilian comms are down. Some of our military communications are still working, however, and we believe we may reroute or restore more. We're protected here, but our computers and phones have nothing to connect to at the moment."

The mood in the room hit a new low.

"We planned for this," James said quietly. "The country is strong. Her power lies not with us in this room, no matter how much we may hate to admit it. No, her power lies in our dispersed government, in part, but mostly in the individual citizen. Sit down, everyone. It's in the hands of the people now, as it was in the beginning, a few hundred years ago. We will get through this. America will persevere."

Outwardly, he presented a commanding, reassuring authority. Inside, his stomach churned. *How much of this can we take?*

As he sat, James' thoughts turned to Haley and Axe, possibly fighting for their lives on the island. If Haley was wrong and someone else was to blame for this situation, he had blown it. The country—and the world—would never recover.

I hope I've done the right thing.

68

PIONEER

Bec flew to her screen, leaving Tina laying dead on the floor.

I have to fix this.

Pioneer had touched the scanner and launched... what?

There has to be a way to recall it. Stop parts of it from happening. Something.

She didn't have access to the correct system.

Gunther's station.

She hurried to the workstation at the edge of the platform. Gunther wouldn't be needing it, judging by the awkward angle of his neck as he lay near the door.

The system had logged him out due to inactivity.

She needed his password, which he could no longer provide.

There had to be another way.

Back at her computer, she explored the internal subprogram which had allowed her to send items straight to Gunther's system, as well as to unlock the door.

Could this be it?

Her fingers raced across the keys, delving deeper into the program.
There!

A solution—or rather, a first step. She looked at the bleeding form of Pioneer laying in front of his precious scanner, obviously dead.

She needed him alive. A body with a beating heart and warm blood.

His body is still warm.

"Give him CPR, quick!"

Haley, covered with blood but still more beautiful than she would ever be, stood over Pioneer's body.

"Bec, he's dead."

"Give him CPR, now! I need his heart to be beating, or at least seem to be!"

Bec turned back to her computer and clicked until the proper subroutine came up.

"Do it!"

Haley assessed the situation. Bec had a plan, and there was no time to explain. Haley didn't argue—she dropped to her knees, flipped the man over, and started rapid chest compressions.

Axe watched Haley uselessly working to keep the man's heart beating but didn't question the hacker. If she had a plan, he'd go along with it.

He nodded to Cody and was about to ask if the kid was okay when he heard a noise from the lobby.

Running to the door, he called to Bec. "Lock the door!"

"I can't right now," she cried, intent on her screen.

He grabbed the knob and pulled the door closed. It latched but didn't lock. A second later, the handle tried to turn. He held on tight.

"Cody, get me Haley's gun—it's over there!"

Cody started to leave the platform, but Bec yelled at him. "Cody, you stay right there or the whole world ends."

Lost, the poor kid looked at Axe for guidance. "Stay there, Cody. I'll figure something out."

He only needed to hold the door closed against whatever guards were in the hallway.

How hard can it be?

Bec looked at the directive on the screen.

TO CHANGE ADMINISTRATIVE ACCESS, USER #1'S PALM PRINT IS NEEDED

"Haley, keep it up. Cody, put his palm against the screen!"

Cody lifted Pioneer's hand and held it toward the scanner. It didn't reach. He and Haley moved the body around, then Haley started CPR again. Cody placed the hand against the scanner.

It flashed red.

"Again. Take it off and put it on it. Make sure all five finger pads and the palm touch."

He did it again, carefully pressing the fingers and palm against the reader.

The light flashed red again.

An alert flashed on her screen.

AFTER THREE FAILED PALM SCANS, ACCESS WILL BE BLOCKED FOR THIRTY MINUTES

The world didn't have thirty minutes.

She took a deep breath. Maybe this wouldn't work. Pioneer was, after all, dead.

"Once more. Haley, really put yourself into it. We have to fool the scanner into thinking he's alive. He's still warm, so it's the hand or the heartbeat it's not accepting."

Haley picked up the pace, her body leaning over Pioneer's.

"Ready, Cody?" She stared at him and smiled. "We can do this."

He held the dead man's hand over the scanner.

Gunshots came from outside, thudding into the metal door, but she didn't allow herself to be distracted.

"Okay, now!"

Axe didn't bother to duck. If he wasn't dead by the time he heard the shots, they had missed.

Thankfully, the door didn't allow any bullets through.

If it's one guy on the other side, I'm fine. But if there are more…

Cody carefully placed the hand against the scanner, covering it with his own and pushing down. His pulse raced.

I've messed up today at every turn. I didn't attack Pioneer when I first had the chance. I let him slip through my grasp when we finally fought. I have to get this right.

A second passed with no light.

The screen flashed green.

They had done it.

A hard tug nearly pulled Axe off his feet. The door opened two inches.

That's more than one guy.

He levered his body back, pulling the door shut.

"I'm going to need some help here or we'll be overrun."

Bec's screen flashed green.

USER #1'S PERMISSION GRANTED. PLACE HAND OF NEW ADMINISTRATOR ON THE SCANNER.

She stood to dash to the scanner when her screen changed to a countdown timer.

3… 2…

"Cody, put your own hand on the screen. Right now!"

Cody followed orders. The only way to make it in the Army—and the surest way to not get chewed out or assigned shit duty—was to always follow orders. Without hesitation, without question, without argument.

He let go of Conroy's hand and placed his on the scanner.

The light immediately flashed green.

He looked over at Bec as she stood bent over her keyboard, staring at her screen. While he wasn't the smartest guy, he could guess what happened. With a deep breath, he stood tall and began to mentally prepare himself.

Time to grow up. I've just been promoted.

ADMINISTRATOR UPDATED. NEW UPDATE ALLOWED IN THIRTY DAYS.

Cody is the new Pioneer.

Bec met his eyes and offered a weak smile.

Sorry. It should have been me.

The countdown made sense. It must be a security device designed by Pioneer to prevent someone forcing him to transfer power. It would take at least a few people to make him do it: one at the workstation who had full system access and one or more to force his hand to the scanner.

Now, with Cody as the administrator granting her total access, how much could she do to reverse the damage to the world?

Axe couldn't hold out much longer.

The door flew open three inches this time.

Found more guys, did you?

"Help!"

If there are four, I'm dead. Three will pull the door, one will shoot me. It's what I'd do.

He fought hard but couldn't pull the door all the way closed. It went from open three inches to two, then four, and back to three as he wrestled with the men on the other side.

Where the hell is Doug? Or Bec?

"Bec, if I close it, can you lock the damn door?"

The door.

Bec switched back to the door lock screen.

"If you can close it, I can lock it!"

Out of the corner of her eye, she saw Haley and Cody move to help Axe.

"Cody, no! Stay away—you're the new Pioneer! I need you."

Haley helped Axe tug on the door. It nearly closed, then flew open an inch.

"Together," Axe said and counted down.

They yanked at the same time and must have caught the men on the other side off guard. The door clicked shut for a moment.

"Now!" Haley yelled to Bec.

The door lock clicked. She and Axe stood, shaken for a moment before she rushed to the side of the room and retrieved the pistol from where the twin sister had kicked it from her hand.

"Here," she said, giving it to Axe. "Just in case."

Cody stood near the platform where he'd been told to stop by Bec.

I'm the new Pioneer.

He had been right. Putting Conroy's hand to the scanner, then his, had changed his life completely.

I'm ready.

His stomach flip-flopped and he nearly threw up.

I hope.

"Keep it together, Cody. We can do this," Bec called. The guy looked like he was about to have a heart attack. "Go back to the scanner, please. I'm going to need your palm print in a second."

I hope.

Bec navigated to a new screen deeper in the access program, clicking the proper buttons as she went.

TO ATTAIN ADMIN ACCESS, PERMISSION IS REQUIRED. CLICK HERE WHEN READY FOR PALM SCAN.

"Ready, Cody?"

He nodded at her, standing in front of the scanner.

She clicked the button and nodded at him.

The system accepted the change. She was in.

The interface made complete sense, but it was new to her. She scrolled through, trying to figure out what she could do… and which to do first.

Bec felt Axe and Haley at her shoulders.

"You're in?" Axe asked.

She ignored him, speed-reading.

"Wait, go back," Haley said. She stopped and scrolled up. "There. USA. Dive in there, please."

Bec resisted her natural urge to rebel. She hated people hovering over her, telling her what to do.

The world is at stake. Maybe I can dial down the hacker side for a minute.

"Cody, get ready," Haley called at her side.

"Do you see a way to abort all future USA strikes?" Haley asked.

She checked, figuring out the system as she went. "Yes, there." She checked off boxes and locked eyes with Cody, giving him a nod. He placed his hand on the scanner and her screen flashed a yellow warning. **ABORT ORDER RECEIVED.**

Bec reversed out the USA subdirectory and back to the overview.

"Priorities?"

Axe frantically considered different strategies.

"Allies first?" Haley asked him.

"No. First is she gives you access on another computer."

"Great idea." Haley moved to the next computer as Bec went to work.

If President Heringten were here, what would he want?

Axe considered the possibilities.

This is way above my pay grade.

He felt enormous pressure. Who was he to decide who lived, who died, and who suffered?

The Navy SEAL Ethos, his guiding light, sprang to mind. "In times of war or uncertainty there is a special breed of warrior ready to answer our Nation's call… I am that warrior."

He leaned over Bec's shoulder, scanning the overview with her.

"We won't be able to reverse them all," the hacker explained. "Even with Haley's help. They are all programmed to go off as they come online—either the missiles fire or the suitcase EMPs detonate. We can't reverse them as a group. We have to do it region by region, sometimes country by country. And Cody has to do his Hand of God trick each time, though I might be able to speed that part up."

Axe looked at the list, running the angles in his head. "Okay, here's what we do."

Cody pressed his palm to the scanner again. He'd lost track of the number of times Bec had smiled and nodded at him to do it. But as long as she kept smiling, he'd keep doing it.

He didn't dare interrupt the intense work she, Haley, and Axe were doing across the room. But Bec had quickly updated him, explaining how the system wouldn't allow a new Pioneer for thirty days.

I have at least a month here. And every day I'll be working with Bec. Things could be worse.

Axe heard an M4 firing outside. He looked at Haley, hard at work with Bec on saving as much of the world as they could. "I've got to help Doug."

"With the pistol? Maybe we get him in here and hole up?"

Not a bad plan. Except for the lack of food, water, and bathroom facilities. It would get very bad, very quickly.

And it didn't count on the mob's ability to figure out a way to tear the door off its hinges.

The only problem was the men on the outside of the door. The second Axe opened it, he exposed Bec, Haley, and Cody. If he lost any of them, they lost the world.

Every part of his soul screamed for him to go to Mad Dog's aid, but there was no way he could. The stakes were too high.

I'm so sorry, brother.

69

SEALS

Mad Dog fired another burst of warning shots over the heads of the approaching mob. The unarmed, khaki-clothed guards in front stopped again for a few seconds but were once more pushed forward by the hundreds behind them.

From his vantage point behind the rear of the orange SUV wedged in the Center's doorway, he could see men filling the parking lot. They continued down the driveway and covered the road from one edge to the other. Several had fallen over the side, down the steep slope, and had to be retrieved by others.

There's no way this ends well for me or them.

Doug didn't want to shoot unarmed civilians, even ones who were going to tear him limb from limb.

Well... when I put it that way...

The crowd surged forward again, driven by those behind.

He considered bargaining, but they didn't look much in the mood to negotiate. The men looked enraged. Mob rule would propel them forward.

In a moment, they would be at the edge of the parking lot. When they stepped foot on the grounds, all bets were off. That's when they would rush him.

I'll give Axe and Haley all I have. I will never give up.

Doug ducked behind the truck to retrieve the gun Haley had left him. He checked the magazine. Almost empty, as Haley had said. Still, it would buy him a few extra seconds before he died.

A shadow fell across him for a second. When he looked up, he couldn't help but smile with relief. Opening above him were about two dozen black parachutes.

HALO operators to the rescue!

Under each high altitude, low opening parachute was a fellow Navy SEAL coming to save his ass.

Or at least prolong the agony by a few minutes.

Moments later, the first landed on the roof directly behind him, gathered up his chute, and lay prone at the edge of the flat roof.

"Mad Dog, right?" the man asked, extending the bipod legs on his weapon and pointing it at the men in the parking lot, who had stopped for a moment to watch the landing troops.

"About time you got here," Doug replied. "Thought I'd have to hold off this zombie apocalypse all by myself."

"The only easy day was yesterday, brother!"

70

PRIME

Bec finished the latest batch of aborts and turned to Haley. "You have to take over. I need five minutes."

"In five minutes, thousands more people will die!"

"No, they won't." She clicked on her screen as she argued with Haley. "In five minutes, a few more electronics will be fried. But if I don't take the time, hundreds will die outside, including the guy Doug you mentioned. The people will get inside here and kill us."

Bec dove into the surveillance footage section of the system, reaching it much more quickly with full admin access than she had when hacking it.

Her workstation had a basic video editing package. She grabbed footage from the control room's cloud server and quickly edited it together as best she could. She didn't make it fancy—the less polished it looked, the better.

A few minutes later, she finished. Bec checked it one last time, then retrieved the tablet Pioneer kept in a holder next to his throne. She turned it on and used Conroy's dead finger to unlock the screen before changing the login to use her finger instead. Thankfully, the device wasn't as smart as the scanner and recognized the dead man's fingerprint. She logged in with her administrative access and downloaded the video.

She got Axe's attention as she finished. "I need her sleeve," she explained, pointing at one of the twin sister's white, long-sleeve blouse. It didn't have any blood on it.

He cut it off and handed it to her. Bec explained what needed to happen, and he agreed.

"If they kill me, you have to figure out how to show it to all of them. It's the only way."

Axe nodded. "Let's hope it doesn't come to that."

"Cody, Haley, get down," Axe said. "I think this will work, but you never know."

He walked to the door and held the white fabric. At her workstation, Bec unlocked the door.

"Truce! We want to talk!" he yelled through the door. He gripped the pistol in his right hand and turned the knob with his left. No matter what, no one could hurt Cody. And either Haley or Bec could die, but not both.

He'd die first to protect them, taking out the attackers, paving the way for Bec to try again.

Axe shoved his hand out the door and waved the white flag.

No one shot him.

So far, so good.

"Pioneer, are you okay?" a guard's voice called from directly outside the door.

"It's Bec—Rebecca." She stood as Axe had asked, back from the entrance, protected from being shot. "I'm one of Pioneer's techs. You've seen me, I'm sure. Pioneer had a massive heart attack. He's dead."

The pause was short. In the background, three other guards' voices murmured. "We don't believe you! The blond and the bodyguard killed him."

"I have security camera footage to show you. It's on Pioneer's own tablet. I'll hand it to you." She slowly stuck her arm through the narrow door opening. "Don't shoot me, okay?"

A guard took the tablet from her hand.

Now we wait.

The rest of the SEALs landed on the roof and formed up. They aimed their weapons at the horde of men still pushing up the roads, forcing the ones in front closer and closer to the building.

Seeing the guns pointed at them, the men in front pushed back, reluctant to move but unable to stop the tide.

"We're going to have to take out some in back first," Mad Dog called up to his guardian angel on the roof above. "That might stop this."

"Copy."

Bec stood safely pressed against the wall in the control room. She narrated the footage from memory and hoped it would convince the guards.

In the silent video, Cody and Bec stood before a focused but pleased Pioneer. He spoke to each of them.

"That's Pioneer earlier this morning. The man, Cody, is a guard from the docks. We met recently and fell in love. Pioneer sensed something in Cody. A connection. You can see it. We're standing before Pioneer, requesting his blessing for us to marry."

Bec didn't look across the room at Cody, unsure how the news of their engagement would go over with him. She knew she wasn't a traditional beauty, but an arranged marriage of convenience with her for a month couldn't be all that bad, could it?

"Next, you see Pioneer collapse." She had edited out the moments before when Cody had fought with Pioneer, and Axe had stabbed Pioneer in the back. Axe's body hid the knife from the camera.

The footage only showed Pioneer falling, placing his hand on the scanner, then collapsing.

"It must have been a heart attack. With his last gasp, Pioneer ordered me to transfer full authority to the new Pioneer. You see him authorizing it with his palm scan. Cody, the loyal guard he had taken a liking to, was meant to be Pioneer."

On the tablet, the guards would see Haley giving CPR to Conroy. "We tried to revive him."

Bec had taken a long clip of the scene, unedited, to show their supposed efforts to save Pioneer's life.

"Pioneer had secretly brought the bodyguard and the blond to the island because he thought Gunther was untrustworthy. He was correct. Both Gunther and the twins were jealous that Pioneer had chosen Cody over them to lead the Movement. They rebelled, fighting the bodyguard and Haley, the blond. "

The video would show Axe killing Gunther and Haley killing the twins. Shown out of order, with this explanation, Bec hoped it would be enough to fool them.

"But the bodyguard killed a bunch of our men today!"

"Pioneer told me that he suspected several men were disloyal. He was worried about rebellion—you know that. And rightly so. It happened, and by his supposedly most loyal guards. But he had no solution except to bring in an outsider—the bodyguard."

The people of the island—including these guards—fell for Conroy's BS. Will they now believe mine?

Bec made herself choke up by thinking of the death and destruction the world was suffering. Her voice broke with sadness and tears flowed from her eyes.

"I'm coming out." She pushed open the door slowly, talking as she went. "Pioneer was all-knowing. All-powerful. He knew what was coming and brought Alexander—the bodyguard—and Haley, the blond, to make it right."

She sobbed. Four guards looked from her to the tablet screen showing the footage on a loop from the beginning.

"Pioneer was betrayed by members of his personal guard detail and his inner circle. That he could have overcome. He planned for it. But in the end, he was also betrayed by his heart. His oversized, unbelievably giving heart."

Tears streamed down Bec's face—for the suffering people of the world—but they convinced the khaki-clothed guards of her sincerity and truthfulness.

"The new Pioneer has taken the reins of the Movement and has declared seven days of mourning. He will address the people tomorrow in the stadium when we have a memorial service for Pioneer Prime."

"Pioneer Prime," one guard said, buying the story.

The others repeated it reverently.

"Pioneer has declared the mourning period. All those gathering outside are confused. They have misunderstood the situation. We have to turn them back to the safety of their homes so they can grieve Pioneer Prime."

The guards looked at each other, not certain what to do.

Cody walked through the doorway, standing tall, his face set. He appeared strong and in command, sad yet warm and caring.

Bec drew in a breath, seeing a new side of him. On instinct, she kneeled.

The guards followed her example.

"Pioneer," she said.

"Pioneer," they repeated quietly.

"My friends," Cody began.

71

DEBRIEF

MONDAY

Central Analysis Group Headquarters
Alexandria, Virginia

Haley had slept a few hours aboard an empty Air Force plane from St. Thomas to Joint Base Andrews in Maryland. She'd also napped for part of the drive between the base and CAG HQ.

But the lack of sleep bothered her less than the strangeness of returning from the field to the real world. The fluorescent lights in the office seemed too bright. Stopping by the refrigerator in the staff kitchen to grab a soda felt too convenient.

The only easy day was yesterday?

This morning wouldn't be easy. She had to give a report to Gregory about her "vacation." And discuss which direction she wanted her career to go.

I can't be in too much trouble. I was right—again. And Axe and I ended up saving the world—again.

Mostly.

Haley stopped in front of Gregory's door and tried the knob. Locked. No light shone from under the door. She was too early.

She'd been too busy Saturday and Sunday advising Bec and Cody to dig into the news of the world. All she knew was that things weren't good, but would have been so much worse if she, Axe, Bec, and Cody —along with Mad Dog and the SEALs—hadn't done their parts.

The SEALs had secured the facility and established communication with the White House situation room, which immediately took over. Experts had worked with Bec to locate all the EMPs—ready to detonate or still in transit—along with Pioneer's militant followers willing to destroy the world.

Bec had steadfastly refused to turn over the encryption keys for the ransomware virus until receiving immunity from prosecution for herself and Cody—in writing. She also demanded, and received, a written guarantee of non-reprisal for the Movement's people who hadn't committed any crimes or acts of terrorism. Haley had whispered those ideas to her in the Ladies' room right before comms were established. Even then, the ability to unlock the world's computers had gone straight to the President of the United States and no one else. Again, at Haley's suggestion.

"Good morning, Haley," Gregory said, startling her out of her thoughts. He unlocked his office door, flicked on the lights, and held the door for her. He walked to his desk and sat down, holding his to-go coffee mug with both hands and nodding to the chair in front of him.

"Restful vacation, I trust?" His face betrayed a wry smile before hiding it with a sip of coffee.

She looked like hell, and they both knew it. She offered a tired smile back but said nothing. Instead, she reached into her backpack and withdrew the fake ID package, including the wallet, and slid them across his spotless desk, empty except for his computer keyboard and monitor.

He left them untouched.

"I realize I should be debriefing you, but it can wait a bit. You've undoubtedly been busy, so let me catch you up." He held up a finger, ticking off the points. "Between the South Koreans and our troops, we stopped the North's invasion."

Another finger. "The Middle East, on its own, worked out a settlement. Iran has agreed to not pursue nuclear weapons—"

She snorted.

"Yes, they've said it before. Whether they mean it or not, with their facilities destroyed and scientists dead, they aren't in a position to continue their program. All the major powers in the area have agreed to a truce while they rebuild their countries."

"They got hit by EMPs too?"

"Yes, but not as many. It appears Conroy was counting on a regional conflict to turn the people against each other and their governments."

He ticked a third finger. "In Europe, few EMPs were detonated—nearly all the attacks came from the ransomware virus infecting the area's computers. President Heringten and his team are sorting that out as we speak."

"China? Russia?"

Here Gregory frowned. "Fortunately, or possibly unfortunately for us, their difficulties came from the computer virus. China began to invade Taiwan for firing EMP missiles at the mainland but was persuaded to stop once they heard we had the keys to their computer systems. In fact, every country in the world is our new best friend. The president is reshaping the attitudes of the world, making offers they can't refuse. Don't worry," he added, "he's playing fair. No need to make everyone hate us."

"What about the United States? What happened?"

"First, Los Angeles. Nancy figured out why it was hit first. Conroy's ex-girlfriend disappeared there years ago. The authorities had opened a cold case and were snooping around. They suspected Conroy of foul play. Conroy enlisted criminal gangs, prepared them, then hit downtown with the EMP. Genius, really. With the bank robberies, cold cases have been put on the back burner. But on Friday, a secretary updated a database and Nancy caught it."

"All that to stop an investigation?"

"We also believe he needed to test the devices. Speaking of which, there were limited EMP strikes in several cities. Destruction, but little loss of life. Relatively easy to repair, though it will take some time. A review of the target list shows the majority were stopped by fast actions taken Saturday morning in the control room at the Center." He nodded approvingly and sipped his coffee again.

Instead of feeling proud of the work she and Axe had done with Bec and Cody's help, she flashed to the feel of her finger pulling the pistol's trigger, sending two bullets into the heart of Emma and the sound of Anna's head cracking open on the tile floor.

"Haley?"

She realized Gregory had continued talking while her mind was elsewhere. "Sorry?"

"I said I received the security camera footage from the control room. Officially, we're going with the story that Rebecca Dodgeson, dedicated employee of Stefan Conroy's legitimate company, tried to save his life when he had a heart attack. Tragically, however, he died. The so-called actual story is similar. Rebecca tipped off the FBI to Conroy's terrorist intent and single-handedly recruited a former soldier named Cody who worked for Conroy's company as a guard. Together, they figured out Conroy's scheme and stopped the worst of it from happening, eliminating him in the process."

Good story.

"President Heringten assigned our group to secure the surveillance camera footage and placed a Code Word Classified designation on it due to its sensitive nature."

"Have you… Did the president…"

"The president and I watched it together, alone in the situation room."

She didn't know how she felt about that.

"We also had a long talk about your… situation… with Admiral Nalen."

That would have been a fun conversation to hear.

"Oh?"

Gregory sipped his coffee and stared past her, lost in thought for a few seconds. "He and I agreed your… extracurricular activities… are yours to pursue, so long as they did not adversely affect your day job."

"I'm not sure…" she began, then hesitated before plunging ahead. "I'm not entirely convinced the field is my calling."

Gregory frowned. She had surprised him.

Great. Uncle Jimmy works it all out with my boss, and I blow it by wanting to just sit in my cubicle and analyze data.

"Your call, of course. But your team of two has excelled while you've been gone."

Her team of two? Axe's tired, bloody face flashed in her mind, and she saw Cody standing confidently on the stage in the soccer stadium on St. John, speaking passionately about his love for the island and his desire to continue the best of Pioneer Prime's legacy.

"Nancy and Dave," Gregory said with a look of concern.

"Of course," she said, attempting to cover but not fooling him.

"I believe they are sleeping a few hours before diving back in to sort out the mess Pioneer left us with, but they took a few minutes to look at the results of their queries from last week."

The Assistant.

Gregory nodded, seeing her recognition. "They have a..." He hesitated, then spoke the word with obvious distaste, "Hunch. They claim to be channeling your abilities and I think—I hope—they're joking."

He leaned forward and slid the fake ID packet back toward her. "Why don't you find them, say hi, and take another week off? Come back fresh next Monday."

Haley hesitated. Gregory had presented it more as an offer, not an order.

Can I do it, or am I done in the field?

She felt the crushing weight of the guard she had stabbed in the mouth as he fell on her in the soccer stadium, his blood splashing her face.

She startled in her chair when Gregory's metal coffee mug clanked on his desk when he set it down. She'd been lost in thought again.

I wonder how long I was gone.

"Get with Nancy and Dave, Haley," Gregory said gently. "Sleep on it for a few hours. I hope to see you next Monday." He turned to his computer and pressed the power button to boot it up. She was dismissed.

She walked the halls of the building she'd left only five days before. It all looked so foreign.

But safe.

Haley stopped at her cubicle, exactly as she'd left it Wednesday night.

Comfortable.

She shook her head.

Soft.

Turning, she left it behind and went to find Dave and Nancy.

72

PEACE

Onboard *Mine, All Mine*
Isla Mujeres Yacht Club
Isla Mujeres, Mexico

Todd sat on the yacht's stern, enjoying the sunset and a fine cigar.

The past few days had been delightful. He'd been right—Kelton had been fired as CEO and booted off his own board of directors.

The stock price of his company continued to plummet.

Todd's bets against it continued to increase. He would soon be able to afford a larger yacht. Or a small army to find and kill Haley and Kelton, just like he'd dreamed. He'd save the warrior for last.

Kelton's fall from grace had calmed him greatly.

He could sail north. He looked completely different with the bald head, bushy beard, more muscular body from the steroids and workouts onboard, and a darker complexion.

Perhaps he could find and handle Haley himself.

He'd miss the peace and calm of the marina, but the burning inside him would return soon. It wouldn't be diminished until the analyst and her man were dead, preferably dying slowly and painfully. If it meant paying more, enlisting the help of less than savory characters, or even risking his own freedom, so be it.

But a few last days here. While he wouldn't be able to fully let go until Haley was dead, at least he could enjoy the sunshine and happy-hour cigars on the back of his lovely yacht.

He'd use the time to scheme and plan.

73

PICTURES

FRIDAY

Isla Mujeres Yacht Club
Isla Mujeres, Mexico

"Both look good," Axe said to Haley, lowering the binoculars. "The sailboat seems too slow, but the yacht is a definite possibility." He took a sip of his non-alcoholic beer, which he hated, but they were on the job.

Haley sat next to him in the shade of the huge umbrella over their table, a fruity drink in her hand, also alcohol-free. She wore a yellow beach coverup and a huge, pale yellow floppy hat. The strings of her black bikini top, tied at the back of her neck, stood out against her skin. Everywhere they went, men stopped and stared.

They had spent four days traveling up and down the Yucatán Peninsula in Mexico, from Cancun to Tulum, hitting the better marinas along the way.

Nancy and Dave had traced calls made during Haley's abduction attempt to other phones, which led to a cell phone in the coastal area of Cancun. They had a hunch Todd "The Assistant" Burkley likely lived on a yacht or sailboat. He'd gotten away from Long Island somehow, and they didn't believe he'd flown, taken a bus or train, or drove himself. An incredible amount of computer processing power had been put to work using facial recognition to comb through footage from bus and train stations, traffic cameras, and toll booths without catching a hint of him.

With other choices eliminated, a boat made the most sense.

Axe and Haley were undercover as a photographer and up-and-coming model, taking pictures for a travel magazine story about the area.

Nancy provided a list of likely marinas for them to check out, in order of probability. Axe approached the owner or manager with Haley behind him, flashing her stunning smile, and paid a location fee—a bribe, really—for permission to photograph Haley in her swimsuit on the dock. He also mentioned a friend of theirs they were hoping to catch up with. Medium height, thin, blond, blue eyes, mid-thirties, kept to himself, owned a boat Axe couldn't quite remember the name of.

A few men had matched the description. None had been the Assistant.

They hid in plain sight, taking real photos and showing them off when necessary to loosen the tongues of the marina operators about their clientele.

"This one and two more tomorrow," Haley said, checking Nancy's list before putting it back in her fashionable beach bag. "If we don't find him, it's back to the computer. We can send a team if we get a lead."

They shared a look. Neither wanted to send a team. They had spoken with Burkley during the attack in New Jersey. He had targeted Haley—twice. It was personal.

"The afternoon light is nice. Let's do this." The owner of the small marina had taken one look at Haley and was more than happy to chat about boats, the marina... and the man who arrived on his yacht about six months before. He was bald but had a bushy blond beard. Another blond man lived on a well-kept sailboat and had arrived a month before. Both kept to themselves. One—the sailor, had a reservation for another week. The yacht owner was due to leave the next morning.

The proprietor didn't know if either was around at the moment.

Axe had browsed his well-outfitted marina shop and bought a spear gun. "For the lady to pose with," he said, miming him taking a photo of her with it. Just in case they needed a weapon. With two real leads, his intuition made him reach for more firepower.

Always trust your gut.

Aside from the scuba diving knives they checked in their luggage, they were weaponless. The days of chartering a jet on Kelton's dime were long gone since he had lost his job and much of his net worth. Instead, they had flown coach class. On a commercial flight, they couldn't bring guns. Axe had stuffed his frame into the middle seat, giving Haley the window, and endured a screaming baby for the entire flight from D.C. to Cancun.

Out on the dock, Axe loaded the shaft in the speargun and showed Haley how to operate it.

They strolled to where both the sailboat and yacht were moored.

Haley stood with her back to the sailboat.

"Leave the dress on this time. I have enough swimsuit pictures."

She put the butt of the speargun on her hip, playing the part of supermodel perfectly. The sun shone through her thin coverup.

That's actually a decent picture.

He took a few shots, pleased with the lighting. Next, he'd take pictures focused mostly on the boat, then they'd switch places so he could photograph the yacht. If they didn't stumble across either of their suspects, Haley would send the photos back for Nancy and Dave to analyze.

"Nice," he said, intent on Haley's next pose. She held the speargun at the low ready position, finger on the trigger, the barbed shaft pointed only slightly downward. Her eyes were spectacular: focused, widening, intense.

He grabbed the shot and stepped back to get more of the sailboat in the next one. He kept his finger on the shutter button. The camera took twenty shots per second, capturing Haley as she raised the speargun higher...

And pulled the trigger.

From behind, Axe heard a surprised grunt of pain.

The man stared at Haley from the deck of his yacht as he twitched. The spear protruded from the center of his chest, its barbed head sunk into the boat behind him. He grabbed the metal shaft and tried to pull it from his body. Blood spurted from the wound when he moved. The spear didn't budge.

A second later, he slumped, his lifeless form held in place by the spear. His glassy eyes continued to stare at her in surprise.

Haley scrutinized his face, no longer sure she had shot a terrorist.

I just killed an innocent man.

"What the..." Axe spun around, primed for a fight, and saw the man die.

Bushy blond beard, but his face is wrong. Dark eyes. Muscular. He looks similar to the guy I remember, but it's not him.

Axe quickly checked the dock, boats, and the patio tables where they had enjoyed their drinks. All appeared deserted.

We have to clean this up and get out of here.

He leaped onto the back of the yacht and raced to the man. "Haley, get up here."

She hurried after him. It took both of them to yank the shaft from the wall, taking a chunk of fiberglass with it. They dropped the body on the expensive looking rug laying across the stern deck. Hopefully, it would soak up all the blood.

"Don't take out the shaft. He'll only bleed more. I'm going to warm up the engines. Get ready to cast off the lines."

Axe moved forward to the bridge and quickly familiarized himself with the controls. They were well labeled. The start-up process was mounted on a laminated card near the helm.

Gotta love rich people who don't know how to handle their boats.

He followed the instructions and called to Haley, kneeling over the dead man. She hadn't said a word.

"Haley, get the bow line, then the stern line. Time to go for a cruise."

They could dump the body offshore. Axe would rig the boat to blow with the spare fuel, and they'd swim to shore.

He pictured the marina office and patio but didn't remember any security cameras. With a little luck, the man wouldn't be missed for a few days. By then, the boat would have sunk. It would be put down as a tragic accident.

Rich guy disappears, and his yacht is missing. Tragic boating accident suspected.

They would get away clean.

Haley released the lines and hopped back on board, still not speaking. Axe gently added power to the engines. They were off.

What the hell happened? And what if the guy from the sailboat was actually their man?

Haley had made her first mistake, and it was huge.

"He looked at me and..." Haley paused, trying to find the words. She and Axe stood over the body. They were safely out of sight of land, motoring slowly against the current. "Most men look at me a certain way. I'm used to it. But he saw me and reacted differently. In that moment, I knew it was Burkley."

So I shot him.

"I get it. He looks a little like Burkley. You reacted in the heat of the moment."

He sounded so supportive, she almost believed him.

Axe crouched down, peering at the face. "What if it is him?"

Haley fought back tears, forcing herself to keep it together. Axe, trying to support her, almost made up for the horror of killing an innocent man.

"It's not. See?" She pointed at the man's cheeks and the area above his mouth. "His face structure is different. He's bald, the eyes are black, not blue. And look how muscular he is."

"It could still be him. Shaving his head would be an obvious move, along with growing out his beard. Some kind of cosmetic surgery could have done this." He poked the man between his nose and mouth.

"Axe, thank you, but we have to face the facts. I killed—"

"Haley!"

She blanched as Axe fished around inside the dead man's mouth with his fingers. Turning away, she took a step toward the side in case she vomited.

"Look!"

She didn't want to see. Axe would keep the murder to himself, for her, but she could never work in the field again. Maybe she'd get out of the intelligence business completely.

This is something I don't come back from.

Axe stood in front of her, holding up a flesh-colored... something.

"It's a prosthesis of some sort. Look at him now." He went back over to the body.

She turned, looked, and gasped.

It's him.

"It looks like him now!"

"You may have been right all along."

They searched the yacht for the man's name, but all the documents listed a corporation as the yacht owner. "There has to be a safe. Let's look again."

It took a while, but they finally found it behind a wooden panel in the galley. The front had both a fingerprint scanner and a keypad. To save them from dragging the body forward, Axe simply cut off the man's finger with his scuba knife, not bothered at all by the gruesome chore.

He pressed the finger to the scanner, which wasn't as sophisticated as the hand scanner Pioneer used on St. John. This one immediately accepted the dead man's fingerprint.

"We need a passcode," Axe announced, nonchalantly setting the finger in the sink. "Do you know Burkley's birthdate?"

I know everything about him.

She tried it. The safe flashed a red light and beeped.

They stood, thinking. After a few seconds, Axe said softly, "Try the date of the New York City attack."

She entered the date. The light flashed green, and the door unlocked.

"That proves it, right?" Haley asked. "Who else would have that date as their code?"

"Inconclusive but looking better for us."

'Us.' We're in this together. A real team.

Stacks of bound hundred-dollar bills lined the safe. In the middle of the piles, a United States of America passport, the familiar dark blue cover peeking out.

The man's picture—including the mouth insert—but the wrong name.

"Damn."

They started the search again. While Haley went through every drawer in the bedroom and bathroom, Axe remained in the kitchen.

He'd gone through the contents of the refrigerator and most of the freezer when he came to a whole frozen fish.

Axe removed the white freezer wrap and unveiled a gorgeous red snapper. He almost wrapped it again when he noticed the slit in the fish's belly. After running it under hot water, he finally forced the fish open. Inside, a sealed plastic sandwich bag held another blue passport in the name of Todd Bryon Burkley. It had an image of the man he had seen and traded shots with on Kelton's superyacht.

After washing his hands, Axe carried the passport into the bedroom.

Haley turned to look as he walked in.

He held up the passport. "I'm sorry I doubted you."

"It's him?"

Axe nodded. "Always trust your gut."

Axe made sure Haley understood how to operate the boat, then scanned the surrounding area with the high-powered binoculars on the bridge. They were completely alone.

"Aren't you worried about sharks?" Haley asked as he unselfconsciously stripped to his boxer briefs.

"I'm more worried about his body floating around, which is why I'm going to cut him open. If sharks don't get him, he'll sink. Other creatures will get to work on him. Either way, he won't last long."

From the kitchen, he grabbed Burkley's severed finger. They wouldn't need it any longer, as Haley had deactivated the fingerprint scan on the safe so it would open with only the passcode.

Finally, he rolled the body up in the rug and carried the dead weight to the stern of the yacht. He let the rug unroll, dumping the body into the water. He tossed the rug in after it. The natural fibers wouldn't last long before sinking and decomposing.

He grabbed his knife and quickly jumped in. It took only a few strokes to reach the dead man floating face down, the shaft from the speargun still protruding from his back.

Axe went to work, slicing Burkley's belly open first.

He eventually removed the spear gun shaft, which he carefully stuck in the side of his briefs. They'd discard it and the speargun elsewhere to be safe.

As the blood spread across the water, Haley called out. "Remember how you weren't worried about sharks?"

She pointed. A fin sliced the water about fifty yards away, coming straight at him.

Yep, that's a shark all right.

He pushed the body away. It sank immediately.

Without splashing, Axe hurried to the small swim platform at the stern of the yacht. Haley met him with a towel and a surprise. "The light's perfect," she explained.

He dried his hands and arms before taking his camera from her.

Laying down on the platform to get the perfect angle, he lined up the shot. The sun set behind him, blazing orange. In front of him, three shark fins now circled a patch of ocean. He fired off several frames as the shark fins disappeared from the surface. Only a hint of blood remained on the water.

74

STORIES

EIGHT DAYS LATER

Axe's Cabin
Rural Virginia

It had been a long week, but Haley could finally relax. Or at least try.

She accepted the bottle of beer from Admiral Nalen, who handed it to her in a way that felt ceremonial. After giving one to Axe in the same manner, he sat down on the tired fabric camp chair on the front porch of Axe's cabin.

He raised his bottle. "To…" He stared into the distance, "A job well done."

They leaned forward and clinked their bottles, then sat back, relaxing after their hard work. Earlier, the men had arrived in Axe's truck at her house. Working together, the three of them maneuvered Haley's chest freezer—filled with the body of her would-be abductor—into the bed of Axe's truck.

Once at Axe's cabin, they dumped the body into a deep grave Axe and the Admiral had dug in the woods, then cleaned the freezer with bleach. Finally, they took it to the recycling area of the local dump.

In a bit, Axe would grill their steaks. Haley would return to her little house in the city, where she'd sit with the lights off, pistol in hand. She'd watch the street through a narrow gap in her blinds, waiting for a team to assault the house and attempt another abduction.

Yes, she'd killed Todd "the Assistant" Burkley, and Axe had killed Stefan "Pioneer" Conroy, but the world was a dangerous place. Both men had followers and a long reach, even in death.

When she couldn't stay awake any longer, she would triple check the security system, deadbolts, and newly installed door bars which could only be opened from inside. She'd sleep for a few hours, get up, and sit watching the street until it was time to return to the office and mine the world's data for the next threat.

Each time, as she sat in the dark, she'd relive the dangerous moments from the mission—and see the men and women she'd killed.

A week earlier, after the Assistant's burial at sea, as Axe called it, he had guided the yacht to Cozumel for her to take a ferry back to Cancun and fly home.

Axe cruised the area until a homeless Kelton Kellison flew in. Fresh from being fired from his job as CEO and chairman of the board —and consequently evicted from his houses and yacht, which were owned by his company for legal and tax purposes—he happily agreed to care for Burkley's yacht while Nalen figured out what to do with it.

"Haley?" Nalen asked gently. She looked up, startled. Once again, she had zoned out. It happened a lot lately. She attempted a smile. "Sorry, what was that?"

"I asked how you're holding up?"

Aside from being constantly on edge, waiting for the next attack? Or the inability to stay asleep... and the nightmares when I do manage to nod off for a few hours? And getting lost in thought while people are speaking? Fine. Absolutely fine.

"Doing great. No worries."

That's not what the bags under my eyes say, or the weight loss, or the brand-new stress wrinkles on my forehead.

The men's eyes drilled into her like they could read her thoughts and see into her soul.

"Get out of my head," she growled, but neither blinked. When she accidentally used that tone of voice on Dave at the office a few days ago, he'd nearly peed his pants. With these two, they sipped their beers and waited patiently.

Haley sighed theatrically, knowing her anger showed despite her best efforts to hide it. "Fine. I'm having a bit of trouble sleeping. Satisfied?"

"We figured. Me too," Axe admitted.

"You?" Haley gave him a skeptical look.

"Probably not for the same reasons. But yeah. I keep waking up, thinking about fighting Gunther. I was too slow. He almost had me twice in the first few seconds. I only won because I used a move I'd trained on with a few other crazy SEALs one slow deployment. Otherwise…" He trailed off, staring at the woods and taking a long pull of his beer. "And at the marina, I got so focused on taking good pictures, I completely lost my situational awareness. I didn't realize Todd was behind me. I'm getting too old for this."

"You're not slow or old. Look what we pulled off!"

Their eyes met. "Knowing the truth doesn't make the feelings go away, though, does it?"

Bastard. He's got me there.

She heard tires on the long gravel road leading to Axe's cabin in the woods. Instinctively, she stood, her hand on the pistol at her side.

"Relax, Haley. It's a few guys from my old Team."

"I thought it was just going to be the three of us."

"No, you need more than that… and so do I. Remember during the mission when you put all those overwhelming feelings into a box to deal with later? Now's the time." He and Nalen stood to greet the guys.

Several trucks arrived. Mad Dog, from St. John, hopped out first with a twelve-pack of beer in each hand. "No horde of angry villagers? Good, because I don't have enough beer to go around!" With Kelton nearly broke and the superyacht taken away from him, Doug's contract had been terminated.

As the others came, Axe reintroduced her. She'd met them before, but it felt nice to be reminded. Red, with his powerful physique and bushy red hair and beard. Thor, aka Hector, the slight Latino with a buzz cut, watchful dark eyes, and a great sense of humor. Ronbo, with an easy smile and obvious intelligence. Finally, Link, a beast of a man with a sweet, quiet demeanor. They headed inside, talking and laughing, leaving Axe with her on the cold porch.

No women.

"I invited Bec and Cody," Axe said beside her. "They're still busy though, leading the Movement. And Connie,"—Axe's girlfriend—"sends her love but thought it would be better to have only the warriors here."

It took her a second to understand—she was one of the warriors.

Axe stood next to her, looking at the woods as darkness fell.

"Every one of these men, including Nalen, has dealt with what you're going through. Hell, they still do. Tonight's a chance for us all to be ourselves. Let it out, and let it go."

"We don't have this kind of event at the office. When it's someone's birthday, we'll meet in the conference room for cake. And we don't socialize outside of work."

"Maybe you should. But don't worry. Tonight will be simple. All those feelings have to be processed or they'll drive you—us—crazy. This isn't a therapy session. We're not going to pass the talking stick and emote. But we can gather and support each other... without making a big deal of it," he smiled.

"Couple different methods to try." Axe gestured through the window to Mad Dog, standing in front of the others, chugging a bottle of beer and talking loudly. "Getting drunk works for some." Thor had his feet on Axe's beat-up, rustic coffee table, his muddy boots making a mess. "Drunk or sober, listening to others' stories and telling your own seems to work well for everyone." He leaned closer, though no one could possibly hear. "And never let the truth get in the way of a good tale!"

She had to smile.

"And in a bit, meet Link out back. I picked up a present I think you'll like, and he'll help you out." He opened the door for her as Doug finished talking. The rest of the men erupted with laughter.

As she walked in, eyes turned to her. Axe closed the door and started talking as he took a seat on the worn couch. "So no shit, there we were. Covered in blood, of course, but only some of it was ours. I'm driving this stolen SUV on a steep mountain road. Haley—get this —is crouched in the foot area of the passenger seat. This captured enemy guard is pressed back against the seat," he imitated the man's stiff body and frightened expression, "because Haley has this huge knife against his family jewels to keep him in line..."

"Oh, Haley, that's cold!"

"Serves the bastard right, going against you two!"

They looked at her expectantly. "Well, he got his in the end," she said.

"No!" they yelled, crossing their legs or cupping their hands over themselves.

She sat in an ancient leather chair near the fireplace. "Not like that. This guy—" she gestured to Axe, warming to the story, "rams the truck into the doorway of a building so we can gain entry," she explained.

"Make use of what you got. Nice one," Link said approvingly to Axe.

"The guards inside start shooting. The dumb prisoner is going to get it any second, so Axe pulls him out of the truck to save him."

"Oh, geez, Axe. Come on," Thor said, rolling his eyes.

"I learned it from you, remember?" Axe asked. "That little village?"

"Couldn't let the poor guy just sit there and get killed," Thor mumbled. "Not his fault he worked for that asshole drug lord."

"Exactly!" Axe said. "But my guy tried to warn his buddies after I saved him."

There was a chorus of disbelief.

"So they shot him by accident, didn't they?" Red asked.

"Yes," Haley said, and suddenly, the story wasn't funny anymore.

There was a moment of quiet, then Thor raised his bottle. "To the ones we save... and the ones we can't."

"Here, here," they murmured, leaning forward to toast.

"Haley, when Axe stole the SUV, did he drive with his elbow out the window, like he didn't have a care in the world?" Red asked her, demonstrating by sitting back in his chair, his elbow on the edge, pretending to casually drive.

She flashed back to the soccer stadium, Axe announcing they were going to attack the Center, his elbow resting on the windowsill of the vehicle.

"As a matter of fact, yes!"

"Papa, remember that time in... where the hell was it?" Red continued. "When you stole the drug guy's three-hundred-thousand dollar car for our getaway? That's how you drove then, too. Like you were out for a Sunday drive, even though the guy's wife—"

"No, she doesn't need to hear that story!" Axe yelled to a great deal of laughter.

"True, true, but you drive like that only when you steal a vehicle. Never in one of ours, you realize that, right?"

Haley laughed and listened to the stories, feeling her burden lighten.

A while later, she looked up at Link's huge frame looming over her. "Come with me."

He led her to the back porch, flicking on a dim light. With the temperature in the forties, she could see her breath. "I need a jacket," she said, turning to go back inside.

"No, you don't." She turned to face him. "I saw you not drinking much," he began. "Smart. Drinking helps, but not for long. Have to keep at it, which can become its own problem. This is better." He nodded at the heavy workout bag hanging from a thick chain in the center of the space. "Done this before?"

She shook her head.

He taped her hands as she shivered, then slid boxing gloves on her hands and laced them up. They were brand new. "Axe got 'em for you," Link explained. "Listen to him. Smart guy."

Definitely.

"First several times, lots of padding. When you get used to it, you can drop to a less padded glove. You've had combat classes?"

"A few."

"Quick review. Punch like this." He showed her the basics. "Try it."

She punched tentatively. It didn't do a thing for her.

"I don't think this is going to work the way you thought."

"Hit it."

She punched harder, looked at Link, and shrugged.

"You gotta open the box. Remember those feelings. Now is the time. Do it." He nodded at her and stepped behind the bag to hold it.

"I don't know…"

"Remember the fear?"

She nodded slightly, holding back the feeling.

"You know what fresh blood smells like."

Her body stiffened, remembering.

"And the moment you realize you've taken a life."

Tears rolled down her cheeks. She brushed at them with the big, dumb boxing gloves, embarrassed.

"Now hit it!"

She swung with all her strength, putting the feelings she had been holding back into the punch.

The bag swung. Link let out a soft grunt as he worked to hold it still. Her other hand lashed out and connected, the sensation flowing up her arm.

It felt good.

Suddenly, she was all over the bag. All the painful, difficult emotions flowed out of her heart, mind, stomach, and soul, through her arms and hands, into the bag.

Eventually, she was done. The box of feelings she had filled during the mission was empty.

She staggered back and slumped against the cabin's wall, spent.

Axe came out, carrying her coat. He hung it on a hook, then took her hands and unlaced the gloves.

"Link's next. I'll hold the bag for him, give you a chance to rest. You'll hold it for me when he's done. Jacket's there if you need it."

Those were the only words said. Link slipped on a pair of thin gloves like MMA fighters wore and started small, punching and weaving. After a few minutes, his huge arms drove into the bag over and over, nearly knocking Axe off his feet as he held it steady. Link grunted and swung. Gradually, he wound down.

Link's eyes sought hers. They nodded at each other. He was a giant of a man. She weighed one hundred fifty pounds less. But they shared a connection.

They had both been there and done that.

75

ART

TWO WEEKS LATER

The Art Gallery
Washington, D.C.

The soft sounds of happy people talking and laughing reached Axe at the rear of the gallery. His favorite photo hung on the wall. The show would open in a few minutes, but Axe had allowed early entry to a few invitees—friends and three of his best clients.

Connie held his hand. She had finally gotten away from a busy time at the hospital to join him for a long weekend, including the night of his second photography show.

His friend Kate, the gallery owner, had begged him for it. Early December was the perfect time, she'd said. People would scoop up his art for holiday gifts. He'd fought hard to keep from rolling his eyes at the description of his pictures as art.

As long as people like them, I guess I shouldn't care what term they use.

This time around, the show was a mixture of styles. Many walls displayed landscape pictures, including several large framed prints of fall foliage.

Another section showed animal photography. His favorite was a buck with a twelve-point rack he'd captured after laying perfectly still in the cold woods all day, waiting until right before dusk to get the shot. Another one, which Kate loved, had an eagle in a nest feeding its eaglets.

There was also one of his most dangerous photos to date: a skunk turned away from him, eyes looking directly back into the camera lens, tail raised high.

A smaller section of the gallery contained a different style of photographs. These were of a beautiful woman, her face hidden, in various locations near the ocean.

In another area, in the back, there was a photo of what looked at first glance to be blankets and trash bags against the wall of a building. Closer inspection would reveal—to the curious—a pair of dark, smiling eyes mostly hidden in the pile.

Also in the back were several pictures taken with a lower quality camera looking up at a dark freeway filled with stationary cars and milling people. The Los Angeles skyline glowed in the distance. Axe had snapped them with the cheap phone from the convenience store on his way to downtown LA.

In the farthest corner of the gallery, Haley joined Axe and Connie. Axe smiled at her and nodded to her date, Officer Derek Johnson.

Haley had asked him out, she told Axe, and they seemed to hit it off. Derek had mentioned the police had no leads on the person or people who shot up the vans at an intersection in the suburbs a month before. Some kind of fugitive apprehension gone off the rails, they figured. It wasn't his problem, he'd told Haley, and it wasn't a priority of the department.

The four of them had a double date tonight. Axe wanted to be anywhere but in the gallery during the show.

Haley, Derek, Connie, and Axe stared at the photograph on the wall in front of them.

It has a certain… something.

Axe looked at it with pride. He'd started his photography journey taking snapshots, recording moments with little technique. Point the camera or phone at a scene, click the button, let the magic of technology grab a decent photograph.

With practice, he'd graduated to better technique, capturing special moments in time. This produced photographs people were eager to pay sums of money Axe couldn't believe for the privilege of hanging his pictures in their homes or offices.

Lately, a few of his shots had a different quality. He couldn't put his finger on it, nor could he consistently make the magic happen. They were, for some undefinable reason, art.

Even to him.

The picture of Chief against the wall of the building in Venice, California, was one of them, despite being taken with his new cell phone.

This was the other. He'd bottled the magic somehow when Haley had passed the camera to him on the stern of the Assistant's yacht in Mexico. Whether it was the angle, the light, the settings he used, the focal length, or the subject, he couldn't say. The picture just worked.

Three shark fins—tiger sharks, he'd learned later—circled in the brilliant blue-green ocean. A few clouds in the distance blazed with an incredible shade of orange.

The sun reflected off the water in the area in the center of the fins, making the ocean seem to glow blood red. It looked as if the sharks had already done their work.

"It's spectacular," Derek said quietly. "I can see why it's already sold."

Axe nodded. "Actually, it's more like a commissioned piece." He and Haley shared a long look.

After the show, he would get it to Admiral Nalen, who would pass it along to President Heringten.

He would understand and appreciate it.

It might take days, months, or years, but eventually, America always caught up with her enemies—and made them pay.

76

PARADISE
MONDAY

The Center Control Room
St. John, United States Virgin Islands

Bec sat at Gunther's old workstation, to the left and in front of Cody, who had reluctantly claimed Pioneer Prime's throne-like chair.

She glanced back at him and smiled. He blushed.

What a cutie.

He had moved from his barracks room into Pioneer's residential wing of the building. And as awkward as it was, she'd joined him.

They were engaged, after all—their union blessed on video by Pioneer himself. Or at least in the fiction she had presented to the people, which all had bought completely.

They are either gullible or don't care. All that matters is they have a leader they can believe in.

Which they did. Cody was a fine man. He'd grown immensely as a person, starting with the battle in the control room. He'd stepped up and became a leader instead of a follower.

She looked at him again and he blushed again.

Bec had slept on the couch for three weeks. Cody had frequently insisted she take the bed. After all the hours spent together discussing their ideas for the Movement and enjoying the island's recreational activities after work, last night she had known it was time.

She took the bed but asked if he would stay. At first, the perfect gentleman, he played dumb. But she quickly put an end to that.

It had been magical.

Love at first sight. And all it took was working for a worldwide cult —that I now help lead.

"Pioneer, I have the plans ready," she said.

"Onscreen, please, Bec."

Instead of a list of potentially vulnerable computer systems, the new spreadsheet contained the top twenty-five poorest, most vulnerable populations of the world.

The nearby techs worked on solutions to each area's problem.

They were putting Conroy's billions—which he'd left in control of the Movement—to good use.

She'd never been happier. She was doing good work, helping people. And the hacking efforts she had made the last few weeks would make sure many world leaders played nice.

Not that they know it yet...but they will if I decide they need to.

Cody examined the list with a critical eye. His mind couldn't compare with Bec's, but he had common sense. The two of them worked well together.

He thought about the previous night in his room.

We work well together in more ways than one.

All he ever wanted was to enjoy the outdoors and be useful. He never thought of the island of St. John or leading a worldwide back-to-nature movement, but here he was.

It might not last, but I'll enjoy every second of it while I can.

He and Bec were already discussing finding the next Pioneer to take over. They were young and probably not the best people to control the organization long-term. But for now, they would do the best they could. Lay the foundation for the next person. Do good work.

And enjoy ourselves.

77

CHAOS

The Dojo
Fredericksburg, Virginia

Axe stood next to Haley as the last of the mixed martial arts students filed out. Haley's intensive hand-to-hand combat classes would resume shortly, taught by one of Axe's old teachers, another retired SEAL.

Her next level of knife fighting instruction would follow.

Not that she needs it. She already held her own in battle, but more training never hurts.

Haley took a deep breath and readied herself. "*Semper Paratus*," she said. "'Always prepared,' right?"

"That's the Coast Guard."

"What did you say in the SEALs?"

"'My training is never complete.' SEAL Ethos."

"Not Sun Tzu?"

Axe smiled at her teasing and quoted the master. "'To not prepare is the greatest of crimes; to be prepared beforehand for any contingency is the greatest of virtues.'"

Her eyes shone as she took another jibe at him. "You are wise."

Only elders are wise. She thinks she's funny.

He frowned at her before his lips twitched, fighting to hold back a smile. "As wise as you are beautiful."

It was her turn to scowl at him. "Touché."

If she comments on my age, I'll compliment her beauty. That'll teach her.

Before they stepped onto the mat, he had to ask. "What's new on the intel front? Anything to be concerned with?"

───────────

Haley struggled with how much to tell him. She only had a glimmer…

Something to do with China… and maybe drugs… or it could be nuclear weapons.

She couldn't make sense of it, or even whether it was worth worrying about. Best not to burden him with details yet. It could be nothing.

Yeah, right.

"The usual. Chaos. Destruction at the gates, with only us to hold it back."

Axe nodded slowly. "So… just another Monday."

She smiled tightly at him and nodded.

Just another Monday.

───────────

───────────

───────────

Author's Note

Thanks for reading! Continue with *A Team of Three*, the next book in the series:

Freedom isn't free.

America's newest enemy launches an audacious plan to incapacitate the country. A never-before-seen danger is about to be unleashed on an unsuspecting public. And the world faces a crisis unlike any before.

Can intelligence analyst Haley put the puzzle together in time from the safety of her office - or is she meant to risk it all as a field asset? Is Axe capable of overcoming a foe with nothing to lose?

The clues are cleverly hidden. The threats are terrifying. And the stakes have never been higher. For the USA, the world, Axe, and Haley. They are on their own, in deep, and desperate.

All they have is each other, their dedication, and their skills... but will that be enough to prevent death and destruction?

Join them for their most dangerous mission yet. Pick up the book on Amazon via: https://geni.us/a-team-of-three

- Also, I use the names of real places but fictionalize some details. I also take inspiration from areas but change names and some features to improve the story. My apologies if you live in or are acquainted with one of the areas and think, "Wait, that's not right." You're correct. License was taken in describing places as well as technology, equipment, weapons, tactics, and military capabilities. Where location details, distances, or technical issues conflicted with the story, I made the story paramount.
- If you haven't signed up yet, get a free Axe/Haley story each month in my newsletter. Go to: www.authorbradlee.com/shortstoryclub
- If you enjoyed the book, please leave a five-star or written review. It helps new readers discover the book and makes it possible for me to continue bringing you stories.
- Find me at: https://www.facebook.com/AuthorBradLee

Finally, please join me in thanking Beth, Hayleigh, David, and Mac for their help. The book is far better because of them.

Made in United States
North Haven, CT
07 July 2023

38687862R00253